MEDICAL

Pulse-racing passion

Home Alone With
The Children's Doctor
Traci Douglass

A Surgeon's Christmas Baby
Deanne Anders

MILLS & BOON

Traci Douglass is acknowledged as the author of this work
HOME ALONE WITH THE CHILDREN'S DOCTOR
© 2023 by Harlequin Enterprises ULC   First Published 2023
Philippine Copyright 2023   First Australian Paperback Edition 2023
Australian Copyright 2023   ISBN 978 1 867 29524 2
New Zealand Copyright 2023

Deanne Anders is acknowledged as the author of this work
A SURGEON'S CHRISTMAS BABY
© 2023 by Harlequin Enterprises ULC   First Published 2023
Philippine Copyright 2023   First Australian Paperback Edition 2023
Australian Copyright 2023   ISBN 978 1 867 29524 2
New Zealand Copyright 2023

MIX
Paper | Supporting
responsible forestry
FSC® C001695
www.fsc.org

Published by
Harlequin Mills & Boon
An imprint of Harlequin Enterprises (Australia) Pty Limited
(ABN 47 001 180 918), a subsidiary of HarperCollins
Publishers Australia Pty Limited
(ABN 36 009 913 517)
Level 19, 201 Elizabeth Street
SYDNEY NSW 2000 AUSTRALIA

Cover art used by arrangement with Harlequin Books S.A.. All rights reserved.

Printed and bound in Australia by McPherson's Printing Group

Home Alone With
The Children's Doctor
Traci Douglass

MILLS & BOON

Traci Douglass is a *USA TODAY* bestselling romance author with Harlequin, Entangled Publishing and Tule Publishing and has an MFA in Writing Popular Fiction from Seton Hill University. She writes sometimes funny, usually awkward, always emotional stories about strong, quirky, wounded characters overcoming past adversity to find their forever person and heartfelt, healing happily-ever-afters. Connect with her through her website: tracidouglassbooks.com.

Visit the Author Profile page at
millsandboon.com.au for more titles.

Dear Reader,

The holidays can be such a fun and festive time for people. But they can also be hard for others for various reasons. In *Home Alone with the Children's Doctor*, I got to explore exactly that kind of situation. What it would be like for two people who don't necessarily have a lot of family or friends to hang out with, who don't really have a lot of traditions or even reasons to celebrate. For Kali, she's still adjusting to her new adult-diagnosed autism and what that means for her. And Dylan is working because work is where he feels most comfortable and in control. He's also Jewish, so the whole Christmas vs Hanukkah thing is a bit messy for him. Neither is looking for company, let alone romance, but when fate throws them together for an unexpected reunion during the month of December, they get to know each other all over again as the people they are now and create some special holiday magic on their own. I hope you enjoy their nontraditional winter romance full of heart and heat and more than a little ho-ho-ho humour.

Until next time, happy reading!

Traci <3

DEDICATION

This is for all the lonely people...

CHAPTER ONE

THE HOLIDAYS WERE hardly *fa-la-la-la*-tastic for Kalista.

And not just because of the usual reasons—overstressing, overspending, overeating, over-everything. Nope. Dr. Kalista Michell had recently discovered that what'd she'd thought were issues everyone dealt with weren't the norm for most people. Which could've been the mantra for her life since she'd hit her teens: "Not normal."

With a sigh, Kali locked her apartment door behind her, tossed the keys into the blue glass bowl on the side table by the door where she and her roommate, Jen, kept them, then leaned back against the wall and closed her eyes. It had been another grueling on-call shift at Boston Beacon Hospital, and she was glad to be home.

She took a deep breath and inhaled the silence—a rarity, since Jen could usually talk the paint off a wall. But Jen had taken a leave of absence from her EMT job this December to travel to Israel to see relatives, which left Kali blissfully, delightedly, uneasily alone for Christmas.

After removing her coat and comfy work shoes, Kali padded into the living room, where Wednesday, the black cat she and Jen had adopted the year before from the local shelter, preened. So, she wasn't *completely* alone for the holidays. Her therapist's voice, forever present now in Kali's head, said that was a good thing. Diagnosed at twenty-seven as having autism spectrum disorder with low support needs. The words still sounded strange to her. They were still too new. But they were hers, and they explained so much about her: all the troubles she'd had when she was little, the things she was going through now—everything. Her diagnosis had been both a blessing and a curse.

A blessing because she finally had a name for the weird feelings she always got when socializing with others. Her penchant for trying to read what other people wanted from her and doing what would make them happy, her strange habit of avoiding looking people in the eye and instead focusing somewhere near the bridge of their nose to make it look like she was holding their gaze even though she wasn't. Her constant "masking"—the name her therapist had given it—where she mimicked what others did emotionally, thinking it would hide her deep-seated insecurity and inability to innately know what was the "right" way to react in a situation. It was exhausting, honestly, and all that on top of being a busy resident had nearly run her right into the ground.

But now she was doing her best to be more real, to tune into her own emotions and reactions and act upon them instead of copying others. It didn't always work, but she thought she was getting better. None of her patients had complained about her bedside manner recently, and her coworkers seemed more cordial, if not less distant, than before, so...

Her autism diagnosis became a curse, though, when Kali still found herself getting stuck in people-pleasing mode, which probably explained her crazy decision to volunteer for extra shifts in the children's ward this month instead of taking some much-needed time off herself. But she figured it was better than sitting alone in the apartment and getting stuck in one of her "loops" again—another term her therapist had coined to explain the times when Kali's anxiety got out of hand,

and she kept repeating the same patterns or actions over and over to avoid making a mistake or failing at whatever it was that scared her. She hated those times. And lately, they'd seemed even worse because she could recognize when they were happening, even if she wasn't able to stop them. Yet.

Kali's therapist had assured her she would get there. It would just take time.

But Kali wasn't the most patient person either.

She was twenty-eight and tired of sitting on the sidelines, watching everyone else have a life. She wanted a home, kids, family, romance someday. And as the years ticked by, the yearning got stronger.

And sure, she'd done enough cognitive behavioral therapy sessions to know that part of that yearning came from growing up without that stability in her life. Her own parents' marriage had been a train wreck of epic proportions. They'd divorced when Kali was just a kid, and she'd ended up shuttled between two chaotic worlds—her father with his new girlfriends, who were usually barely legal—*ew!*—and her mother's "flavor of the month" man. Kali suppressed a shudder at how many times she'd sat through dinners with those monthly guys making inappropriate passes at her mom over the mashed potatoes. She swallowed down the bile burning her throat and scooped some kibble into Wednesday's bowl before refilling the cat's water dish.

"It's just you and me for the month, baby." Kali smiled down as the cat rubbed against her shins. She pulled her cell phone from the pocket of her scrub pants to set it on the charging pad on the counter. A message alert popped up on screen, but it was from Jen, not the hospital, so Kali didn't bother checking it just then. Her best friend had touched down earlier in the day in Tel Aviv, and she probably just wanted to tell Kali how wonderful it was there—sunny and warm and beautiful—while Kali was stuck in cold, gray Boston. It could wait until after she showered and changed.

Kali scooped up the cat in one arm and carried Wednesday into the living room to turn on some music. This month Kali wanted to keep to her schedule as much as possible, even though she had the apartment to herself. She'd learned since her diagnosis that routines were good for her. They helped keep her on track and less stressed, both of which lessened her chances of a "looping" episode. Plus, with being by herself for the holidays, her routines would hopefully make the time pass quicker too. She planned to take lots of walks, bake some cookies and other recipes that had been passed down from her Scandinavian grandmother, and generally avoid too much peopling outside of work. Of course, most of her fellow residents and colleagues at the hospital were gung-ho for the holidays, so she felt even more like a pariah this time of year.

Quiet celebrations worked better for Kali, though, and she was trying to listen to her instincts more these days, so...

Wednesday jumped down and sauntered away. Kali got up and walked over to flip through the channels on the satellite radio. Every station seemed to be playing Christmas carols nonstop, even though the holidays were still three weeks away. She was already sick of most of the songs. Kali finally found the least objectionable station and headed down the hall toward her bedroom, stripping out of her scrubs as she went.

Man, it felt good to relax and let go a bit after spending all day dealing with other people and their emotions. Introverted and studious, Kali had always been on the quiet side, and those tendencies had only worsened during her teens and early twenties when her autism disorder had really started to manifest. At first, Babs—her mother preferred to be called Babs, not Barbara or Mom—had put Kali's "quirks" down to normal teenaged stuff and thought she'd outgrow them. But Kali never did and finally decided enough was enough. Last year, she'd made an appointment with a therapist to figure out what was wrong with her before she dropped out of medical school and ended up in a psych ward somewhere. Having a label for her condition and knowing there were other people like her out there made the autism easier to deal with. Made her feel a bit less isolated and alone. Babs still thought it was something Kali could just "get over," but her mother was who she was, Kali chose which battles to fight and which to let go these days.

Kali walked into the bathroom across from her bedroom and closed the door behind her, then flipped on the shower to let it heat up as she sang at the top of her lungs to lower her stress from the day. She'd forgotten to grab a bath towel from the linen closet in the hallway, but it was fine. There was no one there to see her anyway. She belted out the lyrics to the pop song playing as she opened the door to the walk-in shower.

Clunk.

Frowning, Kali stopped with one foot in the shower and looked back over her shoulder. Sounded like something had fallen in the living room. The cat must've knocked something over.

Click. Clunk. Thud.

"What the...?" She shut off the water and walked back to the bathroom door just as footsteps echoed down the hallway. Footsteps that were far too loud and solid to be Wednesday's. Kali's pulse stumbled and her throat dried.

Someone's in the apartment.

Kali distinctly remembered locking the door when she'd gotten home, so...

Oh, God.

The footsteps drew closer to the bathroom, and blood thundered in Kali's ears.

Her phone was still on the charging pad in the kitchen, where she'd left it, and her scrubs were scattered down the hall. She grabbed the last clean hand towel in sight to cover herself—at least it covered the front parts, if not the back—and tried to find a weapon to use against the intruder.

Razor? No, not very effective. She and Jen both used the kind of cheap razors where the blades were sealed inside the plastic handle part, so it wouldn't do anything unless she planned to shave the intruder to death. Her loofah? Nope. It was wet and soft. It wouldn't do much either. That left the can of hair spray in the medicine cabinet. Not much, but if Kali could spray it in the intruder's eyes, it might give her a chance to get around them and run to her phone.

Hair spray it was.

Armed and ready, Kali held her towel in place with one hand, then placed her other hand on the cold metal doorknob just as the footsteps stopped outside the bathroom door. Eyes wide, she took a deep breath for courage. Three, two, one...

She pulled open the bathroom door, then grabbed the hair spray, still managing to keep her towel in place. Locked and loaded, finger primed on the nozzle, Kali froze a split second before spraying as she stared into the face of the last person she'd ever thought she'd see again.

"Dylan?"

Dr. Dylan Geller had expected a lot of things when he'd agreed to leave his busy practice in Providence in his partner's hands and come to Boston to support the single mother of one of his young patients. He'd expected to get some rest. He'd expected to stay in his sister's apartment. What he hadn't expected—especially on his first night here—was a naked woman. Especially *this* naked woman. He'd known Kali would be here. She lived here.

But he thought she'd be fully clothed. And not ready to blind him with chemicals.

Speaking of Kali, it took him a second to recover from the shock of seeing her again after six years, then the added stunner of realizing she was basically naked, except for that little hand towel she held to her front, barely covering the important parts. He'd forgotten about all those freckles covering her amazing body—all soft curves and creamy skin and...

What? No. Stop it.

But the more he tried to look away, the more he couldn't. Finally, Dylan forced his gaze down to the floor and away from that silly little towel, with its grinning Christmas character that revealed far more than it concealed.

"Uh, hello." He forced the words past his suddenly tight vocal cords. Dylan coughed to clear the constriction and tried again. "I thought you knew I was coming."

"Hell no, I didn't know." Kali still had that can of hair spray aimed at his face, her cheeks flushed and her blue eyes bright with anger. "What are you doing here, Dylan?"

He held up his hands and took a step back from the line of fire. The last thing he needed was to have his vision compromised when he had an important case to consult on at the hospital in the morning. Plus, he'd agreed to volunteer his services at the understaffed pediatric day clinic while he was in town for the month, so working eyeballs were important. "Jen said I could use her room while I was here. She left you a message."

"A message?" Kali frowned, her strawberry-blond brows knitting. "I didn't get a message."

"Well, I don't know what to tell you, Kali. I'm sorry, but all the local hotels are booked for the holidays, so this was my only option. I'm in Boston for a case and—"

But she'd already pushed past him and headed down the hall, her bare butt jiggling as she walked away, grumbling under her breath. And once again, Dylan was speechless. The last thing he should be looking at was her ass, but how could he not? Firm and round, it was a fine butt, no doubt. Memories of those cheeks filling his hands as he'd pulled her closer that night on his parents' deck six years ago flooded his mind before he could stop them. Man, that summer had been a revelation in so many ways. It was the first time he'd dealt with real, true heartbreak because his then-girlfriend of three years had left him for his best friend. The first time he'd sought solace in what he knew would only be a fling. A fling with Kali...

He'd been twenty-six, she'd been twenty-two, and while they'd always been on each other's radar because of Jen, he'd never looked at Kali sexually until that fateful night she'd come out on the deck. They'd sat there alone, listened to the crickets, surrounded by the smell of freshly mown grass, and the air between them had seemed to sparkle with possibilities. Then Kali had turned to him and asked the last question on earth he'd ever expected. "Will you take my virginity?"

To this day, Dylan couldn't shake the feeling it had all been a dream. She'd been beautiful, and vulnerable, and so very willing. There were nights he still dreamed about the way she'd felt, how she'd tasted of the cheap wine they'd been drinking, the sounds she'd made as she came apart in his arms...

Gah! Stop thinking about that!

He'd moved well past that now, and his night with Kali had become one in a string of many one-night stands since then. In fact, Dylan had become quite the playboy over the years, at least according to his sister. Sex for him was a means to an end, a stress reliever. No strings attached.

Give him free and fun any day of the week.

"Crap," Kali called from down the hall, jarring him from his thoughts. "It's here."

Cautiously, Dylan made his way toward her voice, not sure if he should guard his eyes or not. He found Kali in the kitchen, glad to see she'd pulled on the blue scrub top he'd seen lying in the hallway earlier. "What's here?"

"Jen's message," she said, scowling over at him as she held her cell phone to her ear.

The hand towel from the bathroom now sat atop the breakfast bar, the ridiculous reindeer on the front grinning maniacally at him. He'd bet good money his sister had bought that. She went full-out tacky for the holiday, even though they were Jewish. The kitschier, the better for good old Jen.

He started to move into the living room, then stopped as a medium-size black cat climbed his jeans-clad leg like a tree. The cat's piercing green gaze dared him to do something about it as its nails dug into his skin like tiny needles. He would've removed the beast, too, except he couldn't seem to get his brain to focus on anything other than the fact Kali had put her phone down and was now walking toward him with that scrub shirt she was wearing barely hiding her essentials, stopping a few inches above mid-thigh.

God, what the hell was wrong with him? He didn't go gaga over women like this. He was a successful thirty-two-year-old man with a life and a thriving pediatric practice back in Providence, Rhode Island. But he should've known better than to trust his sister when she'd suggested he use her apartment while he was in town. There were always complications where Jen was concerned.

"Stay here." Kali gave him a wary glance as she passed him and headed down the hall again. "I'm going to change. Then I'll be back, and we'll talk."

She disappeared, leaving Dylan with the cat who'd reached his chest and now stared into his eyes like it saw and knew everything. Maybe it did. Maybe he should ask it what the hell was going on here because he sure didn't know.

With a sigh, Dylan sank down on one end of the sofa, the cat still attached to his front. Good thing he wasn't allergic and liked animals. "Hello, kitty. What's your name?"

The cat hissed and let go, stalking away with its tail in the air, like a big middle finger, feline-style. A perfect metaphor for how his evening had gone so far. His drive down, which should have taken an hour at most, had ended up taking nearly three because of traffic. And he hadn't eaten since breakfast because his office had been crazy busy, as usual.

He rubbed his tired eyes, then looked around the place for the first time since his arrival.

No holiday decorations other than the towel. Huh. Normally, Jen would've covered every available surface with gaudy snowmen and stars and all manner of sparkle and shine, like she'd usually done when they were kids.

The stereo switched to a song about Santa hurrying down the chimney tonight, and Dylan rested his head against the cushions and stared at the ceiling, wondering when the day's chaos would end.

A few minutes later, Kali returned, covered from neck to toes in a gray tracksuit and socks. Her long reddish hair was pulled up into a messy topknot, and her cheeks were pink. She looked good. More than good, if he was honest. Healthier, happier, more mature than he remembered.

More direct, too, if their previous interactions were any indication.

He'd always had a thing for confident women.

"So…" She returned to the open-style kitchen, pulling things out of the cabinets and setting them on the counter in front of her. "I'm sorry about the hair spray thing. But like I said, I didn't know you were going to stay here. My schedule at the hospital has been nuts since Thanksgiving and won't get better until January." She held up a mug and a tin of something. "I'm making hot chocolate. Want some?"

"Uh." Dylan's stomach growled. He ran a hand through his messy hair, then shrugged. It wasn't dinner, but it was better than nothing. "Okay. Sure. Thanks."

"You're welcome." Kali turned away to make their drinks. "Then we can figure out this mess of a situation."

CHAPTER TWO

"WHAT CASE ARE you here for?" Kali asked a few minutes later as she set a mug on the coffee table in front of Dylan, then curled into the corner of the sofa opposite him, careful to keep her tone neutral instead of betraying the roiling anxiety inside her.

This was her chance to start over with him. Her last chance. She didn't want to blow it.

They hadn't seen each other since *that night*, the one on the deck behind his parents' house, the one where she'd thrown caution to the wind and gone after what she wanted. Back then, it had been to lose her virginity, finally. She'd been twenty-two with no romantic prospects on the horizon. Dylan, who was four years older, had always seemed so put-together, so sure of himself and confident, and so broken-hearted that night on the deck after his girlfriend had left him. After a couple of beers, he'd confessed it all to her, and she'd felt his emotions as her own—the betrayal, the hurt, the deep ache that came from knowing nothing would ever be the same. She'd yet to get her autism diagnosis, so she'd interpreted her "masking" as something special between them, a resonance she'd never felt with anyone else. She'd vowed then and there to make him feel better. And what better way to do that than sex?

Everyone she knew raved about it, couldn't get enough of it.

Kali wanted to experience that too.

So when he'd turned to her for comfort, she'd given it to him. That, and so much more.

Even now, she'd wake up at night sometimes, hot and sweaty and unbearably turned on from memories of them together. She'd had other partners since then, but none that had rocked her world like Dylan Geller. And not just because he was her first. It was the care he'd taken with her; the way he'd treated her like a precious jewel he never wanted to let go; the way he'd held her afterward and stroked her skin, with awe and wonder in his eyes…

She shook off those memories now, recognizing them for what they were: an illusion.

Looking back now, it had to have been her autism that had made her feel like that about him, right? No way could one night of sex, no matter how spectacular, connect two people over years—unless there'd been a baby involved. And even as a twenty-two-year-old virgin, Kali had known better than to do it without protection. She was neurodiverse, not insane.

Dylan cleared his throat, drawing her attention back to him as he stared down into his mug.

He looked good. Just as handsome as he'd been that long-ago summer. Maybe more so because he'd matured. Thick, tawny blond hair, the longer top tending to flop over his forehead, forcing him to push it back often with his hand. A fit, well-built body. Tanned skin. And those sexy green-gold eyes. Kali was tall for a woman, at five-nine, but Dylan topped her by at least five inches.

He had a good soul too. Jen always called him the playboy with a heart of gold.

Over the years, Kali had figured she'd imagined his knight-in-shining-armor persona, dismissing the way the air had sizzled between them that day as just a fluke in that hot, hazy summer. Then they'd gone their separate ways—him, back to his residency in New York; her, to start medical school in Boston. She hadn't expected to see him again tonight. Hadn't expected to see him again ever, if she was honest with herself. She'd been content to tuck those memories away for safekeeping. She'd never told anyone about sleeping with Dylan, especially Jen. And Kali planned to keep it that way.

"Tetralogy of Fallot," Dylan said.

Kali took another swallow of her cocoa, her cheeks heating when she realized he'd been talking this entire time and she hadn't heard anything. "I'm sorry?"

Dylan frowned a little, his eyes narrowing on her. "Why are you doing that?"

"Doing what?" she said, even as the hairs on the back of her neck stood up and her nerves prickled.

He cocked his head to the side, his brows furrowing deeper. "I remember now. You did that the summer at my parents' house too. Staring at people's foreheads instead of looking them in the eye."

For a second, Kali wasn't sure how to act or what to do. She'd been caught in her act. No one other than her therapist and Jen, the two people she was closest to in the world, had ever caught her before. Did everyone know about her problem? Did all her coworkers know and make fun of her behind her back? Was Dylan making fun of her now? She wanted to sink into the floor and disappear, but since that wasn't possible, she tried to play it off instead. "Don't be silly. I don't do that."

"You're mirroring my actions and expressions too," he said.

"I'm n—" She started to deny it, then realized that yeah, she was. Her head was cocked to the side like his, her expression frowning, her eyes narrowed. Crap. Kali forced herself to relax back into the cushions and gulped more hot chocolate, glad for the heat on her throat to remind herself to stay alert, stay cautious. This was a test. One she was determined to pass.

Dylan continued to watch her closely for a moment, then sat forward to put his untouched mug of cocoa on the coffee table. "Is there something you want to share with me?"

Kali's desire to disappear intensified. When she was a kid and her parents had been fighting, she'd sometimes take out all the pots and pans from the lower cabinet and then crawl inside to shut out the world. They always found her, of course, and dragged her back into the chaos of reality, but man. What Kali wouldn't give for a nice, quiet cupboard right about now.

She managed to choke out, "No. Why?"

A beat passed, then two, before he said, "No reason. Forget I asked."

Dylan smiled then, the same one that used

to melt Kali's heart that summer. It barely touched the iciness inside her at present. Her heart was racing so hard she feared it would beat right out of her chest, and her mouth felt parched as old bone. Her therapist's instructions at the end of their last session rang through Kali's head on an endless loop.

"Watch what you say and do. If it doesn't feel right and true to who you are, if it exhausts you or doesn't make you happy, then ask yourself why you're doing it. And if there isn't a good reason...then don't do it."

So far, Kali had been able to follow those instructions pretty well. At work, she was doing better with developing an authentic bedside manner with her patients rather than telling them what she thought they wanted to hear to make them happy. And with her coworkers, she was trying to let them see a bit more of the real Kali—even if that meant she was blunt and bold and a bit boring sometimes.

Most of the staff at the hospital and those in her residency cohort were used to her odd personality, but newer hires took a bit to warm up to her, if they made the effort at all. That was fine, though. She liked being on her own.

Mostly. Okay, fine. It did get a little lonely sometimes...

Dylan was watching her expectantly, and she realized he'd asked her something else.

Kali opened her mouth, but it took a while for her to say, "Can you repeat that?"

Deep in her marrow, she knew he was going to ask her something she wouldn't like, and she began to sweat a little beneath her tracksuit. Part of her wanted to yell at him that she was too tired to cope with this and couldn't they just go to bed and talk about this later… or never? Another part of her wanted to cry because she was messing all this up so bad. Dylan was looking at her with those kind eyes of his, and if she saw pity there, she might actually die. In the end, she didn't do either, just sat there like a deer in the headlights because that's what she'd always done when things around her got too bad: froze. Sometimes, when her parents turned extra nasty, she couldn't even talk.

Dylan blinked at her a second, then sat back and scrubbed a hand over his face, seeming to come to some decision. Finally, he said, "You asked me about my case. I'm here for a patient of mine. His name is Jiyan Chowdhury, and he's four. He was born with a severe heart defect called Tetralogy of Fallot, but it went undiagnosed until a few months ago, when I found it on an exam. He and his mother are here for a consult with a pediatric surgeon, Dr. Ben Murphy, who'll be performing a procedure to correct the condition. I'm here to offer support to Jiyan's mother and answer any additional questions she might have. Amita is a single mother."

"Oh." Kali flexed her stiff fingers to relieve some tension, surprised her mug hadn't broken under the force of her grip. "Okay."

Dylan yawned, then stretched his arm along the back of the sofa, invading Kali's space a little more. It was a very masculine move, one that made an odd, unwanted tingle unfurl in her core. Dating was hard enough without involving her autism diagnosis, and with her crazy work schedule on top of it, Kali had a hard time meeting people. Add in her social awkwardness and, well, her pool of available suitors had pretty much evaporated. That left mainly the people at the hospital, but workplace relationships were fraught with landmines too. So yeah. She didn't really go out much.

"Or at all," her therapist's voice chided in her head.

"You're what now, a second-year resident?" Dylan asked, the dark shadows under his eyes suggesting he was as tired as she was. "How's that going?"

"It's going." Kali untucked her legs from beneath her and set her mug on the coffee table, forcing a smile. "I'm doing my peds rotation at Beacon. I see Ben Murphy a lot at the hospital and can introduce you, if you want."

"That would be great." Dylan smiled, too, warm and comfortable. "Your specialty's internal medicine, yes?"

"Yes." She stood, wondering how much of Dylan's nice-guy persona was genuine and how much was just politeness. He probably still saw her as that gullible young woman who'd hopped right into his arms on the deck that night. Kali was different, in ways she was only now discovering about herself. She liked things to stay the same, each day essentially identical to the other. Wake up, have her coffee and toast, go to work, see patients, come home. Repeat. Every day. Over and over and over again. Things were safer that way. More predictable.

"I'll show you Jen's room so you can get settled," she said, already walking away from him, leaving him little choice but to follow her down the hall to Jen's door.

"I really am thankful for you letting me stay here, Kali," Dylan said from beside her in the room. "I know you just got my sister's message, but it's a huge help to me to be so close to the hospital and my patient. And I promise, I won't be any trouble at all. I won't even remember I've seen your cute butt. Again."

Kali couldn't help physically recoiling from his teasing, then immediately regretted it when Dylan's smile slipped back into a frown. She wasn't acting the way he wanted, and she didn't want him to feel bad, so she laughed— a strained, tinny sound that hurt her ears.

Frustration burned in her gut, making her queasy. She didn't like lying, but she did it all the time. Her therapist was right: all harmless little lies to make other people feel better around her. Not doing so felt wrong.

"Kali? Everything okay?" he sounded concerned now, and she took a deep breath.

"I'm fine. Just tired."

Off-kilter, Kali stepped back toward the open door, away from Dylan and the past he represented. She'd worked too hard to put all that behind her just to have it all rush back now and overwhelm her. "I'll get you some fresh sheets from the linen closet."

She turned to walk away but stopped abruptly at the sound of Dylan's voice.

"Thanks again, Kali," he said, quieter now. "I really appreciate you helping me out here."

"Sure," Kali said, moving stiffly toward the closet. "No problem."

Dylan went and got his bag from the living room and brought it back to set it inside Jen's room, then leaned against the doorframe, looking far too gorgeous than any man should. "Well, maybe we can get reacquainted while I'm here. I'm sure there's fun things to do. I haven't been to Boston in a while, and especially around the holidays."

The last thing Kali wanted to do was spend more time with Dylan, traipsing around the city, visiting all the cute decorations, getting close to him again. He could stay at the apartment. That was enough "reacquainting" for her peace of mind.

She grabbed a stack of sheets and a blanket, then closed the linen closet with her hip before walking back to him and shoving the bundle into his chest. "Make yourself at home. My shift tomorrow starts at seven a.m. If you want me to introduce you to Ben, you'll need to be ready to go by then. Good night."

With that, Kali walked away with Wednesday hot on her heels, hoping like hell he wasn't watching her ass again but knowing already that he was.

Dylan unpacked, then took a shower, his mind still lingering on his odd reunion with Kali.

Six years was a long time, and people changed. Kali certainly had. Him too.

He pulled on a loose pair of sleep pants and a T-shirt, then crawled into bed, feeling bone-weary. He needed a good night's sleep to be ready for his first day at the hospital tomorrow. Besides making sure that little Jiyan and his mother were comfortable, he also needed to go over the case with Ben Murphy. The details of the boy's case were practically seared into his brain now after having studied them so many times, but he opened the files from his secure cloud storage on his tablet and went over them again just to make sure he was prepared for the consult in the morning.

Despite his happy-go-lucky playboy persona, Dylan had always been completely focused when it came to his work. It was what made him such a successful physician—and what had driven his one and only serious relationship away. At least, that's what Lisa had told him the day she'd broken up with him and walked out of his life forever. To be with his best friend. Whom she'd been sleeping with behind Dylan's back. She'd said it was because he was neglecting her because of his career. Right.

And it was then that he'd decided he couldn't

have both. It was either a relationship or a career.

He'd chosen the latter.

And rather than stay on campus that summer like he'd originally planned and feel sorry for himself, Dylan had gone home to Providence to nurse his broken heart and get his head on straight again.

Those first couple of weeks back home had gone well. Until Kali had shown up.

About a week before he was supposed to head back to medical school, he'd been sitting out on the back deck of his parents' house, drinking a beer and staring into the sunset, thinking about his future. Then Kali had walked out in her short shorts, with all that glorious hair streaming down her back and those long, tanned legs gleaming in the twilight, and he'd been dazzled. Dazzled and dazed and more than a little dumbfounded.

The beer might've helped too.

Sex with Kali had felt frantic and frenetic, like trying to hold the sun in your bare hands. She was hot and hungry, as if she'd needed him more than her next breath, as if she'd die without him. And for a vulnerable guy who'd begun to question everything about himself, Dylan couldn't get enough.

Even all these years later, it had never been

the same as it was with Kali that night. Tender yet ravenous. Sweet yet scorching hot. And when he'd woken up early the next morning, Kali was gone and all he had left were hazy memories.

Dylan sighed and tossed his tablet aside, then rubbed his tired eyes before turning off the light and rolling over to face the wall beside him. Having the past resurface now was nothing but a nuisance. He and Kali were different people. They'd both moved on. That night had been nothing but a one-off, a mistake.

Except as he closed his eyes and tried to sleep, the ache in his chest said that maybe there was more there than he was letting on. He sighed and flopped over onto his other side, punching his pillow with more force than was necessary.

And maybe he'd do well to remember that love brought nothing but pain.

Besides, he was here for one thing and one thing only: little Jiyan and his mother, Amita.

The sooner he got on with his work and back in his safe zone, the better. He had patients to help and people to save. He didn't have time for romance. Especially with Kali Mitchell.

CHAPTER THREE

KALI WOKE UP before her alarm the next morning and stared up at the shadows on the ceiling. Normally, the first thing she did was check her phone for messages. Today, the first thing she did was think about Dylan.

He was there. Sleeping right down the hall. The one man she'd never quite forgotten.

It had taken her forever to fall asleep last night because her mind wouldn't stop. Going over what had happened in the bathroom. Going over their conversation in the living room. Going over their one night together six years ago.

She should've been dragging. Instead, she buzzed with nervous energy.

At first, remembering last night had embarrassed Kali—*mortified* her. Dylan had seen her naked butt again, for goodness' sake! But then her therapist's voice had intervened. Telling her she should use this; telling her this could help her be better, stronger, more able to cope with her life. So Kali became determined. Dylan was staying at the apartment—nothing she could do about that now. She didn't like it, but she liked being rude and uncooperative even less.

So they would make the best of things. She'd use him to improve her social skills. They could talk, go out, maybe even flirt a little. She would not torture herself by watching his reactions and trying to be what he wanted. Of course she'd probably embarrass herself again, because yeah. But she was determined not to care. After all, why should she? They'd had sex once. That was it. And yes, he'd been her first. Arguably, her best, too, but she wasn't going there. He'd be gone soon, and she didn't need or want his approval.

And that made him perfect for her to experiment with, if he agreed.

With Dylan, she could be brave.

Problem resolved, Kali got up and got ready for work, then went out to the kitchen to start a pot of coffee. As she worked, she heard his door open down the hall, his shuffling steps to the bathroom and then the sound of the shower. She got extra interested in the coffee machine after that to avoid picturing a wet, naked, soapy Dylan.

"Morning," he said a short while later as he walked into the kitchen, dressed in a blue button-down shirt, navy tie and navy dress pants, his still-damp hair combed back from his face. He'd shaved, too, based on the little nick just under his chin.

Not that Kali noticed. Nope. Didn't notice at all.

Then he brushed behind her to get to the coffee maker, and her breath hitched without her permission from the brief contact. Her entire body went still as the old recognition hit her. The remembered feel of his body against hers. His familiar scent of sandalwood and soap. Dylan was here. He was real. And she would have to deal with him. Not necessarily on her terms but on his.

That last thought sent a jolt of pure panic through her, and all her resolve and determination from earlier went right out the window. *I can't experiment on this guy. I can't be brave with him. He knows too much about me. He knows me intimately.*

Her muscles tensed, and sensation pinpricked over her skin.

He wasn't just some meaningless one-night stand. He was the man who'd taken her virginity.

She'd asked him to do it.

Oh, God.

She gripped the plastic filter basket for the coffee so tight it threatened to crack. Her face burned. Blood roared in her ears. She had to get it together. She had a full schedule in the children's day clinic today after their weekly residents' meeting, and she was on call. Her lack of sleep and low-grade anxiety did not help at all. But the fact they were stuck together in this apartment for the next few weeks, at least until his patient was taken care of... Ugh. Why couldn't she just pretend like he wasn't there?

Kali jammed the filter basket into the top of the machine and poured the water in, then pressed the start button. Distracted, she turned fast...

And collided with Dylan.

Firm chest. Solid body. Warm. Alive. Real. It was horrible. Absolutely horrible.

He gently gripped her upper arms for an instant to steady Kali, then stepped back to put some space between them as the shock of his touch reverberated through her.

"Whoops," he said, giving her a small smile.

She tried to say "Sorry," but her voice refused to work. She was at eye level with his throat, and all she could seem to focus on was the sleek muscles working as he swallowed.

As a doctor, Kali had seen a lot of throats, but somehow Dylan's was different. Part of her wondered what it would be like to nuzzle her face there, perhaps nibble his earlobe, taste the salt from his tanned skin. An image flashed in her mind of that night on the deck, them entwined, him shuddering and groaning as she'd done exactly that...

"Uh. I was looking for cereal," he said, pointing toward the cabinet beside Kali, his eyes twinkling as his lips curved into a smile, like he had a secret. "Is it in here?"

Her frazzled brain malfunctioned. She'd forgotten how disastrously gorgeous Dylan was when he smiled like that. Something wonderful radiated from the heart of him, realigning his features and transforming him from merely handsome to beautiful.

She blinked up at him for a moment, trying to make sense of his words before blurting out, "There isn't any."

"Oh." He let her go, the sensation of his hands sliding away from her arms distracting her even more. "No big deal. How about toast?"

Toast. Toast. Her brain finally snapped back

to reality as the coffee maker beeped, signaling its doneness.

Kali turned away to fix herself a mug of much-needed clarity, then carried her cup over to the breakfast bar and sat down on a stool to scroll through her messages and emails, not answering his question at all.

If Dylan thought she was weird, he didn't say. Just turned around to fix his own coffee, stirring cream into his cup. "It's December fourth."

Frowning, Kali finally hazarded a glance over at him, taking in the sight of his broad shoulders and back stretching the material of his shirt. She didn't want to notice things like that about him. She wasn't interested in that right now. She had work to do. She didn't care about how nice Dylan looked in the morning or how good he smelled. She shoved those stupid flutters in her stomach aside and continued scrolling through her inbox, her tone a bit harsher than intended when she answered. "Yeah, so?"

"So?" Dylan turned around and crossed his arms over his chest, stretching that stupid material again—this time over his toned pecs—as he sipped his coffee. "Where's your decorations?"

Kali met his gaze with a scowl, scrunching her nose. "What?"

"You know. Christmas. *Ho-ho-ho* and all that. You don't even have a tree up in here."

"I don't want a tree," she grumbled, returning her attention to her phone. Live trees were a nuisance and a potential fire hazard. They got dried out and shed everywhere, and too much pine scent made her sneeze. Fake trees were made with all sorts of harmful chemicals. Besides, as busy as she was, no one would be here much to see it anyway, and it was just another reminder of her loneliness this time of year. At any time of year, really. "Too messy. Bad for the environment."

"Hmm." Dylan stood across the small kitchen, his hips leaned back against the edge of the counter, his long legs crossed at the ankle, his gaze burning a hole through Kali as she continued to ignore him. Or tried to, anyway. "What about wreaths? Garland? Mistletoe?"

"Why do you care?" she snapped, her anxious annoyance outweighing her need to be polite and keep him happy. "What are you, the holiday police?"

Kali noticed she was tapping her top teeth against her bottom teeth again, something she did when she was stressed. She stretched out her jaw, then massaged it, ignoring how Dylan's gaze zeroed in on the tiny movement. He kept watching her, obviously waiting for a real answer, so she finally gave in. "I don't like Christmas, okay? And Jen's not here. She's the one who usually does that stuff. Drop it, please."

Seconds ticked by slowly, and for a moment Kali thought maybe he'd respect her wishes. But then Dylan straightened and came around the breakfast bar to sit on the stool beside her, his knees brushing hers and causing more of those stupid tingles to zing through her nervous system. Kali tried to turn away, but there wasn't enough room to do so without causing a scene, so she kept her eyes locked on her phone's screen and pretended like he wasn't there. It wasn't working.

Finally, after the awkward silence between them got too taut, she asked flatly, "What?"

"Nothing," he said, but she kept catching him watching her over the rim of his cup.

"Seriously?" It was too early in the morning to play these games, and Kali really didn't have the spoons for it. Here came her bluntness again. "You did the same thing last night—watching me. If you have a question, ask."

"I just..." He sighed and set his mug aside,

tapping a finger on the granite bar top. "I noticed some things you were doing last night—the mirroring, not looking me quite in the eye—that I see in many of my young patients with autism, and I wondered if you'd been diagnosed."

Her heart squeezed painfully as adrenaline shot through her system. He couldn't know. She'd only told her parents and Jen, and Jen had sworn not to say a word to anyone. Her stomach dropped to her toes. Was she that easy to read? Was her weirdness that obvious to everyone else? Kali worried her bottom lip, then tried to play it off, her tone trembly and pathetic. "I don't know what you're talking about."

"Okay," he said, shrugging. "But you asked, so..."

Her skin felt itchy and too tight under his scrutiny. She *had* asked; he was right. But she hadn't expected him to guess her problem so quickly. And now that he knew, would that change the dynamic between them? He was a doctor too; he'd mentioned having autistic patients. Did that mean he'd see her in the same light? Or worse, that he'd want to fix her? She'd lost count of the number of times someone had tried to do that. Make her more social, happier, perkier, friendlier and more approachable. And before last year, Kali had taken all that on board, always trying to meet some impossible standard other people seemed to have for her and feeling devastated when she disappointed them again and again. But now that she had a name for what she was, it was supposed to be easier. People were supposed to accept her quirks and move on.

"You can do this, Kali."

Her therapist's voice cut through the noise, encouraging her, emboldening her.

"Does that mean you'll try to cure me, Doctor?" She'd tried to make it sound snarky, but it came out as scared, the lightness she went for in her voice ending up as brittle. A sudden wave of nausea had her breathing in through her nose and out through her mouth, her too-bright smile wavering.

Next thing she knew, he was hugging her. It had been a long time since anyone had hugged Kali, and at first, she was so stunned she didn't know what to do.

"You're shaking," Dylan whispered, his warm breath on her temple making her shiver deep inside. "I'm sorry."

Kali didn't have the first clue what to do, so she just buried her face against his shoulder. She figured he'd let her go then, but his arms tightened around her instead, hard but not hurting. The embrace reached deep into her bones and felt like pure heaven. So much so that despite her wishes, Kali leaned farther into him as her muscles relaxed and her stomach unknotted. Her head spun with relief.

For long minutes, they sat there in each other's arms, the steady beat of Dylan's heart comforting her. His low voice rumbled beneath her ear as he asked, "How are you doing?"

"Better," she said, not pushing away from him yet even though she should. "This is nice."

He chuckled, low and sexy. "I'm an expert hugger."

Kali burrowed closer, couldn't help herself. "You really are."

"Hugging helps when my patients get overwhelmed during their visits, so I've gotten good at it."

Kali peered up at him. He knew. She should have been panicking about that, but with his arms around her like this, she couldn't. It didn't seem like the end of the world. It felt like…a beginning, somehow. Of what? She wasn't sure. But she wasn't terrified anymore at least, so that seemed like progress. And honestly, his easy acceptance meant the world to her.

They each sat back slowly and sipped their coffees as the tension in the air cleared.

Dylan looked around the apartment again, his expression curious as he walked over to inspect the books overflowing the bookshelves. Kali realized he hadn't been there before. Jen usually went home to Rhode Island to see her family instead of them coming to Boston. It felt weird having a man around the place, in her space. And the fact it was this particular man left the air around Kali feeling...charged.

He ended up standing in front of the French doors across the room, staring out at the city one floor down. Kali couldn't help admiring him as he admired the view through the glass panes. There was a confidence around Dylan now, a relaxed coordination that hadn't been there six years ago. He'd settled into himself, she realized. He knew who he was and was comfortable with it in a way he hadn't been the last time she'd seen him. She found it both attractive and enviable.

"Nice place," Dylan said. "I love the balcony. Jen didn't mention it before."

"We don't use it much, since we're both working all the time," Kali said.

He glanced back at her over his shoulder, his look inquiring.

It was enough to push Kali to her feet and

send her fleeing to the safety of the fridge. "You said you wanted toast."

She pulled out the loaf of whole-grain bread they kept there and popped two slices into the toaster, then got out a knife and a jar of peanut butter. Dylan returned to his seat at the breakfast bar, his gaze burning a hole through the back of her. To stay busy, Kali refilled their coffee cups while waiting for her toast to finish. "What about you?"

"What about me?" Dylan asked, sounding confused.

"You celebrate Hanukkah, right?" The bread in the toaster popped up, and Kali spread peanut butter on each slice before giving one to him and keeping one for herself. She stayed near the sink, not trusting herself to sit near him again for fear she'd end up in his arms once more.

He shrugged, wiping his mouth and hands on his paper napkin. "I used to, as a kid, with my parents. But I'm not really observant anymore. I honestly can't tell you the last time I went to synagogue." One side of his lips quirked into a smile as he glanced at her. "It's just hard, with my schedule and everything."

"Yeah, I get it. We were never really a church-going family that I remember growing up. Like, maybe at Christmas or Easter we'd go, but that's it. But that isn't why I don't like the holidays."

Dylan kept his attention on his toast, letting her take her time to continue.

"It's all just too much. Too commercialized. Too in your face all the time. And most years, I'm stuck with my mom and whatever boyfriend *du jour* she's brought home this time, since my dad's been out of the picture for a while now. I'd rather just stay here and enjoy some peace and quiet."

"Hmm." Dylan seemed to take that in, his expression thoughtful. "But not too much, though."

"'Too much'?"

"Alone time." He hesitated, then seemed to come to a decision. "I'm no expert on autism, but I do know that too much isolation isn't good either." Dylan finished his food, then wiped his mouth one last time and sat back. "Maybe me being here isn't such a bad thing after all."

Kali sighed and began cleaning up after herself and Dylan. She couldn't stand a messy kitchen. "Not like we'll see a lot of each other. And I get all the 'peopling' I need during my shifts. I would've been fine here by myself until Jen gets back."

"I'm sure you would." He smiled, and those

fizzy flurries started up inside her again. "But maybe we can make this month enjoyable for both of us."

"Enjoyable how?" Kali asked, wariness creeping up inside her.

You can do this, Kali.

"Keep each other company. Raise each other's spirits when needed."

"How?" she asked again, strangely excited by the prospect of doing social things on her terms, setting her own boundaries, even if it disappointed people—perhaps *especially* if it disappointed people. When she realized Dylan was looking at her funny, her cheeks prickled with heat and she closed her eyes. "Sorry, I—"

"It's fine." He stood and came around the breakfast bar to lean against the counter beside her. "How about we start over?"

Thankful for a respite from the embarrassment threatening to burst her into flames, Kali nodded. "I'd like that."

"Good." He grinned and held out his hand. "Hello. I'm Dr. Dylan Geller, pediatrician."

Kali blinked at him a moment, then shook. "Dr. Kali Mitchell. Internal medicine."

"Nice to meet you, Kali." Dylan's warm fingers squeezed her cold ones gently before letting go. "I have an idea."

"Uh-oh." Kali chuckled. "That's never good."

"No. Hear me out." He walked out into the living room again. "Since this is a new beginning for us, and neither one of us is big on the holidays, let's start new traditions for ourselves."

"New traditions?"

"Yeah. I'm sure there's lots of things going on in the city. We pick the ones that sound like fun and go for it."

The thought of battling holiday crowds made Kali light-headed. "I don't know. I think we'll both have our hands full at work and—"

"Can't work all the time, right?" He held up his hands like it was obvious. "Plus, the more we have to do, the less time we have to sit around and be awkward together."

He wasn't wrong; she had to give him credit for that. Awkward had a way of getting Kali in trouble. "Fine. I'm listening. But make it fast. We've got about fifteen minutes before we need to leave for the hospital."

"Perfect." Dylan pulled out his phone and sat on the sofa, patting the cushion beside him. "Come on. Let's see what fine holiday celebrations Boston has to offer."

Ten minutes later, they'd scrolled through endless browser results. Kali had never realized how many activities there were in the city around the holidays.

"Well, I think attending the giant-menorah lighting this Thursday at Boston Commons is a must. I don't want to lose my Jew card." Dylan added it to his calendar. "And afterward, we can go to Café Landwer, if I can get a reservation. Best shakshuka in town."

She squinted at the screen. Trying new foods wasn't exactly her thing. "I don't know."

"Start with small things and try them in a safe environment."

Her therapist's words looped through Kali's head. When she'd woken up, she'd been determined to go for it; then she'd lost her resolve. Now, with an opportunity in front of her, she had a choice. Considering that Dylan had guessed her diagnosis and was still here, he was probably the safest bet she had right now, despite the past. It was just dinner, after all. She could handle it. She *would* handle it.

"Okay."

"Okay." Dylan grinned, and Kali's world brightened just a little. "And if you feel overwhelmed or don't like it, we'll leave. Promise."

And for the first time in a very long time, she found herself looking forward to the holidays.

Dylan's first time inside Boston Beacon Hospital reminded him of a zoo. In a good way.

People were bustling around as he followed Kali through the chaotic lobby that had been decorated to the hilt. There was even a live reindeer in a pen in one corner near the floor-to-ceiling windows and a giant Christmas tree for the kids to feed a carrot to and have their picture taken with. The jingle bell–encrusted yoke around his neck had the name Tinsel emblazoned on it. Dylan made a mental note to bring Amita and Jiyan down to see it later that day. A glance upward showed a huge artwork mobile hanging from the glass atrium in the ceiling, bright-colored shapes spinning slowly in time to the carols pumped in through the PA system. It felt like a joyous surprise in a place where he suspected a lot of children were scared and unsure. He stopped to admire it before racing to catch up with Kali.

She hurried expertly through the crowds, making a beeline for the elevators, and Dylan followed in her wake. She pressed the Up button, and they boarded the car, along with several other people, to ride up to the second-floor Pediatrics ward. He and Kali stood in a back corner of the elevator, shoulders bumping as the car jerked upward. Knowing she was on the autism spectrum made so much sense now. He saw it in all the little things about her that she covered well but that, as a doctor, he'd picked up on. Her nervous tics, her avoidance, her people-pleasing. He'd have to be on watch for that last one, especially since he'd suggested they do things while he was here. He never wanted Kali to feel like she had to go along with his ideas just to make him happy.

Dylan's thoughts turned toward his busy first day. His top priority was making sure Jiyan and Amita had gotten settled in all right. Then he had a meeting with Dr. Ben Murphy, the surgeon who would be performing Jiyan's complex and delicate procedure in a few weeks, after all the necessary testing had been done ahead of time. And finally, he was due to start a shift in the hospital's day clinic for low-income and indigent children and their families. When he'd first talked to Dr. Javier Pascal, the head of the pediatrics department here, Dylan had expected just to come along for moral support for Amita and Jiyan. Then, out of the blue, Javi had mentioned the staff shortage in the day clinic and asked Dylan if he'd mind helping while he was here. Considering Dylan was an overthinker by nature—a problem that was great when it came to patient cases and not so great in other areas of his life—he'd jumped at the chance to stay busy and help others while staying out of his head.

The fact that he and Kali would be working in the clinic was a bonus.

Ding!

People surged forward as the elevator doors slid open to more controlled pandemonium. Staff dressed in scrubs briskly walked around a large central hub. Parents sat in a waiting room, some knitting, some watching TV, some just looking anxious.

Kali showed him to the staff room, then left to head to her residents' meeting.

Inside, Dylan found an empty, unmarked locker and put his stuff in there before slipping on the white lab coat he'd brought with him from his office in Providence. His name was embroidered over the left breast pocket; he figured it would be easier having his name and credentials right there for everyone to see since he was the new doc on the block. After hanging his stethoscope around his neck, he closed his locker, took the key and then headed back out to the busy nurses' station to see if he could find which room Jiyan was in.

"Uh, hello," he said to a woman in scrubs behind the desk, who was furiously typing on a computer. She was scowling at the screen like she wanted to murder it, and he was glad not to be a keyboard, the way her fingers were pounding it. Under her breath, she kept mumbling about a Dr. MacKenzie and their ridiculous orders. Dylan looked around for someone else to help him, but this woman was it for the moment. "Sorry to interrupt," he said tentatively to avoid getting punched like that computer. "I'm Dr. Dylan Geller, and I'm looking for my patient, Jiyan Chowdhury. He was admitted yesterday."

At first, the woman had no reaction at all, and Dylan started to wonder if she'd even heard him. But then she looked up at him, her bright-blue eyes pinning him to the spot like a bug on a wall. Her gaze flicked down to the name on his lab coat, then back up again. "Right. Dr. Geller. We've been expecting you."

She stood and held out her hand, drill sergeant style. "Linda Wachowski, head nurse." They shook, her grip strong. Then she turned back to her computer and typed some more. "Looks like your patient is in Exam Room 412, Doctor. Down that hall—" she pointed to the left "—sixth door on your right."

"Thanks."

"Anytime," Linda called behind him as he walked away. "And welcome to Boston Beacon."

He knocked briefly on the door to Room 412, then walked in to find Jiyan in bed, his toys spread out on the wheeled table in front of him, and Amita in a chair by his bedside, helping the boy put together what looked like some kind of superhero soldier.

"Good morning," Dylan said as he entered, holding his hand up to keep the mother from standing. Amita was thirty-two and petite, and she reminded Dylan a bit of that actress, Priyanka Chopra. She was also a single mom, doing her best to keep it together during what had to be one of the hardest times of a mother's life—seeing your child sick and not knowing how to help them. But hopefully, coming here would help a lot. If the surgery went well, it should cure little Jiyan completely.

"Hey, Dr. D!" Jiyan said in an excited voice only a four-year-old could accomplish. "Want to see my new Trans-Venger toy?"

"Wow!" Dylan stood near the bed, trying to show the appropriate amount of awe for a half cyborg, half Greek god soldier. "That's impressive, Jiyan. Did you build him yourself?"

"Yep. I did." The kid grinned wide, showing his baby teeth. He was already taking after his late father, who'd been a highly successful engineer. Amita's proud gaze warmed Dylan's heart. "He can fly and jump into outer space and even dive into the depths of the ocean."

"Impressive." Dylan nodded. "A man of many talents."

Amita laughed. "How are you today? Did you get settled into your sister's apartment?"

"I did, thanks," Dylan said, avoiding Amita's gaze. They'd been friends long enough now that she could read him like a cheap paperback. Since her husband had died when little Jiyan was just a year old, Dylan had looked out for Amita and her son. Strictly in a platonic way. There had never been any romantic sparks between them at all. But trying to raise a child on your own was hard enough. Raising a child with a medical condition that required special care and attention was even more difficult. And Dylan admired Amita's strength in handling everything she had on her own. Her dearly departed husband would've been proud.

"And?" Amita asked, raising a dark brow at him.

Dylan frowned as he glanced over Jiyan's digital file on the screen, pointedly avoiding her too-perceptive gaze. "And what?"

Amita shook her head, her long dark hair trailing over her shoulder. "Don't lie to me, Dylan. I can see that there's more to the story."

"There is no story," he said, hoping his firm

tone would be the end of the discussion. "Has Dr. Murphy examined Jiyan yet?"

"No. And don't change the subject."

"What subject?"

This was how their friendship went. One of them would have an issue they needed to talk about but didn't really want to discuss, and the other would pester them until they did. Dylan wasn't exactly the type of guy who wore his heart on his sleeve. More like he wore his heart in a Kevlar vest buried deep inside a locked vault in his chest. Safer that way all around. And probably why he was thirty-two and still single, without a hint of a permanent long-term relationship in sight.

Because that's the way he wanted it.

Wasn't it?

Yeah. It absolutely was. He'd spent the last six years keeping it light and easy and fun. No sense stopping now, right? If it wasn't broke, don't fix it. That was what his mom had always said. Words to live by. He resisted the urge to rub the odd ache in his chest and scowled at Jiyan's file like it was the Rosetta stone.

"The subject of—" Amita started, but she was interrupted by a short, sharp knock on the door before it opened, and in walked Kali.

"Sorry to interrupt," Kali said, her blue

gaze darting between Dylan and Amita. "Dr. Geller, can I have a word with you, please?"

"Uh, sure." Dylan forced a smile to cover the stumble in his pulse. Why did that keep happening to him every time Kali was around? Sure, they'd slept together once upon a time, but he was well over that. Whatever the reason, he felt Amita's interested gaze burning a hole in the side of his head, so he better get it together fast. He stepped around Kali, ignoring the slight fragrance of flowers and mint from her hair as they passed and moved closer to Jiyan's beside. "While you're here, let me introduce you to my favorite patient. Kali, this is Jiyan Chowdhury. Jiyan, this is my friend, Dr. Kali Mitchell."

"Hi," Jiyan said, waving from his bed. "Are you a kids' doctor too?"

Kali looked from Dylan to the little boy, then shook her head. "I'm actually specializing in internal medicine."

"What's that?" Jiyan frowned and scrunched his little nose.

"*Beta*," Amita said, ruffling her son's dark hair, "don't be rude." She then smiled at Kali and held out her hand. "Sorry about that. He's only four. I'm his mother, Amita."

They shook hands, Kali still looking a bit uncomfortable. "He wasn't rude. Just honest.

I appreciate that." Her smile lost the tension at the corner of her lips, and Dylan felt Kali's stiff posture relax. "It's nice to meet you, Jiyan."

"Same." Jiyan held up his toy. "Do you like superheroes?"

"I do." Kali laughed, the bright sound zinging through Dylan all the way to his toes before he could stop it. "Who's your favorite? MCU or DC?"

"Both. But Iron Man's my all-time fave of any universe." Jiyan then went on to tell Kali all the reasons why he was his favorite.

While they talked, Amita came around the bed to stand on Dylan's other side. She tilted her head, narrowing her dark eyes on Dylan. "Something tells me there's more going on here."

"There's nothing going on," he hissed under his breath. "Kali's an old friend."

"Hmm." Amita's smile looked all too knowing for Dylan's taste. "I bet."

"Is there something you wanted to talk to me about?" Dylan said to Kali, attempting to interrupt what had become a fairly in-depth discussion of superhero lore. When she didn't turn to him right away, Dylan called, "Kali?"

She looked back at him over her shoulder

and their gazes locked, and Dylan felt flushed all over. God help him, this was ridiculous. Even worse, Amita was still watching him like a hawk too. "I wondered about dinner tonight."

"Dinner?" Amita said, with far too much interest for Dylan's liking. "Wait," she said, her smile widening. "Is this your sister's roommate, Dylan? You two are sharing an apartment together?"

"Yes," Kali said at the same time Dylan said, "No."

Amita tilted her head. "Well, which is it?"

Kali gave him a quizzical look. He shouldn't have lied. He wasn't sure why he had.

"Yes, we are sharing the apartment while my sister is out of town and I'm here for Ji-yan's case," Dylan clarified. "But that's all. Separate rooms, separate schedules."

"Hmm." Amita sounded as if she saw right through his BS. "Plus dinner."

"It's not what it sounds like," he said, too fast.

"And what do you think it looks like?" Amita was watching him make a fool of himself, and Dylan resisted the urge to run a finger beneath the collar of his dress shirt. When had it gotten so hot in here?

"We're not sleeping together," Kali blurted

out. "We did once, a long time ago, but that's not happening again now."

"Oh?" Amita perked up even more, clearly holding back a laugh as she seemed to enjoy Dylan's burgeoning discomfort. "Wow. Okay. So there is something between you two?"

"No!" Dylan said while Kali said, "Yes."

"I had a sleepover once," Jiyan offered, still playing with his toy. "Johnny Easton ate too much pizza and threw up."

"Kali," Dylan said, hoping to salvage what was left of his dignity and the situation. "Can I talk to you out in the hall, please?"

"Sure." Kali smiled at Amita and Jiyan like nothing out of the ordinary had happened. "Nice meeting you both."

"Same." Amita's grin could've lit up Gillette Stadium. "Look forward to talking again soon."

Not if Dylan could help it. He opened the door and waited until Kali had walked out before he hazarded a glance back at Amita. "Be right back."

"Don't hurry on our account," she responded, her little smirk saying he was far from off the hook.

With a sigh, Dylan walked into the hall and closed the door behind him, nearly bumping into Kali, who stood near the wall off to the side, waiting.

He felt flustered and frustrated and completely discombobulated for no reason. This wasn't who he was. He was Mr. Cool and Calm under pressure. Everyone said so. At least, they *had*, until Kali came back into his life. He took a deep breath, then ran a hand through his hair. "What's going on?"

"Nothing." She blinked at him a moment, looking completely unaware of and unaffected by the chaos now roiling inside him. "Ben Murphy is here. I was going to introduce you. Then, when you're done with him, I wanted to see when you'd be ready to start working in the clinic. There's a patient I could use a consult on if you're available."

"Oh, uh, yeah. Sure." He stepped back, then checked his watch. "I'll be right there. Let me just finish up with Jiyan."

"Great." Kali straightened and walked away, leaving Dylan standing there, staring after her. "Ben's office is this way."

Her hips swayed as she walked away, and he couldn't help remembering the night before, watching her scurry down the hallway of the apartment naked. Gah! When in the hell had his well-ordered life gotten so out of whack?

Dylan hurried after her, rounding the corner in time to see her stop near a door at the far end of the adjacent hallway. By the time he got there, Kali had already knocked and stuck her head inside, saying something to the person within that Dylan didn't quite catch.

A man a few inches shorter than Dylan walked out to greet him. He had wavy brown hair that was shorter on the sides and a neatly trimmed beard. His blue eyes held an intensity that was both arresting and a tad off-putting, like he was too busy to be bothered with most things or people.

"Dylan, this is Dr. Ben Murphy. Ben, this is Dr. Dylan Geller," Kali said before starting to walk away, stopping then to glance back at Dylan. "See you when you're done."

"Uh, hello," Dylan said once he and Ben were alone. "Great to meet you."

Ben gave Dylan's hand a short, strong shake, then gestured him into the office, nearly as no-nonsense as Kali. "Sorry, I don't have a lot of time in my schedule, so let's make this quick."

"Sure." Dylan had come well prepared for this meeting, with all the pertinent information fresh in his head and Jiyan's records sent over to Ben ahead of time. "I suppose this is more a formality than anything else. I just want to make sure my patient gets the best care."

"Of course." Ben indicated Dylan should take a seat in one of the chairs in front of the desk while he took his behind it. "Let's get started, shall we?"

For the next twenty minutes, they discussed the intricacies of Jiyan's case and the other details Dylan would need to know to adequately prepare Amita and her son for the big day. Symptoms of the boy's congenital heart issues, diagnosed by Dylan earlier that year as Tetralogy of Fallot, hadn't manifested until he'd turned three and fallen behind on his growth charts. Then, in rapid succession, he'd begun having a heart murmur and periods of bluish skin as he'd become more active. When he'd passed out one day at home, a panicked Amita had brought him to the ER where Dylan had met them and looked at the abnormal echocardiogram results. That combined with the cyanosis—or "tet spells"—were enough to warrant more tests that eventually confirmed the rare condition. And since it involved not one but four different heart defects—a hole between the two lower ventricles of Jiyan's heart; a narrowing of the pulmonary valve and the main pulmonary artery; an enlarged aortic valve that opened from both ventricles, not just the left one; and a thicker-than-normal muscular wall of the lower right chamber—Dylan's patient needed specialized surgery to correct all four defects at once.

Enter Dr. Ben Murphy.

"So," Ben continued, jarring Dylan from his thoughts, "I believe the best course of action is to replace Jiyan's pulmonary valve, widen the artery and patch the hole in his ventricular wall. That should improve blood flow to his lungs and the rest of his body. As you know, we've booked him for the surgery on the twenty-first of this month, which will allow us to monitor him ahead of time and make sure all the necessary testing is completed first."

"Sounds good. How long will the procedure take?"

"Five to six hours, give or take an hour before or after for prep and recovery," Ben said, standing. "I'll perform the operation in our cardiothoracic OR here in the ward." He checked his watch, then walked around the desk to the door. "Sorry, but I've got another meeting downstairs. It's been great meeting you, though, Dylan, and I'm sure we'll talk more as the surgery approaches. If you have any questions or would like to set up a meeting with the boy's mother involved, just let me know."

Dylan watched the man go, then made his way back to the nurses' station to find out where the day clinic was so he could get to work there. Boston was turning out to be a lot more hectic than he'd anticipated, but he supposed that was good. It would keep him out of trouble. Especially where Kali was concerned.

CHAPTER FOUR

KALI SPENT ABOUT an hour going over charts in the clinic before actually seeing her first patient. It was something she liked to do to make sure she had all the facts straight and clear in her head. Plus, it gave her a chance to get used to the idea of having Dylan there, working alongside her. She was still reeling a bit from their conversation that morning and the fact that he'd read her so easily.

Then there was the hug.

It had been a good hug. Very good. She wasn't usually a fan of being touched unexpectedly, but with Dylan... Kali swallowed hard and stared down at the nurse's notes for a new patient without really seeing them. She could still feel the warm, reassuring pressure of Dylan's arms around her, and it sent a shiver through her before she shoved it aside.

"You're not getting sick, are you?" asked Ailani, one of the new nurses on the floor.

"No. I'm fine." Kali gave her what she hoped was a confident smile, though she'd gotten the impression from their first meeting a few days ago that perhaps she didn't have to pretend with Ailani either. Like Dylan, Ailani just seemed to know how to be around her without overwhelming her. Kali appreciated it more than she could say.

"Well, I'll tell you who else is fine." Ailani glanced over her shoulder toward the open-concept exam area, where Dylan was standing and talking to a young patient's mother. "Our new visiting pediatrician, Dr. Geller. You guys arrived together today, yeah? He seems nice." She turned back to a mortified Kali, and her dark eyes widened. "Oh, sorry. Didn't mean to be unprofessional."

Kali quickly went back to studying her notes, her face burning hot. "No. I mean yes. I mean…" She took a deep breath, wondering why she was getting so flustered over Dylan. It wasn't like they were a couple or anything. And nothing Ailani had said was unprofessional at all. Not wanting the nurse to be upset—or worse, hate Kali—she hurried to reassure her. "You weren't unprofessional. Dylan is very attractive."

Totally objective observation. Yep.

When Ailani kept watching her like she expected Kali to say more, she added, "And yes, we arrived together because he's staying with me during the holidays. Well, not with *me*," she went on, aware she was starting to babble but unable to stop herself. "I mean, Jen is my roommate and his sister, and she told him he could use her room at the apartment over Christmas since she's out of town, even though she didn't tell me about it, but it's all good. I mean, Dylan and I see each other a lot now, and since we slept together six years ago it's awkward, but we'll get over it and..."

By the time Kali stopped to take a breath, Ailani was blinking at her like she had no clue how to dig herself out from beneath the word avalanche Kali had unleashed on her. And she'd blabbed about being with Dylan too. Great. Her first shot at maybe a new friend in years, and she'd blown it already. Way to go. Autism: one. Kali: zero.

Finally, Ailani chuckled a little under her breath, then shook her head. "No worries. I think we all have things we'd rather forget in our past." She jotted something in the chart she was working on, then set it back in the rack on the desk. "I'll start prepping your first patient in exam space one, okay?"

"Okay." A torrent of relief flooded Kali's system, and she leaned against the desk when her knees wobbled. She hadn't blown it; Ailani still liked her. That was good. She felt better. "Yes. Thanks. Be right there."

The nurse left and Kali took a deep breath, glad for a moment alone to gather her thoughts again before starting her shift. The way the day clinic was set up was unusual, but it worked for them. They'd taken what had been a large secondary waiting area slash break room in the ward and converted it to be used as a clinic for low-income, uninsured kids and their families for routine and acute care. It took a bit of the burden off the ER downstairs for cases that weren't urgent, and it allowed those who needed medical care to get it without worrying about how to pay for it. Generous donations from some of the hospital's wealthy donors allowed them to keep it up and running year after year. Kali liked working there during her rotation here in peds. She liked working with kids too. They were easier to read. Easier for her to relate to as well. No walls. No ulterior motives. They said it like it was.

Which was something Kali had been accused of on more than one occasion too.

She'd just picked up her chart and was heading toward her first patient when a cheer sounded down the hall. Kali stepped back and began clapping and shouting, too, as was tradition in the children's ward. Whenever one of their young patients was headed into a serious surgery, all the staff lined the halls on the way to the OR to clap and cheer and wish them good luck on their journey. Today it was a little boy named Timmy. He was four and had a brain tumor, which the surgeon was going to remove today. He'd been on the ward for the past month and a half, going through chemo and radiation in prep for his procedure, and they'd kept him in isolation due to his lowered immune system. As the gurney wheeled past, even from inside the clear protective shield, little Timmy's grin was huge as he waved to all the staff he saw on a daily basis and everyone cheered and waved back to him as he passed, warming Kali's heart. Such a brave boy. She blew him a kiss and said a silent prayer for him to make it through and have a swift recovery. His oncologist and the nurses who took care of him flanked the gurney, smiling and laughing and doing their best to make what could've been a terrifying experience one of hope and joy.

Once the parade passed, Kali crossed the hall and entered the clinic area. Dylan stood nearby, waiting for her.

"What was that?" he asked as they walked toward their first patients of the day.

"Just a little something we do for the kids when they have surgery," Kali said, keeping her attention on where Ailani stood with a mother near her son, who was seated atop an exam table. According to the notes Kali had seen, the boy had a sore throat and slight fever. Probably a cold, but best to check.

"Hello," Kali said, shifting into her "on" professional mode. It was like she was two people: the Dr. Kali who worked at the hospital and the Kali at home. One of the reasons, her therapist kept telling her, that she was probably so tired and close to burnout all the time. Her therapist had given Kali brochures to read about it and suggestions on how to slow down, but she'd been too busy to read them yet, so...

"I'm Dr. Mitchell." She took the chart Ailani handed her and watched as the nurse walked away to help the next patient in line. Kali glanced at the paperwork, then smiled at the little boy. "And you're Adam, right?"

When the little boy didn't answer, just frowned down at his shoes, his mother stepped in and said, "Hi. Yes. His name is Adam. And I'm Yolanda, his mother. He's two."

"Nice to meet you." Kali set the chart aside,

then snapped on some gloves and got a tongue depressor from the jar on the mobile cart nearby. "Okay, Adam. Can I look inside your mouth for a moment?"

Whatever had been going on with the boy's throat didn't stop him from wailing at the top of his lungs, then kicking and biting and flailing on the table like Kali had tried to cut his leg off. She'd seen her share of the "terrible twos" during her peds rotation, but this took the cake. Plus, she knew better than to put her hands anywhere near the kid's mouth until he'd calmed down for fear of getting bitten.

Kali hazarded a glance down the room of exam spaces to where Dylan was finishing up his first patient. A nice quiet baby, sound asleep in his mother's arms. She wasn't eavesdropping but could overhear Dylan telling the mother not to worry about how much the baby was eating. As long as she was happy and keeping it down and the baby's bowel movements were normal, it was all good.

Lucky guy.

She turned back to her tiny terror of a patient. Yolanda, the mother, stood off to the side, seemingly unfazed by her son's outburst. Right. Kali took a deep breath and tried again. From her studies, she knew that temper tantrums at that age were usually triggered by fear or frustration. Two emotions Kali was more than familiar with herself. So, for a minute, she let Adam do his thing, thinking he'd wear himself out. But when the rest of the clinic started watching the show, the pressure to act grew unbearable.

There was a sudden lull in the chaos and Kali seized it, stepping forward and leaning down, using her gentlest voice to say, "This won't hurt at all, Adam, I prom—"

And that's when she got decked by a two-year-old. One little fat fist on her cheek before the enraged wailing started anew.

Kali straightened and rubbed her sore cheekbone, her desperation growing. "Does he behave like this at home?"

Yolanda sighed and shrugged. "At least a couple of times a day."

"How do you handle it?"

"All the books I've read say to just let him have at it. Eventually, he'll tire himself out."

"I see."

Adam, meanwhile, was turning a mottled shade of dark red, and Kali was starting to worry. If he kept going at the rate he was, he'd hyperventilate and pass out. Not exactly a stellar outcome for a resident at her next review.

You can do this, Kali.

The words snapped Kali out of her anxiety spiral. Maybe they'd work with a petulant toddler too.

"Stop it, Adam!" Kali said sharply, straightening her posture to stand tall and strong.

It shocked the kid enough for him to stop, for about three seconds. Then his wailing went up an octave or ten. Kali was about to walk away when Ailani walked by, dropping off a small Bluetooth speaker on the mobile cart. Soon, opera music began to play, and Adam stopped crying, his attention now focused on the speaker.

Both Kali and Yolanda stood there stunned as Adam smiled, then laid down on the table, calm as a clam. When Ailani passed by again, en route to another exam pod with a new patient, Kali pulled her aside to ask, "How did you know that would work?"

The nurse laughed. "I didn't. But opera always puts me to sleep, so I thought I'd try."

After collecting the necessary swabs and doing a quick exam, Kali wrote a prescription and sent Yolanda and Adam on their way, then moved on to her next patient. This one was a six-year-old girl named Lian Muang. She and her father, a Burmese man named Cetan, waited quietly in the pod beside Dylan's. Kali had seen Lian a few months back for some vaccinations.

"Hello, Lian," Kali said, greeting the little girl, then her father. "Cetan. What brings you in today?"

"I don't feel good," Lian said, looking miserable and lethargic. Her skin was pale, and her eyes were red-rimmed.

Kali updated the girl's medical history and began her exam, palpating Lian's neck and finding the lymph nodes there were swollen. Then she looked in the girl's mouth—without issue, this time—and found, unsurprisingly, that her tonsils were red and inflamed. Seemed strep throat was the order of the day.

"Lian," Kali said as she changed her gloves and took a swab pack from the cart. "I'm going to take a culture from the back of your throat. Is that all right?"

Both the little girl and her father nodded. Lian opened her mouth, and Kali gently swabbed her tonsil area before sticking the culture in a plastic tube to hand off to the lab nearby.

Five minutes later, the results were back. Positive.

Kali jotted notes in the chart as she talked to her patient. "Lian, you have strep throat. I'm going to place you on antibiotics. Dad, make sure she eats something before she takes them, otherwise they could upset her tummy."

Kali finished with her notes, then turned to Cetan. "Strep throat is highly contagious. I'd keep your daughter away from other children for a minimum of twenty-four hours, preferably thirty-six to forty-eight. That means no school, no play dates. Basically, she should stay at home and rest in isolation. Adults are susceptible, too."

"But, Daddy." Lian's voice turned plaintive. "What about my sleepover this weekend?"

Cetan looked from his daughter to Kali. "They've been planning it for months. She'll be so disappointed."

"Well, it's Monday now." Kali did the calculations in her head. "If she starts the antibiotics today and her fever and sore throat are gone by Friday, I'd say she should still be okay to go. She shouldn't be contagious anymore."

"Thanks, Dr. Mitchell!" Lian threw her arms around Kali, hugging her around the waist and making it all worth it.

"You're welcome." Kali smiled and patted the girl's back before handing the prescription to Cetan. "They can fill that for you at the dispensary down the hall before you leave."

"Thanks."

"You're welcome."

The rest of the day went by in a busy blur of patients, and between Kali and Dylan, they saw an array of shots, skin rashes and sore throats. No more tantrums, thank goodness. Kali took a short break around noon, hoping to talk to Ailani about going to the football game with her and Dylan over the weekend, but the nurse was nowhere to be found. So she sent off a quick text instead, saying she had two extra tickets and asking if Ailani would like to bring a friend to the game with them. She grabbed a granola bar out of the vending machine and ate it standing at the nurses' station, too restless to sit. Luckily, she got a response from Ailani that she'd love to go to the game before Kali returned to see more patients that afternoon. One less thing on her plate to worry about.

Her last patient of the day was a young couple, the Marshands. Patty had given birth to her second child, Miley, a week earlier, and this was just an incision check from her C-section. She sat on the exam table, breast-feeding the baby, while Jon, her husband, sat in the chair beside the table, absorbed in his phone. Their three-year-old son, Gage, played on the floor with some plastic blocks from the waiting room, surrounded by a field of Cheerios he'd evidently been eating and also smashing with the blocks.

"Good afternoon," Kali said.

"Hey," Jon said, still distracted by his phone.

"Shh," Patty chided him. "Miley likes quiet when she's feeding."

The day clinic was probably one of the least quiet places in the entire hospital.

"I need a five-letter word," Jon said, ignoring his wife. "Starts with a K and ends with a TZ."

Before Kali could answer, Dylan leaned around the curtain. "Klutz."

All three adults looked at him in amazement.

Dylan shrugged and grinned. "I'm a Wordle fiend. Carry on."

"Right." Kali shook her head and went over the patient's chart again. "How are you doing after the delivery, Patty? Any questions or problems for me today before I examine your incision?"

"A couple." She handed Kali a list.

As Kali read through them and prepared to answer, Gage smashed a Cheerio with a loud thwack, sending cereal bits flying into the surrounding exam pods. One disadvantage to the day-clinic setup.

"Stop it!" Patty scolded her son. "Miley's sleeping. You don't want to disturb your sister."

"Yes, I do." Gage scowled as he smashed another Cheerio.

To avoid another noisy conflict, Kali jumped into the list. "How about we start with this one: What temperature should the baby's room be? Between sixty-eight and seventy-two degrees is a good range."

"What about bathwater?" Patty asked.

"Lukewarm." Kali glanced down at little Gage beating the heck out of his cereal with blocks. "Miley is your second child, and you obviously did okay with the first one. I'd suggest following the same blueprint."

"Dammit," Jon said, glowering at his phone, his expression nearly identical to his toddler son's. "Game timed out. The Wi-Fi here sucks."

Kali couldn't argue with that. One of the reasons they went back to using regular old paper charts in the day clinic was because of network issues in this part of the ward. Also it was cheaper.

Patty gave her husband a quelling look, then focused on Kali again. "Yes, this is my second baby, but a lot has changed since Gage was born. I just want to make sure I do everything right."

Gage smashed more cereal, then threw the block under the curtain into Dylan's exam pod. "When is Miley going back where she came from?"

"I believe this is yours," Dylan said, coming around the curtain and crouching in front of the little boy to hand him his block. "And who's Miley?"

The boy pointed up at his mother, then crossed his little arms. "She's my sister and I hate her."

"Hmm." Dylan looked up and met Kali's gaze, silently asking permission. She gave him a tiny nod to continue. He sat on the floor beside Dylan like it was the most natural thing in the world. "You know, I have a younger sister too. Her name is Jen."

"Do you hate her?" Gage asked, brimming with a level of affront only a three-year-old could achieve.

Dylan appeared to consider that a moment. "There are moments…" He winked up at Kali. "But no. I don't hate her. Why don't you like Miley?"

"She always needs something. And she takes up all the time and attention. Mommy used to sit and read me stories and play with me, but now Miley cries and she runs to take care of her."

"Ah." Dylan nodded, looking very serious. "That is definitely a problem. Miley should be able to handle that stuff herself, huh?"

Gage's brow furrowed as he frowned at Dylan. "She's a baby. She can't do that stuff."

"Oh." Dylan seemed to think on it some more. "Then your dad should do it instead, so your mom can spend time with you."

"Dad's at work. He's super busy."

Dylan and Kali both looked at Jon to find his phone put away and his attention finally focused where it belonged: on his family. "Okay. I see. So if Miley can't do stuff and your dad's super busy, I guess Miley will just have to do without whatever she needs. Seems reasonable. If she's hurt or hungry, too bad."

"No." Gage glanced at his baby sister, then the floor. "Not if she's hurt or hungry. She needs help."

"But you just said there's no one else to give it but your mom, and you hate your sister anyway, so…"

"I don't hate her," Gage finally said, a tear running down his little red cheeks. "I just…" He sniffled. "I miss my mommy."

"Oh, sweetie." Patty stood and handed the baby off to Kali, who took it without reservation because she was so distracted by what Dylan had just done. She'd always known he was good with kids and a great doctor, but she hadn't seen him in action until now. While Patty knelt down to hug her son, Kali cradled

Miley in her arms and looked down at the newborn's tiny body, her chubby limbs and amazing head of flaxen hair, her bright-blue eyes looking up at Kali with innocence and curiosity. She could smell Miley's sweet baby smell, and while she'd never really thought about having kids herself, a surge of wonder still swept over her that she was holding a tiny human in the first weeks of its life. Then, quickly, the anxiety rose. Miley was so helpless, so young, so trusting. She could be hurt so easily. By the time Patty stood back up, Kali couldn't hand the infant over fast enough.

Kali didn't miss the way Dylan looked at her, either, a mix of curiosity and concern at her actions. She turned away to fiddle with putting on gloves at the cart. "Let me go ahead and exam your incision so we can get you on your way."

At the end of clinic, Kali found Dylan waiting for her at the nurses' station, looking far too relaxed and happy for Kali's taste. She felt drained and stretched thin, like a toy wound up too tight. How did he act so...engaged all day? It baffled her mind.

"Hungry?" he asked as they walked to the staff locker room together.

She thought about it for a moment, realizing that yeah, she was starving. "We can pick something up on the way home."

"Or," Dylan said, "we could stop at the grocery on the way home and I can cook."

"You cook?" Kali scrunched her nose. While their apartment had a nicely appointed kitchen, neither she nor Jen used it much. "What do you make?"

"Lots of things." He held the door for her as they walked back out into the hallway and down to the elevators. "But tonight I'm in the mood for latkes."

"Latkes." The elevator dinged and they stepped inside.

"You know. Potato pancakes. You had them at my house growing up, I'm sure."

"Yes. But aren't they a lot of work?"

Dylan looked over at her and winked again. This time, Kali had the feeling he was talking about more than food as the elevator doors slid closed. "The best things in life always are."

Two hours later, they were back at the apartment, Dylan grinning when he saw the preparations Kali had made in her kitchen. All the food items they'd bought at the kosher grocery store down the street were neatly laid out—Russet potatoes, a large onion, eggs, kosher salt, baking powder, black pepper and oil for cooking. Over by the window, Kali had already set the kitchen table for two. She hadn't forgotten a single thing.

Dylan liked knowing this stuff about Kali. Liked being one of the few people who knew about her autism diagnosis. Looking back, he was kind of shocked he hadn't realized it sooner. But he'd always been fond of different and quirky, and he liked stowing away secret traits about people in his mind like treasure. It was what made other people real to him, what made them special, and Kali was no exception. His dad kept two Swiss army knives attached to his key ring. It always made Dylan grin when he saw that. Why *two*? How would his dad ever use both? No one else Dylan knew did that. His mother had so many quirks that they were a quirk in and of themselves. And his sister, Jen, would never admit it, but he knew she planned out her outfits to match the color of the day based on some magical almanac thing she got every year. When Jen finally settled down and had kids one day, they'd be that obnoxious family who were all color-coded to match. He couldn't wait for it. Now Dylan had Kali back in his life, and he was excited to learn everything he could about her.

Talking so fast she could hardly breathe,

Kali took a wine bottle from the freezer and peeled the metal wrapping off the end. "I wasn't sure what kind of wine went with latkes, so I got a bottle of red, too, if you think that will work better. I put it in the pantry." She walked past him and over to the opposite counter, still talking. "Where do you put wine when you don't have a wine cellar? Is the pantry the right place? I've got no clue. I don't drink much." She yawned, then pulled out the cork with a corkscrew. "I'm beat. If I fall asleep at dinner, it's no reflection on your culinary skills. Just warning you."

Dylan just smiled and worked on washing, then cutting the potatoes lengthwise into quarters. Today at the day clinic had been enlightening for him. Seeing his new digs for the next month, meeting new colleagues, seeing little Jiyan and Amita and reassuring himself they were settled in okay. Then, later, observing Kali as she worked with patients. It was the first time he'd seen her as a physician, and he had to admit, he'd been nervous. Social skills weren't exactly her forte, but with her patients, she was kind and caring and hyper-engaged. It was even more admirable because he knew now what strength it took for her to put on that show. The fact she seemed to be a nervous wreck now only endeared her to him more. He wanted to put her at ease and help her relax, so acting on instinct and his experiences with little autistic patients, Dylan dried his hands, then moved behind her to squeeze her shoulders before running his palms down her arms. Kali went completely still.

He leaned down to whisper in her ear, "Is this okay? Touching you like this?"

Kali had pulled her hair up into a messy topknot again after they'd gotten home, and they'd both changed into comfy clothes. This close, Dylan could see goose bumps standing up along the length of her neck. They were running down her arms below her short-sleeved T-shirt as well. A good sign, he thought.

Kali swallowed with an audible click, then nodded. Dylan couldn't help lingering a little longer, inhaling deep to draw her scent into his lungs. Clean, feminine, with something he couldn't quite name. Wait. No. Cinnamon. That was the scent. He stood close enough now that his lips brushed the shell of her ear, and Kali's breath hitched as the corkscrew fell from her hand to clatter onto the countertop.

She managed to set the bottle down, then touched a flustered hand to her ear before meeting his eyes over her shoulder. Her cheeks were flushed, her eyes dazed, her breaths

quick, and Dylan bit back a smile. He'd just
learned something new.

Kali's ears were sensitive, and she liked to
have them kissed. And perhaps nibbled too.

"M-maybe you should keep cooking," she
said, putting the corkscrew back into the
drawer.

"Yeah. I probably should." Dylan acci-
dentally brushed against Kali again when he
moved back to his spot, and her entire body
jumped in reaction. He felt the weight of her
stare burning into him as he peeled and sliced
the onion, then put it, along with the potatoes,
into the food processor to coarsely grate them.
Dylan might be lost in a maze when it came to
Kali and their past together, but if there was
ever a woman who needed to be kissed, it was
her.

He hazarded a glance over at her, and she
quickly looked away, but then, almost against
her will, her gaze returned to his mouth. Yep.
Definitely time for a kiss. And while they'd
made an agreement—strictly professional—it
was just a kiss. No big deal. No...

Dylan leaned toward Kali, completely focused, but she turned away at the last second
and filled the sink with water. "We can wash
up as we go along. More efficient that way."

"Sounds good." His voice sounded husky to

his own ears, and Dylan cleared his throat before turning off the food processor and dumping the contents out onto a clean, dry dish towel to squeeze and wring out as much of the liquid as possible. He'd been making these latkes since he was a kid, learning the recipe at his Nana's knee. Now he could practically make them with his eyes closed. Good thing, too, since he was a tad distracted tonight.

Kali filled two wineglasses with chardonnay and handed one over. Dylan watched with wide eyes as Kali finished hers in two large gulps, then wiped her mouth with the back of her hand. When she noticed him watching her, she blushed and explained self-consciously, "I'm trying to relax."

"Take it slow," he said before sipping his own wine from his glass. It was good. Crisp, not too sweet, nice. Then again, he didn't know much about wine, so... "You don't want to go overboard."

"I won't." For a second, something flickered in her eyes, and he wondered if she was remembering that night on the deck. They'd both gone overboard then. Kali looked like she wanted to say more, but she turned away again. "How long will this food take?"

"Not long," Dylan said, torn between relief and disappointment at the missed opportunity.

He shouldn't want to get involved with Kali like that again. It would be messy and complicated, and someone was bound to get hurt. And yet he couldn't seem to stop thinking about it again now. He distracted himself by pointing to the frying pan. "Especially if you help. Heat that on medium heat, then pour in a quarter inch of oil, please."

Some of the tension leaked out from her. Kali stood straighter and nodded. "I can do that."

Dylan smiled and poured the potato-and-onion mixture into a bowl, then added two eggs, half a cup of flour, a teaspoon of baking powder, and some salt and pepper. He then stirred it all together.

While they worked, they talked about their day and their patients, then Kali added, "We're going to the Patriots game at Gillette Stadium on Sunday."

"We are?" Dylan frowned. He didn't remember that being mentioned before. "Why?"

"Babs sent me tickets in the mail the other day." Kali rolled her eyes. "Her boyfriend of the month had them, and now they won't be here, so he thought I might like them." She stared down into the oil heating in the frying pan. "I asked Ailani to come with us. She's bringing a friend."

"Okay. She's the nurse from the clinic this morning, right? She seems nice."

"She is. She guessed my diagnosis too. Same as you." Kali fiddled with the silicone spatula on the counter. "She says she's got an uncle back in Hawaii with autism."

"A lot of people are on the spectrum, Kali. And more are diagnosed every day. It's not such a stigma anymore." Dylan dropped a bit of test batter into the oil to make sure it sizzled, then used a heaping teaspoon to place the batter into the pan. Once the first batch was going, he used the spatula to flatten and shape the drops into discs. "There are some studies that suggest that one in every one hundred adults is on the autism spectrum—they just don't know it."

"I know. It's just a lot to take in," she said, still staring down into the pan. "Those are starting to brown around the edges."

"Yep." Dylan flipped them over carefully to cook the other side. He wished he'd been around when she was diagnosed the year before. Kali obviously didn't have an ideal support system in place. When the first batch was done, Dylan reached around her to grab the platter she'd set out for them and found himself right behind her again, close enough to touch her, though he was careful now not to. He'd gone a little too fast earlier, but it had been difficult to resist the curve of her shoulder, the graceful arch of her neck, the fine line of her jaw. She even had pretty ears. Dylan wanted to trace them with the tip of his tongue.

Rather than go overboard, though, he tried to keep his thoughts on neutral things as he fried up a second batch of latkes, then placed them on the platter next to the first ones. One got stuck to the bottom of the frying pan, and he leaned closer to get a better look at it and—

Kali's lips pressed to his.

Dylan's heart jumped as electricity jolted through his nervous system. His blood rushed and he tried to be gentle, tried not to get carried away, but Kali was so soft, so perfect, and he couldn't get enough. Summoning all his restraint, he swept his tongue into her mouth and tasted wine, only sweeter. Kali gasped, and he could have gotten drunk on the sound. Maybe he did because he deepened the kiss as her tongue slid against his. Everything in him tightened and clamored to be closer to Kali, and he poured that aching need into the kiss.

It seemed to go on forever. It was over too soon. When they parted, their breaths were ragged. Kali looked like she'd been kissed long and hard, and Dylan didn't think he'd ever seen anything more beautiful. The last latke was still on his spatula and the rest were getting cold, but he didn't care. All he wanted was more Kali.

Before either of them could think better of it, Dylan kissed her again, greedy this time, and Kali seemed right there with him, kissing him back, letting him in. Until she turned away and pressed clumsy fingers to her mouth.

"We shouldn't do this." Her voice was throaty and so damn sexy. "We agreed, Dylan."

He heard her, but he couldn't stop himself from swaying toward her anyway, craving one more taste. It took a herculean effort, but he stopped himself, barely. "You're right. We did."

Her chin went up a notch, and her expression turned stubborn. After a long pause, where she seemed to struggle against herself, she finally said, "If we do this, it couldn't be more than a fling."

Dylan's eyebrows shot up, and he stifled a surprised laugh. "Uh. That's…pretty much all I do. You know that. No strings for me."

He should've felt relieved. She was basically giving him exactly what he wanted: all sex, no commitment. And they had a definite time limit because he'd be gone as soon as his young patient was on the road to recovery after surgery. So why did that niggle of doubt burst his happiness bubble?

Because he was an idiot, that's why.

As if sensing his inner conflict, Kali narrowed her gaze, her expression skeptical. "Are you sure?"

"Of course I'm sure." He turned to dump the cooling oil into a disposable container, put the whole thing into the trash, then stuck the dirty fry pan into the soapy water of the sink. "Mr. Playboy, remember? I'm King of the Fling. You won't get any argument from me there. And if that's not what you're looking for, then no big deal."

"You're wrong. It *is* a big deal. I'm supposed to want a long-term relationship. Commitment is supposed to be my primary concern. According to my mother, I should already have one kid and another on the way. Never mind my issues. I should want marriage and kids and an orgasm every night."

"Well, I've never had any complaints before, and—"

She ignored him and kept talking. "On the flip side, I don't want someone clinging to me, around all the time…you know. I want someone there, but only when I want them there.

Does that make sense?" He started to answer, but Kali blushed sunburn red and clarified awkwardly, "I just mean that I've got a lot of things to work out myself, and I don't want to burden anyone with all my issues. Until I can figure out who I am now and what I want, it wouldn't be fair to bring someone into this." She gestured vaguely around herself. "Right?"

That almost seemed like a challenge to Dylan, so he asked, "But what if they wanted to deal with your stuff? What if they like things messy and complicated?"

Not that he was talking about himself, because he wasn't. He'd been there, done that, had the skid marks on his heart to prove it.

Looking pained and frustrated, Kali said, "That person doesn't exist. Trust me. I'm…a lot to handle. That's why I think maybe flings are better for me right now." She traced a finger over the lines in the quartz countertop. "I don't know why I kissed you, Dylan. I'm sorry."

"Don't be," he said quickly. "I kissed you back too."

She searched his face. "And you're okay with that?"

"Obviously."

Her eyes narrowed again. "Are you joking?"

"Never." He smiled and trailed the back

of his fingers down her cheek. "I never joke about sex, Kali. I just like to be up front and open from the start. So everyone knows where they stand. It makes things a lot easier."

She released a long, shaky breath and finally relaxed against him.

For a while, they both stared down at the platter full of yummy latkes; then, when their gazes connected and his stomach growled loudly, they both busted out laughing.

"Let's eat before these get cold," Dylan said.

CHAPTER FIVE

THURSDAY NIGHT, KALI stood beside Dylan in a crowded Boston Commons, waiting for the lighting of the huge, golden, twenty-foot-plus menorah erected there. The place was packed, and everyone had their cell phones out, taking selfies and shooting video of the scene. Local Rabbis gave speeches about tolerance and perseverance through hard times of persecution and strife, and everyone waited for the governor to arrive to light the first flames—lanterns set atop each of the branches of the menorah—to kick off eight nights of Hanukkah festivities in Boston. There was live music and dreidel games for the kids and plenty of treats and outdoor activities to keep everyone occupied until the big moment.

The weather had been cold, but that didn't seem to dampen anyone's holiday spirit. Kali stuck close to Dylan's side so they wouldn't get separated and, well, because it just felt good being with him.

Not that she'd tell him that. Bad enough she'd thrown her sanity out the window the other night in her kitchen and kissed him. Not once but twice, and quite passionately too. Neither of them had discussed it since, but it still lingered in the air between them like a coiled cobra waiting to strike.

Or maybe that was weird, to think about what had been some of the best kisses of her life in such a menacing way. And honestly, it wasn't the kisses that bothered her; it was what they could lead to. She'd steered clear of serious relationships since starting medical school for a reason. They took too much time and effort and could easily overwhelm her and knock her completely off-balance.

They could also break her heart.

And maybe, deep down inside, Kali also believed she might not deserve forever with someone.

After all, her parents hadn't been the best role models, and now, with her diagnosis… It was a lot, both for Kali to deal with and for a potential new partner in her life to accept and agree to take on. Of course, Dylan didn't seem to have a problem with it, which was great—but then, he wasn't forever material either. He'd been very clear on that the other night, and she'd been around him long enough and had heard enough from Jen over the years to know Dylan wasn't relationship material.

A good fling? Yes. A good boyfriend or husband? No way.

But Kali was getting ahead of herself, as she often did. One kiss did not a relationship make. And even if they did decide to sleep together again while he was here, it could—and would—be just that.

Sex. Nothing more.

Considering her therapist's challenge for Kali to mix things up and try something new and different, maybe Dylan was the perfect choice after all. If he was game. Based on his reactions the other night, he was, but if Kali was going to do this, she needed to be sure.

"Ladies and gentlemen," an announcer said from the dais at the front of the crowd on which the giant menorah was located. "May I introduce Rabbi Rabinowitz from Chabad Boston, who will say few words before Governor Healey and Mayor Wu light the first lights of Hanukah. Then Rabbi Rabinowitz will lead us in the first night blessing. Rabbi, take it away."

A man dressed in all black, midforties, with a yarmulke, took the mic and began talking about unity in times of trouble and division. It was a message Kali could certainly get behind. Dylan, too, if the way he put his arm around her shoulders and tugged her into his side was any indication. It was nice there, snuggled against him. Warm and safe and cozy. A girl could get used to that.

To distract herself from those forbidden thoughts, Kali focused on the happenings at the front of the crowd. A group of people were being loaded onto an elevated work platform and slowly raised up toward the top of the giant menorah. Another Rabbi fiddled with a blowtorch that would take the place of the traditional candle used to light the menorah.

Dylan, who'd been fairly quiet so far, leaned down to whisper in Kali's ear, "Mayor Wu is lighting the Shamash. It's the center candle in the menorah and sometimes called the helper candle. According to tradition, only that flame should be used to light all the other flames."

Kali suppressed a shudder of warmth from his breath against her skin and glanced up at him. "You remember a lot for someone who doesn't practice his religion."

"Once a Jew, always a Jew," Dylan said, grinning down at her, his teeth white and even in the twilight. "I spent years going to Hebrew school as a kid, had my bar mitzvah when I was thirteen. I was raised with all this stuff. Just because I don't observe all of it anymore doesn't mean I've forgotten it. It's part of who I am. It's in my blood."

"Makes sense." Kali sometimes wished she'd been part of something like that. Something that would help define her, give a community of other people who were like her that she could relate to. Then she supposed her autism did that, but not really in the way she'd wanted. The Rabbi on the elevated platform began singing in Hebrew, and Kali leaned closer to Dylan. "What's he saying?"

"The first night Hanukah blessing," Dylan said, his gaze trained on the Rabbi as he translated the words for Kali. "'Blessed are You, Lord our God, King of the universe, who has granted us life, sustained us, and enabled us to reach this occasion.'"

His reverent tone filled her with awe, too, and she blinked hard against the sudden sting of tears in her eyes as she watched the governor take the blowtorch from the mayor and light the leftmost lantern on the menorah signifying the first night of Hanukah. Once that was done, a huge roar of applause and cheering went up from the crowd as the music started up again and the festival of lights was officially underway. Caught up in the moment and the excitement, Kali turned to Dylan and hugged him tight. He squeezed her back, and they just stood there, holding each other, until Kali finally pulled back a little to look up at him. Dylan watched her, his lips slightly parted, and she knew, deep down in her pounding heart, that they were going to kiss again. His head started to lower, and gone was the awkwardness that had set in since their last kiss. Gone was her anxiety and his adamant rule about no strings or emotions. Because right then, Kali would've sworn the light in his green-gold eyes burned with more than just lust or adrenaline or desire. They were close enough now that their breaths mingled, close enough for her to see the hint of dark stubble just beneath the surface of his jaw. Close enough that if she went up on tiptoe, she'd be kissing him right that very second and...

"Chag Sameach!" someone shouted nearby, jarring them out of the moment.

Feeling more than a bit dazed, she stood there as Dylan stepped back and scrubbed a hand over his face. Then he took her hand and started leading her through the crowd toward the exit, saying over his shoulder, "Let's get a cab to Café Landwer. Beat the crowds."

* * *

The whole quick cab ride over, Dylan berated himself.

Why the hell had he almost kissed her again? He'd sworn to himself he wouldn't. The more time that stretched between the night in the kitchen and now, the more certain he was that it had been a mistake. Yes, it had felt incredibly, gloriously right at the time. But no. Just no.

He had no right to burst back into Kali's life again now—especially when she had so much happening—and seduce her back into bed with him. Because clearly that was what had happened. He had six years and a boatload more experience than her sexually. And even though she'd kissed him first and rocked his world off its axis, he was still in charge. He had more experience. At least, he thought he did.

Dylan frowned out the window as they headed down Newbury Street toward Exeter, the holiday lights reflecting the happy faces of the pedestrians crowding the sidewalks this time of year. He ran through the conversations he'd had over the past six years with Jen where Kali had come up, and he couldn't for the life of him recall his sister mentioning Kali dating anyone. Granted, she could've had a series of one-nighters like him, but Kali didn't seem the type. So he had to assume she didn't sleep around.

Plus, it made him feel better to wallow in his guilt. Better than wallowing between the sheets with Kali, because that would only get them both in trouble. And the last thing he needed on this trip to Boston was trouble. He had enough to deal with at the hospital.

And speaking of the hospital...

He glanced over at Kali in the shadows. "How's your face?"

"Fine," she said, looking at him, her strawberry-blond brows knitting. "How's yours?"

Dylan snorted. "I meant where that kid hit you the other day."

He'd not noticed a bruise, but makeup could hide a multitude of things.

"It's fine. He was only two." Kali reached up and rubbed her cheekbone as if to show him it was all good. "No harm done."

"I'm glad." The cab swerved to the curb, and Dylan paid the driver, then got out on his side while Kali got out on hers. They stood in front of the restaurant's vintage black-and-white facade at the base of the Charles Mark Hotel. It sounded kind of corny, but Café Landwer Back Bay was one of Dylan's favorite places in the city. He loved the old-world feel of the place. The black-and-white tiled floors and the banquettes. The melting pot feel of its menu, which offered everything from Austrian schnitzel to Tunisian/Yemen shakshuka and Italian pizza. The crowds inside were just as diverse as the food, drawing on the community around the place and the Israeli owners' backgrounds. The first Café Landwer had been opened in Berlin in 1919 and was still going strong today, with locations in both Israel and the United States.

They walked inside and were immediately surrounded by the scrumptious smells of freshly brewed coffee and grilled food. They were open for breakfast and lunch, too, but dinner was what Dylan was after now.

"This place looks awesome," Kali said as she looked around with wonder.

"Wait until you taste the food," Dylan said, leading her to a small, open table for two near the back. They checked out the menus and ordered their food—schnitzel for him with a side of crushed potatoes and za'atar-spiced salmon for her with couscous and a green herb salad—then took off their coats and settled in. Neither of them mentioned their almost-kiss at the menorah lighting. Kali tilted her head back to gaze up at the white geometric hanging design near the ceiling, but what captivated Dylan was her profile. The way her lips parted ever so slightly; how nice it was to be here with her.

Determined to stay on track, though, he said, "Have you been here before?"

"Nope." She looked back at him, grinning, the light dancing in her blue eyes. "Do you always come here when you're in town?"

"Yes." Trying to play it cool, even as his stomach turned a bit queasy with nerves, he shrugged. "It's one of my favorite spots in Boston."

"Nice," she said, sitting back. "Thanks for sharing it with me."

They held a look a beat or two longer than normal before sitting back as the server brought their drinks. When the Asian waiter left, Kali took a sip of her ginger-and-lemon iced tea and Dylan drank his Sanpellegrino straight from the bottle.

"So, football game on Sunday, huh?" he said for lack of anything better.

"Yep. Patriots playing the Saints. One o'clock at Gillette Stadium."

"Cool."

"Cool."

Several more minutes passed in which they looked at anything but each other, and Dylan felt like a complete ass. Any game he might have developed over the years seemed to vanish whenever Kali was near. He didn't want to think too hard about why that was, but he also didn't want to walk on eggshells around her the for the rest of his time here. One of them had to confront the gorilla in the room, and it seemed like it was going to have to be him.

"Look, Kali," Dylan said, leaning forward over the table, eager to get this over with before their food arrived. "About those kisses..."

Kali held up a hand, her cheeks blushing pink. She met his eyes for the barest fraction of a second before glancing away. "I think we should have a fling."

Stunned didn't begin to cover how he felt just then. He blinked at her while his mind struggled to comprehend her words. "I'm sorry?"

She cursed under her breath, then shook her head. "I'm trying to be brave here, and my therapist said I should break out of my comfort zone and do new things, and you're here and I thought since we'd already done it once a long time ago and you sleep around all the time that you'd be a safe bet and—"

Her tone had grown steadily louder as she'd babbled on, and now people at surrounding tables were looking over at them. Dylan flashed what he hoped was a "nothing to see here" smile and took Kali's hand across the table to get her attention. "Hey. Slow down a minute. Take a breath."

They both inhaled deep, then exhaled slow. *Courage,* Dylan told himself, even though his heart felt like it might pound out of his chest. He could handle this. He'd been with a lot of people over the years. This was just another date. No strings. No emotions. No need to get all worked up about it. Steeling himself, he reached over to tuck a loose tendril of her hair behind her ear. When her cheek twitched, he asked, "Do you mind when I do that?"

Kali started to shake her head, then stopped. "I like the sentiment, I guess."

"But?" he prodded.

"But…" She looked up at the ceiling again. "It bothers me when people touch my hair."

"Okay. Noted." Dylan stored that information away and ran the backs of his fingers along her cheek, then cupped her jaw in his hand, gently forcing her attention back to him. "What about this?"

Kali took another shaky breath and let it out slow. "It's okay."

"Okay *good* or okay *bad*?"

Her lips curved. "Okay *good*."

"Good." Without realizing it, Dylan leaned in, the need to press his mouth to hers an ache inside him, but instead, he grazed his nose against hers, the small caress making her eyes drift shut.

Finally, he went for it. His lips brushed hers, and when she moved a little closer to him to prolong the contact, his control snapped, and he took her mouth the way he'd been craving. She made a tiny sound in her throat, and Dylan was lost. He deepened the kiss like a man drowning. He wanted to memorize everything about that moment, kissing her in his favorite restaurant, but Kali's mouth was all he could think about just then. Her intoxicating softness, her taste, the way she seemed to pull him deeper into the moment. He couldn't get enough. He couldn't stop—at least until a discreet clearing of the server's throat announced the arrival of their dinners.

Reluctantly, they both sat back as their food was placed before them.

"Can I get you anything else right now?" the waiter asked.

They both shook their heads.

Dylan wasn't sure he was capable of speech at that moment, his throat tight with need.

Kali kept her focus squarely on her plate, fiddling with her napkin and silverware before taking a huge bite of her food.

He did the same but couldn't taste a thing as her words looped in his head endlessly.

I think we should have a fling.

Dylan was beginning to think so too. Or, more precisely, a specific part of him was. He shifted in his seat and placed the napkin on his lap to make himself more comfortable. But somehow, having a "fling" with Kali just seemed wrong. Then again, he didn't do anything other than flings, so what else would this be? It hurt his brain to think about, but it was necessary if they were going to move forward with this.

They both ate their dinners in silence for a while, and finally the tension between them dissipated enough for Kali to say, "This is really good."

The food was delicious, as always, but he couldn't enjoy it. Not until he said what needed to be said. "I really like you, Kali."

"I like you too," she said, and there was a weight to her words that told Dylan she meant it.

"And I'd be lying if I said I didn't want to sleep with you again," he confessed. "After what just happened, I think that's obvious. But instead of labeling what's happening here, why don't we just see where things go?" He had a hard time concentrating over the loud rush of blood in his ears. He wasn't sure if he was saying all this for her benefit or his.

"Right…" She frowned and brushed the hair away from her face with an impatient swipe of her hand. "I want you too. I'm just trying to deal with all this and my diagnosis and what my therapist thinks would help me, and I—" She gave up trying to explain.

It took him a moment to understand what she was saying, but then a weird mixture of feelings boiled inside him. Maybe he was wrong. Maybe Kali didn't want to sleep with him. Maybe he was just a new diversion. It stung more than he expected. It shouldn't matter why she wanted to have sex with him, just that she did. They weren't supposed to mean anything to each other; that was the whole point.

"Are you angry?" she asked at last.

Dylan didn't know what he was feeling, so he asked instead, "When do you want to start this thing?"

Kali worried her bottom lip, then shrugged. "I don't know. Now?"

His heart jumped. His hands ached to touch her, but he gripped his fork tighter. "Like tonight?"

"Tonight works," she said, holding his gaze in a way she rarely had before.

Oh boy. Dylan forced down another swallow of Sanpellegrino before responding. "How long have you thought about...doing this?"

"Since we kissed in the kitchen the other night," she said. "For the record, I'm not seeing anyone right now, so..."

He had to smile at that. Some deep place inside him felt glad that he was the only one who'd get to see her naked gorgeous butt. Then, just as quickly, that queasiness from earlier returned. He huffed out a breath, hoping it would go away. "And we're clear that this is just sex."

She nodded. "Crystal."

For some crazy reason, Dylan wanted to tell her she was worth more than that, but his eyes felt scratchy, and there seemed to be a fist lodged in his throat, blocking his words. No matter how many times he swallowed, it refused to go away. He didn't want to show too much in front of her. He wanted to be the person Kali thought he was, the carefree, confident playboy who was allergic to commitment. But right then, for reasons he didn't want to explore, Dylan didn't feel that way. He wanted to be more. He wanted to be enough— for her, for himself, for all the people in his life.

Kali reached over and touched his face like

he had hers earlier, her gaze concerned. "You okay?"

"Yes, fine," he managed to croak out. "Great."

She laughed, surprising him. Honestly, it burned a little.

"Sorry, I'm not laughing at you," she said at last. "But I've never seen someone look so confused."

Her words were insensitive in a way, but Dylan knew she didn't mean them to be. She just wanted him to know that it was all right, that it really didn't matter to her that this whole situation was awkward as ass.

Pretty soon, Dylan was laughing too. At them. At all this craziness.

He didn't think he'd ever had this much conversation with someone before sleeping with them, but leave it to Kali to be different. He felt vulnerable in a way he'd never experienced before with her. Normally, he'd have run far and fast. But tonight, he wanted to stay. Maybe he was finally outgrowing his old playboy ways after all.

"Okay," he said, hailing the waiter for their check. "Let's go back to the apartment and get it on."

She pursed her lips, apparently trying to look disapproving at his choice of words, though a smile hinted at the corners of her mouth, and Dylan couldn't resist leaning in until his forehead touched hers, then whispered, "Let's do this—you and me, together—and see what happens."

"Okay." That was all she said, but it was more than enough.

Now that it was decided, he couldn't wait to get out of the café. Dylan felt hyperaware of Kali, the building around them, the lights above, the night beyond.

And all of it, every single thing, felt absolutely perfect.

CHAPTER SIX

KALI HONESTLY DIDN'T remember anything about their trip back to the apartment. Dylan followed her into the building and up three flights of stairs to their front door. Inside, she stepped out of her shoes while Dylan removed his jacket and draped it over the back of the sofa. Anticipation suddenly turned to anxiety as they stood there, ill at ease. Kali knew what came next but had no clue how to get them there.

She walked into the open kitchen. "Want something to drink?"

"No, thanks," Dylan said.

Great. She took her phone out of her pocket and set it on the charging pad in the kitchen, then walked around to stand on the other side of the breakfast bar, facing Dylan. "You can turn the TV on, if you want."

His lips quirked in amusement. "I don't feel like watching TV right now."

He stepped toward her, and Kali's breath caught. The way he moved, deliberate and determined, appealed to her in a way she hadn't noticed before. Probably because he was moving toward her.

"This isn't our first time together, but it feels like it is. To me, at least." He smiled. "I think I figured out how we need to do this tonight."

"How?"

Dylan was close enough now that she could feel the heat of him penetrate her clothes. He bent and kissed her temple, her cheek, the soft spot behind her ear. "With the lights off."

Considering how nervous she was, darkness sounded good to Kali. She nodded. "Okay."

They walked down the hall to Kali's room, and in the doorway, she automatically fumbled for the light switch before he stopped her, whispering, "Lights off, remember? Unless you changed your mind."

"No," Kali said, more breathless than she'd intended. "I just forgot."

She wandered into the shadows of her bedroom until her knees bumped against the side of her queen-size mattress. Kali turned around and smacked right into Dylan's chest.

"*Oof!* Sorry."

"Okay?" he asked.

"Yes, but this is a little awkward. Last time we did this, we'd both been drinking."

"True," he agreed, his hands a warm, reassuring weight on her shoulders, grounding her. "But I like it this way too. I get to experience you in a whole new way this time."

"Yeah." She snorted. "The clumsy way."

In response, Dylan leaned down and kissed her on the forehead, then her eyebrow, then the tip of her nose, ending on her mouth. He sucked her bottom lip, licked, then claimed her mouth with bold strokes of his tongue as his hands swept over her body.

When he palmed her behind and squeezed, her inner muscles clenched tight, and moisture flooded between her thighs. Logically, she knew he wouldn't ease the ache in her body—there's no way he could know how—but she wanted him anyway. Wanted his kisses, his caresses. Wanted him close. Most of all, she wanted him to want her again.

Her kisses acquired a wild edge. She slipped her hands under his shirt and traced the firm muscles of his abs, chest and back. Even without the light, she could sense how strong he was. He must've started working out more over the years. Kali didn't have a lot of time or inclination to go to the gym, but her constant working kept her in shape. Still, where her soft curves met his toned body, she delighted in the differences. When she felt his hardness pressing against her lower belly, Kali rose instinctively onto the tips of her toes until they lined up...just right.

Dylan gave a hoarse moan and rocked against her, slowly. Sensation arrowed straight to her core, and Kali's knees buckled. He didn't let her fall, though. He held her up, pulling one of her thighs over his hip so that his body rubbed against hers between her legs as he kissed her deeper. The rawness of the action, the friction, his mouth all overwhelmed her senses to the point that she barely registered when he picked her up and settled her on the bed. All Kali knew or cared about was that their bodies were closer now. And closer was better.

She pushed Dylan's shirt out of the way, impatient with the layers of fabric between them, and he broke their kiss to yank it off. Their mouths came back together like they couldn't stand to be separated. Kali supposed that was true, at least for now. In just a few short days, she'd gotten addicted to his kisses. And his taste, his scent, his skin. She slid her hands down his back, trailing her fingertips along his spine, luxuriating in the feel of him. When she encountered the waistband of his pants, she slipped her fingers underneath and ventured down so she could fill her hands with the perfect round globes of his butt, and instantly she was obsessed.

"You're in trouble," Kali whispered between kisses.

"Why?"

"Now that I know what you feel like, I won't be able to stop touching you here. I'm going to do it all the time." She was being completely honest, so when Dylan started laughing, she didn't understand, but then she decided it *was* a little funny.

"I'm glad you like my butt," he said, and even though Kali couldn't see him, she heard the smile in his voice. "Touch me as much as you like."

"Anywhere?" she asked, needing to be sure.

He paused for a moment; then the bed shifted as he moved away. Kali heard his zipper as he undid his pants, then the thud when they hit the floor. It didn't make sense, but she suddenly felt intensely self-conscious as she undressed and stripped off her bra and underwear. It seemed ridiculous to feel that way. It was dark. He couldn't see her. She couldn't see herself. And even if he could, they'd done this all before. But it was like her mind still hadn't accepted that the darkness was real. Like she was still waiting for someone to judge her, her body, her actions.

Then Dylan stretched out beside her again and pulled Kali to him so their bodies were flush together, front to front, skin to skin. His erection felt hot and heavy against her hip, and she did her best to ignore it.

"You feel so good," he whispered, running his hand up her leg and over her hip.

"So do you." Kali touched his face, his neck, then rested her palm against the center of his chest. "I can feel your heart beating. It's fast. Are you nervous?"

"A little," he admitted. The fact someone so experienced felt the same as she did helped ease her anxiety.

She smiled. "Me, too."

"Do you want to stop?" he asked.

"No."

His lips brushed softly against hers. "Should I stop talking and get back to kissing you, then?"

"Yes, pl—"

His tongue stroked between her lips, and Dylan kissed Kali with so much feeling her toes curled. For ages, that was all they did: kiss until they were both breathless. They touched each other, too, but their hands remained in safe places—arms, legs, stomachs, backs. And yeah, she grabbed his butt again, too, because she couldn't help herself, but that's where her brazenness ended. Then she shifted restlessly, and Dylan's length slid between her thighs, rubbing against her, and he groaned against Kali's neck, his entire body stiffening.

"I'm sorry."

"Don't be sorry." Breath rough, Dylan nuzzled her neck and nibbled on her earlobe before asking, "If I show you how I like to be touched, will you do the same?"

"Can't I just touch you?"

He gave a small, frustrated growl, then pressed a hard kiss to Kali's mouth. "I want us both to enjoy this."

"I am." She'd had sex with a few other men after Dylan, but it felt like work—physically, mentally and emotionally. Probably, she now understood, because she was always trying to be what they wanted, trying to be something other than what she was. But tonight, with Dylan was...something else.

"You know what I mean," he said. "Talk to me, or show me, anything."

"I can't. I *want* to. For you. But I can't. It's embarrassing. Just do what you did before and—"

"We're different people now, Kali. Things change."

"I know, but…" She didn't finish. She couldn't because she didn't know how to explain.

"You want me. Unless I'm imagining things."

"I do." Kali turned her now-burning face away from him but then remembered he couldn't see her anyway and felt silly.

Dylan gathered her closer and kissed her temple. "I can't leave you unsatisfied. That's Fling Rule Number One. Everyone gets a happy ending."

Now it was her turn to laugh. "Seriously?"

"It's totally a thing. You just hadn't heard because you aren't usually a fling-type woman."

"Right."

"Tell me how you like to be touched," he whispered.

Her face burned hotter, but she made herself answer. That was the whole point of all this, right? Breaking out and trying new things. Just like her therapist wanted. "I don't know. I don't really think about it. I just do it."

"Like this?" He ran his fingers lightly up the inside of her thigh, making her shiver.

"That's nice."

"Or this?" His fingers went higher now,

brushing over the heat between her legs before he cupped her.

It took Kali two tries to get the word out this time. "Maybe."

"What about here?" He raised his hand to trail a fingertip from her collarbone down to her breast, then teased her nipple until it hardened into a tight peak.

Kali's throat locked, leaving her unable to speak. She arched against him instead, her body all but begging for more.

Dylan chuckled. "Guess that's my answer." He adjusted his position slightly, and in the next instant, the heat of his mouth closed around her nipple. He sucked and stroked with his tongue. She couldn't help the sounds she made—half gasp, half moan. "Do that again. I love the noises you make." Next, he switched to her other breast and mirrored his actions there. Kali couldn't help herself; she made more sounds, grasping the bedsheets, clenching them tightly as she writhed beneath his mouth.

"Let's see if I can get that sound when I touch you here."

He smoothed his hand over her stomach, down between her parted legs again, stroking her with languid motions. Her hips rose against his hand, needing more. She was close to what she needed, so close, and yet so far away.

"Faster?" Dylan asked in a low voice.

She couldn't answer.

"Harder?"

Kali stared into the darkness, quietly raging against…everything. But mostly against herself. Why did she have to be like this? Why did her autism diagnosis have to affect everything? Why couldn't she name and ask for what she wanted?

"Should I stop, Kali?" he whispered.

Tears flooded her eyes, then slowly spilled down her face to soak into the pillow beneath her head. "I don't want to stop."

Dylan stayed silent for a while before taking one of her hands, kissing her knuckles and guiding her hand down between her legs, placing her fingers so they pressed against her most sensitive place. "How about we try this, then? I can't see you. I won't know what you're doing. You don't have to say a single thing."

"Dylan, I can't—"

He silenced her with another kiss, as his hand covered hers and slowly began to stroke her slick folds. As before, it felt so close to what she needed but not quite there. Except now it was her own fingers, right there, and the temptation to do what he'd suggested was nearly unbearable. She fought it and succeeded. For a while.

But the longer Dylan kissed Kali, the harder the temptation was to resist. Soon, she ground against their joined hands, seeking the kind of contact that eluded her. She couldn't tell Dylan what she liked or needed because she didn't know. But somehow, her body knew. Every muscle in her body drew tight as a bowstring, and she cried out against Dylan's lips, her arousal sharpening painfully.

"That's it," he whispered as he pulled his hand away, leaving her to touch herself freely.

She did. Then again, moaning his name. Her core clenched hard, and her hips jerked.

"Don't stop," he encouraged her, kissing Kali's temple, cheek, mouth, jaw. "You're so hot."

Kali glowed inside at his praise.

Driven by desire she leaned up and kissed Dylan deeply, biting his bottom lip, his chin, then nipping the strong cords of his neck. She quickly reached the brink, then hovered at the edge, unable to go over as insidious thoughts invaded her head.

She must look ridiculous right now. She should have sex the right way, the normal way. She should be easier to please. People would laugh if they saw her.

Dylan kissed her, whispering more encouragement as she trembled in his arms, but he didn't quite drown out the voices in her head. They'd become too loud. Her body twitched, yearning for the release that remained frustratingly out of reach until her skin was slick with sweat.

He stroked her inner thigh again, and Kali's heart lurched. She froze, afraid he'd discover how weird she'd become. She didn't want him to know. He couldn't find out.

"I can't—it's not—we need to stop," she said at last, and it sounded like pleading.

"Okay. We'll stop." Dylan's words were husky, rough, but he did as she asked. He stopped. He rolled onto his back and pulled Kali partially onto his chest. She heard the steady, wild beat of his heart, felt his deep breaths.

Her sense of failure made Kali want to cry. "I'm sorry."

"Don't be," he assured her.

"But I didn't. And you didn't. Nobody got their happy ending."

"It was still nice."

"You're not angry?" she asked. In the past, Kali had found that the men she'd slept with were less than friendly when they didn't get what they wanted from her. And they usually never returned.

"Of course I'm not *angry*." He hugged her tighter. "I'm proud of you. I'm honored you trusted me enough to do all that. I'm not angry, not even a little."

"But what about..." She shifted her leg and moved her hand downward from his chest. Dylan stopped her, though, pinning her hand against his stomach.

"Next time," he rasped.

"There'll be a next time?"

"I hope so. We've still got weeks to go before I leave."

"Oh. But won't you get..." Kali frowned, not sure how to phrase it in a way that sounded not horrible. "Bored if you keep waiting for me?"

"I'll deal with it," he said.

She sighed. It almost felt like him choosing to wait for her put more pressure on things, but then she reconsidered. They'd both agreed to this fling idea, so it wasn't just about her. It was about them both. He was a grown man who obviously knew what he wanted, and she should respect that.

Wrung out and exhausted, Kali wasn't sure what the next step was. "Do we sleep now?"

"Are you inviting me to sleep here in your bed?"

Kali flashed a tired smile. "Yes."

"Then yeah, let's sleep now."

The alarm on Kali's phone dragged her back to consciousness several hours later. Her hair felt damp and mussed on the side where she'd slept with her head pressed to Dylan's chest. Groaning, she pushed herself up into a sitting position.

"Hit the snooze button," Dylan murmured sleepily.

"Can't. My phone's in the kitchen, remember?" She slipped out of bed in the predawn gloom, then groped around on the floor for her shirt to pull on. Finally, Kali grabbed what she thought was it, but once she'd pulled it on, she realized it was Dylan's. Perfect. Wrapping it around herself, she fumbled her way to the door and down the hall to the living room to grab her phone, turning on a lamp as she went. By the time she got the annoying alarm shut off, Dylan stood at the end of the hall. He'd tugged on his pants and nothing else. Her heart sighed. Kali couldn't stop thinking about how she'd touched all that skin without seeing it. Maybe doing it in the dark hadn't been such a great idea after all.

Except if it hadn't been dark, she never could've done what she did.

His gaze swept over her—dark; intense; possessive, even—and Kali realized how she was standing: slightly bent over, her elbows on the counter, revealing her lack of underwear and giving Dylan quite the view. She straightened fast and pulled the hem of his shirt down farther, embarrassed and self-conscious. But she also felt weirdly sexy and immensely desired, things she wasn't sure she'd felt since the last time she and Dylan had slept together.

Seeing Kali naked that first night had been shocking and sexy. But seeing her now— wearing his shirt that showed more than it hid of her gorgeous figure; staring at him with wide, startled eyes; her hair disheveled—was almost enough to bring him to his knees. He took a deep breath and scrubbed a hand over his face, her scent still clinging to his skin, as he groaned, then dropped his hands to his sides.

"Kali, about last night. I..." He shook his head, unsure what to say.

She pulled his shirt tighter around her and seemed to shrink in on herself. Her face turned away from him, she asked, "Is this it? Are we done?"

"Can we talk through this?"

She opened her mouth like she wanted to speak, but nothing came out.

Dylan stepped toward her. She was so clearly struggling with all this, and he hated seeing that. He wanted to make things better, to help her—because that's what he did. Who he was. He walked into the living room and sat down on one end of the sofa, then gestured for her to join him.

"I know you're going through a lot right now, Kali. With your residency, your new diagnosis." Dylan paused, considering his next words carefully. "I don't want to add to your stress here. If we're going to have a fling, then I need to know it's because you want to have one, too, not just because you think it will make me happy. Because if you're not feeling it, I can't—" He glanced her way and saw her guarded expression. Dammit. He was not making things better here, but it needed to be said. "Do you understand? I need you to be just as into it as I am."

She frowned at him for a long moment before she said, "Okay."

"Okay." He sat back. "So, is there anything that I could have—"

"Can we not talk about this right now?" She covered her face with her hands. "I have a shift at the hospital to get ready for."

"Me too. But we can't move past it until we confront it."

"Now you sound like my therapist," she groaned.

"Look. Sex isn't anything to be ashamed of." He tilted his head as he searched for the right words. "Asking for what you want is the only way I'm going to know what you like. I tried the regular stuff, and it didn't seem to do it for you."

She made a miserable sound and shrank deeper into her corner of the sofa.

Because he couldn't stand her discomfort, Dylan moved down the sofa until he sat next to her, and Kali immediately curled up against him, pressing her face to his neck. He wrapped his arms around her, and the same feelings he always felt around her swamped him—tenderness, protectiveness.

"I don't really see why talking about sex is so embarrassing. I do it all the time," he said, trying to lighten the mood, and she laughed, her body shaking against his. "I mean, we are doctors, so…"

"It's different outside the clinical setting,"

she said, hitting him lightly on the chest with her hand. "Don't even go there."

He smiled and kissed her knuckles. "I won't. Don't worry. But if you can't tell me what you like, you could show me."

She inhaled sharply, and her face flushed an even deeper shade of red. "I could never, ever, ever…"

"Why?"

"Dylan…" she said, her tone accusing, like he should know why.

"It's just you and me here. It's not like anyone is watching."

Kali shook her head quickly and looked away from him.

"So you're okay with never having good sex, then?" The idea horrified him. "And what about all the other people you've slept with since me? They can't all have been terrible."

She didn't respond.

"Kali, it would have been so easy just to—"

She tensed and sat up, glaring at him. "No, Dylan. That's the point. It's not 'easy.' Not for me. If it was, we wouldn't be sitting here now."

"I'm sorry. I thought—"

"I think this conversation is over." There was a finality in her tone that told him she was done.

A sense of loss threaded through him. Their

fling was over before it had started. All because he couldn't keep his mouth shut. It wasn't how he'd wanted things to end. Neither of them had accomplished what they'd wanted here, but they were at a standstill. They both wanted things the other wouldn't give.

He stood and started back toward the hall, aware of Kali's gaze on him. He could tell from the look in her eyes when she watched him that she liked what she saw. That was something, he supposed, even if it was completely superficial. Maybe someday, Kali would open up with the right person, and it would be glorious. But that person wasn't him.

"I'm going to take a shower," he said, turning back at the door to his room. "I know it was rocky in the end, but I had a great time last night."

She joined him in the hallway. "Same for me. Thank you—for being you."

It seemed like the right thing to give her a final hug. When she was in his arms, it *felt* like the right thing. She fit against him like she belonged there. Dylan didn't mean to kiss her, but it just happened. And Kali kissed him back. There was a moment when they hesitated, both unsure of what they were doing, but then their lips came together again. He wasn't sure who initiated it, her or him—

maybe both—but he kissed Kali like it was their last kiss. For all he knew, it was.

When they finally separated, her eyes were dreamy, her lips red. He ran his thumb over her swollen bottom lip, unable to stand the fact that this was the last time he'd be able to do this.

Without stopping to think, Dylan said, "What if we tried again?"

Kali blinked several times, her brow wrinkling. "You think we can finally have a proper fling if we try one more time?"

He huffed out a laugh. "Third time's a charm."

"But you—I—we…"

"I think there are things we both could work on. Why not try it together?" Dylan held his breath and waited for her to answer.

She concentrated on a floral painting on the wall beside him then said, "I don't think I can do…the things you wanted."

"Maybe we can figure out another way, meet in the middle somehow."

"Do you have any ideas?" she asked.

"Not yet," he admitted. The thought of leaving her unsatisfied like he had the night before left a bitter taste in his mouth. But there had to be another way, something else they could do. They couldn't be the only people in history to deal with the problems they were having.

"Okay." Kali squared her shoulders, a determined glint in her blue eyes. "Let's try one more time."

Dylan couldn't stop himself from smiling. "Okay."

"This weekend?" she asked. "I'm off both days. We have the football game on Sunday, but otherwise..."

"That works."

"Are we completely ridiculous?"

"Maybe." He laughed.

She laughed along with him, and for a moment, they stood in each other's arms, just looking at one another.

Eventually, Dylan pulled away. "I need to get ready. So do you."

"Yep." She headed for her room, flashing him a smile over her shoulder. "Meet you in the kitchen."

As he stripped and showered, Dylan started brainstorming different ways they could approach their intimacy problems. Nothing seemed quite right yet, but he thought they'd get there. He was a doctor, after all. They both were. They'd figure it out. And probably have some fun along the way too.

Happy holidays ahead, for sure.

CHAPTER SEVEN

"How about these?" Kali asked, holding up a pair of handmade stuffed blue Hanukkah gnomes, one holding a dreidel and the other a menorah. They both had on tall pointed hats that covered their little faces and long white beards. "They're cute."

It was Saturday and they both had the day off, so they'd decided to check out the Seaport Holiday Market instead of sitting around the apartment feeling awkward about their promise to try and have meaningless sex again that night. Or at least, that's what Kali was doing. Dylan seemed fine, as always.

He tilted his head and wrinkled his nose. "Everything we get doesn't have to be Jewish themed, you know."

"I know." She handed the gnomes to the woman behind the table at the booth and got out her wallet to pay. "But I like these. Jen's stuff is all loud and garish and in-your-face

Christmas. These will help balance it all out. We can have a hybrid holiday."

"Hmm." He waited off to the side as she paid for her purchase; then they continued down the aisle, the whole place buzzing like a hive of holiday bees getting ready for the big day, which was now only a little over two weeks away. Pretty much anything you could think of that had to do with Christmas or Hanukkah or Kwanza or Diwali was here. Decorations of every size, shape, color and taste level. There was even a live-tree vendor at the far end of the market, and despite Kali's earlier aversion, Dylan had convinced her to stop there on their way home to get one for the apartment. Normally, crowded spaces like this were too overwhelming for Kali, but having Dylan by her side helped.

And she'd agreed because, again, new and different.

That was her mantra these days. Especially since the night before. Stop masking. Stop people-pleasing. Figure out what she liked and wanted, and go for it. And if it was uncomfortable or messy, well, that was part of the process.

"Well, if we're going hybrid, then we should get some gelt too," Dylan said, leading her over to a booth with locally made chocolates.

"Gelt?" Kali frowned.

"Yep." Dylan picked up a large net bag of what looked like gold pirate coins and handed them to the attendant at the register. He smiled at Kali as he took his change and purchase, then led her down the aisle again, his free hand warm and comforting on her lower back. "There's a lot of history behind this candy for the Jewish people. Basically, they represent victory over oppression, prosperity and freedom." As they walked, he reached into the bag and pulled out two coins, one for each of them. "Plus, chocolate. Always a good thing in my book. And you can gamble with them playing dreidel."

Kali laughed, unwrapping her coin and popping the chocolate in her mouth as Dylan did the same. Funny how those words kept reappearing in her life the past week: *Freedom. Victory. Good abundance.* For some reason, spending time with Dylan made her feel like all of that was flowing toward her again, finally. Maybe it was. Without thinking, she slipped her mittened hand into his as they stopped at another booth, this one with hand-carved wood ornaments and decorations. She picked up a pair of brightly painted dreidels and grinned. "Gambling, huh? What do I get if I win?"

"Whatever you want, darlin'," Dylan said, swooping in fast to kiss her before taking the dreidels and paying for them. "But you have to beat me, which is pretty much impossible. Ask Jen. I used to whoop her butt every year."

"Whatever."

As they neared the tree market, Kali stopped a couple of times to buy more stuff. Yes, all Jen's stuff was there in a basement storage locker, but she felt like this holiday was different, and she wanted it to look that way too. She still planned to dig out Jen's lights and some garlands and wreaths, but Kali wanted to start her own traditions too. She ended up with two big shopping bags over her arms filled with several sets of handcrafted wool felt stuffed red-and-white Yule goat ornaments, a Father Odin Norse statue and even a large Grinch wreath for the front door. A little bit of everything. Just like her.

"Happy Holidays," the tree lot attendant said as they approached. It took Kali a second to realize it was Cetan Muang, the Burmese man whose daughter, Lian, she'd treated in the day clinic the other day. "Dr. Mitchell! Great to see you."

"Hello, Cetan. How's Lian doing?" Kali said, smiling.

"Much better, thanks to you. The medicine

seemed to do the trick. She's feeling good and her fever's gone, so according to what you said, she'll be able to go to her sleepover. She's very happy."

"I'm so glad." Kali stood there awkwardly for a moment, not sure where to go from there, conversationally, until she remembered Dylan was standing there beside her. She gestured toward him and said, "And this is Dr. Geller. He's helping out at the clinic over the holidays."

The two men shook hands and Cetan grinned. "You like our Boston Christmas?"

"It's very festive," Dylan said, sliding his arm around Kali's waist. "And I've got a great tour guide too."

Kali couldn't help the rush of warmth that flooded through her system. Touching wasn't usually something she enjoyed, but with Dylan it felt different. It felt right and real and remarkable. She snuggled closer to his side and didn't miss the surprised, pleased glance Dylan gave her.

Cetan's grin widened as he noticed their closeness. "You are wanting a tree to celebrate your happiness. We have just the thing. What size are you looking for? Tall or small?"

"In-between?" Kali said.

"Good." Cetan led them back through rows

of pines, the pungent smell bringing memories of holidays past for Kali, before the divorce, when her dad would bring home a live tree and they'd decorate it together as a family. She hadn't realized how much she'd missed that until now.

"Here we are," Cetan said, stopping in front of three trees near the back corner that were about six foot and varying widths, from thin to plump. "Which one do you think?"

"Don't forget we have to carry this back to the apartment," Kali said when Dylan went for the plumpest one, her breath frosting on the chilly air. They still hadn't had any snow yet in Boston, but the temps were already down in the thirties. "It's two blocks away."

"Right."

They ended up choosing the medium-width one and split the cost. Cetan offered to have the tree delivered for them, but it could be a few days due to how busy they were. Kali wanted to decorate that day, so she declined. They were both young and healthy; a little exercise would do them good. Dylan agreed. They hoisted the tree over their shoulders and headed out of the market for home. Walking single file, Dylan took the lead, securing the trunk on his shoulder with one hand and holding the stand in the other. Kali took the rear, supporting the lighter treetop while juggling her many bags as well. They must've created quite a spectacle, because lots of people stopped and stared as they passed, with a few tourists even taking pictures or videos with their phones.

Once they got back to the apartment, Kali unpacked her purchases while Dylan fit the tree into the stand. Then they went down to the basement storage closet and got out several boxes of stuff Jen had packed down there and brought them upstairs. After a debate, they decided the best place to put the tree was by the windows overlooking the Back Bay area. They had to move some furniture, but it was all good.

They untangled the lights and strung them on the branches, then started putting up the first decorations. She handed Dylan a red felt Yule goat and took a white one for herself to hang, along with the card that had come with the ornaments, explaining their significance. She read it aloud to Dylan as he continued to hang more goats around the tree. "It says these represent the ancient Norse tales of Thor eating two goats but they come back to life the next morning. Magical immortal goats. This rebirth metaphor also fits in well with the winter solstice, as on solstice night, the sun goes through its own rebirth."

"Perfect." Dylan chuckled. "I love it."

"Me too."

Once they'd hung all the goat ornaments, they moved on to Jen's boxes of stuff.

Kali set her new blue gnomes on the windowsill beside the tree, then stepped back to admire their handiwork. "We did a good job. Your sister would be proud."

"I think so too." Dylan slung his arm casually around her shoulder as they stared at the tree. A little bit gaudy, a whole lot messy and one hundred percent theirs. "What next?"

Kali shrugged. "Lunch? I can make us some sandwiches and cocoa and we can watch *Die Hard* on streaming?"

"Sounds wonderful." He followed her to the kitchen to wash up and help with lunch. As they assembled their food, he asked, "What about tonight? Are we just going to stay here? Or maybe we can go see a show."

She'd been thinking a lot about what they'd do that night in the back of her mind all day. How they might get into sex again without her freezing up. She really wanted this to work with Dylan because it would signify a new beginning for her too. Plus, they'd already had sex once before, and it had been amazing, so she hoped for the same outcome again. And yeah. She liked Dylan. A lot. More than she probably should. He was handsome, kind, sweet. And he got her. He just knew her. That was rare, in Kali's book. They had so much in common, so many shared interests that went beyond work. Music. Food. Decorating, even. With him, she felt comfortable, special, wanted. It was heady stuff, and she wasn't ready to let that go yet.

Kali swallowed hard, then put forth the idea she'd been considering since she'd seen an email about it earlier that morning. That long-ago night on the deck, they'd both been relaxed and comfortable, and part of that, Kail thought, had been because they'd been drinking. Not that too much alcohol was a good thing. As a physician, she knew that could cause its own problems in the sex department for men. But just enough to ease the wheels, get things rolling. And to that end...

"I was thinking maybe we could go to a pub crawl instead," Kali said, putting her dirty knife in the sink, then grabbing her phone from the charging pad to show him the email she'd received about it. "Everyone wears ugly Christmas sweaters, and it's super casual. You can go to as many places as you want and then leave when you want to. But if you don't want to—"

"No. I like it!" Dylan laughed. "Not sure I have a sweater ugly enough, though."

"No worries." Kali walked over to the small coat closet by the front door and pulled it open to dig through the shelves near the top. She pulled out two of the most revolting garments she'd ever seen and held them up. Both sweaters were extra-large and extra-ugly; one had huge neon-colored ornaments and boxes stuck to the front, and the other had twerking elves all over it. She and Jen had worn them to a staff party at the hospital a few years back— had won first place for Best Costume with them too. "I've got us covered."

Dylan shook his head, still laughing. "Then yes. Let's go crawling!"

They made it as far as Sissy K's that night. It was the fourth pub they'd been to, and the bars were starting to blur together in his head. Not because he'd had too much to drink, but because all he could think about was getting Kali home to the apartment and getting on with their fling idea.

Buzzed and slightly bemused, he watched Kali dancing in time to the person performing a horrifyingly bad rendition of "Santa Baby" up on the karaoke stage. People were milling about with various drinks in their hands, all dressed for the holidays. He and Kali had ended up placing fifth out of the twenty or so people who'd entered the pub crawl organizer's best ugly sweater contest, and they'd won a free round of frozen drinks. Neither of them were blind drunk, but he'd slowly watched the tension in Kali's posture dissolve as the night went on. If they were going to try again, now was the time. First, though, they had to get back to the apartment.

"I'm ready to head home," he called to her over the music and off-key singing blaring through the bar's speaker system. "How about you?"

She nodded and set her half-finished drink aside before turning to him. "Yep. Let's go."

Dylan took her hand and led her out of the bar to the sidewalk, where he pulled out his phone to call an Uber. Afterward, he tucked his phone away in his jeans pocket, then put his arm around Kali and pulled her into his side to share body heat while they waited. That's the excuse he was going with, anyway. Man, it felt good to hold her. He glanced down to find Kali watching him, and Dylan couldn't resist dropping a quick kiss on her lips. "This was fun tonight. Thanks."

Kali grinned and nuzzled her face into his chest. "The night's not over yet."

His body tightened before he could stop it, need sizzling through his veins. He was happy to slow down and wait for her, but it had been a while since he'd been with anyone, and he wasn't used to that. He also wanted it to be special for Kali, knowing what a big deal it was for her to have sex with him again. It was a big deal for him, too, if he was honest, but he didn't feel the odd pressure he usually did when things went beyond just the physical. Maybe it was because he knew her. They were friends. They'd done this before. They both knew what was happening. Or maybe it was something more...

Whatever it was, those thoughts were pushed aside as their Uber swerved up to the curb and they climbed inside. Dylan gave the driver their address, and it was a fairly quick trip back to the apartment.

He'd figured they'd relax a little bit. Talk. Hang out first.

But nope. Kali surprised him again.

He'd barely closed and locked the door behind them when she was on him, kissing her way down his neck. She tugged down the crew neck of his sweater to expose the sensitive spot where his neck met shoulder, and when she scraped her teeth over his skin, he gasped and held her tighter.

"I want you, Dylan."

"Pretty sure you have me..." he whispered near her ear, enjoying her answering shiver.

He kissed her then, deep and hungry, both of them seemingly swept away. Despite his considerable experience, Dylan felt weak with wanting. He couldn't get enough of Kali, sneaking his hands under the hem of her sweater, skimming his palms along her hot skin. He loved the way her muscles tensed beneath his touch, the way she moaned and kissed him deeper.

"Ready to try again?" he asked, running his hand up her jeans-clad thigh to cup her butt possessively and pull her against him, letting her know how much he needed her. "I am."

"Yes." The word broke as he slid his hand down until his fingertips grazed the heat between her legs.

Her eyes closed and her head tipped back as Kali lost herself in sensation, and Dylan didn't think he'd ever seen anything more erotic in his life. Watching her come to life beneath his hands was the most powerful aphrodisiac in the world to him.

"God, I want you so bad," Dylan groaned,

then nuzzled her neck, nipping and kissing, just like he wanted to down lower on her too.

She sought out his mouth again and kissed him as she arched into his touch, rubbing against his hand through her jeans, seeking satisfaction as she had the night before. Tonight he intended to make sure she got it. That they both got it.

"Bed," Dylan said roughly, toeing off his shoes and waiting while Kali did the same. "Need to get you in bed."

He picked her up and carried her down the hall to her bedroom and laid her down on the bed before joining her. He cupped her cheek, and Kali touched his face almost reverently before pressing her lips to his. They undressed quickly, and Dylan put on a condom, then gathered her into his arms again, a charge going through him as he stretched out beside her on the bed.

Usually, these encounters for him were fast and furious, both partners eager to get what they wanted, then go on their way. But with Kali, it was different. It had always been different. Her warmth heated him, and his mind and body and all his good intentions about keeping things light and purely physical unraveled. He held her for a while, noticing the fine tremors running through her.

"Okay?" he whispered against her temple, praying it wouldn't be a frustrating repeat of the night before.

She took a deep breath, then nodded. "Things just got really noisy in my head for a second."

He leaned down to kiss her nose, then her mouth. "What kind of things?"

"Like I need to prove to you that I'm sexy. Like I need to please you. Like I need you to like me."

His heart clenched painfully at her confession. "You do please me. And I do like you, Kali. I think you're sexy as hell."

She hugged him tighter and pressed her cheek to his, and for a stretch of time, that was all they did—just breathe together.

"Where do we go from here?" Kali asked at last.

"I don't know. Where do you want us to go?"

She kissed his lips, his chin, nipped at his ear; her sharp teeth coupled with her warm, sweet breath had him covered in goose bumps. "I want to kiss you."

"Just kissing?"

"To start." Her mouth opened against the side of Dylan's neck, and her tongue traced his skin, making his breath catch.

"Kissing is good," he said.

"Very good."

His mouth found hers again, and he licked her, sucked her bottom lip, then plunged his tongue deep, claiming Kali's lips with a drugging kiss. He couldn't seem to stop touching her, his hands roving over her body, squeezing and stroking all her curves until he palmed her breasts. He teased her nipples with his thumbs until she gasped against his mouth and dug her nails into his shoulders, responding to him fully and uninhibitedly. Maybe the drinking had helped after all. Her legs moved restlessly against his, and she ran the soles of her feet along his calves. He was painfully hard now, and when the heat between Kali's legs brushed against his erection, he couldn't contain a hoarse groan of need.

"Dylan—"

He took her mouth in another deep kiss to keep her distracted, keep her in the moment, with him.

That seemed to work for her because her tongue stroked his. He reveled in the taste of her—sugar from their drinks earlier and spicy passion. He gloried in the feel of their bodies together, skin to skin. He couldn't stop himself from thrusting against her slightly. It felt so good, so tempting. She rocked into him more forcefully, and his tip entered her.

His eyes flew open, finding her above him, watching him. They hadn't bothered to turn on the lights again, so the only illumination was the glow from the streetlights streaming through the windows. "You said just kissing, Kali. Do you want more?"

She bent and kissed him, tiny, teasing things before pulling back slightly, her smile white in the shadows. "I want you, Dylan."

As if to prove her point, she rocked against him once more, and they both moaned as another inch of him penetrated her.

"Are you sure?" he asked, panting with the effort to control himself. She was in charge tonight, and he planned to keep it that way, even if it killed him. And considering how hard his heart was pounding just then, it might.

"I am." She kissed him lightly and undulated her hips, her tight heat stretching to accept him.

Thank God he'd put the condom on earlier, because it would be agony to stop now. With a moan, he pushed all the way into her, then held still. Breathing hard, shuddering, gripping her hips tightly, he said, "Nothing has ever felt as good as you do right now, Kali."

Even in the semidarkness, he saw the happiness light her beautiful face. She smiled into the dark, then leaned close to his ear to whisper, "Thank you."

When she started moving on him—slow, sinuous movements; pulling away, then returning like waves on the shore—it was so sexy that he wished the lights were on so he could see her face. He wanted to watch her enjoying him. She arched against him, sinking him deeper inside her. They wouldn't finish this way, but for now it was what they both craved.

When his desire built too high, Dylan finally took charge, rolling her gently beneath him. Even then, he wanted her to tell him what she wanted, to keep her in control, because that's what she needed. He thrust into her slowly, gently, thoroughly, reaching between them to stroke her most sensitive spot with his fingers. "I want you to feel so good, Kali."

She hid her face in his neck as her body tightened around his.

"That's it, darlin'. Let go for me," he whispered, kissing her temple, sucking on her earlobe, nipping her neck, then licking the sting away.

She did, rocking against him as he moved faster, harder, deeper. Pleasure tingling low at the base of his spine, sharp and irresistible, even as he held himself back.

Soon, Kali cried out as Dylan praised her, pushing them both closer and closer to the edge. He was proud of her, so proud. He couldn't get enough of her, might never get enough of her. He could happily die now inside Kali and never regret a thing. Her hips met his thrust for thrust, her body clenching hard around him.

"Are you with me?" he asked Kali between ragged breaths. "I'm close, darlin'. I don't know if—"

Kali pulled his head down to kiss him, and he groaned, kissing her back. She grasped his ass with both hands, pulling him closer, and he drove into her faster and faster. Her desperation was what finally ruined him. She cried out and stiffened beneath him, trembling, as she said his name over and over again, completely undone.

For Dylan, there was nothing more powerful than Kali coming apart around him. He felt invincible, indestructible and impossibly close to oblivion. He was right on the edge but held back and slowed down to draw it out for her. He wanted to brand her, make her remember him as the best she'd ever had, replace all those old memories with these new ones. He didn't want her to ever forget tonight.

Dylan knew he wouldn't.

When her body finally relaxed beneath his and she sighed, he began to move again. The feel of her, the sound of her moans, was almost more than he could take. Sensation coursed over his scalp and down his spine, and everything he was concentrated low, clamoring to rush into her. He became pure desperation, pure need, pure emotion, but Dylan refused to give in. It wasn't until Kali began to peak again, her soft cries reaching a crescendo as her body did the same for a second time, that Dylan finally let go. He might not be able to give her forever, but tonight he could give her what she needed.

Kali fell over the edge into ecstasy, and this time Dylan fell with her.

CHAPTER EIGHT

"REMIND ME AGAIN why we're walking a mile to get to the game when we could park at the stadium?" Dylan asked as they walked along the road toward Patriot Place, the collection of restaurants, bars, shops and vendors surrounding Gillette Stadium. They were holding hands, and the sun was warm on Kali's face, and for the first time in maybe forever, she felt great. Great about herself, great about life, great about what was happening with the man beside her.

They'd woken up early in the morning and made pancakes, taking selfies as they cooked, bedhead and all, then made love again and showered together before hitting the road. Looking back now, it almost seemed like a dream. And if it was, Kali didn't want to wake up.

She glanced over at him and grinned. "Because the dirt lot only costs thirty dollars. And the exercise will do us good."

Dylan laughed, low and sexy, and Kali felt the sound straight to her core. "I think we got more than enough exercise last night."

Face hot, Kali gave him a playful swat with her hand as they turned to follow the rest of the people filing into the entrance to the stadium complex. At the gate, they each showed their tickets to the attendant, then passed through. Years of attending Patriots games meant she had it down to a science: Arrive an hour early so you had time to eat and sit in the end zone to watch the players warm up. Wear your ticket in a plastic cover on a lanyard around your neck for easy access when someone asked you to show it; since purses weren't allowed in the stadium, it was really the only reasonable choice. And since Kali was the designated driver for their ride home, she was free to accept all the soda coupons passed out as they made their way through Patriot Place.

She'd texted Ailani earlier, and they were going to meet her and Javi in their seats on the fifty-yard line. She'd offered to let them ride with her and Dylan in Dylan's car, but Ailani had said they were getting an Uber instead. So, until the game started, she and Dylan were free to do as they wanted. They had wings and egg rolls from one of the vendors, stopped at the bar for a couple of beers for Dylan and a soda for her, then walked down to sit near the end zone on the Patriots' side to watch as they warmed up. Of the two of them, Kali was by far the biggest football fan. Which was probably why her mom's boyfriend had given her the tickets in the first place—to try and butter her up before dropping another bombshell on her, like her mom was getting hitched again.

Honestly, it made what she and Dylan were doing seem even more reasonable and perfect.

Who needed long-term commitment? Not Kali. Nope.

It all ended in ruins anyway, so what was the point?

"Who's your favorite player out there?" Kali asked Dylan as they stared out across the huge artificial-turf field in front of them, where guys were throwing footballs and practicing tackles and runs. Above them, cameras zipped around on wires, quick to capture all the action for people watching at home.

"Tom Brady?" Dylan said, shrugging. "I'm just here for the free food."

Kali laughed and shook her head. "Brady left in 2019."

She then went into depth about her favorite

players and plays and predictions for the next season until finally, Dylan nudged her with his shoulder, then kissed her quick.

"You know a lot about this stuff," he said, chuckling.

"I like football." She grinned, then glanced around to make sure Ailani and Javi weren't lurking around to see them canoodling. Coast clear, she concentrated on the field again. She loved spending time with Dylan. She just didn't love the gossip machine at the hospital or how quickly her personal business could become part of it if they weren't careful. People had already noticed Dylan, as evidenced by Ailani's comment the other day. If they knew Kali was sleeping with him, she'd never hear the end of it. Without thinking, she took his hand and tugged. "C'mon. Let's find our seats on the fifty-yard line."

"Hey," Kali said as they reached Ailani and Javi. "How are you both doing?"

"Great," Ailani said, her dark gaze flicking between Kali and Dylan, then back again, far too perceptive for Kali's comfort. "You both look very well rested."

"Hi," Javi said, holding up a hand in greeting. He was wearing a Patriots jersey, the same as Kali. "Thanks for the tickets. I haven't been to a game since before the pandemic."

"Me neither." Kali sat down next to Ailani, with Dylan on the other side of her, in the end-row seat.

"Dr. Geller, glad to see you again," Javi said, leaning forward to see Dylan around the two women.

"Likewise. And call me Dylan, please." Dylan lifted his beer in greeting to Javi, then sat back, stretching his arm casually across the back of Kali's seat. She froze, hoping no one noticed, but of course Ailani glanced over at the gesture and smiled.

It felt both nice and weird being there with Dylan. If it had just been the two of them, she'd have snuggled into his side, held his hand, kissed his cheek. But the constant awareness that there were two coworkers not that far away kept Kali in her seat, hands clasped in front of her most of the time, other than when she was cheering for a good play or standing to yell at the referee for a bad call. In the end, the Patriots won, twenty-six to eighteen in overtime.

"Well, that was fun," Ailani said afterward, standing and stretching. Kali couldn't help noticing how Javi watched the nurse's every move, and from his expression, she wondered if maybe her and Dylan wouldn't be the only two people hooking up soon. Javi was clearly interested, though Ailani seemed oblivious. "Guess we'll go wait for our Uber home."

They went their separate ways outside Patriots Place, with Kali and Dylan hoofing it back to Dylan's car.

"Did you have fun at least?" she asked, taking Dylan's hand again when they were a safe distance away.

"I did." He chuckled. "Would've been better if you weren't so embarrassed to be seen with me."

"I'm not embarrassed." She frowned. "I just didn't want to start any gossip at work about us. That's all."

"Hmm." He raised her fingers to his lips and kissed them. "Who cares what people think?"

Kali started to say she did but then stopped herself as her therapist's words ran through her head again. She did care, but maybe she shouldn't. Her and Dylan were both adults, having consensual sex and enjoying it immensely. No shame in it. Or there shouldn't have been, anyway. But years of conditioning and trying to do what she thought other people expected of her had made Kali believe differently. Her goal was to change that, so…

She stopped and turned in front of Dylan, blocking his path as she cupped his cheeks and kissed him deeply. At first, he stiffened against her, probably from shock; then he returned the kiss enthusiastically. Kali had never been one for public displays of affection before, but now she couldn't get enough of Dylan, even going so far as to jump up and wrap her legs around his waist. His hands cupped her butt to keep her there. Spectators be damned. He was right. Who cared what other people thought?

"Get a room!" someone muttered angrily as they pushed past them.

Both Dylan and Kali burst out laughing. He slowly lowered her to the ground, then took her hand and tugged her onward toward the car. "That's exactly what we're planning to do."

Later, back at the apartment, they were lounging around the sofa, eating the leftover latkes from a couple of nights prior and figuring out what they wanted to do for the night. The game had been an early one, so it was only four p.m., according to Dylan's smart watch. He took another bite of latke dipped in sour cream and shoved it in his mouth, chewing and swallowing before asking, "Maybe we just stay in? Watch some more movies? Play some games?"

"Maybe. We both have busy weeks next week at the hospital." She set her empty plate aside and leaned back against the arm of the sofa, her stockinged feet in Dylan's lap and her bare legs looking impossibly long as they stretched out from beneath the hem of the shirt he'd worn earlier. Dylan wasn't sure if it was the outfit that was doing it for him or the woman in his clothes, but he couldn't seem to get enough of Kali. Worse, it didn't bother him at all.

Which was odd for a man who changed partners like other people changed their clothes.

He wasn't playing the field, per se—he just got too restless after a while to stay still. It felt like an annoying buzz, building ever stronger until he had to leave, had to run, had to move on to the next new thing. It never occurred to him to ask why. Until now.

These days with Kali so far hadn't made him buzz at all. Not in the annoying way, at least. He liked her. Liked talking to her. Liked hanging out with her. Liked sleeping with her. It was comfortable, easy.

And even though they both knew it was only temporary, a guy could get used to their arrangement.

While she took their plates to the kitchen,

Dylan checked his phone for updates on Jiyan.
He'd called the hospital earlier that morning
to check in with Amita, and she'd said Bryn,
one of the nurses Dylan had met the other
day, had stopped in with her service dog,
Honey, to see Jiyan. He remembered the big,
goofy golden retriever in the Santa sweater
and made a mental note to ask Amita to see
the photos she'd said they'd taken of the visit.
Dylan couldn't wait for the boy's surgery to
be over and Jiyan to be on the road to recovery. He deserved a normal life. With the help
of Dr. Ben Murphy, hopefully he'd have one.

"How about we compromise?" Kali said,
returning to the living room.

Dylan set his phone aside as Kali strad-
dled him, her hips rocking against him in all
the right places through the sweatpants he'd
tugged on after they'd made love. Her palms
skimmed down his bare chest, stopping over
his pecs. The only compromising he was interested in now as he placed his hands on her
hips to keep her from squirming against him
and getting him too excited too fast involved
them ending up back in her bed, sooner rather
than later.

He cleared the lump of lust from his throat
and asked, "What did you have in mind?"

"Let's hang out here a little longer." She leaned in to nuzzle his neck, and Dylan bit back a groan. "Maybe nap or whatever, stream a show. Then we'll go out later for a walk to see the lights at Faneuil Hall."

The rush of blood in his ears had basically blocked out everything after her saying they should hang out at the apartment a little longer, and he was good with that. Instead of responding, he quickly tipped her backward so she lay flat on the sofa; then Dylan stretched out on top of her, his body naturally settling between her parted thighs.

"What are you doing?" Kali asked, laughter in her tone.

"You said napping or whatever." He smiled down at her as he tugged up the hem of the oversize shirt of his she was wearing, then bent to kiss her bare stomach before heading lower. "This is my idea of 'whatever.'"

Soon her soft sighs of pleasure filled Dylan's ears and set off fireworks of need in his bloodstream, his body rising to attention and letting him know he'd definitely made the right choice of activities.

Making love with Kali had quickly become his favorite thing to do while he was in Boston. Maybe his favorite thing ever. And later, as they both snoozed on the sofa, naked and satisfied, beneath a blanket with a huge snow-man on it, Dylan realized his time here so far hadn't been anything like he'd planned and better than he'd ever dreamed.

CHAPTER NINE

THE NEXT WEEK passed in a bit of a blur for Kali. Between work and home, her head was swimming. The day clinic was packed, as usual, and between her and Dylan and Ailani and Bryn, they kept the patients moving and treated as necessary. She and Dylan had consulted on more cases together, and Kali was surprised how well they worked as a team. At first, she'd been a little worried their sleeping together outside of work might affect their professional relationship, but so far it hadn't. If anything, they seemed even more attuned to each other, often recommending the same treatments or diagnoses before the other could say it. Life was surprisingly good.

Perhaps too good.

Kali felt like she'd lived so long expecting the other shoe to drop that when it didn't, she wasn't sure what to do. The logical portion of her brain told her to just enjoy the ride. It was the holidays. Joyous times. In a few weeks, the new year would start, and things would return to normal. Dylan would return to his life in Providence and his practice, and Kali could get on with her residency.

She thought she'd feel happier about that than she did.

Last night at the apartment, she and Dylan had cooked again, this time making treats to bring in for the annual staff bake sale. Kali had chosen to make her great-grandmother's solstice cookies. They were basically short-bread cookies dusted with powdered sugar and were seriously delicious. And Dylan, keeping with his whole Hanukkah theme, had made *sufganiyah*—Jewish jelly doughnuts. Deep-fried dough injected with strawberry jam and topped with powdered sugar.

"Ready to go?" Dylan asked, coming up to her, looking hotter in his lab coat than a man had a right to. The day clinic was drawing to a close, and the waiting room was finally empty. "Don't forget we need to stop by the break room and collect our leftovers."

Kali snorted. "If you think there'll be any food leftover from what we brought in, you haven't been paying attention. Especially with the bake sale. Staff on the children's ward love to eat. And if they can support a good cause at the same time? Forget about it."

Dylan laughed. "True."

"I just have one more patient to see. Want to help me?"

"Actually, I think I'll go check in on Jiyan again. It's been so crazy today I haven't looked in on him and Amita since we first got here this morning." He started to back away, his little smile making her core tingle. Man, hard to believe how quickly she'd fallen right back into lust with the guy. The twinge in her chest was new, though. And dangerous. Her feelings for Dylan didn't go beyond the bedroom. That was what they'd agreed to, and if Kali was anything, it was a rule follower. "Meet you at the locker room?"

"Yep," she said, turning away. "Give me half an hour."

They parted ways, and Kali grabbed the last chart from the holder at the nurses' station. One of the other pediatricians on the floor, Dr. Izzy Jeong, was finishing up with a patient in the pod next to where Kali was working. They exchanged a brief smile as Kali passed, and she noted Izzy looked better today than she had earlier. They didn't know each other well, but Kali liked Izzy a lot. She was nice and always positive and upbeat, which helped make the atmosphere in the ward better. Kali hoped poor Izzy hadn't caught that nasty bug that was going around among their young patients but didn't feel comfortable enough to say anything. So she just smiled at Izzy in passing, then concentrated on the young girl waiting for her in the exam pod.

Kali swished open the curtain and smiled, expecting to see the girl and her parent, but twelve-year-old Amy Walker was all alone, sitting on the exam table with her thin legs dangling over the side, looking pale and wan. From the paperwork Kali had, her father was a long-haul trucker, which explained his absence. But it was the notes about the mother that broke her heart. According to the chart, Amy's mother had died eight months prior of a brain aneurysm while on her way to pick up her daughter from school. Kali's relationship with her own mother was tenuous at best, but she couldn't imagine what her life would've been without her mom there, especially at such a young age.

"Hi there," Kali said, keeping her voice light and friendly despite the ache in her chest. "My name is Dr. Mitchell, and I'll be treating you today. Did someone bring you into the clinic?"

"My aunt Shelly. She's down in the cafeteria." The girl shrugged, then gave Kali the sweetest smile—sad and a little bit lost. It pinched Kali's heart because it was so familiar. She'd seen it in the mirror for years growing up. Memories of her standing in front of school with her backpack, waiting for her mom to pick her up, hoping she hadn't forgotten about Kali again...

"Okay. What am I seeing you for today?" I asked.

The girl shrugged, staring down at her sneakers. "I feel weak and tired a lot."

"Anything else?"

"No, not really. I just feel tired all over."

"All the time?"

"Pretty much."

"How's your appetite?"

"I don't have one."

"Can you tell me how long you've been feeling this way?"

Amy sighed heavily, a faraway look in her eyes, and Kali's heart hurt anew. The girl had to be remembering the day her mother died. She wanted to talk about that with Amy, suspecting it likely had something to do with the girl's condition now, but wasn't sure how to bring it up. The last thing Kali wanted to do was cause her patient more pain.

Finally, Amy said, "I'm not sure."

"All right." Kali pulled on some gloves. "Let's start with a complete exam, then. Is that all right?"

Amy nodded.

Kali examined her patient with the gentlest touch, trying to communicate to Amy that she was cared for and safe. She found no swollen lymph nodes, no tenderness over the bones and joints, no liver or spleen enlargement, no heart murmur. The girl's neurological exam was negative, and her lungs were clear. But despite the fact there were no obvious signs of systemic disease or inflammation, her pallor and listlessness were troubling. Of course, the psychosomatic response to her mother's death was foremost in Kali's mind, but she also needed to rule out all other possible disease etiologies.

"Amy, we'll need to take some blood to test. Would that be all right?"

"Yes."

"Thank you."

Usually one of the nurses drew the blood, but since it was late, Kali decided to do it herself. It saved time, and she was good at phlebotomy. For kids, having blood drawn could be frightening, even traumatic, and she wanted to show Amy that she took a special interest in her. Amy turned her head away but otherwise sat stoically through the process.

"You were very brave, Amy," Kali said afterward, putting the vials into a special pouch to be sent off to the lab, stat. "I'm going to do everything I can to help you feel better. There are just a couple more things I need first. First is a urine sample. And then I'll give you a kit to take home for a stool sample that you can send back to us. I can go over all of this again with your aunt when she gets back."

"I'll do it." Amy said, taking the kit from Kali. "Do you know about my mother?"

"I do. It was in your chart."

There was a slight pause; then Amy nodded and stared down at her shoes again. She looked so fragile, her arms and legs thin and pale—a little girl in a big city—that Kali wanted to hold her and protect her from the world.

"Thank you for being so nice to me," Amy said, her voice tiny and quiet.

Kali's heart broke a little more. "It's my pleasure."

"I know why you're doing it."

"You do?"

"Because you feel sorry for me. Just like everyone else."

This was familiar territory for Kali. Growing up different, she'd been acutely aware of people being nice to her because they didn't know how to act normally around her. Honesty here seemed like the best policy. "I am sorry about what happened to your mom, Amy. But I'm also your doctor, and I know you're not feeling well. I want to find out why and help you to feel better."

"Do I have a disease?"

"I'm not sure. What I do know is that something very hard and very sad happened to you."

"Did you know my mom?"

"No, I didn't. But I'm sure she was a very special person."

Amy frowned down at her lap for what seemed like a small eternity; then she looked back up at Kali with angry eyes. "Shut up. You don't know anything about me or my mom." Her cheeks flushed, and her breaths turned fast and shallow. "She was my mom, not yours—so just shut up!"

Amy's hands were balled in her lap now, and Kali wondered if she was about to get punched again. Then, gradually, the tension in the girl's body relaxed, and her breathing evened out. "I'm sorry. That was rude."

Despite her autism, every fiber of Kali's being urged her to hug the girl, but instead, she said, "I accept your apology."

A long silence followed, and Kali felt like Amy was testing her to see if she could trust her, if she really cared. When their gazes met again, Amy said at last, "I wrote a report on the flora and fauna of Boston for school."

"That sounds interesting."

"Do you know that there are foxes living in the city? There was a gray fox a few years ago on Commonwealth Avenue. Someone tracked it and posted on social media about it and everything."

"Really? Did it have a name?"

"No. They never got close enough to find out if it was a girl or a boy, so it didn't feel right to give it a name." She shrugged. "Red and gray foxes are actually found all throughout Massachusetts, except for Martha's Vineyard and Nantucket, because they have coyotes there instead."

As she spoke, Amy's voice grew livelier and more animated, and her eyes brightened.

"That's amazing, Amy. Thanks for teaching me something new today."

"You're welcome," she said.

Kali squeezed the girl's hand reassuringly. "I've got your and your dad's cell numbers on file. We'll call as soon as we get your test results back."

* * *

"Dr. D!" Jiyan said excitedly when Dylan walked into his room after knocking. "I got to see Tinsel today."

At first, Dylan thought the kid was talking about a Christmas tree; then he remembered Tinsel was the visiting live reindeer down in the lobby. "Cool! Did you feed her a carrot?"

"Nah. She likes bacon better."

"Don't we all," Dylan said, snorting. He pulled up the boy's file on the computer in the corner, then glanced over at Amita. "How are you holding up?"

"Good," she said, setting aside the knitting she'd been working on. Amita was making what she called a recovery blanket for her son. By the time she was finished, Jiyan should be well on his road to recovery from his heart condition, she'd told Dylan last month. He hoped she was right. "You've been busy."

"Have I?" he said distractedly as he scrolled through pages of test results onscreen. She was right, of course. He had been busy. Busy with Kali. Not that he planned to tell Amita that. She'd already guessed too much about them from that first meeting. He didn't want his personal business clouding their friendship. That was the excuse he was going with, anyway. He stopped at the MDCT results and frowned. Between Dylan and Ben, they'd decided to do a multi-detector CT scan of Jiyan's heart in addition to echocardiography to evaluate the severity of the defects in Jiyan's heart rather than immediately jumping to the more costly, high ionizing–radiation burden and invasive nature of a cardiac catheterization. Not to mention the risks of prolonged sedation on a patient as young as Jiyan. It was still a new technique, but so far the pros had far outweighed the cons in Dylan's opinion. MDCT gave them better, more accurate pictures of what was going on inside Jiyan's heart and lungs without them having to put him under and open him up. And anytime those things could be avoided prior to his big surgery was great in Dylan's book. From the results he could see on screen now, his initial diagnosis stood.

Dylan checked the boy's latest lab-test results as well to make sure he was stable and saw that things had remained the same: diminished oxygen saturation, hematocrit between 65 and 70 percent, and low platelet counts and coagulation factors. Not great, but at least he wasn't getting any worse as the surgery approached.

Once he'd finished with that, he shut off the computer and faced Amita at last. She was watching him like a hawk from across the room, her gaze far too perceptive for his comfort. Dylan resisted the urge to run a finger under the collar of his white dress shirt and leaned back against the counter behind him. "What?"

Amita raised a dark brow at him. "What's been keeping you so busy?"

"Work," Dylan said, shrugging one shoulder.

"Uh-huh." Her tone suggested she didn't believe him in the least. He'd thought with Jen out of town, he would avoid people poking into his private business. He'd been wrong. "How's Dr. Mitchell doing?"

"Fine." The answer emerged too quickly, and Dylan hid a wince, then changed subjects. "So, tell me more about Tinsel."

Jiyan, who'd been playing his Nintendo Switch, set the game aside to grin at Dylan. "Did you know reindeers are the only deers who don't have fur on their noses?"

"I did not know that," Dylan said, smiling as he pulled up a chair on the opposite side of Jiyan's bed from Amita. "Tell me more."

"Their hooves change with the seasons."

"No!"

"Yes!" Jiyan's little face lit up with excitement. "And they can't fly, but they can swim."

"Whoa. Wait a minute." Dylan frowned and sat forward. "So you're telling me Rudolph is a myth?"

Amita shook her head and sat back, picking up her knitting again as her son said, "Rudolph is just made up. Everyone knows Santa uses jet engines now."

"Really?" Dylan looked over at Amita and saw her biting her lip to hold back a laugh. "That's good to know. Probably makes landing on roofs harder, though, yeah?"

"That's what the elves are for," Jiyan said, like Dylan should have known that. "Air traffic control."

Dylan did laugh then. He thought he could probably live to be a thousand, and his young patients would still surprise him. He stood and ruffled Jiyan's hair, then said to Amita, "Can I talk to you in the hall for a second?"

"Sure." She set her yarn and needles aside again, then kissed her son's cheek before following Dylan out of the room. "What's going on? Jiyan's okay, yes? Dr. Murphy said everything looked good for surgery, but—"

"No," Dylan said. "I mean, yes. Jiyan is doing as well as expected under the circumstances. The surgery should proceed as planned, in my opinion."

"So what did you want to talk to me about, then?"

Honestly, he wasn't sure. He just wanted someone to talk to that wasn't Kali or his sister, for obvious reasons. "How are you holding up?"

"You asked me that already." Amita crossed her arms and leaned a shoulder against the wall, her long black hair glinting midnight blue under the overhead lights. Her crimson turtleneck highlighted her complexion and looked festive at the same time. "What's going on with you, Dylan?"

He took a deep breath, then raked his hand through his hair. A knot had formed between his shoulder blades throughout the day, and he rolled his shoulders now to relive it. "Nothing. I just…"

"What?"

Good questions. He was happier than he'd been in a long time. Spending his days here at the hospital and his nights with Kali was damn near perfect. Dylan should be thrilled he'd landed in such a great spot for the holidays. There was a week left until Jiyan's surgery, then his recovery would take another week maybe; then Dylan could get back to his practice and his home and get on with his life. He'd gotten exactly what he wanted. Amazing sex. Fun times. The ability to help others while he was here.

But he kept getting these weird pains in his chest. At first, he thought it was heartburn, but it didn't happen after he ate. It only happened when he thought about leaving Kali behind. And that was a problem. Because he would leave her behind. That had been their agreement.

Besides, long-term anything wouldn't work between them. They were both too busy. Kali had her life here in Boston; he had a busy practice in Providence. He didn't want a relationship. Neither did she. They were both in it for the fling. That was all.

It was probably just the normal holiday angst playing with his head.

Once Jen got home after New Year's and he got back into the swing at home, he'd forget all about Kali and how she felt in his arms and how she sounded when she came apart around him and the sweetness of her kisses to start the day, morning breath and all.

"Nothing," he said when he realized Amita was still waiting for an answer. "I'm just up to my neck in patients at the clinic and worried about you and Jiyan."

"We're okay. Don't worry about us." Amita shifted her weight, jutting her other hip out as she tapped a toe on the floor. "Dr. Mitchell seems nice. I think you two would make a good pair."

"We're not a pair," Dylan said. "We're just friends."

"Friends with benefits, maybe?"

Dylan looked away fast, and heat flooded his face. He was a grown man. He was single. He could do whatever he wanted. Yet, standing here, lying to Amita, made him feel ashamed. To distract himself, he checked his watch, then took a deep breath. "I need to go."

"Okay." Amita shook her head, clearly laughing at him. "Run away like you always do. But one of these days, love will catch up with you, Dylan. When you least expect it."

He stared at her as she walked back into her son's room and closed the door behind her. Love? He wasn't in love. That was ridiculous. And he didn't run away. He steered clear of the L word altogether. Better that way. Easier. Less messy.

And speaking of mess, he should get to the break room to collect his and Kali's pans from the bake sale so they could take them back to the apartment tonight and refill them for the next week. Warmth filled him as he remembered cooking with Kali in the kitchen. Being with her was nice, easy, fun, exciting.

But none of that equaled love. Nope. No way. And while Kali was much different than his cheating ex Lisa, he just couldn't go there with her. Dylan's experience with emotions in romance hadn't been good, and he wouldn't allow himself to be that vulnerable again, despite what Amita thought.

CHAPTER TEN

"WHAT'S THAT?" DYLAN asked when they got back to the apartment that night.

After seeing her patient Amy and catching a late train home, Kali felt dead on her feet. She picked up the package left by her front door and handed it to Dylan without fanfare. "Here. Happy Hanukkah."

He frowned down at the cardboard box while she unlocked the door. "Is this a gift?"

"Open it and see," she said, holding the door for him, then closing and locking it behind them before tossing the keys into the blue bowl and toeing off her shoes. All she wanted was a hot shower and a good night's sleep. But what she got instead was Dylan blocking her path with more questions. "What?"

"I just..." He sighed. "I didn't get you anything."

"It's fine." She shook her head and sidled around him to put her phone on the charging pad in the kitchen. Thank goodness she wasn't on call tonight, because she didn't think she could do it. When she could see he was still watching her, she stopped at the end of the hallway and faced him. "Seriously. It's just some stuff I got you because..." Her brain couldn't even find words anymore. She'd been doing a lot of masking and people-pleasing at the clinic today, and it had left her drained. Plus, the case with Amy was bothering her. She wasn't sure if it was because she'd missed something or because the girl reminded Kali so much of herself at that age. Absently, she said, "Hanukkah."

"You got me Hanukkah gifts."

"Eight nights and all." She waved a hand vaguely, then swiveled toward the hall again. "I ordered them late, and then with delivery snafus and whatnot, they just arrived. I need to take a shower. Be right back."

She left him standing in the living room, frowning down at the box in his hands. He called after her. "Should I open it?"

"If you want," she said, stopping at her bedroom door. She removed her scrubs and stuffed them into the laundry basket, then wrapped herself in her fluffy robe for her trek across the hall.

Standing under the hot spray of the shower,

she knew something was wrong, but she couldn't pinpoint what exactly. Things with Dylan were good—at least, she thought they were. They were sleeping together every night, working together at the clinic during the day, spending pretty much all their off time together, too, these days. She saw him more now than she saw anyone, honestly. That was a good thing since her therapist said she should socialize more. But it was also not so good because Kali was used to having more time to herself to process, and she hadn't really done that since they'd started this whole affair. Or fling. Or whatever they were calling it.

Kali soaped up, then rinsed off, her mind still looping endlessly through her time with Dylan up to this point like one of those cheesy montages in those sappy rom-coms Jen loved watching so much. They'd visited pretty much everything in Boston that had to do with the holidays: the menorah-lighting, the Seaport Christmas Market, the lights at Faneuil Hall. Hell, they'd even put up a tree. It was more than Kali normally did in a whole year, let alone one holiday season. No wonder she was exhausted.

But as she shut off the shower and got out to dry off and wrap her damp hair in a towel, an uncomfortable restlessness buzzed through her system. Had buying him gifts been a mistake? She'd done it on impulse, thinking that he could just open them all at once since they were late. She hadn't expected him to feel obligated to buy her anything. But maybe she'd violated another social rule she wasn't even aware of. That always seemed to be her problem. Other people operated under a set of instructions she either had never received or couldn't interpret. The confused, concerned expression on his face as she'd walked away flashed in her face, and the buoyant balloon of happiness that had been riding high inside her since she and Dylan had gotten back together sank a bit lower.

Maybe it was too much. She'd specifically bought things that were silly so he couldn't misinterpret them as meaning anything more than she'd intended. Fun. Festive. That was all she wanted.

Wasn't it?

Her scowl deepened as she padded back across the hall and changed out of her robe and into a pair of blue flannel PJs with white snowflakes all over them since they were the only clean thing she had in her drawer. She hadn't had a lot of time to clean around the apartment since Dylan arrived, and her laundry basket was overflowing. She pulled on a pair of socks, then walked back into the living room while she pulled her hair up into a messy topknot to dry. Her look couldn't be called *sexy* by any stretch, but she was comfortable and warm, and that was her current top priority.

Dylan was still sitting there on the sofa, staring at the box in his hands, but his expression looked a million miles away. The happy balloon in Kali deflated further. Yep, she'd screwed up somehow, but she wasn't sure when or where or what.

She walked into the kitchen and got out the stuff to make hot cocoa, then glanced back at Dylan over her shoulder. "Want hot chocolate? I'm making some."

He grunted, which she took as assent.

After fixing two mugs, she carried them into the living room and set them on the coffee table before curling into the corner of the sofa opposite from him and pulling her feet under her. She grabbed a throw pillow to hold on her lap, then picked up her mug and sipped the warm sweetness of her cocoa. None of it seemed enough to shield her from whatever he was about to say. She wasn't great at reading people's emotions, but it was clear something wasn't right with him.

Several beats passed in silence before finally Kali couldn't stand it anymore. "What's wrong?"

Her words seemed to jar him out of whatever thoughts had been filling his head, because he sat up straighter and glanced over at her, his eyes a bit unfocused, like he'd been lost in a dream. Or nightmare. He frowned then and smiled, though it looked a bit forced. "Sorry?"

"I asked you what was wrong," she repeated, then lifted her chin toward his mug. "Better drink that before it gets cold."

"Yeah," he said, looking from her to the mug like he'd never seen one before. Then he shook his head and set the box on the floor and picked up his cocoa. He took a long drink of it, then sat back, looking almost as tired as she felt. Shadows marred the skin beneath his eyes, and there was a shadow of stubble on his jaw. "Sorry. Just tired, I guess."

They'd stopped to eat on the way home, so at least that was done. If either of them would have had to cook that night, Kali thought she'd start crying. She nudged the box with her toe. "If you don't want these, I can send them back."

He rolled his head and looked at her then, those green-gold eyes warm and drowsy. *Bed-*

room eyes, she thought. And suddenly sleep wasn't her top priority.

Dylan caught her foot in his hand to massage it. If she hadn't been sitting down, she'd have probably ended up in a heap on the floor because it felt so good. She bit back a moan of relief as he worked a tight knot in her arch. He was watching his handiwork with her foot—not her—his handsome face frowning in concentration. She wasn't sure she'd ever seen anything sexier in her life. "We're still on the same page here, right?"

It took her brain a second to comprehend his words past the pure ecstasy of being touched where she needed it most in just the way she needed it. And now it was her turn to frown. "Yes, same page," she said, having a hard time putting words together just then. All she wanted was for him to keep doing that forever. "Don't stop that."

Her commanding tone made him grin, and up went that balloon inside her again, flying higher than before. Or maybe that was lust. Either way, she wanted him to keep touching her. She wanted to touch him too. Until neither one of them cared about silly gifts or rules or anything but what they had right there and then.

Dylan pulled her other foot into his lap and

chuckled, low and sexy. She shifted, her toes brushing against the growing evidence that he was just as into this as she was, and their eyes met. "You look beat," he said, his talented fingers massaging higher now, beneath the hem of her PJ pants.

"You too," she countered, shifting again so she brushed against him once more.

He groaned and Kali closed her eyes, and she wasn't sure who moved first, but soon they were naked on the sofa, and no one was worried about anything anymore.

Not the past, not the future.

And if her therapist's words kept haunting her that night after they'd made love and Dylan was snoring softly beside her, well, that was something Kali would deal with later.

Dylan made her feel good. He made her happy, at least for now. Wasn't that enough?

Kali rolled over to stare at the wall, unable to sleep despite her fatigue because deep down inside, she'd begun to wonder if it was enough for her now.

By the time Saturday arrived, Dylan knew he was in trouble.

It wasn't that he wasn't grateful or that he didn't appreciate that Kali had taken the time to buy him something. It was more his growing concern that this whole thing between them had gotten way out of hand. Or at least, it felt that way to him. No one had bought him Hanukkah gifts since he'd been with Lisa, and it was an unwelcome reminder to him of everything that had gone wrong back then. It raised major red flags and warned him to take a step back from things with Kali and reassess.

And yes, he'd asked her point-blank, and she'd told him their rules were still in place.

No strings. No mess. No emotions involved.

But if he was honest with himself, it wasn't Kali he was worried about there. It was himself.

This time with her in Boston, sharing the apartment and their lives, had come as a revelation to him.

For the first time since the day his world imploded when Lisa had told him she was leaving him for his best friend, Dylan had let himself imagine a life with Kali. It was a gorgeous, glorious future indeed. And it terrified him more than anything else he'd ever encountered.

Because if he let himself, he could easily fall in love with Kali, and then where would he be?

They had an agreement. She'd abided by the rules. She wouldn't love him back.

He'd end up heartbroken, rejected, alone.

The same as before.

All of it messed with his head, too, at a time when he couldn't afford to lose focus. Not with Jiyan's surgery coming up and Amita having more questions every day, and the never-ending stream of patients at the day clinic, and his own practice waiting for him back in Providence, and...

Stressed out didn't begin to cover his current state of mind.

So maybe it was good that he and Kali had signed up to participate in the Santa Dash this morning—a charity 5K run/walk to benefit Camp HeartLight, a summer camp for kids with serious heart conditions. It would be a chance for them to get some fresh air and space and raise money for a good cause.

The chilly air nipped at his cheeks as he stood off to the side of the start line and began stretching. In general, Dylan wasn't a runner unless he was being chased, but he went to the gym regularly because it was good for him, and he was in decent shape. He lunged to the front to stretch his calves and hamstrings and glanced up at the sky. For someone who'd lived in New England his whole life, he knew

that those dark clouds near the horizon fore-
casted snow ahead. Which was good since
they'd had basically none yet for the year. He
wasn't necessarily a huge winter fan, but a
white Christmas was always nice, especially
for the kids.

"Nick!" Kali called from somewhere behind him, and Dylan turned to find her in the
crowd, lining up at the starting line. She'd insisted they wear these stupid Santa hats. His
head itched underneath it, and he was constantly having to fiddle with it to keep it from
falling off. But now that he saw the man next
to Kali wearing full Santa garb, including
wooly beard, he was glad just to have the hat
to contend with. As he moved in beside her,
she gestured toward the man, one of her colleagues from the hospital. Dr. Nick Walker,
if Dylan remembered right. He'd met the guy
during his first week there, but after a while
all the names became a blur. Kali nudged him
in the ribs and lifted her chin toward her colleague. "And I thought wearing Santa hats
made us festive."

"Festive enough for me," Dylan said under
his breath. "A full Santa suit, huh?" he asked
Nick. Nick gave him a look over the top of his
beard that screamed "Help me!" Dylan swallowed a chuckle and rubbed his gloved hands

together instead. His nose felt frozen already, and they hadn't even started, reminding him again why he normally avoided these kinds of winter events like the plague.

"You don't think it's too much?" Nick asked no one in particular.

From the glowing look on Bryn's face, the nurse Nick was dating, it was clear he'd done it for her, so Dylan wisely kept his opinions to himself. Not his circus, not his monkeys. He had enough to deal with on his own, anyway, sorting through the complications of his fling slash not-fling with Kali. Considering what a mess he was inside about the whole thing, he had no room to advise anyone about being stupid in love.

The last word caught him up short.

No. No, no, no.

I do not love Kali Mitchell.

Nope. Not possible.

While Dylan was stewing over this, Ben Murphy, Jiyan's surgeon, stepped up beside Dylan at the starting line, stretching his limbs like this was the Olympics or something. He was wearing just a Santa hat too. When no one else answered poor Nick, Ben said, "Not at all. Maybe you should stop and see the kids when we're done. I bet they'd love that."

"Did I miss the memo on Santa hats?" Nick

asked, looking around and realizing he was the only full Santa present.

"Nah." Ben shrugged and readjusted his hat. "It was Izzy's idea."

Dr. Izzy Jeong was another pediatrician working at the hospital. Even in the short time he'd been there, Dylan had sensed vibes between the two—but again, not his business. Even more reason to avoid workplace relationships, in his mind. Love messed everything up.

"Runners ready!" The announcement came over the large speakers set up on either side of the start line. An excited roar rose from the crowd—a good two to three hundred people, if Dylan had to guess. A great turnout for the charity. The others crowded around him and Kali.

"Is this a joke?" Nick asked, jumping in place to keep himself warm despite the suit, before yelling back, "Of course we're ready!"

"On your marks, get set…go!"

The crack of the starting gun echoed through the air, and the crowd surged forward. He and Kali both shot out of the gate, hoping to get out of the tangle of people early. Dylan wasn't an expert, but he was hungry. He hadn't missed the table of doughnuts and baked goods set up near the finish line, and he figured the sooner they were done, the more he could eat. Kali must've thought the same, because she matched him stride for stride. Soon, they'd left most of the crowd in the dust, including her coworkers.

He was feeling pretty good about things until she blindsided him with a question out of the blue. "Why haven't you opened my presents?"

Dylan fumbled his steps and nearly tripped over his own feet.

Just enough time for Ben Murphy to dart past them, heading for the finish line doughnut–table.

Dammit.

Suddenly more out of breath than the exercise warranted, he shook his head and raced forward toward the end. "Can't we talk about this later?"

"It's a simple question," Kali countered, keeping up with him, her cheeks flushed and her eyes bright. Maybe too bright, if he was honest. But lately, honesty hadn't really been a top priority for Dylan, at least where Kali was concerned. If he told her the truth—that he was scared to open it because of what it might reveal about her and him and this thing they had going—he'd sound like an idiot, so he kept his mouth shut and sprinted forward like he could outrun it all.

But Kali wasn't having it. She darted around him and jogged backward in front of him. "Answer me, Dylan. Why won't you open my gifts? If you don't want them, I'll send them back."

He started to say that he did want them, that that wasn't it, but then he realized there was no way out of that conversation that ended well for him, so instead he just shrugged. "Do what you need to do."

Anger flashed hot in her eyes before she turned around and ran off, leaving him in the dust.

Great. Way to go. Now you hurt her feelings.

And damn if his own chest didn't ache because of it.

It was ridiculous. The whole thing. He shouldn't care about hurting Kali, because they'd both agreed not to get their hearts involved in the first place. If they'd both stuck to the rules, there wouldn't be awkward gifts and even more awkward talks like this to have. This was exactly why he didn't do all this relationship, emotion stuff.

After a full-body shake to rid himself of the crawling sense of despair and disappointment prickling his skin, Dylan charged ahead toward the finish and the food. But as he crossed the line to cheers and congratulations, the last thing in the world he felt like was a winner.

Because winners didn't break other people's hearts.

He knew what that felt like. Knew what it was like to have your whole life, the whole future you'd planned, upended because of one stupid, thoughtless decision. Knew what it was like to open yourself up and be vulnerable and have your heart ripped out and stomped on like so much trash.

Dylan refused to go through that again. Not for Kali, not for anyone else.

He liked Kali—more than liked her. But he couldn't love her.

It wasn't in him. Not anymore.

So they'd stick to the rules, and in two more weeks, he'd be gone for good, and this would all be over.

Joyful tidings, indeed.

Now, if someone could just tell his aching heart that, he'd be all set.

CHAPTER ELEVEN

THURSDAY, DECEMBER TWENTY-FIRST, started off busy and only got worse from there. Kali was on call that day, and Dylan was on edge because of his patient's surgery. Things between them had gotten decidedly chillier since the Santa Dash the weekend before, but Kali couldn't explain exactly how or why.

Physically, they were still close. Dylan slept in Kali's bed every night, though they hadn't had sex since the night of the charity run. And even then, it had seemed more rushed and distant than before. She was honestly trying not to think about it too much because, depending on how the surgery went today for little Jiyan, Dylan could very well be gone the following week, and she'd be left to deal with the aftermath. A few short weeks ago, that would've suited Kali fine. Being alone had been fine with her. But now she wasn't so sure.

In fact, she'd been thinking a lot lately

about what her future might look like, and now, thanks to Dylan, she thought maybe—if she met the right person—it might not be alone after all.

He'd shown her that she could be with someone, really be with them, and it wasn't scary or awful or annoying. Okay. Fine. Maybe he did get on her nerves a little bit when he left a mess in the kitchen or didn't clean the sink in the bathroom after shaving, but still. That was normal.

For the first time in her life, Kali felt...*normal*.

And speaking of normal...

She stared at the lab results on the computer screen for Amy Walker, the young girl she'd seen in the day clinic the week before. They weren't what Kali had expected. The girl's erythrocyte sedimentation rate was elevated—thirty-five instead of where it should be, below twenty. Which indicated either a current or recent infection, or it could be an early marker for systemic inflammatory disease. When Kali had first seen Amy, she'd assumed the girl was like her—introverted, withdrawn—and that her symptoms most likely were psychosomatic. She'd even gotten hold of the girl's father at long last and had recommended therapy for Amy. But now it looked like there might be a real physical cause for the girl's pallor and weight loss. Based on their conversation, her patient might still benefit from therapy, but she also needed further testing to determine why these lab results were abnormal.

The children's ward was buzzing with activity around her as she went over the rest of Amy's results and added them to her patient file; then she handed it all over to Linda Wachowski, the head nurse for their shift, to call the father and see if he could bring Amy by the clinic later to chat with Kali.

She'd just turned around to head back toward the clinic when the familiar claps and cheers of a patient on their way to surgery echoed down the corridor. Today was extra special because it was Jiyan's big day. Kali took her place beside the other staff lining the hall and began clapping and cheering as Jiyan's gurney rounded the corner to head past the nurses' station on his way to the OR. Ben Murphy was there, of course, along with the various surgical nurses and techs, and following at the other end of the gurney, near Jiyan's head, was his mother, Amita, and a worried-looking Dylan on the other side.

As they passed, Dylan caught Kali's gaze and held, his green-gold eyes filled with an odd mix of concern and resignation. It sent that balloon inside Kali plummeting again because she wasn't sure if those emotions were directed toward his patient or her.

He hadn't slept much the night before, pacing the living room and going over all his notes repeatedly well into the early-morning hours. When he'd finally come to bed, Kali had looked at the clock: 3:30 a.m. They'd gotten up at five to get ready to be at the hospital at seven. It was a bit after eight now, and the fatigue showed on Dylan's face, his complexion a bit gray under his usual tan. She hoped he wasn't getting sick too. There'd been a nasty strep throat bug going around the ward lately.

Once Jiyan's parade was over, Kali returned to the clinic and worked on patients, preferring to stay busy rather than overthink her situation with Dylan. Yes, she cared about him, probably more than she should because of their rules, but she'd also realized that she deserved more than an occasional fling when they were both free. They were good together, yes, but good wasn't good enough for her anymore. She wanted the best. She wanted hearts and flowers and happily-ever-afters.

Or at least, happily-for-now. She deserved that.

And she planned to tell him as much that

night when they got home, depending on how Jiyan's surgery went today. He needed to know that she'd be fine when he was gone, even if it hurt her heart to say so. Yes, it would be hard letting him go. He'd become such a big part of her life so quickly the past few weeks, but that probably had as much to do with the holidays as anything.

That was what she was telling herself, anyway.

Because you didn't fall in love with someone in a few weeks. That only happened in corny movies and pulp-fiction romance novels. She was too analytical for that. Too detail-focused and cerebral. Kali didn't lose her heart easily—or at all, some would say. And while Dylan had gotten closer than just about anyone else, ever, she would let him go because that's what she'd promised to do.

And Kali always kept her promises.

"Hey, Doc," Linda called from the nurses' station as Kali finished up with a young boy who had an ear infection and his mother. "Talked to Mr. Walker. He'll be in with Amy around two."

"Great. Thank you."

The rest of her morning passed in a blur of routine exams, vaccinations and the occasional stomach bug. By the time she took a quick break for a granola bar, it was one forty-five, and the Walkers were due in any minute. After a visit to the bathroom, Kali returned to the clinic to find Amy and her father waiting for her in pod three. She smiled as she entered and shook the man's hand.

"Dr. Kalista Mitchell. Nice to meet you in person at last."

"Agreed."

"And hello, Amy." Kali smiled at the young girl.

Amy gave her a small smile in return as she sat atop the exam table again. She still looked pale and too thin, which brought Kali to the reason for their visit. "We got the lab results back for your daughter, and it looks like she has an elevated sedimentation rate."

"What's that mean?" Mr. Walker asked, his nose scrunched. "Sounds like dirt or something."

Kali snorted. "Actually, it's the rate at which red blood cells in whole anticoagulated blood descend in a standardized tube over a period of an hour. Long story short, it's a way to measure inflammation in the body."

"Oh," the man and his daughter said in unison.

"Now, when that rate is elevated, it could mean anything from a recent infection to something more serious, like an autoimmune disorder like lupus or juvenile rheumatoid arthritis." Kali focused on the girl again. "How are your symptoms now? Better or worse?"

"Worse," Amy said, shifting on the table.

"Do you think it's arthritis, then? She's only twelve."

"I know, Mr. Walker, and honestly, at this point, I can't tell you for sure what's happening. We need to get more tests to figure out exactly what's going on."

Amy nodded, then stared down at her toes again. She didn't look well. Her color was pallid, she was listless and her eyes were dull, with dark circles beneath them. When Kali had her step up on the scale, it showed she'd lost more weight since the week before too. Her father sat in the chair in the pod, looking anxious as Kali cupped the girl's cheek. Her skin felt clammy. Next, she gently palpated the lymph nodes in the girl's neck. No enlargement. No joint swelling or tenderness, and she had full range of motion. Amy's lungs were clear, and no sign of enlargement of the liver or spleen. The neurological exam was negative too. If there was inflammation in Amy's body, it wasn't showing up for Kali on exam. She felt stumped. Perhaps she should get her attending involved. Or Dylan.

"Amy, I'm going to have one of my colleagues examine you, too, just to confirm my findings, okay?"

She got permission from both the patient and her father before setting off in search of Dylan. As far as she knew, he hadn't planned to see any patients today, devoting his time to supporting Amita when she needed it most. So she went back to the smaller, quieter waiting area for the families of surgical patients and, sure enough, found Dylan pacing the floor near the wall of windows looking out at the city of Boston. Amita sat nearby, knitting as she listened to something on her earbuds. Kali didn't know the woman well, but from what she'd seen and knew about Amita, she admired the woman's calm fortitude and ability to continue in the face of adversity. Those were things Kali was working on herself.

Kali caught Dylan's eye from across the room and gestured him over. He stopped to whisper something to Amita when she removed one of her earbuds, then headed over to Kali.

"What's going on?" he asked. He looked stressed and tense, and she wanted to hug him and tell him everything would be okay, but that would be inappropriate, so she kept her arms by her sides instead.

"I wondered if you might have time to check one of my patients quickly." Kali explained Amy's case to him as they walked back toward the clinic. "It shouldn't take long, but I can't figure out what's going on with her, and I don't want to let it go over the holidays in case it's something serious."

"Understandable," Dylan said, following her to pod three and snapping on a pair of gloves himself. "Hello," he said to Amy and her father. "I'm Dr. Dylan Geller, a visiting pediatrician, and I'd like to examine your daughter by request of Dr. Mitchell, if that's all right."

Once again, both Amy and her father nodded, and Dylan got to work.

"Right," he said once he was done. "Let me talk with Dr. Mitchell for a moment, then we'll be right back."

They walked over to the nurses' station, where Dylan went over the patient's file.

"What are you thinking?" Kali asked after a long moment.

"Well, you were right to get a second opinion, because if I went by the exam alone, I'd be confused too. Maybe start her on a course of steroidal medicines. If her symptoms improve, then you're on the right track."

"But the steroids could mask more serious

problems by artificially increasing her appetite and decreasing her pain. They will also give her an artificial boost of energy."

"True. What do you want to do?"

"I don't know. That's the problem." Doubt nagged in her gut. Kali felt like she was missing something but couldn't see what. She went back over the chart again, including the initial history and physical where the nurse had asked Amy about any trips she'd taken. Her finger stopped over one line. "Wait a minute. I think I found something."

Before Dylan could respond, Kali was on her way back to the pod, leaving him to follow behind her.

"Amy, I saw in your chart that you went up to Connecticut to visit your father on one of his long-haul trips. You said you spent the weekend camping in the woods. When was that?"

"Early summer, the third weekend in May, I think," the father answered. "Why?"

"Did you notice any unusual bites or rashes when you got home, Amy?"

The girl thought a moment. "Now that you mention it, I did have an itchy bump on my leg for a while, but it went away, and I didn't think about it anymore."

Kali smiled at the bewildered-looking girl, then glanced at Dylan. They'd developed a sort of silent communication over the few weeks they'd been together, and he nodded now, telling her he was on the same track she was. "I want to take another blood sample and send it to the lab, stat. I'm willing to bet good money that Amy has Lyme disease, which a simple course of antibiotics should cure."

Sure enough, about an hour later, Kali got the positive results and sent Amy and her father on their way with a script for amoxicillin. Today was a good day for Kali. Now all she had to do was get through the staff party, and she'd be all set. Once they'd seen the last patient in the clinic, she went in search of Dylan and found him still sitting in the surgical waiting room with Amita. Jiyan's surgery was a long, delicate one that normally took five to six hours, plus prep and recovery time, so it wasn't unusual for people to spend all day in the waiting area. She felt bad for Amita and wondered if she should give Dylan a break, but she also didn't want to disturb them and wasn't sure what she'd say, anyway, so she went to the staff locker room instead to change out of her lab coat and put her stethoscope away before heading to the break room to check out what free food might be had.

Inside, it looked like Christmas had basically thrown up everywhere. Lots of streamers and garlands and decals of elves and Santas and snowflakes everywhere. If Kali didn't know better, she'd have thought Jen was back in town. But she'd gotten a text from her best friend earlier that day with pictures attached of lovely sunny Tel Aviv. Must be nice, since the temps were falling again in Boston and the first big snow of the season was on the way. *Ho, ho,* not. Kali was not a fan of shoveling.

She helped herself to a plastic cup full of cheer from the punch bowl on the counter nearby, then turned to find Bryn standing close by. Kali hoisted her cup to the nurse in a toast. "Happy Holidays!"

"Happy Holidays," Bryn said, toasting her back before zeroing her attention back on Nick near the window again.

Kali focused outside and laughed. "It's snowing."

"It is," Bryn said, her happy tone sounding forced to Kali.

Leigh walked by and handed Bryn a small box. "Delivery for you."

"I didn't do Secret Santa." She frowned and started to hand it back to her.

"Has your name on it," Leigh said, shrugging.

Kali stared at the garish wrapping paper. "Are you going to open it?"

"No."

The sight of sudden tears had Kali taking the nurse's wrist out of concern. "Bryn?"

She swiped a hand across her cheeks, then gave a dismissive wave. "It's fine. I'm fine. I'm just going to wait until I get home." She sniffled and shook her head, obviously trying to play it off. "I...um... I didn't get a gift for anyone else, so..."

"I didn't either," Kali said, though she knew it wasn't exactly the right answer. Then, because the whole thing had gotten awkward and she needed an escape, she excused herself.

Dylan stood on the roof of Boston Beacon Hospital, staring out at the twinkling city below as snow began to fall. Jiyan's surgery was over, and Ben had come to talk to him and Amita in the waiting room about half an hour earlier. Everything had gone well, and the boy was recovering and stable. The next twenty-four hours would be crucial to determining whether he'd come through the process unscathed, but once tomorrow arrived and Jiyan had made it through the night uneventfully, then he should be well on the road to a healthy, happy future. He wished he could say the same about himself.

The slight breeze blew his lab coat around

him, and Dylan tugged the white cotton material closer to his body. A wise man would've stopped to get his winter coat before coming out here. Then again, a wise man probably wouldn't have made the choices he had since coming to Boston either.

He should never have started sleeping with Kali again, knowing what it had done to him last time, searing her into his heart and his mind forever. But he couldn't bring himself to regret it. At least not yet.

That might change once he told her that it was over between them. Which he planned to do as soon as he bolstered his courage in the cold, wintry night up here. He took a deep breath, the icy air stinging his chest and easing the ache in his heart. Because yeah. Despite all his wishes and efforts to the contrary, he'd gone and done the one thing he'd sworn he'd never do again.

He'd fallen for Kali Mitchell.

Hook, line and sleigh bell.

For a crazy second, as he blinked away snowflakes from his eyelashes, he wondered if they could give it a go for real, try to make it work. After all, Kali was a far cry from Lisa. He knew in his heart Kali would never cheat on him. She was too blunt and honest for that. But then, no. It wouldn't work. Dylan couldn't let himself be that vulnerable again. He couldn't risk getting his heart broken, so it was better to end it now. Keep to their agreement. Chances were good he'd be heading home to Providence next week, anyway, right after Christmas. Best to make a clean break and be done with it.

Right. Fine.

He took another deep, brisk breath for courage, then turned to head back inside, when the door opened and out came the woman topmost in his thoughts. Kali had on a parka and mittens, a red plastic cup in each hand. She walked over and handed him one.

"I was looking all over for you," Kali said before sipping from her cup. Dylan tried his as well, then wrinkled his nose. It was fruity and sweet and made him wince from the tart cherries floating in the neon orange liquid. "Ben said Jiyan is doing well. I saw Amita with him too. I'm glad for them."

"Me too." Dylan said, contemplating where he could dump the awful punch. "Did you make this?"

"God, no," she said, making a face. "But it's free and I was thirsty, so…" She looked around, then shrugged. "The staff party is in full swing."

"Great."

"Yep."

They stood there, looking anywhere but at each other as the seconds ticked by and frostbite encroached. Finally, Dylan said, "Listen, Kali. About us. I—"

"Wait." She held up a mittened hand to stop him. "Before you go on, I have something to say."

"Okay."

She hesitated, her brow furrowing like she was thinking hard about it. Then she blurted out, "We need to stop sleeping together."

Dylan blinked at her, feeling the wind knocked out of his sails. He'd been about to say the same thing himself, but hearing it from her hit differently for some reason. He frowned. "Well, that was always the plan. Once I leave, life will go back to normal."

"No, I know. But I mean now. Effective immediately," she said, watching him over the rim of her cup. "I don't think we should sleep together anymore, starting tonight. I don't see the point when you'll be gone soon."

"Oh." Screw it. He tossed the rest of his yucky punch in the corner, then put the cup in the recycle bin by the door. "Well, I guess if that's what you want." His voice sounded normal despite the fact his pulse pounded loud enough to thud right through his eardrums. His chest felt hollowed out, empty, yet full of hot, prickling...*something*. Why? He couldn't say, didn't want to name it, but it was there, and it hurt worse than having his heart stomped on all those years ago by Lisa. He cleared the sudden thickness from his throat and forced out a question, glad for once that Kali couldn't read people's emotions well because his were currently a mess. "What made you change your mind?"

"You, honestly."

"Me?" He heard his tone rising, along with the level of adrenaline in his system. So much for sounding normal. "How so?"

She took a deep breath, then exhaled slow before explaining. "You made me see what I really want, Dylan. You helped me understand that I deserve more. By helping me open up and showing me that it's not as scary as I thought it would be and that someone could actually understand me and accept me and want me, you showed me that I'm not broken. That I can be different and still be loved. I know it sounds crazy, and I know that I might never actually find it, but I want to try for my happily-ever-after, Dylan. However that looks for me."

When he didn't say anything, couldn't say anything, she continued.

"I know that's not what you want. You've made it clear these past couple weeks that your heart's off-limits. And I understand. I do. And maybe, in a way, that's what allowed me to feel safe and open with you all this time. Knowing that you'd never reciprocate. You took the risk away for me. Thank you for that."

Stunned, all he could do was blink at her, dumbfounded.

He should be thrilled. This was exactly what he'd wanted. Sex with no strings.

But it felt lousy.

Worse than lousy—it felt wrong.

"So yeah," she said, stepping close to cup his cheek and kiss him gently on the lips. "Thanks for helping me move forward, Dylan. It's the best gift I could've gotten this holiday."

Then she was gone, leaving him standing in the snow, wondering when in the hell his entire world had turned upside down.

CHAPTER TWELVE

NEW YEAR'S EVE arrived far too quickly for
Kali. In fact, the time between her leaving
Dylan on the roof of the hospital and now had
passed in mostly a blur. She'd been working in
the clinic as much as possible to keep herself
busy, and when she wasn't at Boston Beacon,
she was holed up alone at the apartment with
Wednesday, reading or sleeping. It felt like
she was sleeping a lot since Dylan had moved
out and into a hotel. That night, after the roof
thing, he'd come back to the apartment late
and said a room had become available unexpectedly at the same hotel Amita was staying
at, and they'd called him first because he'd
been on a waiting list. Kali wasn't sure she
believed him, but whatever the reason, it was
probably for the best he was gone.

Even if deep inside it felt awful.

Which was weird because her therapist had
told her that choosing what she wanted and

needed instead of trying to do what pleased everyone else would free her. Because Kali didn't feel free.

She felt exhausted. Exhausted and hurt and horny and just generally horrible.

A vague sense of guilt and a deep sense of rejection plagued her. Why? She couldn't say. All she knew was that her efforts to follow her therapist's instructions and build a new life for herself, a life of her choosing, hadn't gone the way she'd wanted. She didn't feel better than before. In fact, she felt worse. Her appetite was gone. She couldn't focus. Even music didn't help silence the critic in her head.

She missed Dylan.

And despite all the sleep she was getting in her off hours, it wasn't restful slumber, the kind that left you feeling rejuvenated and well rested. Nope. It was the fractured tossing and turning through the night, an hour here, two hours there, her waking up from some dream or nightmare she didn't remember, sweating, her PJs stuck to her.

She'd contemplated taking down the tree and decorations they'd put up weeks ago, but Kali didn't have the energy. Rather than mess with them, she streamed nature documentaries on Netflix and let the narrator's voice keep her company as she scrolled through all the selfies of her and Dylan cooking latkes they'd taken on her phone. She'd thought about texting him a couple times, pretending to need advice on a case or whatever, but couldn't bring herself to do it. Because in those moments, all she saw was the confused, hurt look on his face as she walked away from him on the roof. They weren't supposed to care. No strings. No emotions.

But Kali had broken the rules. And now she was paying the price.

Maybe this was always going to happen. Maybe Kali had *needed* it to happen. Change was painful, her therapist had warned her at the outset of all this, but necessary. Setting appropriate boundaries would be tough at first, she'd said, but in the long run, they would benefit Kali more than anything else.

Still, she felt like she owed Dylan an apology. For bringing him into her life experiment. For using him as a distraction from the real work she needed to do on herself. For violating the terms of their agreement and falling for him despite her promises to the contrary. But even if she did tell him she was sorry, it wouldn't make things right between them. He'd been clear that he didn't do love, didn't want it in his life, that he was fine without it.

To force hers on him now would only make things more terrible.

She sighed and stared up at her living room ceiling as Wednesday turned in circles on her stomach before finally curling into a ball for a nap. Or maybe she could tell him she was sorry without being specific as to why. Just a general commiseration for things not working out like they'd planned.

Kali blinked hard and tears rolled down her cheeks, the ache in her heart enough to take her breath away. She missed Dylan's warmth, his laugh, the way he knew how to hold her and touch her when she didn't even know she needed it herself. The way he never questioned her actions or responses, just accepted her without judgment. And now he was gone. Again. For good, this time.

Her eyes drifted shut as memories of the past few weeks bombarded her tired brain. The menorah-lighting. Dinner at Café Landwer. The Seaport Christmas Market. The Santa Dash. Eventually, she must've drifted off, because next thing she knew, Kali woke up on her stomach on the sofa, with her phone stuck to the side of her face and Wednesday nowhere to be found. Groggy, she pressed herself up on one elbow and rubbed her eyes, then squinted at the smiling face of Jen on her caller ID.

Scowling and sleepy, Kali answered. "Hello?"

"Happy New Year!" Jen sounded far too cheerful. From what Kali could see on the screen, people were partying behind her best friend to start the new year off right. Jen held an icy green drink with a sparkler stick stuck in it. Her wide grin faded into a concerned frown as she squinted at Kali. "What the hell happened to you? You look awful."

"Thanks." Kali winced, her head pounding, as she forced herself to sit up. Wednesday reappeared, meowing for food. She checked her smart watch and saw that it was late afternoon now, which meant she'd slept away most of the day. Good. "How's your vacation?"

"Good. I wanted to share some festive cheer with my best gal back home, but looks like I'm out of luck there. Seriously, Kal. Are you all right? Do I need to come home early?"

"No," Kali grumbled, then restated more clearly, "No. I'm fine."

She wasn't really, but she would be. Someday. Eventually.

Jen did not look convinced but thankfully let the matter drop. Instead, she asked, "Where's my brother?"

"He moved into a hotel over a week ago."

"He what?" Now it was Jen's turn to scowl. "Why?"

"Well..." Kali shrugged, and an intangible thread broke in her mind, and she mentally collapsed. She'd read enough stuff about her condition to recognize the symptoms of autistic burnout, and it hit her hard. Suddenly, all the weeks with Dylan were swept away under years of masking and people-pleasing, and she couldn't hold it in anymore. She started crying, sobbing, raging...all while Jen watched over the phone. Her EMT skills helped then as she coached Kali through it, breathing with her, getting her to relax and let it all flow through her and out of her, until she was empty again, until she could function again. In between the start and the end of her episode, she told Jen everything. Starting with that long-ago summer night on their parents' deck to the current situation with her and Dylan. It felt good to put it out in the open, honestly. It also made Kali feel completely eviscerated and raw. Thank God she wasn't on call and didn't have to work the next day.

When it was all over and quiet had settled again, Jen finally said, "So, you and my brother, huh? I always kind of sensed something there."

"What?" The surprise was enough to jar

Kali out of her pity party. "Why didn't you say anything?"

"Why would I?" Jen countered. "Besides, I'm not mad about it. I'd much rather have Dylan settle down with you than some of those other people he was with."

Those words took a moment to penetrate Kali's overtaxed brain. "You would?"

"Sure. My two favorite people in the world together forever? What's not to like about it?"

"Oh." Kali frowned and uncurled a little, rolling her stiff ankles. "Well, it doesn't matter, because we aren't together. Dylan doesn't want that."

"Do you?" Jen asked, one brow raised.

Kali shook her head. "Doesn't matter. We agreed."

"Agreed?"

"Yes. This thing between us was just supposed to be for fun, temporary."

"But it wasn't. Not for you."

It wasn't a question. Which was good because Kali didn't think she could answer without crying again.

"Did you tell him?"

"Of course not." Kali scowled at her friend. "I promised."

"Promises are meant to be broken. I still think you should talk to Dylan."

"Why? What's the point? We've both moved on."

"Uh-huh." Jen gave her a look that told Kali she didn't buy it for a second. "What did my brother say when you told him it was over?"

She thought back to that night, the hurt in those green-gold eyes, Dylan's shocked expression. "Nothing, actually. He just stared at me, then I walked away."

"Right." Jen snorted. "He was probably amazed that someone finally dumped him before he could do the honors. Dylan's such a control freak."

"Is this supposed to make me feel better? Because it's not working."

"Sorry." Jen sat down at a small café table before continuing. "I know you two, and I know that what you both need is more love in your life, not less." Kali opened her mouth to argue, but Jen held up a hand to cut her off. "I know you're working on not people-pleasing, but this is something you need to hear, Kali, and I'm gifting you this advice, okay? You can thank me later."

"I don't think—"

"I know you don't, Kal, but you're so wrapped up in your diagnosis and trying to process it and everything around you that frankly, in this area, you don't know what you need, because you've never had it. Same with my brother. So, this New Year, I'm acting like your fairy godmother and giving you advice to get moving again."

"How can I get moving when I don't know what to do?" Kali groaned and covered her face with her free hand. "Or worse—I know what to do, but I'm afraid to do it."

"You need to talk to him, Kali."

"But I know what he's going to say. It was fun while it lasted but he's glad it's done."

Jen took a deep breath. "Well, at least then you'll know, and you'll have closure on the whole thing."

Kali sighed, breathing slowly and evenly to calm the chaos in her head. Jen was right. She needed to figure out what she wanted, then go for it. She stared at the unopened box of Hanukkah gifts she'd bought for Dylan still sitting on the floor near the coffee table. He should at least have those, no matter how things turned out for them in the end. Kali had picked them out with him in mind. She hated the idea of being rejected again to her face, but she needed to know. Deep down in her heart was that certainty she'd been look-ing for. Regardless of what Dylan chose to do afterward, she had to talk to him and tell him exactly how she felt and what she wanted from him and let him decide, once and for all. Decision made, she sat forward and straightened her shirt. "I'm going to see him."

"Great. When?" Jen asked.

"Tonight," she said.

"Perfect." Jen was smiling now, nodding her approval. "Where?"

She could invite him to the apartment, but that was a loaded location for them both now, seeing as how it was where the fling had taken place. The hospital was always an option, but Kali really didn't want all her coworkers having more fodder for the gossip mill about them. So someplace neutral, then. Boston's annual First Night celebrations were going on that evening to celebrate the New Year. Maybe one of those would be good. Nothing too crowded or noisy, though, so they could still talk.

"Trinity Church," Kali said, squaring her shoulders. It would force her out of her comfort zone, going to such a busy place, and the ice-sculpture exhibit there would give them something to look at besides each other if things got too uncomfortable. "I'm going to text him right now, after our call ends."

"Wonderful." Jen was grinning wide now, looking tanned and relaxed. "Be sure to let me know how it goes tomorrow. I'll be back home next week. Love you. Be safe. Shalom, hon."

Kali said her goodbyes, then messaged Dylan that she wanted to see him, along with a time and the location before shutting off her phone. It was in the hands of fate now, but Kali somehow felt more empowered anyway. She'd made her choice and acted on it. And she knew she'd be okay no matter what Dylan decided, but her heart yearned for him to say he wanted to try with her too.

She got up and tidied the living room, then went to her room to change. After feeding and watering Wednesday, she pulled on her coat, hat and mittens, then grabbed the cardboard box from under the coffee table and headed out the door, ready to meet her destiny, one way or the other.

Dylan had somehow managed to avoid seeing Kali since he'd moved out of the apartment the night of Jiyan's surgery. Which was good because he didn't know what he'd say to her, anyway. He was still a mess inside, torn between beating himself up for being such an idiot by getting his heart involved and feeling like a schmuck for not beating her to the punch.

He had no business loving Kali Mitchell.

She didn't want him to, and he didn't want to, either.

And yet he did.

Story of his life.

Not seeing what was right in front of his face until it was too late.

Served him right, her walking away from him. Hell, Dylan would've walked away from his pathetic self, too, if he could have. But he was stuck with himself, so he sought distraction in the best way he knew how: by focusing on work instead.

After he'd moved into a vacant hotel room just down the hall from Amita's, he'd volunteered to work in the ER over the holiday and the week after, thinking it would keep him away from the day clinic and trouble with Kali. So far, it had worked. And he'd been busy, too, seeing everything from car accident victims to food poisoning when someone's holiday dinner didn't go to plan. He liked the variety and, as always, liked the fact that he was helping others. Even when his own life was a dumpster fire, he could prevent someone else's from becoming one through medical intervention.

Little Jiyan was doing well, too, healing quickly, and was expected to go home the day after New Year. Then Dylan would return to

Providence and his old life there and get on with things.

He'd expected to feel more excited than he did.

But he refused to show anyone anything other than his usual carefree, easygoing self. It was his own fault he was in this emotional predicament, and he'd get himself out of it too. Just as soon as he figured out what the hell he was doing.

He saw another patient, then another and another, until it was well after five and time for him to go home. His shift was over. He went to the locker room and pulled on his parka, then went outside. They'd gotten some snow, finally, but the sidewalks were clear, as were the roads. His hotel was just a few blocks from the hospital, and the walk would do him good, even as the chilly air stung his cheeks and the end of his nose turned numb. He walked on through the darkness, determined to get back to the hotel, to put the last few weeks behind him and move the hell on with his life. That's when he slipped on some ice and fell on his butt. Nothing was broken— just his pride. And his heart.

Kali would be so upset if she saw him like that, but she'd be even more upset if she knew why he was acting this way. As he sat on the pavement, staring up at the cold, glittering stars above, his eyes burned, and he blinked hard.

Shit.

Even as crappy as he felt now, he couldn't bring himself to regret the time they'd spent together this past month. In that moment, with his sore butt and his stinging pride, he knew that regardless of what had happened at the end, for a while, he'd loved Kali Mitchell. More than he'd loved anyone ever. And he'd do it all again, if given the chance.

Not that he'd get a second one.

A few flakes fell, sticking to his face and eyelashes and Dylan climbed to his feet finally and continued toward the hotel. As he neared Boston Commons, where the big fireworks display was set to go off at midnight, there were more people milling around. Music echoed in the distance, and the air smelled of fried food and chemicals from the sparklers all the kids were waving around.

It was in that moment that Dylan knew he owed Kali a huge debt of gratitude. Because she'd shown him that he could open his heart, be vulnerable, risk it all and still survive when it didn't work out. He didn't have to be Superman. He didn't have to be everything to everyone all the time. He could just be himself,

face his failure, face his pain and still find a
way to keep going.

He'd just reached the entrance to his hotel
when his phone buzzed with a new message.
He pulled it out and stepped off to the side to
avoid blocking the path of people coming and
going from the lobby, expecting to see a message from the hospital about one of the patients he'd seen that shift. But instead, it was
a message from Kali.

We need to talk. Trinity Church. Near the ice
sculptures. Eight p.m.

Pulse pounding, Dylan stared at the message.

We need to talk.

Yeah, they did. Or, more precisely, Dylan
needed to come clean with her. Come clean
about his past, about what he wanted for the
future. Come clean about his real feelings for
Kali and his fears about being vulnerable. He
needed to put it all out there, finally, and take
whatever she gave him in return. If that was
her heart, he'd be overjoyed. He'd guard it,
protect it, keep it safe forever. If not, he'd have
to survive without her. He'd done it before; he
could do it again. Maybe better this time be-

cause he had experience with heartbreak. It wasn't the end of the world.

He could survive Kali telling him goodbye for good.

But in his gut, he hoped she wouldn't.

A volatile mix of anticipation and apprehension warring inside him, Dylan sent a single word response—Yep—then went up to his hotel room to shower and change before heading out to meet Kali.

With any luck, the fireworks over Boston Harbor wouldn't be the only things lighting up the night.

CHAPTER THIRTEEN

KALI HADN'T REALLY thought through bringing the box to Trinity Church because when she got there, security wouldn't let her into the exhibit with it. So she ended up sitting on a bench outside the exhibit area, keeping a lookout for Dylan so he wouldn't think she'd bailed on him at the last minute.

People and kids ran all over the place, laughing and joking, lit sparklers fizzing in their hands. She tucked the box farther beneath the bench with her feet, not wanting a stray spark to set it on fire. That was all she needed to cause her already simmering anxiety to boil over into a full-blown panic attack.

She pulled her phone out of her pocket and tugged off one of her mittens with her teeth, checking her messages to see if he'd sent an update. So far, all she'd gotten was an inscrutable "Yep" in response to her original text. Kali inhaled deep and tried not to read too much into it. "Yep" was good. "Yep" meant he was at least coming. Right?

But the longer she sat there, the more she began to worry maybe he wasn't. Maybe *Yep* meant they did need to talk but not now. Later. Much later. By email, when Dylan was back in Providence. And while Providence wasn't that far away, it was still not the same as now, in Boston, in the same city.

"Excuse me," an older man asked, stopping before Kali and indicating the other half of her bench. "Is this seat taken?"

"No." She shook her head and snuggled farther down inside her poofy parka, tugging her hat down to cover her ears. Once Christmas hit and the first big snow had fallen, the temperatures had plummeted down to where they should be this time of year. Twenties and below for highs. But just because it was normal didn't mean it was comfortable. She blew into her mittened hands, avoiding looking at her new bench partner as she rubbed them together, then glanced around the area again. Dylan should be here by now. It was quarter past eight.

Oh God. Maybe he really isn't coming.

Her throat tightened with tension and unshed tears as an image of Kali schlumping back home with her box filled her mind. So pathetic. She shut off her phone and shoved it back in her coat pocket. Stewing over his responses wouldn't solve anything. Best not to worry about it.

"Are you waiting on someone?" the old guy asked, his nose and cheeks red from the cold. He had a bright red scarf around his neck and rested his hands atop his cane in front of him. Clear blue eyes sparkled from beneath his white bushy brows and his white beard hung down the front of his dark coat to the top of his rounded belly. If Kali didn't know better, she'd think she was sharing a bench with old St. Nick. He gave her a kindly smile. "I'm waiting on my wife. She's always stopping to talk to someone or another."

Kali gave him what she hoped was a polite smile. "Yes, I'm waiting on someone."

"Well, hopefully both our people show up soon before we turn into popsicles."

"Agreed."

The man's laugh was infectious, and Kali found herself chuckling, too, some of her earlier tension fading. "How long have you been married?"

"Seems like eons," the man said, then shrugged. "I honestly can't remember a time when my wife wasn't there. She's like the other half of me. I'd be lost without her."

Kali knew the feeling.

"How about you, young lady? Certainly someone as pretty as you has a partner waiting for them at home?"

She sniffed, then looked around again. "Not yet, but I'm hoping to change that tonight."

"Oh!" The man's blue eyes widened with joy. "Well, then. This is a special night, indeed." He looked over at a group of women chatting nearby, then pushed to his feet. "I'll leave you to it, then. Best of luck, Miss. And Happy New Year."

"Happy New Year to you too."

Kali watched him walk over to the group and put his arm around one of the women, who snuggled into his side, then leaned up to kiss his cheek. They looked so happy and comfortable together that it warmed Kali from the inside out.

"There you are!" Dylan said, walking up to the bench, looking relieved. "I've been searching the ice exhibit trying to find you. I texted you twice."

She cringed. "Oops. Sorry. The signal here isn't very good."

Dylan took a deep breath before sitting down on the bench beside her, fidgeting with his coat and his gloves and his hat. He looked as nervous as she felt and was still the most handsome man she'd ever seen. Her heart squeezed in her chest, and she coughed to cover the surge of anxiety inside her.

"Thanks for coming," she said at last, the words emerging squeakier than normal past her tight vocal cords. "I'm sure you're busy, with work and Jiyan and—"

"It's fine, Kali." He stared across the square toward the crowded area where they'd shoot the fireworks off later that night. "I'm glad you texted."

She nodded and watched the older man and his wife as they moved away toward the fireworks area too. Then, for lack of anything better, she pulled out the box and set it between them. "You left this at the apartment. It's for you. You should have it."

"Oh." Dylan looked at her then, his gaze dropping to the box before meeting hers again. She wondered if he'd had trouble sleeping like she did. There were shadows under his eyes, and his cheekbones were more pronounced, like he hadn't been eating well either. Her chest ached a little more, her arms yearning to reach out and hug him despite all the things between them they'd yet to discuss. Finally, he sighed and shifted on the bench to face her, placing his hands on the box. "Guess I should open this, huh?"

"Yeah, you should." It wasn't exactly the conversation she needed to have with him, but it was a start. "Go ahead. Hanukkah's over, but…".

He used his car keys to slice through the packing tape on top, then opened the flaps to see inside. Kali had ordered each of the gifts to be wrapped, saving her the time, so the larger box was filled with eight smaller packages. Dylan pulled out the first one and tore through the plain blue paper to reveal a coffee mug covered in Yiddish insults.

"Oy vey," he said, grinning. "I like it."

He set the box with the cup inside aside, then took the next package. A bag of blue raspberry dreidel jewel pops. "Oh my God. I haven't had these since I was a kid." He opened the plastic bag and took out one for Kali and one for himself, then knotted it up again. "Seriously. These things are so good. They turn your tongue blue, though. Fair warning."

As they each sucked on their candy, Dylan opened the next several packages. There was a Hanukkah Mad Libs game, a Hanukkah T-shirt with the word spelled out in the same lettering as the band Metallica's logo, a Jewish Wisdom Eight Ball, a set of Light My Fire boxers with a flaming menorah set in a particularly advantageous spot, and a Jewish Card Revoked game that was similar to Cards Against Humanity that she'd bought for Jen, too, because she hadn't shut up about wanting it for months now.

Finally, there was just one package left, and Dylan reached in to grab it. He started to tear through the paper, but Kali stopped him, her pulse tripping as she realized what this one was and how it might be misconstrued. Or not.

"Wait!" she held Dylan's wrist, and even through all their layers of outwear, it still felt so good to touch him again. She swallowed hard, her throat feeling raw now. "I need to tell you something. I need to apologize for that night on the roof."

Kali took a deep breath for courage and closed her eyes, centering herself. This time, she wasn't just going through the motions. No one had pressured her to be there. No one had pushed her other than herself. She was here because she'd intended to be. She was exactly where she needed to be, wanted to be. Tonight, she was fully Kali, and there was something she needed to say.

Dylan stiffened beneath her hand, his expression hardening. Kali looked off now—washed out, almost; her skin nearly translucent. He could tell she was nervous. Hell, he was too. But there was a fierce glint in her blue eyes and a stubborn tilt to her chin that Dylan was both stunned and awed by. She was beautiful, breathtaking. And for a full two seconds, she knocked the breath out of him. Then he forced himself to say, "You already made yourself clear, Kali. You don't need to do it again."

Her words had brought everything back to him—the pain, the rawness, the hurt—and his need to keep looking at her warred against his need to look away.

She bit her bottom lip, her tone quivering, her gaze uncertain. "Does that mean we're okay? I'd like to try again, Dylan. For real this time. Not a fling. A real relationship. You and me. Together."

"Kali..."

She looked over his shoulder at something or someone behind him, then exhaled slow. "I love you, Dylan. I know I wasn't supposed to and it goes against our agreement, and I'm really sorry about that, but I've been working with my therapist on recognizing my real emotions and acting on them, and then when I talked to Jen earlier she said I need to tell you and—"

"You told my sister about us?" Dylan's brain was still several beats behind, trying to take in everything she was saying. Including the fact that she loved him.

Kali Mitchell loves me.

Someone set off a huge firework early near the venue on the commons, and the enormous bang shook the ground beneath their feet before the sky filled with iridescent sparkles of red, green and gold. They both ducked instinctively, then stared up at the light filled sky with *ooh*s and *ahh*s along with the rest of the people around them.

When Dylan looked back at Kali she was watching him again. "Uh, okay," he said, still a bit dazed and confused. "So you love me?"

She nodded, her expression brightening slightly. His gaze dropped to her hands, where she was twisting her mittens around between her fingers. Dylan felt like he needed to comfort her somehow, to calm her down, and he shoved his hands in his coat pockets so he didn't do something dumb like hug her too soon. His arms twitched at the thought, though, aching to hold her. Stroke her. Make love to her.

He had to remind himself that they were in a very public venue, and there were still a lot of things to discuss before they moved forward. But still.

She loves me.

Dylan opened his mouth to tell her he loved her, too, but she cut him off.

"I'm sorry," Kali continued. "I'm *so* sorry for screwing everything up. I know I should've kept my heart to myself, but you've been so great to me and made me feel so safe and secure, and I have trouble talking about myself and my emotions, especially in public, and especially when romance is involved. I know that's a horrible excuse, but it's true. I'm determined to change, though. I promise you that if we try this out for real, I'll never stop communicating with you where our relationship is concerned—if I have the chance. You'll always know where I stand. And I won't be like your ex. I promise. I'll never cheat on you. I'll protect you and stand up for you and speak up for you when it's right. I'll keep your heart safe. And I'll do the same for me. Because I matter, too."

Her words, the expression on her face, her body language, it all begged him to give in. To let go and be vulnerable with her. Part of him wanted to. But another part of Dylan still remembered all too well what it felt like when he'd been blindsided out of the blue, betrayed, belittled. He sighed, doing his best to slow his raging pulse. "I know you mean what you're saying, Kali. At least you do right now. But when things go wrong or get hard—because they always do—will you shut down again?"

"I promise I'll try." She sucked in a sharp breath as tears spilled down her face. "I *love* you, Dylan. I don't know how I would have gotten through this month without you. I thought I could handle the holidays on my own, and maybe I could have, but it was so much better with you there. Until you showed up, I didn't realize how much I was missing out on. But you showed me differently. You've been my bright spot. You've pulled me into the light. The only good thing in this broken heart of mine is love for you."

At first, her words hit Dylan so hard all he felt was shell-shocked. Deep inside, he knew she'd told him the truth. He heard it in her voice, saw it with his own eyes. He reached over and took her hands. "I didn't know what I was missing out on, either, all these years. All the hook-ups, the meaningless sex, the short-term flings," he whispered. "I thought that by keeping my heart out of it, I'd be safe. But I wasn't. I was just lonely." The words were right on the tip of his tongue—that he loved her too. It was what he'd longed to hear, but he was afraid of what their future might look like. They each had separate lives, in separate locations. Neither could pick up and leave.

Long-distance relationships rarely worked, even if it was just an hour or so away.

Kali looked away as another early firework went off. This time blue and silver, the long streaks trailing through the sky and lighting up the night. She pulled one of her mittened hands free and swiped it across her damp cheek. "I should have told you sooner, but I didn't know how to talk about it. I'm sorry."

"Stop saying you're sorry, Kali," he said. "You have nothing to be sorry about."

"But I broke the rules," she said, her face crumpling with such intense hurt that he cupped her cheek and smoothed his thumb along her cheekbone. "We weren't supposed to care."

"No, we weren't." He sighed, then inhaled deep and came out with it. "But we did."

She blinked several times, then narrowed her gaze on him. "'We'?"

This time, instead of hesitating, he grinned, secure for the first time in years. "Yes, *we*, Kali. I fell for you too." Dylan swallowed hard, feeling the world shift, slow, freeze around him as he let the words out at last. "I love you, Kali."

For several beats, she just looked at him, apparently as stunned by his admission as he was. But now that the words were out there, they felt good, right. Perfect. He kissed her mittened palm, then leaned in to kiss her chilly lips. Now that he'd said it, he couldn't stop. "I love you, Kali. And I have no clue where we go from here, but I want to try. Whatever you want for the future, we'll give it a go."

She laughed then, the sound drifting around him like joyous chimes, ringing in a bright new year. A bright new future, together. They hugged and kissed again, things heating up until Dylan forced himself to pull back. The last of his unwrapped packages sat atop his lap.

"Can I open this now?" he asked, grinning. "Before we both freeze to death out here?"

"Yes." Kali clapped and laughed. "Go ahead."

Dylan tore through the paper and pulled out a bright blue oven mitt and matching pot holder, both emblazoned with the words "I love you a latke!" across the front in white.

They both laughed then before kissing again.

"I do, you know," Kali whispered against his lips, her smile lighting up his world brighter than any fireworks ever could. "Love you a latke."

"Me too, Kali." He hugged her tight, the way he'd been wanting to since he arrived, knowing that at long last, he'd finally found his person. The right person, who'd be there for him always. The person who'd been there all along. "I love you a latke too!"

CHAPTER FOURTEEN

Eight months later...

SIXTEEN THOUSAND SCREAMING FANS. The first Sunday in August. Kali and Dylan sat side by side in their regular seats on the fifty-yard line at Gillette Stadium, eagerly awaiting kickoff for the Patriots preseason-game opener against the Cincinnati Bengals.

Sun beat down from the clear blue sky and the temperatures were near ninety, their jerseys stuck to their skin and the beer was warm, but Kali didn't think she'd ever been happier.

Even knowing Babs and her new monthly man du jour sat on the other side of her couldn't deflate Kali's joy. Not anymore. Things between her and Dylan had taken some time to settle in. Between their hectic jobs and the inner work they needed to do on themselves with the help of Kali's therapist, the first six months of their "relationship"—it had taken a while for either of them to feel comfortable calling it that—had been slow burn to the extreme.

But now that they were fully bonded and fully open and trusting of each other, life was moving forward at a speed that was good for them both. In fact, they'd looked at houses before coming to the game today. Foxborough was exactly halfway between Providence and Boston, making it an ideal location for them to put down roots. Plus, easy access to Kali's favorite NFL team. What could be better?

Dylan's practice was thriving, and little Jiyan had made a full recovery. Amita and her son still kept regular appointments to make sure the boy was on the right path, but his surgery had been a success, his heart was working properly now and Jiyan hopefully had a long, healthy future ahead of him.

The Bengals won the coin toss, and their quarterback kicked off to start the game. A huge cheer rose from the crowd, and Dylan took her hand, entwining their fingers together before bringing her hand to his lips to kiss her knuckles. His green-gold eyes glowed with contentment and care, for her, for this new life they were building together. Maybe they'd have kids one day, maybe they wouldn't. Maybe they'd get married, maybe they wouldn't. They were together. They were happy. They were committed to each other, regardless of whether they had a piece of paper proclaiming it or not. Whatever they did, it would be a mutual decision between them and take both of their wants and needs into consideration.

Babs was still confounded by what they were together, occasionally pressing Kali about when she and Dylan would get engaged, but Kali didn't care. It didn't matter if other people understood. Besides, if the alternative was a revolving door of people traipsing in and out of your life like her mother had, no thank you. Kali much preferred her small circle of close friends and family and coworkers.

It was enough. More than enough.

And Kali felt understood by Dylan in ways no one else ever had.

"Okay?" he asked, leaning in slightly so their shoulders brushed, letting her know he was there for her. That he would always be there for her, no matter what or how she needed him to be.

It was perfect. Exactly what she'd always wanted. Unconditional love and support, even if she still had trouble putting it into words sometimes. The best gift of all.

"Way more than okay," she said, giving him a quick kiss on the lips. "Thank you."

"For what?" he looked puzzled.

"For everything."

* * * * *

A Surgeon's Christmas Baby
Deanne Anders

MILLS & BOON

Deanne Anders was reading romance while her friends were still reading Nancy Drew, and she knew she'd hit the jackpot when she found a shelf of Harlequin Modern in her local library. Years later she discovered the fun of writing her own. Deanne lives in Florida with her husband and their spoiled Pomeranian. During the day she works as a nursing supervisor. With her love of everything medical and romance, writing for Harlequin Medical Romance is a dream come true.

Dear Reader,

Like a lot of people, I have a love for all things Christmas. As I've been a Florida resident most of my life, writing about Christmas in a wintry Boston was especially a lot of fun for me.

While Dr. Izzy Jeong didn't get to experience Christmas like most children, due to having workaholic parents, she is determined to make up for it by going all out on the holidays. Having her drag the grinchy Dr. Ben Murphy with her made this even more fun. From Christmas decorating to Christmas movies, these two disagree about everything except the importance of caring for their young patients. Add in a surprise baby, and their story has all the makings of a Christmas romance.

I hope, like me, you enjoy Izzy and Ben's journey as they discover how the magic of Christmas can lead to their own happily-ever-after.

Happy holidays,

Deanne

DEDICATION

This book is dedicated to my editor
Hannah Rossiter and the medical team
for giving me the opportunity to fuel my
addiction to Christmas.

CHAPTER ONE

"GOOD MORNING, DR. MURPHY," Dr. Izzy Jeong said, her cheerful voice making it impossible for Ben to ignore her.

Did the woman have to be so happy every morning? How was he supposed to concentrate on his work when she was standing there, all smiles and bubbling with happiness?

He forced his eyes back to the computer screen, but he'd already lost his train of thought.

The nurses' station on the pediatric ward was busy today, and it was hard enough to ignore the insistent beep of monitors and the sound of stretchers and wheelchairs as they rattled down the hallways. Add in the sound of crying babies and laughing toddlers coming from the patients' rooms, and it was all he could do to keep his mind centered on the progress note he was trying to enter into the computer.

And now he had the exasperating, though beautiful, pediatrician to deal with. There was something about her dark wavy hair and those deep brown eyes that drew him in. It was a daily battle that he had to fight when she was around. Which was why he was trying to ignore her.

Unfortunately, there was no way for him to do that this morning without appearing rude to another coworker in front of the staff. The chief of surgery was already on the warpath for feeling that Ben had slighted him.

Ben hadn't, he'd just chosen to ignore one of his ridiculous rules.

"Morning, Dr. Jeong." Even to his own ears his reply sounded stiff and snotty. It hadn't used to be this way between the two of them and if he was honest with himself, he did miss the comfortable camaraderie they had once shared.

But that was before he'd learned that he wasn't immune to the pediatric ward's overly cheery pediatrician. Danger lay in getting too close to Izzy. He'd made that mistake once and that had been a disaster he didn't plan on repeating.

Well, not all of it had been a disaster. The night they'd spent together had been unbelievable. Amazing. And totally unacceptable.

As the sun had come up the next morning, he realized what a mistake they'd made. He was totally wrong for Izzy. She would want a man that could give her the whole white-picket-fence life and that wasn't who he was anymore. He'd lived that life once, before he lost his wife and unborn son, and he would never be able to do that again. The loss had been too much.

Which was why he'd avoided her for the two years they'd worked together on Boston Beacon's children's ward...until one night when they'd gotten carried away by emotions and a passionate connection that he still didn't understand. Never mind the consequences of sleeping with a colleague.

That night they'd spent together still haunted him three months later, and he had to make sure it didn't happen again. It was best for both of them that he continue to ignore her and concentrate on his job.

"I just put in a consult on a three-year-old girl named Janie who was flown in last night from Northampton," she said as she took the empty chair next to his. The sweet smell of honeysuckle floated over to him, bringing memories of a night filled with a sensual passion he had never experienced before.

Was she purposely trying to drive him crazy? He'd chosen to sit at the nurses' station to review his charts instead of the doctors' lounge in order to avoid this. Avoid her. She couldn't be that naive. She had to know what he was doing.

How was it that he'd been able to run off every other well-meaning member of the staff but Izzy? For the last two years, the woman had refused to stop her insistent attempts to fix him. There was nothing wrong with him: he was one of the most highly acclaimed pediatric cardiothoracic surgeons in the country. Couldn't she see that was enough for him?

After the way he'd left the morning after they'd slept together, he thought she'd stop being so friendly with him. But she'd chosen instead to pretend, like he did, that the night never happened.

"I'm about to see her now," he said as he stood. It wasn't like he was running away from her. He had planned to see her patient next before Dr. Jeong appeared.

"I wanted to be present when you spoke with the parents," Izzy said, her hand coming to rest on the sleeve of his white scrub jacket. "A week ago they thought their child had just come down with a virus or the flu then they found out they were facing something much worse. Now they're freaking out."

He'd read the chart. Of course the parents were freaking out. Their child had been showing signs of shortness of breath when they'd taken her to their pediatrician. Unfortunately, instead of the pneumonia their doctor had suspected, an X-ray had shown a lung mass. He didn't envy the person who'd had to tell them. Breaking that kind of news was his least favorite part of his job, and he'd rather perform an eight-hour heart and lung transplant. Relating bad news to a child's parents was one of the few things he wasn't good at now. He'd been there and experienced that heartache himself. He knew the pain that cut through you no matter how kind and understanding the physician tried to be.

And now it would be his turn to possibly give these parents more devastating news if the MRI he was going to request came back showing that the cancer in the little girl's lung had metastasized.

"I'm not a monster, Izzy. I do know how

to handle my patient's family." Okay, maybe he wasn't good at it, but he could do it. Just because the hospital medical board seemed to question every interaction he had, didn't mean he didn't know how to do his job.

"I don't think you're a monster, Ben. I was planning on seeing them this morning anyway," Izzy said, the words short and sharp. "Though I did hear you were already trying to run off our new staff member from Hawaii."

"Who?" he asked. He remembered Javi trying to introduce him to someone, but he hadn't caught the name.

"Exactly," she said.

While her eyes never left his, her smile was gone and he realized he hadn't angered her, but hurt her feelings. "I'm sorry, Izzy. I didn't mean to imply that you did."

"You didn't imply it, you said it." Izzy's gaze seemed to bore into him as if looking for any sign of weakness inside the thick armor he wore to protect himself from prying eyes. "Does this have anything to do with the board meeting they held last night?"

A hot rush of embarrassment shot through him and he quickly looked away. Even though he tried to convince his colleagues that he was unfazed by the chief of surgery's meeting to discuss his defying hospital policies, it still stung that he was being reprimanded for simply doing his job. Everyone thought a doctor's life was all glamour and fortune. It wasn't. The pressure of knowing how much impact your decisions had on someone else's life could be overwhelming. He'd found bottling up all his fear of failure worked best for him. Maybe it didn't make him the most popular doctor, but it did allow him to be one of the most successful in the operating room.

And wasn't that what all of this was about? To successfully save a child's life? And if sometimes he had to break a few rules, wasn't that worth it?

"No, I just don't appreciate being treated like a toddler who needs someone to hold their hand," Ben said before standing and looking back at Izzy, refusing to show any weakness. "But, if it would make you feel better, I'll be glad for you to accompany me. After all, you are the attending."

"Yes, I am," she said, giving him a bright smile that almost made him feel guilty for the hard time he was giving her. If it had been anyone besides Izzy, he would have come up with an excuse to put off this visit until later in the day so he wouldn't have to feel like he was being supervised like a first year resident.

"Hey, Dr. Ben," a young boy called out as they passed the door of his room. "Are we still on for a game tonight?"

"Sure, Max, I wouldn't miss it. Let's plan for nine."

"A game?" Izzy asked.

"An online fantasy game," Ben said, then smiled. "He beats me every time, but it takes his mind off being here in the hospital instead of home with his friends."

"I don't understand you, Ben. You go out of your way to help the kids while you avoid the rest of us. You're a nice guy, so why are you so determined to make everyone think you're a grouch?"

Unable to answer that question, he decided to ignore it. The resulting silence seemed louder than all the noise surrounding them. There was no way Izzy would understand. He didn't even understand it himself. Maybe it was because the kids didn't ask you questions like that. Damaged? Broken? They didn't care. They accepted you the way you were.

The moment the two of them walked into Janie's room, all his thoughts focused back on his new patient, exactly where they needed to be. In one of the larger hospital cribs, the tiny girl lay curled up asleep, a worn brown teddy in her hands while a small tube ran from the oxygen machine on the wall to her nose. On a couch pulled up close to the crib sat what he assumed were the child's parents. Not much more than thirty, the young couple looked up at him the moment he walked into the room. Dark circles surrounded both pairs of brown eyes that were now looking at him with a desperate hope that he always dreaded no matter how much he understood it. He wanted to share that hope. He wanted nothing more than to promise them that he was the answer to all their child's problems. He wanted to assure them the nightmare they were living was just temporary.

Unfortunately, that was something he couldn't do. He was always honest with his patients' families. If nothing else, they deserved that much. Of course, honesty was not always pleasant. Not when your child was sick and you were simply holding on to that small sliver of hope that any moment a miracle would fix everything.

"This is Dr. Murphy, the cardiothoracic surgeon I told you about," Izzy said as the couple rose to meet them. Their eyes swiveled from Izzy to him, then back again. "How about we take a seat?"

When the parents settled back on the couch and he and Izzy had pulled up chairs around them, Ben began. "I've reviewed the records from your doctor in Northampton and spoke with Dr. Jeong. I know your doctor has discussed the results of the lung biopsy that was done last week, but I want to go over it with you again."

He then launched into an explanation of the test results and the specifics of neuroblastoma, which the biopsy from the little girl's lung tissue had shown. When he finished, he paused for a moment to give the two of them time to process all the information.

"But you're going to operate and take out all the cancer, right? That's what our doctor told us. You'll operate and Janie will get better." The little girl's father said, his fear cutting through the silent room as sharp and dangerous as a fine-honed scalpel.

They were counting on him. Someone was always counting on him. The weight of this man's desperation was almost more than Ben could stand. He remembered being this desperate. He remembered having complete assurance that everything would be okay.

And he remembered when the trauma doctor had told him there was no hope for either his wife or their unborn child. No chance for the life he had dreamed of sharing with Cara and their son.

The memory of his own loss had him forgetting the response he'd memorized years ago when he found himself in the position of dealing with a desperate parent. They were empty words that were used to neither promise nor deny that he could make everything right.

"Dr. Murphy and I will be working together to make sure all the tests and procedures are performed so that the surgery can be scheduled. We want Janie to have the best outcome possible," Izzy said, then looked at him. "Maybe we should discuss exactly what we'll be looking for."

Shaking off the bad memory, he focused on the parents who were giving him their full attention. "Dr. Jeong is right. We need to do a few more tests. I'd like another MRI which will be performed with me present. I want all the information I can get on the tumor's location before the surgery. Also, we'll run some blood tests to make sure there isn't any infection. Something as simple as a viral infection can cause problems with recovery from a major surgery."

"Fortunately," Izzy said, in that reassuring voice he'd heard a hundred times as they'd worked together with families, "Janie is a healthy little girl except for the neuroblastoma. She's had an uncomplicated medical history until now and that is in her favor."

"She's barely had a cold before now." The young father's body relaxed as he took his wife's hand in his.

"She's always been at the average percentile for growth. She's very active and a real good eater." The young mom's eyes darted over to her little girl before returning to Ben's, then moving quickly to Izzy where they settled.

The woman was obviously more at ease with Izzy than she was with him. Not that he could blame her. Izzy had a comforting way about her that drew in people quickly. It had even worked on him once.

And just like that he was remembering the night they'd shared.

Ben's phone vibrated with a text, giving him a good reason to excuse himself. After reassuring the couple that he would be back later in the day to examine their daughter more closely, he dug his phone from his pocket and read the message from Javier, the head of Pediatrics.

We need to talk. Now.

Well, that didn't sound ominous at all. Sighing, he put the phone back in his pocket. It was time to face whatever the board had decided would be his punishment.

Izzy watched as Ben left the room. He'd answered all Janie's parents' questions, but still, there was something missing when he talked to them. He was so comfortable with the technical aspects of the surgery. Maybe it was because of the way he'd cut off everyone except for his patients since the death of his wife. She could easily understand how losing the person you loved, especially so suddenly, might cause that. And the fact that his wife was close to term in her pregnancy didn't help either. He'd suffered a terrible blow the night he lost his family.

He'd shared some of his feelings about his loss with her the night they'd met to celebrate a successful case. It had been enough for her to understand that he still felt a lot of guilt because he'd been in the OR saving someone else's child instead of with his pregnant wife when she'd had her car accident.

"He's very intense," Janie's mother said as she joined Izzy at the door where she watched Ben retreat down the hall.

"He's very dedicated to his job and I can tell you that he is one of the best surgeons there is to perform the surgery Janie needs," Izzy said. If it sounded like she was defending Ben, she couldn't help it. No matter what anyone in the hospital thought, she knew Ben was a good man inside that stone exterior wall that surrounded him. On the one night she'd spent with him, she'd seen a man who was considerate and caring. They'd shared an intimate night that would forever change their lives. And she had three positive pregnancy tests to prove it.

She just wasn't sure how to tell him, especially since he seemed determined to pretend that the night they'd shared had never happened. What was she supposed to do? Hand him the pink lined pregnancy tests and tell him to stop being thickheaded and accept that they'd not only had sex together, but they'd also conceived a baby?

She just couldn't do that. Not yet. She'd ignored all the signs, a light period one month and then none at all the next. She'd had only a few days to accept this herself. Even with the positive tests she hadn't believed it until she'd visited her ob-gyn and had it confirmed. In some ways she'd been acting like Ben and ignoring what happened between them.

But now, no matter how much the two of them tried to overlook the big elephant in the room, things between them were about to change. All she could do was hope the man he'd shown her that one night was the real Ben. Because right now, she wasn't sure how she was supposed to share her baby's life with the detached surgeon he portrayed to the rest of the world.

Ben wanted to slam the door. Slam it hard and walk away without ever looking back. That was his first instinct, one he couldn't allow himself to indulge in.

And why not? He was one of the most sought-after cardiothoracic surgeons in the country. One phone call and he'd have a new position at any of the hospitals in the region.

But storming out would only prove to Javier that the administrative board was right about him. So, no matter how much he wanted to slam the door and stomp away, he carefully closed it behind him before stopping and leaning back against it.

He couldn't really blame Javier. He'd only been the messenger. Ben didn't doubt the man's claim that he had tried to talk the board into being more lenient. The man had always been a good department head and fair with the staff. It wasn't him that Ben had problems with. It was the unnecessary rules and regulations of the hospital's administration that tied his hands when he was just trying to do his job.

"Are you all right, Dr. Murphy?"

Ben looked up to find a young starry-eyed resident standing in front of him. What was his name? Joe? Joseph? Did it really even matter? In a few months this one would be gone and a new one would replace him.

"I'm fine," Ben said, starting to walk away before turning back. "No matter what, always remember that you have to live with every mistake you make, even if it was the right mistake to make. Somehow it still comes back to you."

As the young man stared at him, jaw slack and eyes wide, Ben turned and walked away before he told the boy to get out of the medical field while he still could.

And the board thought he was short on

self-discipline? He'd just proved twice in the last five minutes that he had plenty of self-discipline. Their shortsightedness had created the mess he was in now.

Couldn't they see he had been right about accepting that kid from one of their own sister hospitals for their ECMO program? A life-saving therapy that provided oxygen for children with lung or heart conditions. Yes, it was protocol to get administrative approval for all ECMO patients before they were accepted for the expensive program. And yes, it had to be confirmed that there was enough specialized staffing available to handle a one-on-one patient, something he had done himself by contacting the nursing supervisor. Why waste the time it took for all those administrative types to get together and make that decision when with one phone call he had the problem handled? So he hadn't gotten the chief of surgery's approval. Neither he nor the little boy had the time to waste on unnecessary phone calls. The boy had been in critical condition with his young lungs exhausted from fighting a particularly bad case of influenza.

And even if it did cost him his practice in Boston, wouldn't it be worth it to have saved that little boy? He'd bypassed all the red tape that continually tied his hands and now the boy was improving every day thanks to the rest his lungs could receive due to the hospital's specialized equipment and training. Wasn't that the reason they had developed the program to begin with? To help children who needed the specialized treatment?

It would serve the board right if he turned in his resignation and walked away today. Straightening his shoulders, his mind halfway set to do just that, he headed down the hallway leading to his office, sidestepping a volunteer pushing a wheelchair in front of him. It was only after he passed them that he recognized the little girl in the wheelchair. She'd been born with a heart valve defect he'd repaired earlier in the week. Her parents had spent months going from specialist to specialist before she'd been sent to him.

Suddenly changing his mind, he altered his route and took the hallway that would lead him to the children's ward.

He paused outside Elly's room. She was waiting for a heart transplant. Ben had been consulted on the case weeks ago, and all they could do now was wait for a donor heart. Eight years old, the girl was not much bigger than the size of a child half her age. Ben was working with donor registration to get the little girl pushed to the top of the transplant list. It was her only hope.

He stopped at the next door where a teenage boy was up working with physical therapy. Ben had turned to walk away when he heard Jake call after him.

"Dr. Murphy, come see what I can do," the boy said, his voice full of excitement.

Entering the room, Ben was almost as thrilled as Jake as he witnessed him walk from his bed toward the bank of windows on the farthest wall. Six months ago when Jake had arrived, he'd been a scrawny kid who couldn't walk from the bed to the bathroom without being hooked to an oxygen tank. His lungs had almost been destroyed by a vicious virus. The boy had sank further and further into depression while he waited for a lung transplant. Watching the boy smile now as he turned from the windows and swiftly made his way back across the room, Ben felt something close to happiness light up inside him. It had only been two weeks since Jake's transplant and he was growing stronger every day.

He could continue down the hall where he would see patient after patient whose care he was involved in. This was what it was all about. This was why he had gone into medicine.

With a light pat on the boy's back, he left him with the physical therapist and headed back to his office.

He wasn't going to let some stuffy "everything by the rules" medical board that didn't know the difference between a scalpel and forceps stop him from doing what he was meant to do. Hadn't he already lost enough? The hospital was the closest thing to a home he had now and he wasn't giving it up without a fight. So he just had to figure out how he was supposed to become the rule-abiding, perfect-attitude doctor they were demanding.

He needed help. He needed someone who understood what it would take to change the board's opinion of him, and only one person came to mind. No matter how much he wanted to avoid her, he needed Izzy's help to ingratiate him to the board.

He just hoped that asking her to help wasn't as big of a mistake as the night they'd shared together. Walking away that morning, leaving her there alone, had been hard. He knew that walking away from what they had shared had been the right thing to do for both of them, but he wasn't sure he had the strength to do it again.

If his career was the only factor, he might be able to leave Boston. But it wasn't. The kids on the ward needed him.

CHAPTER TWO

NOT FOR THE first time that morning, Izzy's stomach did a sickening summersault. Taking a sip of the ginger ale she'd disguised in a stainless-steel coffee mug, she willed the cool liquid to stay down this time. Puking her guts out at the nurses' station would be sure to get her a lot of unwanted attention. Trying to hide her pregnancy was getting harder every day.

Her mind should be on the lab results from the young girl she'd had admitted to her service the night before, but instead she caught herself listening to the other staff members talk about this year's Secret Santa gift exchange. At least that was better than thinking about her rolling stomach.

"I think it's so cool that all the staff gets involved here. At the last hospital where I worked, the doctors wouldn't dream of taking part in something like this. Especially not with all the regular staff members," Ailani, a nurse from Hawaii, said.

"The doctors are always involved, with things here. They even bring in baked goods for our bake sale," said Leigh, the head nurse.

"Not all of them," added Natalie, a nurse that Izzy hadn't known long. "Dr. Murphy never gets involved."

Izzy's ears perked up at the mention of Ben's name. She had become obsessed with learning everything she could about him since their night together, looking for any sign of the man he'd been that night.

And now that she knew that she was pregnant, she was even more determined to find out more about her baby's father.

"There's always one Scrooge in the bunch, isn't there?" Ailani said before heading down the hallway.

Lizzy tried to ignore the normal hospital gossip. Most of the time it was just innocent comments, but whether it was her queasy stomach or the little life growing inside her, she didn't like the way this conversation was going. Listening to Ben being called Scrooge just didn't sit well with her. She still remembered the pitying looks she'd received from her classmates when she'd had to read her "What I Did on My Winter Holiday" essay.

Besides, none of these people knew him. Not the real him. Not the man who'd managed to rock her world in just a few hours. She wasn't sure there was anyone who really knew him. He was complex in a way she'd never seen before.

"Not everyone celebrates the same way," Izzy said before she could stop herself.

"Dr. Jeong is right, though before Dr. Murphy's wife passed the two of them were very involved in the unit's Christmas activities," said Leigh.

"Dr. Murphy was married?" asked Natalie, the disbelief in her voice surprising Izzy. Yeah, Ben could be more than a little abrasive, but that didn't mean he was unlovable.

"Actually, he's kind of hot. You know, in that *Beauty and the Beast* kind of way," said a nurse who'd recently transferred from another floor. Her freckled face began to turn a deep shade of red that clashed with her auburn curls.

If only they knew just how hot the man could be. Where had the tenderness and passion they'd shared that night come from? And where had it gone the next morning when he'd walked away?

Her mind screeched to a stop with those memories. Nope, she'd worked hard to avoid those particular memories for weeks now, and she wasn't about to go back there. What was important now was to figure out exactly who the real Ben was. And how she could tell him that he was going to be a daddy in six months.

Shaking her head, she concentrated on her job instead of the conversations going on around her. There were too many important decisions to be made in her life right now to let her mind get flooded with what might have been. She needed to focus on the here and now.

When she was a child, her parents had drilled into her that choices in life came with consequences. Now she was beginning to see that the consequences themselves came with choices. And the choices she made now could determine her and her baby's life forever.

And the first one she had to make was when to tell Ben about the baby they were expecting. Then she'd worry about how to tell him.

"Izzy, can we talk?" Ben asked, his question startling her out of the deep trance she'd let herself fall into.

He'd called her by her first name, something he'd not done in weeks. It had been another way of erecting a wall between them. Another way to show her that what they'd shared was not something he wanted to continue. So why was he suddenly changing tactics now?

"Sure, Dr. Murphy. Does this have anything to do with Janie's MRI you ordered this morning?" Or maybe he'd come to apologize for all the times he'd avoided her the last three months.

"Actually, no. I'm still waiting on those results. Apparently one of the radiologists is out sick and there's a backlog of images to be read," Ben said. "Can we talk somewhere privately?"

Izzy eyed him as he glanced around the nurses' station. There was a strange energy coming off him today. A nervousness that was so not the Ben that she was familiar with. Her stomach did another summersault that had nothing to do with morning sickness. Was it possible he'd somehow learned that she was pregnant?

No, that couldn't be it. Unless the man had dug through her bathroom trash can and found the three positive pregnancy test sticks, he had no way of knowing. She'd only been to her obstetrician once and she hadn't seen anyone she knew on that visit.

"Are you okay?" Ben asked, his eyes now trained on her with an intensity that made her want to squirm in her seat.

"I'm fine." She had to get ahold of herself before she spilled her secret here in front of the whole pediatric ward. "How about the doctors' lounge? It was empty a few minutes ago."

She stood and led the way down the hall, all the while trying to come up with something that would explain Ben's sudden interest in her. If it wasn't because of the pregnancy, it had to be because of one of the patients she'd consulted him on. Unless her first instinct was right and he was here to apologize to her.

She waited until he shut the door before turning around and facing him. Maybe it was best if he did know she was pregnant. Getting everything out in the open would take a lot of pressure off her. It wasn't like she could keep the secret forever. Best to just get it over with. If he was suspicious, it would be better to come clean and tell him the secret she'd been keeping. "What's this about?"

"I need your help," Ben said, his words startling her once more.

"Is there a patient you'd like me to see? You know all you have to do is put in a consult," Izzy said, making sure she kept her voice pleasant, not letting her disappointment show. She should have known he hadn't searched her out for something personal. It was all work with Dr. Murphy.

"This doesn't have anything to do with a patient," he said.

For a moment her heart stuttered. Maybe this wasn't about work or the pregnancy. Maybe he did want to apologize for the way he'd acted after they'd spent the night together. Was that possible? Would he finally admit after the last three months that they'd had something special that night?

"It's the medical board. They're giving me till Christmas to quote 'change my ways' or they'll end our contract."

Izzy pulled out the closest chair and sat down. "Are they serious? I know you've had some problems with Dr. Bailey but from what I've heard it's not unusual for you to have problems with the hospital's chief of surgery. Have they ever threatened to fire you before?"

He ducked his head and looked down at

the floor. Embarrassed? Ben? Well, that was something she never thought she'd see. Maybe there was still some hope for him. "What exactly did you do?"

"I didn't get permission before I accepted an ECMO patient," he said, then looked back at her, his eyes hot with the anger that had probably gotten him into this mess. "I'm not sorry I did it. The boy would have died sitting at a hospital that doesn't have the equipment we have here. I didn't have time to wait for all the powers that be to approve the boy's admission."

"Did you try apologizing? I know they have strict rules about getting approval on all our ECMO transfers, but I'm sure if you explain how critical it was to the child's survival they'd understand."

Ben pulled out the chair across from her, sat, and rested his arms on the tiny table that stood between them. Now he looked like he'd lost his best friend. "I tried to explain it to the chief, but it didn't go well."

"Exactly how unwell did it go?" she asked.

His shoulders slumped and his head dropped into his hands. "I might have told him what I thought he should do with all his rules and regulations."

This was worse than she'd thought. Boston Beacon Hospital's chief of surgery had been a medical officer in the marines before he'd begun practicing as a civilian. He didn't take crap from anyone.

"I'm so sorry, Ben," Izzy said. And she was. No matter how things had ended between the two of them, he was one of the best pediatric cardiothoracic surgeons in the country. That was why it was shocking that the board would even consider letting him go. Losing him would hurt the whole pediatric department.

And what would that mean for their baby? If Ben left Boston, everything would be more complicated. Instead of co-parenting as she hoped, they'd have to share visitation rights. Holidays in one city, summers in another. That wasn't what she wanted for their child.

Ben needed to stay here. They had to fix this.

"I'm not giving up. They've given me till Christmas. That's why I need your help. I need you to help me convince the board that I've changed my ways. I need them to think I've become the most meek and obedient doctor on the ward."

Izzy looked at the man in front of her, the sincerity in his face was more than she could take. Meek? Obedient? Ben didn't even know what those words meant. Laughter began to bubble out of her, the kind of laughter that shook your belly and took the breath out of your lungs. She tried to take a deep breath, but thoughts of Ben sitting in front of the board, his hands resting meekly in his lap, was just too much. The whole situation was anything but funny. Ben was right, he did need help.

The hysterical laughter dried up. No, what he needed was a miracle. A Christmas miracle? Was it even possible? Every year she took part in granting a child's wish. Maybe this year, it was Ben that needed his miracle wish granted most of all.

Or maybe they both needed a Christmas miracle. Because they had to find a way to keep Ben in Boston. Not just for the hospital, but for their unborn baby's sake. She needed him here with them, no matter what she had to do to make that happen.

She was suddenly all in on this plan. She didn't have a choice.

Ben leaned back in the chair, crossed his arms and waited as the only hope he had to save his life, as he knew it, finally stopped laughing.

"I'm sorry," she said, her words coming between taking a couple of deep breaths.

"I'm glad you find this all entertaining," he said. He didn't even try to keep the sarcasm from his voice.

"I know it's not funny." Her voice sounded serious now. "I just don't understand why you'd think I'm the one to help. Wouldn't Javier be the best one to help you with the board?"

"He's already tried. I suspect that's the only reason they gave me this last chance." Not that he really had one. Izzy was right. No one was going to believe he'd made a one-eighty transformation in less than a month.

"Okay," Izzy said, taking another deep breath before straightening in her chair. "So Javier is out. But why me? I want to help, but I'm sure you know someone that has more experience dealing with the board than I do."

"But that's just it. They never have a problem with you. They love you. Everybody loves you. You're perfect. You are the one who can show me what I need to do to make these guys think I've really changed." Ben wished there was someone else that could help him. He'd let Izzy into his life for just a few hours and they'd connected in a way he hadn't with anyone since Cara. He'd even opened up to her about losing Cara, and he hadn't done that with anyone else. Now if she agreed, they'd be spending more time together. He was playing a dangerous game, but the hospital board's threat gave him no choice.

"*Think* you've changed? So you don't want me to help you actually make any changes. You just want me to find a way to fool the board into thinking you've changed. Is that what you're saying?" The look she gave him left no doubt that she wasn't happy with him.

"I'm not asking for a miracle. I just want to keep my job." Why did everyone think he needed to change? All he needed was to get out of the situation he was in right now.

"And what happens next time you get in trouble? Because if you're not serious about changing, it will happen again." She stood and his heart sank down to his toes. She was going to refuse to help him.

"Look, Ben, what you need is a complete makeover, but what you're asking for is just an image change. It won't be enough. If I help you, you have to commit to more than that. I need you to trust me and I need you to at least be open to trying to make some real changes. I'll come up with a plan and you'll have to agree to it or we'll just be wasting our time."

Ben stood. Asking for help didn't come easy for him. But if it meant continuing his work here, he'd have to make the sacrifice.

"I'm always open to making changes, if I agree they're needed," he said before holding his hand out to her. "So we have a deal?"

"Not quite yet," she said. "I need you to do something else for me. With all the time I'm going to be devoting to your project, I won't have enough time to work on granting the wishes of one of the children on the ward, so you're going to have to help me."

"You mean granting a child's last wish? You know I don't believe in that. It's like telling the kid it's all over."

"It's a Christmas wish, Ben. It doesn't mean we're giving up on them. It just means we want them to experience the joy of having their wish come true. Yes, sometimes that might be the last wish they're granted. But that just makes it more important." It was the plea in those deep brown eyes of hers that did him in.

"Okay, I'll help. But, if I'm going to, I want to pick who we help." He didn't know why that was so important to him, but it was.

"Okay, then. We have a deal," she said, then took his hand.

The moment her soft skin touched his, he knew he had made a mistake. A big mistake. As his body reacted with exploding fireworks, he pulled his hand back. He'd been so consumed with the need to keep his job that he'd totally tuned out the number one rule he had when Izzy was around. No touching and no thinking about touching. His mind just didn't work right when she was around.

And now, until Christmas, he was going to be around her all the time. What could he have been thinking?

"What was I thinking?" Izzy murmured to herself as she rushed out of the doctors' lounge, clasping her still-tingling hand to her chest. Didn't she have enough to worry about with a baby on the way? And now she'd agreed to "fix" Ben while she fought against all those feelings she'd had the night they'd been together.

"Are you okay?" Leigh asked, as she quickly moved out of Izzy's way. The older charge nurse was one of Izzy's favorites. While sometimes the younger nurses got caught up in their duties, Leigh understood that it was just as important to listen to their young patients and their parents' concerns. Her gray hair and bright blue eyes quickly drew in a shy child and she was the best at giving hugs to crying toddlers. Izzy might not be a toddler, but right then she could have used a hug.

"I'm so sorry. I wasn't looking where I was going," Izzy said, quickly dropping her hand to her side as the lounge door opened and Ben followed her out into the hallway.

"Text me when you want to get together to discuss…uh…that new case," Ben said before nodding his head to her and Leigh and hurrying away.

Leigh's eyes narrowed as they darted back and forth between her and Ben. Izzy didn't have to look over at the nurses' station to know that everyone there had also witnessed their interactions.

When Leigh's mouth twisted into a smile and she winked at Izzy, she knew she was in trouble.

It seemed they'd done it now. Rumors would fill the halls the moment she left the ward. Of course, those rumors would only be a minor blip in the gossip mill when the news of her pregnancy and the baby's father came out.

It looked like Boston Beacon's children's

ward would be full of surprises this Christmas and not all of them would be concerning the staff's Secret Santa exchange.

CHAPTER THREE

Izzy sealed the last envelope and let out a sigh. Sending Christmas cards had been one of her family's few Korean Christmas traditions and it was still one of her favorite things to do each December. She spent months searching for the perfect card for each person on her list and started addressing them as soon as Thanksgiving was over. There was just something about putting up her Christmas tree on Thanksgiving weekend and preparing Christmas cards that awakened her holiday spirit.

She looked across her office to where her tree, all six and a half feet of it, stood next to the fire she'd set as soon as she'd gotten home. After the day she'd had with Ben asking her for help while she was still coming to terms with her pregnancy, she needed the peace and quiet she always found in this room. While the rest of her apartment was dressed in her favorite colors of pink, blue and purple decorations, she'd gone with traditional red ornaments and gold ribbon for the tree here. It was large for the size of the room, but that only made it more grand-looking as far as she was concerned.

Growing up in a home where decorations were kept to a minimum, she'd adopted the motto of more is always better. Each year since college, she had expanded her decorations. Her parents would be horrified by the number of Christmas elves she owned alone and the gingerbread decorations in her kitchen would send them running right back to their modern, and distinctly cold, California two-story. Fortunately, she didn't have to worry about that happening. Her parents were more likely to dance naked in a field of wildflowers than to make a trip to the East Coast to see their only daughter.

Her phone rang beside her and she groaned. Speaking of her parents, it was Monday night. Also known as the weekly night of awkward conversations with her parents. How had things gotten this way between them? Oh, wait, it had always been this way. She covered her flat abdomen with her hands. It would not be this way with her own child. She'd make sure that they knew they came first in her life and that they could always talk to her about everything.

"I got the results from Janie's MRI," Ben said the moment she answered.

It was so like him not to even bother with a simple hello. Well, she'd agreed to help him change so she might as well start now.

"Good evening to you too, Ben."

"Oh, yeah...good evening...like I said, I've got the results—"

"What am I doing? I'm so glad you asked. I'm just having a nice quiet night at home enjoying watching the lights on my Christmas tree. What about you?" While there was more than a hint of sarcasm in her voice, he was so caught up in his own world that she wasn't sure if he would even notice. She found herself wondering exactly what it was that the man did when he wasn't at work. Did he spend his evenings with a good book? Did he watch a favorite show? There was so much of Ben's life that was a mystery to her.

Shouldn't she know these things about the man that was going to have such an important place in her baby's life?

"Right now I'm trying to tell you about the MRI results for a patient you requested a consult for." He paused a moment before his voice became one of concern. "Are you okay?"

She started to bang her head onto her desk. The man really didn't have any idea how to interact with people. Had he always been this way? Or had the last three years of shutting himself off from the world done this to him?

Instead of banging her head against it, she laid her head down on the cold, mahogany desktop and closed her eyes. She was too tired for this.

"I'm fine. I just thought it was a good time to point out how normal people carry on conversations, but I guess we can let that wait for later."

There was another pause before he replied. "No, I think you're right. We don't have a lot of time to change the board's mind."

We? So this had become a team project now. She liked that. It would be a good opportunity to see how well they could work together since that was what the two of them would be doing for the next twenty years. Only Ben had no idea exactly how long they were going to be in this team together.

She opened her eyes and looked at the calendar on her desk where she had circled the day she was scheduled for her twelve-week ultrasound. No matter what happened, she had to tell him once she'd made that visit and was assured everything was going as it should.

"Are you still there?" Ben asked, more concern in his voice now.

"I'm here. I'm just trying to decide where to begin. I need to know if it's really your intention to alienate people, or if you don't know that you're doing it."

"I don't alienate people. People call me from all around the world asking advice on cases and I always answer their questions to the best of my ability." Ben's voice had taken on a defensive tone that told her she'd hit a nerve. Was this one of the things the board had accused him of?

"So I'm going to take that to mean that you don't know that you're doing it," Lizzy said, then continued when Ben started to interrupt her. "It's okay. My parents are the same way. I think it's common in people who are so focused on their work that they don't notice their interactions with others. I was like that, too, when I was young. You just have to learn how to look outside the box you've built around yourself. There are other people in the world that you need to interact with. Some of them you'll enjoy more than others, but you have to learn to acknowledge all of them."

"Did you just read that from some book? Because that sounds like something from one of those self-help books," Ben said. Izzy was surprised to hear the teasing in his voice.

"No, I didn't read it. I lived it. When I left home and went to college I found out there was a whole new world where people actually talked to each other and enjoyed it."

"I'm not an ogre," Ben muttered. Was that pain she heard in his voice?

"I know that. I've seen you with the kids at the hospital. You're amazing with them and they all love you."

Ben cleared his throat on the other end of the phone. She'd embarrassed him. She heard some shuffling around and Izzy imagined him straightening his lab coat as he once again donned his uptight doctor persona.

"Which brings me back to why I called. Janie's MRI results came back and there were no other masses found. I'm going to talk to her parents tomorrow between my surgery cases about plans for the surgery.

I thought you might want to be there since they seem more comfortable with you."

"I'd like that. And maybe we could get together after work and discuss my plan for your board ordered makeover."

They agreed on a time to meet with Janie's parents the next day and after much grumbling from Ben about his time being limited, they had decided on a quick meeting at the local coffee shop after his final surgical case.

They'd just hung up when Izzy's phone rang again and she unexpectedly hoped it was Ben calling back. She'd enjoyed talking to him more than she would have guessed. Ben was a good person, he just lived in his own world too much. She needed to find a way to get him to step out of that place and interact with others more.

It was time that he expanded his world to include other people, because in a few months it was going to include not only a baby, but also Izzy. Because no matter what happened in the next few weeks, the two of them would be tied together by the little one they had made. Not that she could tell Ben that. Not yet. She didn't think Ben would be upset about the baby. Of course it was un-expected, but she'd seen how he interacted with their patients. He loved children. He'd love his own child even more.

So though it might be a shock at first, everything inside her told her that Ben would quickly embrace the idea of being a father. She'd decided that afternoon to wait until she had an ultrasound to confirm that everything was good with the baby before telling Ben. With the loss of his wife and his unborn child, Ben had suffered enough. It was better to wait than to have him disappointed if something was to go wrong in the first trimester which was the most crucial time of a pregnancy.

She glanced at her phone and saw her mother's number displayed.

Raising her head, she gripped her phone in her hand and prepared to hear all about her parent's latest business deal. At least she didn't have to worry about lying to her parents. It wasn't like they'd be asking about how her own life was going. And for once, that was a good thing. "Hello, Mother."

Ben walked through the hospital making a point to at least nod to each person he passed. If Izzy wanted him to acknowledge all these people, he would do it.

He thought of the new nurse Javier had

tried to introduce him to and how he'd rushed past them. He needed to apologize for that. Not that he'd meant to be rude, he'd been in a hurry. If it had been him instead of Javi, he would have assumed that Javi had something more pressing at the time, but he didn't think Izzy would see it that way.

"Good morning," he said to the resident he'd seen after his meeting with Javier. The young man gave him a wary glance before hurrying off down the hall. Maybe he should ask Izzy to talk to him. It wouldn't do for the kid to start alienating his coworkers this early in his career.

"Good morning, everyone," Ben said as he came up to the pediatric ward's nursing station before starting his rounds. A little boy had been flown in the night before from a hospital two states away and Ben was anxious to see him. According to the cardiac surgeon Ben had spoken with, the boy had a cardiac mass that had been deemed inoperable by several surgeons at his local hospital and the pediatrician wanted a second opinion. After Ben had reviewed the MRI, he could see why the other surgeons had refused to operate. The size of the tumor and its location at the interventricular septum would be a challenge. Even with his own experience, Ben wasn't sure if it would be possible for him to operate. But before he could meet the new patient, he and Izzy were scheduled to meet with Janie's parents.

He could hear the little girl crying before he opened the door. Crying children in a hospital were very common, but the sight of Izzy sitting in a chair holding the pre-schooler in her lap while a young lab phlebotomist held the child's arm surprised him. "Where are her parents?"

"I sent them to get some coffee. They'll be back in just a moment. They needed a break before we discussed the surgery," Izzy said, then grunted when Janie tried to twist in her arms to get away from the stick of the needle that she knew was coming.

"Woo, there, little buckaroo," Ben said, as he crouched down next to Janie. "Look what I have."

Ben pulled out his penlight from his lab jacket pocket and held it out for the little girl as he pushed the button making the tip light up. Izzy made encouraging murmurs when the little girl's attention turned to him as Ben held the light up for her to see as he flicked it on and off. Izzy's arms tightened around the child as the phlebotomist found his mark and began to draw a tube of blood for the lab work that needed to be done prior to surgery. When Janie let out a small whimper, Ben handed her the light to hold. In seconds, the job was done and the girl's body relaxed.

"Do you mind holding her a few more minutes so I can examine her?" Ben asked Izzy. The pediatrician had always been good with the children on the floor, which made him wonder if she had plans of having any of her own someday.

"Of course," Izzy said as she used the child's blanket to wipe away what was left of her tears. "Janie and I are becoming fast friends, aren't we?"

The little girl bent her head back and smiled, showing twin dimples in her chubby cheeks. But when Ben adjusted his stethoscope, Janie's big brown eyes widened as she gave him a wary look. "I'm just going to listen to your heart and tummy. It won't hurt."

As he put the bell of the stethoscope against her chest, some of the wariness disappeared, though her eyes never left him. As it always did, the fact that this little one should be out running and playing, instead of trapped here in a hospital being stuck with needles and examined over and over by doctors, tore at him. His job was to make her able to return back to a childhood that wouldn't be filled with hospital stays and needle sticks. Fortunately, it looked like this time he would be able to make that happen.

He was just finishing his exam as Janie's parents returned. Once they were seated and Janie was back in her mother's arms, Ben gave them the news they were waiting for.

"The MRI I ordered yesterday didn't show any other tumors so that is great news. I see no reason to postpone the surgery. From the location of the tumor and the lack of any other masses, that would put Janie in the low-risk category and her prognosis is very good. So let's talk about the surgery and getting Janie well."

Twenty minutes later, Ben walked out of the room with consents signed and surgery scheduled for the next day. He checked his watch and saw he only had a few minutes before he would have to head to the operating room. Not as much time as he'd like to see a new patient, but if he needed to, he could stop back again after he finished with his surgeries.

The young boy he found sitting all alone in his bed looked up at him with eyes that were too astute to belong to any six-year-old. Miguel's doctor had explained that his mother would be unable to travel with him for now due to having younger children that had to be cared for at home. Unfortunately, there had been no mention of a father so the burden of the family seemed to be on the mother alone.

"Hello, I'm Dr. Murphy," Ben said. The boy's eyes might appear older than his age, but he was of average height and weight. His skin was a golden brown and showed no blue from being cyanotic. Except for the IV fluids he was hooked up to and the oxygen tubing running to his nose, the boy looked as if he was in perfect health. But Ben knew better. What he didn't know was how much this boy knew.

"My name is Miguel Contreras Palmero." He pronounced each word distinctly as he sat up straighter in the bed. "Are you the new doctor that is going to tell my momma my heart cannot be fixed?"

His frankness stunned Ben. Who had told this child such a thing? And why? He was only six years old, much too young to deal with the issues of life and death.

"I tell you what, how about you call me Dr. Ben," he said pulling up a chair next to the boy's bed. The matter-of-fact way the child had accepted there was nothing to be done shook him more than anything he'd ever experienced before. "I'm the cardiologist that you were sent here to visit. I'm going to order some more tests and then we'll see what we can do."

"My buddies at home call me Miguel. You can call me that if you want to." The boy laid the book he'd been reading down by his side.

"What's the book about?" Ben asked as he looked at the bright colored cover that displayed pictures of cartoon animals.

For the first time since Ben entered the room, the boy smiled. "It's about a man who works at the zoo. His name is Bernie and his favorite friend at the zoo is a snake named Sam. He gets in trouble sometimes because of Sam, but they're still friends."

"Friends have to look out for each other, right?" Ben's phone buzzed with a text that he was sure was from the operating room letting him know his first patient was ready. "That sounds like a good book, though I'm not really a fan of snakes. I tell you what. I've got to go now, but I'll be back later to see you and you can tell me all about this snake named Sam."

"Okay," Miguel said. "He's not a bad snake. He doesn't bite."

"Well, that's good to hear. I'm going to

have someone do an EKG on you this morning. Do you know what that is?"

"I've had a hundred of those things. They just stick these patches all over you and hit a button on a machine. You have to be still, but they don't hurt," the boy said before picking his book back up.

As soon as Ben left the room, he texted Izzy asking her to do a consult on Miguel just so he could make sure he covered all the bases. He sent another text to the ward's social worker. While the boy might try to give the impression that he was tough and strong, he was away from home and all alone. Hopefully, the social worker could help introduce him to some of the other children on the ward that were able to leave their rooms and visit. Ben knew what it felt like to be all alone and while he didn't know if he would be able to fix the little boy's heart, he could at least make sure he didn't spend the next few days isolated in his room.

Something special about this child spoke to Ben. The kid was so serious, yet so brave too. As often happened, Ben thought about what if this was his own little boy. His son would only be three, all chubby cheeks and legs, full of energy and happiness. He would have moved mountains to protect his son from going through what little Miguel was experiencing. He could do no less for this child.

Ben hadn't been very optimistic when he'd talked to the boy's hometown pediatrician, but now, more than ever, he needed to find a way to operate on him before it was too late. Ben just prayed that he could find a way to do that without losing Miguel in the process.

CHAPTER FOUR

Izzy spent the time she waited for Ben going over the plan she'd come up with the night before. She didn't expect Ben to go along with everything she had scheduled to help him make the changes she thought he needed, but she wasn't going to waste her time if he wasn't serious about changing his attitude either.

She saw him the moment he came in the door, towering over the hostess. He looked up when the hostess pointed her way and his bright blue eyes met hers. For a moment she thought she saw a smile tug at his lips, but then it disappeared as fast as it had appeared. He had a sophisticated air about him, his clothes always well-fitting and his dark brown hair and beard trimmed to perfection. But it was the smile that seemed to play around his lips, always held in check, that drew Izzy's attention. What would it take to get him to relax that tight hold on his emotions?

She'd had a glimpse of that man once. She hadn't known what to think the night Ben suggested they go out for a drink to celebrate a patient's successful surgery. Seeing that part, the excited part, of Ben had been a rare but eye-opening experience. Though he'd never shown any personal interest in her, she'd always felt there was more to him than the grumpy doc that he showed the world. Ben had been so relieved that the little girl survived, that he had revealed a part of himself he usually kept locked away. He'd opened up to her about how important it was to him personally that he be able to help the children on the ward. He hadn't been able to do anything for his wife or baby after Cara's car had crashed into a pole, but he could help others like this child.

He'd been so earnest and honest, they connected that night in a way she had never experienced. She'd even shared her own memories of feeling left out as a child by her parents.

Then there had been the walk to her door and the kiss that started out as a friendly peck but turned into more, surprising them both. It felt like one minute they were discussing a successful surgery and the next they were caught up in a kiss that destroyed all her inhibitions.

Nothing could have surprised her more than the change that came over Ben the next morning when he walked away from her without any explanation. He let down his barriers for just one night, and the world he found was too much for him.

Oh, Ben, what is it going to take to drag you out of this self-imposed loneliness and back into the real world?

"Hey," she said, as Ben took the seat across from her. While the coffee shop was popular with the night staff grabbing an eye-opening cup of caffeine on the way to work, the lull between shift change provided quiet for a private conversation. It wouldn't do for the board to find out that Ben was having to take lessons on relating to his coworkers, especially his boss.

"Sorry I'm late. It's been one of those days. I had a consult with a couple new patients this morning and it set my surgery schedule back a bit," Ben said before turning toward the menu listed above the shop's counter. "I'm going to get a coffee and a sandwich. How about you? Want something else? Another cup of coffee?"

"No, I'm fine, thank you," Izzy said as she warmed her hands against her cup of green tea while the smell of fresh brewed coffee saturated the air. How could something that smelled so good turn her stomach into a swirling pit of acid? Only three months ago she'd lived on the stuff and now it was intolerable.

She took a sip of tea and relaxed. At least her stomach had found something it liked.

"So, you met with the new pediatrician, Dr. Geller? I heard he arrived today with a patient you've agreed to operate on," she said, as Ben returned carrying a multilayered sandwich and a large cup of coffee. Her stomach picked that moment to let out a growl that could be heard all the way to the hospital campus.

"Excuse me," she said, her face heating with an unbecoming hue of red that she knew clashed with her light complexion.

"Here," Ben said as he lifted half his sandwich from its wrapper and pushed the rest over toward her. "It sounds like you might need this more than I do."

She started to refuse when her stomach made another embarrassingly loud rumble. Looking at Ben, she was surprised to see him smiling this time. It would be so like him to find humor in her embarrassment, though she couldn't hold that against him. Shrugging her shoulders, she picked up the sandwich and took a bite, and almost groaned when the rich taste of Italian meats and cheeses filled her mouth.

"Thanks," she said, as she let the memories of their last time meeting like this fade. Things were different now. Her hand slid across her stomach, a protective gesture she found herself repeating lately.

Still, she couldn't help but wonder what his memories of the night were. Did he remember that night too? Did he remember the kisses? The intimate touches?

Her face flushed again as her mind replayed things better forgotten.

"Are you okay?" Ben asked, his eyes filled with concern.

Should she tell him? Was this the opening she'd been waiting for?

No. She'd decided to wait till after her twelve-week ultrasound, and that was what she was going to do. Still, wouldn't it be better if the two of them could talk about that night like two adults instead of pretending it never happened? Once she told him about the pregnancy, he wouldn't be able to do that. "I'm just tired. It's been a busy day, you know."

"And you stayed up late staring at your Christmas tree, I guess?" The disapproval in his voice destroyed all the kudos she'd been ready to give him for at least noticing someone else's feelings.

"It was just one of my many Christmas trees. And no, I wasn't up late admiring my decorations. What about you? Do you even have your tree up yet?"

"It sounds like you've got enough trees for the both of us," Ben said.

"You don't even own a tree, do you?" she asked. She wasn't really surprised. Ben had not been anxious to take part in any of the hospital holiday celebrations since the death of his wife. But that was going to change this year. She'd already decided that he needed to find his way back to living in the present if he was truly going to make some changes to his life. What better way to put the joy back in your life than to celebrate Christmas?

"It's a silly tradition, don't you think? You drag in a bush that you'd never give a second look at normally and you put it up in the middle of your room. You string up lights and dress it up with colored balls and you ooh and aah over it. Then a few weeks later, you drag it out to your curb where some poor city worker has to load it up on their truck and carry it away."

It was like the voices of her parents were coming out of his mouth. Was this how he would be with their child? Never experiencing the simple pleasures of life? "Where is your Christmas spirit? Didn't you enjoy Christmas when you were little?"

"Of course I enjoyed Christmas when I was a kid, but I haven't been a kid in years. I'm an adult with adult responsibilities now and Christmas doesn't really fit into my life."

"There is so much wrong with that statement, but it would take too long for me to tear it apart. So instead, let's get started on what we need to do to change this whole attitude problem you have." She pulled out a notebook from her purse.

"An attitude problem certain people on the board *think* I have," Ben corrected. He'd finished his half of the sandwich and was leaning back in his seat, as far away from her as possible it seemed, as if he thought he might catch some deadly Christmas illness from her. It would probably be easier to create that pathogen in a lab and give it to him than to change the arrogant way he looked down at anything Christmassy.

But that was about to change. She'd spent a lot of time thinking about this opportunity to get to know the father of her baby better and maybe help him find more in life than just existing for his job. She knew all about dealing with workaholic parents. She didn't want that for her own child. "It sounds like the first thing on our list is to get you into the Christmas spirit and that should start with us getting you a tree."

She looked up to see Ben staring at her, his mouth set in a stubborn scowl that she was only too used to. Being a cardiothoracic surgeon brought with it the belief that you always knew what was best and Ben had been subject to this more than once. She'd been expecting this reaction to her plan, but she wasn't about to let it put her off. She'd drag Ben kicking and screaming into a better attitude no matter what it took. And what better way to change someone's perspective than with the festive cheer that came along with decorating a Christmas tree?

"You want my help, right?" she asked, then waited for his nod of agreement. "Okay, then, this is where we start."

"I don't understand what this—"

"That's just it. You don't understand what it is you need to change. That's why you asked me for help, remember? So you're just going to have to trust me. Agreed?" If Ben had his way, he'd make just enough effort to satisfy the hospital's administration and then he'd revert right back to his old ways.

"Izzy, it's a Christmas tree. No one is going to see it but me."

"I'll help you decorate it. You'll see. It'll be fun." At least it was supposed to be fun. It was hard to imagine the uptight Ben that sat across from her right now lowering himself to something as human as having fun. If she hadn't experienced that one night with him, she'd think this was all doomed to fail. But she'd had that one glimpse into a man that was passionate and caring and she couldn't help but hope she could somehow find that man again.

"Okay. I'll call one of those Christmas lots and have them deliver a tree." He didn't sound happy about it, but it was a start.

"I guess that will have to do, but if we had more time I'd insist we go pick one out. It's the only way you can be sure that you are getting the perfect tree. Fortunately for you, I have plenty of leftover decorations that I can bring over so we don't have to go shopping for those," she said. "I don't have clinic tomorrow so I can make it around six if that's good for you."

"Tomorrow? I already have my day full with surgeries and I have the new patient, Jiyan, who Dr. Geller brought in for me to start assessing for surgery. He has a complicated heart defect."

"I heard. Tetralogy of Fallot. It's a rare one. One of the nurses was telling me he's a sweet kid and his mother is just so worried," Izzy said.

"That's why Dr. Geller came along. He's friends with the child's mother. I've studied the images and it looks like I can make the repairs needed, but it's going to be a very complex surgery."

"I'm glad. It sounds like both the kid and the mom have had a hard time. Maybe they can get back to a normal life soon." Not all the children they saw got that opportunity.

"And then there's the little boy with the heart tumor that I asked you to see. He needs to be worked up. I don't have the time for this nonsense. I can't do it." He sat back in his chair and crossed his arms.

Leaning back, she copied his movements, folding her arms across her chest. Everyone thought she was sweet as sunshine, but she could be as hard as nails if she needed to be. One of the few things she had in common with her parents was her stubbornness when she set her mind to something and knew she was right.

They stared at each other, her brown eyes never leaving his blue ones. If this was a showdown, she would win. "We only have three weeks till Christmas, Ben. It's now or never. My way or no way. You decide."

"Okay, okay," he finally said, his arms dropping to his side. "I'll see what I can do."

"Good. That's a start. We want the board to see you out there joining the rest of the staff in the holiday celebrations. It will make you a lot more personable and show them that you can get along with your coworkers."

"I run in the Santa Dash every year. That should count for something," Ben grumbled.

"Oh, you run, all right. You run away as soon as you cross the finish line. That's not celebrating with your coworkers. You might as well be on a solitary run. You have to interact with people, Ben. Ask them questions about their lives, their kids. All the normal stuff people talk about."

She'd won this round, but he wasn't happy about it.

"Also, I went by to see Miguel, the boy that came in last night."

"What did you think of him?" Ben asked, all signs of his annoyance at her gone now.

"He's adorable, but a little sad. He misses his mom and siblings. I talked to the social worker and they've arranged for him to be able to call her whenever he wants. He just needs to tell the nurses. As far as physically, I think he's in more pain than he's willing to admit. I noticed him flinch a few times. Would that be normal for his type of tumor?"

"It can cause some muscle and joint pain. I'll order something to help with that." He became quiet and his mind seemed to wander away from her. She knew he was thinking about that small boy.

"You're worried about him," she said. "Is the tumor non-operable?"

"I don't know. According to his pediatrician every other surgeon has turned him down. I'm his last hope. I think we should get him on the transplant list as soon as possible, in case I can't remove the tumor. It's a long shot that I can get him moved up quickly enough to make a difference, the fibroma isn't going to get any smaller and he's just going to get worse, but I need to try.

There's just so much paperwork and testing necessary to get him moved to the top. It takes time." Ben looked half-defeated, something she'd never seen in him before.

"I can help with some of that. Just send me the paperwork and contact information and I'll get all the tests ordered and sent in."

"Thanks," Ben said, a smile, though a sad one, flitting across his face. "I'm going to head back to the hospital. I promised him I'd stop in again."

"Sure. I need to get home too." She rose from the table.

"Of course. Those Christmas lights won't watch themselves," he said, in a teasing tone that surprised her.

"You just wait. Tomorrow night you'll be oohing and aahing over your own tree."

She pulled the collar of her coat up around her as she watched Ben leave the shop, his head bent down against the cold wind, as he headed toward the hospital. His dedication to his patients could not be rivaled. He was a doctor any parent would want for their child.

But she didn't need a doctor for her child. She needed a father. A loving and giving one. One that would share giggles late at night while reading bedtime stories. One that would sneak her a cookie before dinner.

And one that would gladly string popcorn and make silly paper snowflakes to decorate a Christmas tree. Was it even possible that Ben could be the kind of father she wanted for their baby?

And if he wasn't, how would she protect her child from the pain she'd felt as the daughter of two workaholics who couldn't be bothered to give her the love she'd needed?

CHAPTER FIVE

IZZY STEPPED INTO Miguel's room, surprised to see the him awake so early. She'd come in before clinic hours especially early in order to check on Janie's parents during their daughter's surgery, but seeing Miguel's door open and lights on she'd decided to check in on the boy. She knew that Ben had stopped by the night before, but the thought of this young child all alone made her own heart hurt. Loneliness was something she'd been quite familiar with as a child. Not that she'd been neglected. Her parents had always ensured she had everything she needed. Everything except their time.

"Good morning," she said as Miguel looked up from the book in his hand. She noticed that there was now a pile of new books sitting on the table next to his bed. Apparently she wasn't the only one taking a special interest in him. But it was always that way on Ward 34. The staff was always eager to help out a child or parent in need. "I see someone brought you some new books."

"The lady who helped me call my momma brought me some and Dr. Ben brought me a book on an animal doctor."

Dr. Ben, huh? It seemed Ben had made a stop by the gift shop on his way to see Miguel last night. It was like Ben was another person when it came to the children on the ward. While he was too busy to stop and interact with the staff, he had taken the time to look for a special book for this little boy. But how could she get the board to understand that about him? In some ways, Ben was right. There wasn't anything wrong with him, he just needed an adjustment to his priorities sometimes.

"Is that the book?" she asked as she pulled a chair up to the bed.

"It is. It's about a vet...er...inarian, Dr. Ben says that's an animal doctor. He only takes care of cats and dogs and birds though, not snakes," Miguel said as he shut the book. "Don't tell Dr. Ben, but I like my book about the zoo animals more. It has a snake named Sam."

"A snake named Sam? That sounds like a good book. And I won't tell, though I bet there are a lot of veterinarians that make snakes feel better too." The boy's serious brown eyes met hers and she knew she was a goner. She'd seen that look many times in Ben's eyes. That assessing and measuring look, as if he was trying to figure out exactly why she was choosing to spend time with him. With Ben it was expected: he wasn't one to stop for small talk. He always seemed to have something more important that had him rushing off. But with this little boy, it was startling. She knew he had spent much of his time alone in hospitals as other doctors had tried to figure some way to operate and save his life. Had there never been anyone at these other hospitals that had taken an interest in him?

She decided then and there that this little boy wouldn't fall through the cracks here in Boston. She'd make sure of that. Which gave her another idea. She usually used the Christmas season to grant the wish of one of the hospital's most critical children. She'd been so thrown off from learning that she was pregnant that she hadn't taken the time to find out which child needed their wish granted the most. Ben had insisted that he help choose the child and the wish, but looking at the solemn little boy in front of her, she knew she'd found the recipient. Now they just had to find out what Miguel wanted his wish to be.

She was about to ask him directly, but she wanted to get to know him better. She spent a few more minutes talking to him, trying to find out his interests and figuring out what she could do that would make the most impact in his life.

Some people, like Ben, thought the fact that you were granting a wish for a critically ill child meant you were giving up. She didn't want Miguel to think that, so she'd have to be careful. Neither she nor Ben were giving up on this little one. She'd already set aside a part of her day to contact the hospital's transplant liaison and she knew Ben was still assessing whether there was a way to remove the tumor safely.

Twenty minutes later, when she walked into the surgical waiting room, she was no closer to deciding what they could do to grant Miguel's wish. The anxious looks on the faces of Janie's parents made her switch gears quickly. She couldn't even imagine what these two had been through the last few weeks. Ben had given them hope that their little girl would make it through the operation, but it was normal for them to have some doubts.

"Have you heard anything from the operating room?" Izzy asked. It was protocol for the circulating nurse to keep their patients' families up-to-date during the surgery by calling when the operation began and ended.

"Not since they started," Janie's mother said, her hand visibly tightening on her husband's. "Can you find out anything? I know Dr. Murphy said that it would be around two hours for the surgery, but I just need to know she's okay."

"Let me see what I can do," Izzy said. It wouldn't be the first time she'd wormed her way into the OR sanctuary.

She made a beeline to the operating area and swiped her badge for clearance. But when the doors opened, she was immediately met by a large man dressed out in green scrubs. The charge nurses for the OR always took their responsibilities seriously. There would be no one getting past them and endangering the sterility of their operating rooms.

Izzy stepped up to the red line that designated where those who were not properly dressed out had to stay. "I just wanted to look at the screen for the room Dr. Murphy is currently operating in."

The man looked down his nose at her then stepped back, his hand pointing down to the red line. "Wait here."

Minutes later, he returned with a plastic outer gown, hat and shoe covers. When she'd finished donning the clothes, he turned and she followed him around the corner to where over twenty screens displayed assorted operating rooms, with some screens divided and displaying more than one room. It was amazing just how many surgeries the hospital performed each day.

"Dr. Murphy's in suite twenty-five," the man said, then stood next to her like she was going to suddenly dash off into one of those rooms. She started to tell him that the last thing she wanted was to find herself inside an operating room, but she knew he'd never understand the way her knees wanted to buckle just seeing the operations from this screen. Both she and her medical school adviser had realized quickly that she was not meant to be a surgeon.

She scanned the numbers, finding Ben's room. He was bent over Janie, his body blocking her from seeing what he was doing while a surgical microscope covered his eyes, but from his concentration she assumed he had located the tumor and was working on removing it. At the top of the bed, an anesthesiologist studied the monitors, showing no signs of alarm at anything he saw.

"Thank you," Izzy said, then reached out for something to steady her when she looked down from the screens. For a moment her head spun and bright flickering lights seemed to bounce up and down in front of her eyes.

"Are you okay?" the charge nurse asked as he reached out to steady her. As fast as it had hit her, the dizziness subsided and the disturbing light show disappeared.

"I'm okay. There's a reason I didn't go into surgery." And there was a reason she needed to come clean with Ben about the pregnancy, too, before something like this happened and word got out.

After assuring him that she would be fine, Izzy left the OR and returned to the waiting room. With the news that the surgery seemed to be going well, Janie's parents settled back into their seats to wait. As the minutes ticked by, Izzy's mind returned to Miguel. While Janie was lucky to have her parents with her, Miguel's mother was unable to leave her other children, so he had to face the hospital alone. What if something happened to Izzy and her child was left alone? Would her parents step in and take care of her little one? Was that what she wanted for her child? There was so much to think about, so much to worry about, when you were having a baby. How did single moms do it every day? How could she be the mother she hoped to be with the hours that were required for her job? It was one more reason for her to want Ben to take an active part in their baby's life. It was why she hoped to discover that the version of Ben she'd seen that night wasn't an anomaly.

And if she was honest, it wasn't the only reason she wanted to know if that man really existed. A part of her, a silly, romantic part of her, had fallen for that Ben. He'd been so interested in her. He listened to her thoughts on their patients' care and responded with his own insight while still valuing hers. And later, when they found themselves still talking and laughing at her front door, it seemed just natural that he would kiss her goodnight. When the kiss continued into her front entry and then into her bedroom, Ben was so tender, asking for her consent before they took things further. And when she not only agreed, but begged him not to stop, he made her feel wanted in a way no man ever had before.

Janie's parents stood and rushed across the waiting room. She followed them to where Ben stood and heard him reassuring them that everything had gone well and the tumor had been removed. Unable to meet his eyes after reliving the sensual memories, she slipped away and headed back to the children's ward to finish her morning rounds. She needed to put the memories of her night with Ben behind her. It had been a fluke, a once-upon-a-time kind of thing that they wouldn't be repeating. Ben had made that clear the morning he'd rushed from her home and then proceeded to ignore her from that day forward. While what they shared was special to her, Ben had made it clear he wanted to forget about it.

So how was he going to take it when she told him that soon there would be a baby who would make it impossible to pretend that night never happened? And how was she going to accept that their baby might be all they ever shared?

Ben straightened the tree that stood in the corner of his living room for what seemed like the hundredth time. He knew Izzy was going to step into the room and immediately think he'd purposely sabotaged what she thought was an important part of her plan to help him fix his image. Not that he agreed with her. There was no way this tree, or any tree, would make any type of difference in his life.

He walked over to his bookshelf and pulled out a book, placed it under one end of the tree, then stood back. It still leaned to the right slightly, but at least it didn't look like it was about to topple over onto its side now.

The doorbell sounded. Izzy was here. At his house. And they were going to be all alone. Together. He still had flashbacks from the last time they'd been alone. This was such a bad idea.

He swiped his hands against his jeans and straightened the collar of his white button-down. He was more nervous than if he were going into the operating room to perform a lung and heart transplant, one of the most difficult surgeries he had ever performed.

"Hey," Izzy said, the moment he opened the door. "I thought maybe you'd decided to stand me up."

Only a fool would stand up a woman like Izzy. She was so beautiful with her long, dark hair flowing down her back and her deep brown eyes that were always kind and understanding. Add in how smart the woman was and yes, a man would have to be a fool. Of course, he'd been called a fool more than once when it came to interacting with women. Except, for Cara. Sweet Cara had always accepted him the way he was.

"Can I come in?" Izzy asked, standing there on his doorstep, her arms filled with bags of what she presumably considered necessary for a properly decorated Christmas tree.

"I'm sorry, of course. Let me take those." He grabbed the bags and held the door open for her.

"I had the delivery men set the tree up in here," he said as he led the way into his living room. The large brownstone he and Cara had bought after marrying was still in need of some renovations, but Cara had insisted the main living areas be completed before they moved in. The wood floors on the bottom level were refinished and the dark oak paneling in the living room was painted a crisp white, leaving only the built-in bookshelves finished in the dark stain that spoke of the home's stately history. When they'd discovered they were expecting their son, they started updating the second floor. Now a nursery sat half-finished, the door closed so that memories of the family he'd planned were shut away from his sight.

He stopped in front of the poor lopsided tree and sat the packages down. "Before you start, it's not my fault. This is the way they delivered it to me."

"Which is why you never have a Christmas tree delivered. You have to go to the lot and search for the perfect tree. It's all part of the Christmas tradition," Izzy said as she walked around the tree, the wrinkles between her brows getting tighter and tighter.

"It's not that bad," Ben said, feeling as if he needed to take up for the pitiful thing. "It's not its fault that it grew a little sideways."

Izzy looked at him then nodded her head. "You're right. It's a true *Charlie Brown Christmas* tree and it can still bring you lots of joy."

Ben studied the tree. He felt sorry for the thing and he didn't want to hurt Izzy's feeling when she seemed so excited at the prospect of decorating it, but the only joy he could see him getting from the tree would be the day after Christmas when he took it out to the curb and put them both out of their misery.

"So what do you want me to do?" he asked as he watched Izzy pull out packages of multicolored lights.

"You can take these and plug them in so we can make sure they work before we wrap them around the tree. I didn't know what your Christmas colors were so I brought the multicolored ones."

"My Christmas colors? I don't think that's a real thing, Izzy." He was beginning to think maybe she had a real problem with all this Christmas stuff. Maybe he should check and see if there were support groups for that?

"Yeah, you know. Like your Christmas theme." Izzy pulled out boxes of colored ornaments in bright red, green and blue.

"Are you sure you're not making this stuff up?" he said as he unwound the first string of lights and walked over to the closest electrical plug. Bright colored lights lit up the moment he plugged them in and he unplugged them quickly before they could fry his corneas. He took the next string out of the box and plugged it in, then looked back at all the boxes of lights he still had to test. It wasn't joy this tree was going to bring him, it was a severe headache from its glare.

"Didn't your parents decorate a tree? Put lights on the outside of the house? Place blow-up Santa Clauses out in the yard?" She'd stopped opening the packages and was now studying him, both hands on her hips and her lips turned down in a frown. She looked so cute he wanted to grab her up and kiss that frown right off her mouth.

He took a step back. Better to argue about the senseless decorations than to let his mind wander down that path. "My parents did a tree."

He could still remember his dad fussing about all the trouble as he toted the thing inside while his mom just laughed and pointed out the perfect place for him to set it up. Except it always took him moving it three or four times before she finally was satisfied. Now that he was grown, he wondered if his mom had just been playing with his dad.

"So, what was your favorite color on the tree? Red? Blue?"

It was blue, he remembered. His mother had those big blue glass balls that broke if you knocked them off the tree. The color had always reminded him of the deep blue of the ocean.

"Or was your tree a themed tree?" Izzy asked. She'd started winding a string of lights around the branches of the tree now, carefully covering each limb with lights, her brown eyes narrowed as she made each twist and her perfect lips pursed in concentration.

"If our tree had a theme, it would be middle-class American. What about you? I bet you had the biggest tree in town." He bent down and picked up the next string and handed it to her, then forced himself to glance away.

"You'd lose that bet. Christmas at our house was just another excuse for my parents to invite their coworkers over so they could discuss business. Except for a little pre-lit tree in the corner of the living room, they didn't bother to go out of their way for Christmas. Our tree was so small it had to sit on a tabletop."

He looked back over at her and could see the hurt in her eyes as the colored lights reflected off them. This was why Izzy always made such a big deal about Christmas. She had missed all this when she was growing up.

And here he was complaining about spending a few moments decorating this rickety little tree when she would have been happy to have had it, even as disappointing as it was, to decorate when she was a child.

"I like the blue ornaments," he said, deciding then and there that he wouldn't give Izzy any more trouble when it came to the decorations. "What do you think? Maybe the blue and red ones?"

An hour later, they sat on the floor, surrounded by empty ornament boxes, surveying their work. Despite the fact it still sat off-center, it didn't look half-bad.

"So, admit it. You're enjoying the tree, aren't you?" Izzy said before taking a bite from a slice of pizza he'd ordered while they finished hanging the last of the ornaments.

What he enjoyed was spending time with Izzy, and he wasn't about to admit that. "It's nice, I guess."

She snorted and some of her pizza went down wrong, bringing on a series of coughs that alarmed him.

"Hold on," he said as he moved over to her side, putting an arm around her. "It's okay. You're still moving air so you're not choking."

"I'm okay," she said, her voice hoarse. She cleared her throat then reached for her bottle of water.

He pushed her hair back from her face,

enjoying the soft, silky feel of it as it moved between his fingers. So mesmerized by the feeling, he didn't notice she'd leaned her head against his shoulder until he turned his face to find her lips much too close to his. He could still remember how soft they felt against his. How they'd traveled across his body leaving him hard and desperate for more. How demanding they'd become when he'd made love to her.

"It might not be what you expected, but it's still beautiful," Izzy said as she stared at the lit, lopsided tree.

Ben looked at the tree and then back at her. No she wasn't at all what he had expected and she was definitely beautiful, only he wasn't sure he was ready for this at all. He wasn't sure if he would ever be ready. Which made the catch in his breath whenever he looked at her a really bad idea.

"Didn't you and your wife put up a tree?"

Cara. Yes, that's who he should be concentrating on instead of one night of passion that he knew he couldn't repeat. Cara. The wife taken away from him by a fate he didn't understand.

He moved away from Izzy, then looked over to where his new tree sat exactly in the spot where Cara had planned to put their tree. Sometimes he wondered why he stayed in this house with its memories.

"We had one at our old apartment. She died before our first Christmas here." They'd planned to spend that first Christmas at home instead of traveling to see family as they'd done in the past. But that had never happened. Instead, Ben had spent his first Christmas there alone.

"I'm sorry, Ben," Izzy said.

He appreciated that she didn't feel the need to say more. He'd heard it all before. Her simple, sincere words meant more to him. But that was Izzy. She was always honest and caring. He thought Cara would have liked her. His wife had always had an appreciation for someone who didn't need to spout out words that were hollow and insincere just so they could hear themselves talk.

Izzy stood and began to gather the leftovers, stuffing the uneaten pizza back into its box.

"I've got this," he said, standing and taking the pizza box from her hands. They stood there for a second and the silence surrounding them felt awkward.

"I need to go. I have an early day at the clinic tomorrow," she said, bending to pick up the bag of leftover decorations she brought, then started toward the door.

This was the part where he was supposed to walk her to the door, but he knew that it would be just one more temptation to kiss her good-night. They'd already proven that there wasn't any such thing as a friendly kiss between the two of them. One brush of her lips against his would be all it took for him to forget that sleeping with your coworker was not a good decision.

He walked her as far as the entrance then stopped. As she closed the door behind her, Ben's body protested at the lost opportunity while his brain congratulated him on making a wise decision.

Because no matter how much he wanted Izzy Jeong, he knew he wasn't the man she deserved.

CHAPTER SIX

IZZY'S HAND SLAPPED the top of her nightstand as she searched for her phone. One moment she'd been wrapped up in Ben's arms while they watched the lights twinkle across their Christmas tree after a passionate interlude under its branches, and the next thing her phone was waking her up from her most excellent dream.

She opened only one eye, still hoping to be able to slip back into sleep and discover what else she and Ben could enjoy under the Christmas tree, then she looked at the clock. It was 3 a.m. It shouldn't be the hospital—it wasn't her night to be on call. Was it her parents? Was something wrong in California?

Pushing herself up in the bed, she located her phone lying beside her. Seeing Ben's number, she accepted the call. It took her a moment to clear her sleep-fogged head enough to understand what he was saying.

"Izzy, are you there? If you can hear me, I need you to meet me at the hospital." Ben said, his words rushing out. She could hear him breathing heavily and wondered for a moment if maybe he'd been having some of the same dreams she'd had that night.

She shook her head. He wanted to meet her at the hospital, not at some clandestine destination for a romantic tryst. "What's wrong? Is it Miguel?"

"No, it's Elly. They've found a heart for her, but her parents are panicking. I don't know what's wrong with them. We've been waiting for this for months. It's the girl's only hope, but now they're refusing to sign the consent so we can accept the donation unless they talk to me in person."

Elly. The eight-year-old with heart failure had almost become a permanent fixture on the children's ward. They'd been waiting so long for this that everyone had begun to think a transplant donor would never be found for the child. The girl's parents could be a handful to deal with, always anxious and sometimes demanding, not that she could blame them. No one knew how they'd handle being in their place. Elly had suffered from a congenital heart disease. From what she'd heard, more than one doctor had told them to prepare for the worst when she was born. But Elly had survived and now she had a chance to get better. They had to convince her parents to take that chance.

"I'll be there as soon as I can," Izzy said as she jumped out of bed and headed to her closet, grabbing the first thing she saw. "How long do you have before you have to give the transplant center an answer?"

"I've got an hour before they move on to the next client," Ben said. She could hear him start his car over her phone.

"Don't talk to them before I get there, okay? They know this is the right thing, they're just scared. We'll get them to sign the consents once they have a moment to realize what this will mean for their daughter." Izzy pulled on a pair of old jeans, and was surprised to find them a little snug. Her body was already beginning to change. She pulled out an old college sweatshirt that hung past her waist, then grabbed her bag.

"They'll sign those papers if I have to threaten them with child endangerment charges," Ben said. "It's the only chance the child has. By the time we get another donor offer it could be too late."

"It won't come to that. Just wait for me before you go to see them," she urged as she rushed out her back door toward her car. "Promise me you'll wait, Ben."

"Okay, I'll wait. Don't worry. Just promise me you'll drive carefully. I can try to buy some more time with Organ Procurement if you need it." The fact that Ben was worried about her made her feel all warm and mushy inside. No one had ever really worried about her before. Then she remembered that his wife had been killed in a car accident due to someone not driving safe. Of course something like that would affect him.

"I'm only ten minutes away. I'll park near the emergency room and meet you up on the floor."

By the time she turned the corner, Ben had begun to pace the hall outside of Elly's room, sick with worry over Izzy. He shouldn't have called her in the middle of the night and demanded that she come to the hospital. What if something had happened to her as she'd rushed here to help him out? The thought chilled him to his bones.

He knew he was being ridiculous, but he couldn't help the panic that had set in while he'd waited for her. Something in his body had taken over his common sense and his brain had started playing a loop of disasters that could have happened to her.

It was just one more sign that he was letting himself get too involved with her. He had to find a way for the two of them to continue to work together without him losing control of his emotions.

He shouldn't have even called her in the first place. Why had he instinctively called Izzy when he'd needed help? Handling the transplant patients was his job. Yes, Izzy was one of the pediatricians that took care of Elly, but it was up to the surgeon to handle everything that had to do with the transplant process. Getting Izzy up in the middle of the night had been selfish.

He'd handled challenging parents before, he just hadn't expected Elly's parents to get cold feet when every hope they had for their child living a normal life was finally being offered to them.

"I made it," Izzy said, her breath coming in shallow gulps as she jogged up the hall.

"Whoa, slow down," he said, catching her by the shoulders. "Are you okay?"

"I'm fine, just not in as good shape as I thought I was," she said, before bending over and taking in several deep breaths.

"Here, I'll find you a seat so you can sit

and catch your breath. I didn't mean for you to run all the way here." He shouldn't have said anything to her about being afraid the heart would be offered to someone else. He shouldn't have disturbed her at all.

"I'm fine. I just didn't want you going in to speak to Jenny and Trey by yourself."

The fact that she was on a first-name basis with Elly's parents didn't surprise him. This was Izzy. She had a talent for connecting with people. Wasn't that what she'd been doing with him the night before? She'd gotten him to talk about himself. To relax. And he'd have to admit that he enjoyed the time they'd spent together decorating, even if it meant that he now had a somewhat misfit of a tree to take care of.

"Okay, I'm ready now," Izzy said, straightening. "Let's go."

Izzy entered the darkened room first, after knocking softly on the door. Even in the shadow filled room, Ben could make out Elly's parents, one on each side of the bed as if surrounding their daughter with love. Or protecting her from what they feared was to come? Protecting her from him and the dangerous surgery that their daughter desperately needed? How could he make them see that the risks outweighed the danger? Where did he find the right words to get these parents to trust him with their daughter's life?

"Is it okay if we interrupt?" Izzy asked, moving closer to the bed with Ben following closely beside her.

"Izzy," Elly's mom said, standing to meet them. "I didn't expect to see you tonight."

"Dr. Murphy called and told me the great news. I wanted to be here in case you had any questions that he couldn't answer. I'm not the surgeon, but I have been involved with Elly's care since she was sent here."

"I thought you might be more comfortable with Dr. Jeong here," Ben said, truthfully. "I know my phone call tonight was a shock. It was to all of us. We've been waiting a long time for this call and I wish I could give you more time to discuss this, but unfortunately there are other children in the same situation as Elly. If we can't give the transplant procurement center an answer, they have to go to the next child." He was surprised when Izzy took his hand and squeezed it as they stood in the darkened room. Did that mean he had said the right thing or the wrong thing? His phone rang and he saw that it was the transplant liaison.

"I need to take this," he said, breaking his connection with Izzy as he moved away.

* * *

As Ben took his call, Izzy joined Elly's parents at their daughter's bedside and watched her sleep. Small in frame, the little girl was a spitfire when awake. She was always entertaining the staff as well as the other children on the ward with stories she made up about her stuffed animals. Izzy had a feeling that the little girl would grow up to be a great author someday. A day ago, Izzy feared that wouldn't be a possibility. But now Elly had a chance to be whatever she wanted to be.

She looked back to where Ben was deep in conversation on the phone. Was it the organ procurement center? Was there a problem? Or were they just anxious for an answer?

"Dr. Murphy. I hear he's the best at what he does," Elly's mother Jenny said, as she came to stand beside her.

"He's one of the best pediatric cardiothoracic surgeons in the country," Izzy replied.

"Is okaying the transplant what you would do, Dr. Jeong? If this was your child, would you agree with the surgery?" Jenny asked.

Izzy had been asked various versions of this question many times by many parents in many different situations, but this was the first time she'd really understood what they were asking. The life of any child was precious. The life of your own child was an invaluable treasure that could never be replaced. It was a part of you. Elly's parents would give up their own heart, their own life, for their daughter. She understood that now because she already felt that way about the small life growing inside her. How much more would her love grow as she felt her baby move or held them in her arms?

"Yes," she answered, "I'd do anything to save my child. Even with all the risks, I'd have to give my child the chance to live the life they deserve."

Jenny nodded her head, then motioned to her husband. "Okay. You can tell Dr. Murphy that we want to give Elly that chance. We want to go ahead with the transplant."

After getting all the paperwork taken care of and making the arrangements with the transplant center team, it was almost dawn. Too late to go back to sleep and too early to start rounds on their patients. The thought of the hospital cafeteria's food didn't appeal to either of them, so they found themselves back at the Full of Beans coffee shop.

"I don't understand what happened. Why would that child's parents suddenly have doubts about going through with a transplant after months of hoping that this day would come?" Ben stared down into his coffee cup, but the brown magical brew held no appeal for him at that moment. He still couldn't understand what could possibly have gone wrong. Was it him? Had he said something that made them question proceeding with the transplant? "If I'd had the chance to save my own son, I would have moved heaven and earth to make it happen."

The words surprised him. Not that he didn't feel that way. No, the words were true. He would have given anything to save his wife and son after the accident. But saying it out loud? He never discussed the night he'd lost his family. What good did it do? He'd had enough of the pitying looks from the hospital staff when he'd returned to work afterward. He hadn't needed anyone's sympathy. What he'd needed was to be left alone while he tried to figure out how to continue to live after his whole world had been shattered. What he hadn't needed was a bunch of prying eyes that might see just how close he was to falling apart.

"I'm sorry, Ben. I can't imagine what you went through that night." Izzy's hand covered his on the tiny café table. "If you ever need to talk about it, I'm here."

Her skin was so soft and warm against his. Surprising himself again, he turned his palm up and squeezed her own. They sat there for a moment, their eyes meeting, and it was as if everything and everyone in the coffee shop disappeared.

What was it about this woman that caused him to expose the most painful part of his life to her? There was just something about her calm and reassuring manner that made him want to open up to her. He'd felt this connection to Izzy once before when he'd let himself forget all about the pain and the guilt he'd carried around for the past four years. For one short night the guilt he felt for his wife's death had lifted. Izzy had made him feel like a new man. A healed man. But in the light of the day, he'd discovered there was only more guilt to add to what he carried. Izzy deserved someone better than him. He'd found happiness with her for only a short moment, but that was all they could have.

He pulled his hand away and straightened in his chair. He had enough on his plate today without diving back into the past. He had to keep his mind on the job. Others depended on him and it was important that he didn't let them down. He might have let his wife down by not being with her when she needed him, but that was something he couldn't change. All he could do now was be there to make a difference in the life of his little patients. That was his mission now. That was all that really mattered. Not his past. Not his future. Just the children he could heal so they could go on to have a better life. It was *their* future that mattered.

"I'm not sure what happened with Elly's parents. Maybe they were still in shock. It's possible that they'd given up hope, even if they would never have admitted to it. And when the shock started to wear off, I think their fear of losing Elly might have sneaked in," Izzy said, moving back in her own seat. Had she felt the same connection as he had?

Even after getting up in the early hours of the morning, she still looked beautiful with her dark hair pulled back in a tight knot on her head. And though she was a bit pale, her eyes were clear and her smile just as sunny as if she'd enjoyed a full night of sleep, though he knew she hadn't. She was a very special woman. One who'd rushed from her bed when he'd asked for her help even though he should have been able to handle Elly's parents by himself.

She deserved a man much better than him. A man who she could count on. One that would be there when she needed him. Instead, he was the one always counting on her for help.

"You sure you don't want another cup of tea?" he asked, needing to steer the conversation back to a more comfortable one. "It's going to be a long day today."

"No, I'm fine," she said, though she still studied her empty cup as if hoping it would magically refill itself.

"I don't know how you can drink that stuff this time of morning. I always thought you were a coffee drinker."

"What time are you expecting the team back with Elly's new heart?" she asked, as she mournfully slid her empty cup away and reached for the bottle of water she'd also ordered.

"Organ Procurement is still working on it, but for now the donor retrieval is set for four this afternoon our time. The team should return just after five so we'll start prepping around four thirty," Ben said, relieved that she was willing to drop whatever it was they'd just shared. Now he needed to do the same. Besides, it had probably only been his imagination. She'd probably only meant to comfort him.

"Do you mind checking in on the parents today? They're much more comfortable talking to you." The surgery would go into the late evening and he was already thinking of ways to move his cases around so that he'd have the chance to catch a nap before he headed into Elly's case.

"I'd already planned to. I have clinic today, but I'm not on call for admissions so I should have some free time. Keep me up—to-date on your OR time and I'll come see them in the waiting room too."

"Only if you promise that you won't go back into the OR. The charge nurse told me you came in there during Janie's surgery and he thought you were going to hit the floor." While the nurse might have thought it was fun to watch one of the hospital's doctors get squeamish, Ben did not. Not everyone was made for the intense environment of an operating room.

"There's a reason I didn't go into surgery," Izzy said, standing. Did her smile seem to be a little less bright? Was that because of him? It seemed he was having a bad effect on everyone today.

"I do appreciate everything you did, Izzy.

I'm sorry I called you though. I should have been able to handle those parents on my own."

"It's what I'm here for. It's what all of us are here for. We all need each other. I certainly couldn't do her surgery tonight. I need you to do that. And during your case, you'll need anesthesia to do their job. Look at Dylan. He left his own practice during the holidays so that he could be here for Jiyan and his mother. Should he apologize for asking you for help?" The spark was back in Izzy's eyes and he was glad to see it.

"Of course not. He came to me because that's my job," Ben said, standing as he and Izzy picked up their cups to dispose of them.

"They say it takes a village to raise a child. It also takes a hospital full of team members to care for them. We're all part of the same team. You just think you need to be the quarterback all the time but sometimes you need to hand the ball off to someone else."

As they headed back to the hospital to start their day, he thought about what Izzy had said. How did someone hand a sick kid off to someone else to handle? How did they trust that someone else would do the right thing? He'd especially felt the need to be in control of his patients' care after he'd lost Cara. Everything else in his life was totally out of his control, but he could make sure his patients were safe. It wasn't that he didn't trust his coworkers. They were all great doctors. Was it possible that the chief of surgery had been right when he'd told the board that Ben had trust issues?

If so, why was it that he didn't have those problems with Izzy? There didn't seem to be anything that he couldn't trust her with. He'd shared things with her that he'd never felt able to share with others. He instinctively knew that he could tell her anything and not be judged. At the same time, she wasn't afraid of giving her own opinion or telling him when she thought he was wrong. She was honest with him, instead of tiptoeing around his feelings like everyone else.

Or was he the one tiptoeing around others? He'd been so raw when he'd come back after losing Cara, that he'd tried to disappear into his job hoping everyone would leave him alone to grieve. Maybe, he needed to be more like Izzy.

Or maybe he just needed to be the man he'd once dreamed of being.

CHAPTER SEVEN

WHAT WAS THAT NOISE? It sounded like a bunch of high-pitched varmints had gotten into his operating room. And they were singing Christmas music. He held back a groan as one of the operating techs assisting him with his gown hummed along with the music. Every year at this time, no matter how much he complained, the operating staff insisted on changing the music streaming into the room to all the holiday hits. "Can someone please either change the channel or shoot those poor animals and put us all out of our misery?"

The circulating nurse went to the intercom and a few seconds later the sound of Kenny G's saxophone filled the room. At least that was better than listening to a chipmunk sing about what he wanted for Christmas, though somehow he knew that Izzy would have enjoyed the chipmunks more.

He glanced behind the sterile blue drapes where tiny Elly lay sedated and intubated, almost unrecognizable due to the number of tubes and lines that were attached to her. He'd stopped by to see her parents before dressing out for surgery and had been disappointed not to see Izzy.

Not that *he* needed to see her. He had just hoped she would be there to help Elly's parents.

A voice came over the intercom. "The team is here. They're on their way to the room."

Ben looked at the clock at the end of the room. The donor had been at a hospital located only one hour away. With travel to and from the hospitals, it was less than two hours since the heart had been harvested.

The circulating nurse began the necessary time out per protocol, calling out Elly's full name and birth date while checking the child's hospital ID along with the consent her parents had signed earlier in the day, then stated the procedure that they were about to perform. When everyone acknowledged that they had the correct patient and were consented for the correct surgery, they each took their places.

Ben looked at the anesthesiologist. Nodded. And then held out his hand for the scalpel he'd use to make his first incision. Once his operating assistant had placed it in his palm, he held it in his hand for a moment and took a deep breath. As the door opened and the circulating nurse accepted the plastic cooler that held Elly's future heart, he glanced around the room making sure everyone was ready. Once satisfied that his team, though he'd never really thought of them as being *his* till now, was as prepared as possible, he let himself relax. He had to separate himself from the weight of knowing that this child's life depended on him and instead concentrate all his talent on making this surgery successful.

"Okay, everyone. Let's get started." His hands steady, his breathing even, and his heart rate regular, he made his first incision.

Less than four hours later, he walked out into the waiting room to find Izzy sitting beside the anxious parents. He'd sent word out through the circulating nurse all through the procedure to update them, but he was glad that Izzy was there for them too.

"She's really okay?" Elly's mother asked as he took a seat next to them.

"She's doing great. There were no problems getting her off the bypass machine and the donated heart responded perfectly to re-perfusion. As soon as they get her settled into the intensive care unit, they'll let you back to see her. We'll keep her there for a couple days before she returns to the pediatric ward."

Elly's father's phone buzzed with a message. "She's arrived in the PICU and they'll let us back in fifteen minutes."

"Do you want me to walk you around there?" Izzy asked.

"Elly's spent enough time there that I think I can find my way in my sleep," Elly's mother said.

"But this might be the last time she has to stay there," her husband said, taking her hand and pulling her up into a hug. "We have our Elly back, Jenny."

Ben watched as the two of them rushed out of the waiting room. "Well, those two sure look happy."

"They'll be praising your name for the rest of their lives," Izzy said. "So everything went well?"

"Textbook perfect. The donor heart was in perfect condition," Ben said.

"The donor?" Izzy asked, her eyes suddenly losing their sparkle.

"Vehicular accident," he said, losing his

own high spirits from the successful surgery with the thought of another child lost. And another family grieving from that loss. He was all too familiar with that type of pain.

"How old?"

"Just a few months older than Elly," he murmured, thinking about his own son, as he always did in these situations.

"I hope the gift they've given to Elly and her family helps them," Izzy said, her eyes damp with unshed tears.

"It helps some." He remembered the letter he'd received from a transplant recipient assuring him that Cara's donation had given a young man a new chance at life. "At the time you have to make the decision whether to donate or not, I think most people are still in shock. I know I was. But the knowledge that some part of Cara lives on, that she helped someone else, that just confirms that I made the right decision. The only decision that was right for me. It brings me some peace."

"I'm glad," Izzy said, as she wiped her eyes, then smiled at him. "You want to take a walk with me?"

Her question surprised him. It was late and she had to be tired. But he owed it to her to keep her company after the way he'd dragged her out of her home that morning. "Sure. Anywhere particular?"

"I just want a chance to see the tree at the commons. It's late enough that it won't be crowded and I'm off tomorrow so it seems like the perfect time. But if you're too tired I'll understand."

"Just let me change and I'll meet you in the doctors' lounge," he said. "Then we really need to have a talk about this obsession you have with trees. You might need counseling."

"It's not an obsession," Izzy insisted.

"Keep telling yourself that," Ben said before hurrying down the hall to change. He tried to ignore the fact that his steps were a little higher and his spirits a little lighter after speaking with Izzy. He had to remind himself that they were only working together so he could continue to practice here. Once Christmas was over and they'd managed to change the board's mind about letting him go, things would return to how they'd been between them before.

Fifteen minutes later, Izzy and Ben walked outside where the rest of the city appeared to sleep. She hadn't realized how late it was until she saw that the front entrance of the hospital had been shut down for the night with a sign posted saying visitor hours would resume at 7 a.m. She pulled her coat closer as the cold air stung her cheeks and ruffled through her hair.

"Okay. Out with it. What is it about a Christmas tree that would make you want to get out on a cold night like tonight?" Ben asked, adjusting his own coat.

"Like I told you, I never had a real tree when I was growing up. It wasn't until I went to boarding school that I decorated my first actual tree. I guess that's when I caught the Christmas tree decorating bug."

"I knew it was an illness. Maybe we can find a cure," Ben said. "I'll see if they're willing to donate some of the bake sale money to get you help."

She nudged his side with her arm, liking the teasing. When he grunted and grabbed his side, she had to laugh.

"I'm not looking for a cure. I like Christmas, especially Christmas trees. And I refuse to let your negativity ruin that." Once she'd been a lonely little girl dreaming of having her own tree to decorate with popcorn strings and cheap silver tinsel like the other kids in her classroom. Now she was a grown woman who could have as many trees as she wanted and decorate them any way she wanted to. No one was going to change that.

"I'm just joking. I've found the tree in my house almost painless," Ben admitted. Then it happened. His lips turned up into a grin so charming that it transformed his whole face. Not that Ben wasn't always good-looking, she had to agree with the nurse on the ward that Ben Murphy was hot. But now, with his full lips turned up in a smile that lit his blue eyes and his dark hair swept back by the cold breeze, he was hotter than hot. He was downright scorching.

But she'd been caught up in his spell once before and look what it had got her. She glanced down at an abdomen that would soon be expanding.

She looked away and saw the lights from the tree come into view. Maybe Ben was right. Maybe there was something wrong with a grown woman getting this excited to see a tree. And maybe she just didn't care.

"Isn't it magnificent?" she asked once they made it to the commons. "I read that this year's tree is a forty-five-foot-tall white spruce."

"It is big," Ben said, his head tilted back.

"My poor tree isn't even the size of one of its limbs."

Could it be that Ben was actually feeling sympathy for his little crooked tree? Maybe he wasn't a lost cause after all. She sure hoped so. "This is the first time I've had a chance to see it. I planned to make it to the lighting this year, but as usual when I make plans I got called into work. You know how that is."

The moment the words were out she knew she'd said the wrong thing. Everyone knew that Ben had been working the night his wife had been killed in a car accident. She'd always felt that it was not only his grief from losing his wife that had caused him to become so disconnected with the outside world, but also, in part, a misplaced guilt.

"I'm so sorry, Ben," she said, knowing the apology could do nothing to ease the pain she'd just caused him. "I shouldn't be complaining about something as trivial as missing a tree lighting."

Ben didn't look at her and her heart sank more as they headed back toward the hospital. She'd started to see a crack in that tough-as-iron armor he wore around himself and now she'd ruined everything.

"It's okay. You didn't say anything wrong.

We all work too much," he said, his voice sharp and brittle.

"Maybe," she said, though the fact that they could make such a difference in a child's life seemed to even the score.

But what about now that she would have her own child? Things were bound to change. Even if Ben wanted to be part of their lives, it would be a lot to get used to. She'd seen lots of other single moms—and dads—have a career and a family. If they could do it, couldn't she?

"I saw Miguel today. He has me worried. He's talking less and less every day," she said, as her thoughts turned back to all the children that depended on her for their care. There had to be a way to help them while still providing all the time and love she could to her baby.

Maybe they should look into providing day care at the clinic for the staff.

"He has me worried too, though not just because of his not communicating. I think that has a lot to do with being away from his family. I talked with his mother earlier today and she's also worried."

"Did you discuss the possibility of a transplant? I completed the paperwork and sent it in this afternoon. I emailed you a copy."

She crossed her arms across her body. The temperature was falling and they still had another block to walk.

"Thanks, I appreciate that. I told Miguel's mother that might be our only option. She's willing to do whatever is needed to get her son well and back home with his family," Ben said.

"Do you really think it will come to that?" Did the little boy even have time to wait for a transplant?

"I've studied the images over and over and this tumor is not like anything I've ever seen before. It's grown so deep into the interventricular septum that I don't know how I can remove it without damaging the septum. It would have to be removed precisely and I'm not sure I can do it. And I don't know if Miguel would even survive the surgery." Ben's shoulders slumped.

Her hand took his arm and stopped him as they entered the hospital parking garage. "I know you're going to do everything you can to save that boy. But if you can't, it's not all on you. We aren't miracle workers, even though we wish we were. And if you need any help, let me know. We can rally the troops and fight together."

"You can do me a favor. The organ procurement team should have received the application in the morning. Can you contact them and see about getting Miguel bumped up on the waiting list? If you can handle the transplant side of things, I can spend more time trying to come up with the best way to operate on him. Meanwhile, I'm going to talk to some of the other surgeons and see if they have any recommendations."

"Of course, I can do that. I'd planned to follow up tomorrow, anyway, to make sure the application made it to the right people." Izzy let go of Ben and pulled out her keys.

She'd hoped their walk to the tree would be good for both her and Ben. And for a moment it had been. But the worry and stress that Ben constantly wore had returned. She had no doubt he would spend the rest of the night worrying about Miguel. He was determined to take on all the responsibility of his patients, though at least this time he had asked her to help. Maybe this was a first step. Dr. Bailey had been right to have concerns about Ben. If he kept taking all the burden of his patients onto himself while bottling up the rest of his emotions, he wouldn't last long. No one, not even the great Dr. Murphy, could continue to work with that kind of stress.

And maybe it was time for him to take another step out of his Christmas comfort zone too.

"How about we get together tomorrow night at my place and I can update you with what I find out from the organ procurement team?" She wouldn't tell him that she had already designated her day off as Christmas movie day. He'd definitely run for the hills if he knew he'd be expected to watch *It's a Wonderful Life* with her. It was one of her favorites. "Also, I want to talk to you about the Christmas wish we need to work on granting."

He hesitated for a moment, and she thought he was about to refuse. Not that she was going to let him. She could always remind him she was working to help him learn to be less antisocial.

"Sure, what time?" Ben finally answered. "I have a light surgery day tomorrow so I should be able to make it anytime after six."

They agreed on a time and headed to their respective cars. Once Izzy had climbed into hers and ramped up the heater, she remembered that she hadn't told Ben her address. Of course, he'd been there once before on the night that neither one of them had the nerve to bring up. She wanted to say something about it, just to clear the air, but she wasn't sure how she could do that without telling him about the baby they were expecting. The two were just too intertwined now. If she brought up that night she'd need to tell him about the baby and she didn't want to say anything till after her ultrasound when she could confirm that everything was going as it should. He'd had too much sorrow in his life already. She needed to make sure everything was right with her pregnancy, then she'd feel free to tell him.

Besides, Ben had enough to worry about with Miguel. Telling him about the baby and about how their lives were about to change would just add to his worries. For right now it was best she kept her secret. Soon she wouldn't have a choice. She just hoped Ben would be ready to open his heart up for their baby when that moment came.

CHAPTER EIGHT

BEN STARED AT the black-and-white movie on the big television screen hanging above Izzy's fireplace. He couldn't help but feel like he'd been conned into this. It had been awkward enough standing at Izzy's front door remembering the night he'd basically plastered her against the door while they'd kissed. And then there had been the even more awkward moment when he stood in the foyer where three months ago they'd both shed their clothes in an effort to get even closer. Thank goodness Izzy's television was in her family room and not in her bedroom. Those memories would have been the death of him for sure, his blood pressure already rising with the memories of Izzy in his arms while he trailed kisses down her body.

"Maybe I should go, now that you've caught me up on everything that is going on with Miguel's case. It sounds like you have everything under control there." He never should have agreed to come. Izzy could have told him over the phone about her conversation with the organ procurement liaison. Or better yet, she could have just texted him about it. Hell, communicating by smoke signals would have been better than having to sit there beside Izzy while all his body wanted to do was to repeat the night they'd made love.

"And miss watching *It's a Wonderful Life*? It's a classic," Izzy said as she held out the bowl of popcorn she'd made him.

He shook his head. His stomach was already tied up in knots. It didn't need any more reasons to complain. "I had you figured as more of a comedy person."

"I like comedies. But I have to schedule my favorite Christmas movies in order to get to see them all and this is the movie scheduled for tonight." She pointed to the calendar sitting on her coffee table where she had written down all her favorite holiday films. "I start the season off Thanksgiving night with *Rudolph*. You know, the old Claymation one from the sixties. Then I work my way through the more serious dramas like this one and *A Christmas Carol*. Next week

I'll start on the *Home Alone* and the *Santa Clause* series."

"So your obsession with Christmas doesn't stop at trees," he said, smiling at the thought of Izzy sitting in front of her television watching children's Christmas cartoons.

"Oh, no, my love of Christmas movies, not to be confused with an obsession, started when I was a child. I used to hide in my bedroom and watch Christmas movies while my parents were entertaining all their business associates. Not that they cared. They were too busy with work for decorating or celebrating Christmas the way most people do. They didn't really care what I was watching on the television. Actually, there was one thing we did as a family. Every Christmas my mother would get tickets for us to go to see *The Nutcracker* at the ballet."

He was beginning to see that Izzy's parents were nothing like their daughter. Where Izzy was always interested in others and helping everyone with her contagious smile, her parents sounded like they were just interested in making business contacts for their own benefit while ignoring their daughter's needs. How had such a spontaneously happy woman come from parents like that?

"So what's your favorite holiday movie?"

Izzy asked, pausing the movie on the television.

"I don't know that I have a favorite, but if I did, it wouldn't be this one," Ben said. He hadn't watched a movie in so long that he couldn't even name one. Cara hadn't been much on Christmas movies. It had been Christmas music that she always loved. The Christmas before she'd died they'd just learned that she was pregnant and she'd talked nonstop about all the holiday traditions she wanted to make with their baby, most having to do with baking cookies and singing Christmas carols.

"What's wrong with *It's a Wonderful Life*?" she asked, turning toward him now on the couch they shared with a look that he was coming to know all too well. She thought she was right and she was prepared to defend her decision. "It's a great Christmas movie."

"The lead actor in the movie is about to jump off a bridge because his life has fallen apart and he doesn't know how to fix it. Just how can you say that is a good Christmas movie? Am I the only one that thinks contemplating suicide might be a Christmas joy killer?"

Izzy's gaze dropped to the couch before

looking back at him, concern replacing the stubborn glint he'd seen just seconds before. "I'm sorry. Maybe I should change the movie. I haven't watched *How the Grinch Stole Christmas* yet."

"Are you suggesting I'd relate more to the Grinch?" he teased, feeling bad that he'd ruined Izzy's fun. Maybe the movie was hitting a little too close to his heart, but it was no excuse for him to make her unhappy. "It's okay. I'll watch this one and I won't say another thing about your poor judgment in movies."

"My poor judgment? There happens to be a lot of people that love this movie. I bet you can't even name a Christmas movie," Izzy said before picking up her popcorn bowl and stuffing her mouth full of the messy buttery stuff that promised to clog your arteries by the time you reached middle age.

"What about *Die Hard*? That's an excellent Christmas movie," he said, happy now that Izzy had relaxed back into her usual cheerful self.

"*Die Hard* is a great movie, but the only Christmassy thing about it is that it takes place during a Christmas party. There's no caroling, no baking, no Rudolph or Santa. There's only a bunch of bad guys shooting at the good guy for two hours." She offered the popcorn bowl to him and this time he took a handful.

"What about the *Home Alone* movies?" he asked. "That's about a couple of bad guys trying to hurt a kid."

"Ignoring the fact that his parents didn't realize they were one child short when they loaded on the plane, it's also about how families feel the need to be together on Christmas. And there is caroling and the all-important decorating of a Christmas tree." Izzy faced him now, challenging him with a wide smile on her face.

"You have to admit there are a lot of movies that are considered Christmas movies only because they take place at Christmas. If you accept them as holiday movies you have to accept *Die Hard*." He wasn't going to lose this argument. He'd been a proud member of the debate club his last year in high school. "I bet you have *Love Actually* listed on that calendar as one of the movies you watch every year. That movie could easily been set around any holiday."

Izzy's eyes narrowed at him. He'd scored a point.

"Maybe, but it's still a great Christmas movie and nothing you can say will change my mind." She gave him a wicked smile. "So, while you claim no interest in Christmas movies, you seem to know a lot about them."

Score one point for her. Maybe it was better that he settled for a tie. "Just turn the movie back on."

Settling back in his seat, he ate his handful of popcorn while Izzy sat beside him with that winning smile of hers and decided maybe it wasn't a tie after all. Something about seeing Izzy smile like that made him feel like he was the real winner.

He was surprised to find himself so drawn into the movie, that he hadn't realized Izzy was crying until it ended. Before he could think about what he was doing, he moved over to her side of the couch and put his arm around her shoulders. Seeing tears in her large brown eyes did something to his heart. "Are you okay?"

"I'm fine," she said, sniffling and wiping her eyes against her shirt before laying her head against his shoulder. "Isn't it a wonderful movie?"

"It made you cry." The warmth of Izzy's body curled up against his was too much to resist. Maybe it was the sentimentality of the movie or maybe it was just Izzy herself, but sitting here with her in his arms seemed so right. She turned her face up to his. The tears were gone now, replaced by a small, wistful smile.

His eyes couldn't leave her lips. He could still remember how they'd tasted and he wanted to taste them again.

"I just love a happy ending. Don't you?" Izzy asked.

A happy ending? If that was what Izzy was looking for, he wasn't the man for her. But then, he'd never been the man for her. Izzy was filled with sunshine and happiness, his life had been filled with darkness for the last four years.

"It's just a movie, Izzy. Everyone doesn't get one of those in the real world." He needed to leave before he did something that would complicate things between them even more. They'd both managed to put their one-night stand behind them by ignoring that it had even taken place. If they crossed that line again, that would be impossible.

He forced his body to move away from her and stood. "It's getting late."

"I know, but we still need to discuss granting this year's Christmas wish. We have to agree on who needs it the most. You said you wanted to decide on whose wish to grant and I think we can both agree that Miguel needs a wish most of all," Izzy said as she stood beside him.

What Miguel needed was for Ben to figure out how to save his life before it was too late. "No gift is going to replace the child getting to return to his family, and right now that's impossible. I'm still trying to find a way to operate and it's going to take a miracle for Miguel to get a transplant before it's too late."

"I know, but we still can make at least one day in his life special," Izzy said.

As she walked him to the door, his body relaxed. Talking about Miguel reminded him how important it was to concentrate on their working together instead of how right holding Izzy had felt. Children like Miguel needed their attention. That was where his concentration had to be.

Still, walking away, with Izzy standing in that open door smiling at him, had to be one of the hardest things he'd ever done.

Izzy glanced around her obstetrician's office. It seemed so quiet and organized here after leaving her own clinic where children and toys littered the floor and crying babies filled their tired mother's arms. Did any of these people know what they were getting into? Did she?

She noticed that several of the women had brought men with them. She felt she was safe in assuming that most of the men were the women's significant others, though some could be friends there for support. Knowing what a hands-on doctor Ben was, she was sure he'd want to be present for most of her visits.

And if this ultrasound looked good, she'd have no excuse for not telling Ben about the baby. She'd thought of calling and changing her appointment, but that would be the cowardly way out and her baby didn't deserve a coward for a mother.

It was just that after last night, it seemed that she and Ben were getting closer and beginning to form a bond. She couldn't help but hope there was a possibility the two of them could be more than friends. More importantly, she was getting to see a part of Ben that he kept from the rest of the world. That secret part that he protected as if he was afraid someone might notice he was human. She liked knowing that while he might want everyone to think he was superhuman, he was just a man trying to figure things out like the rest of us. The fact that he'd trusted her by sharing his deepest wound was a big step. Confiding in her about his wife being a donor had to have been hard for him. But he'd done it anyway.

Then during their teasing while watching Christmas movies she'd noticed the difference in him. He was more relaxed around her now. It was like a weight had been lifted off him. He had been funny and almost flirty with her.

And she probably was reading more into it than she should. They'd just been colleagues sharing some downtime. But then there was that one moment when she would have sworn he was going to kiss her. A part of her had been disappointed.

No, every part of her had been disappointed. She had wanted that kiss.

"Dr. Jeong," the nurse called. Glancing around, Izzy saw that some of the other patients were looking at her. What if someone knew who she was? Any one of these women could have a child she saw in clinic. If word got out that she was visiting the obstetrician before she told Ben she'd feel awful. She hoped that when the time came to make the announcement that she was pregnant they could do it together.

Ducking her head, she made her way into

the doctor's office where she was asked to remove her clothing and put on a gown. She had to say, she didn't like being on this side of the exam table.

But once the ultrasound technician came into the room and the images began to show on the screen, she forgot all the anxiety she'd had while waiting. Even at just twelve weeks, Izzy could see the silhouette of a little nose and chin as the baby moved its tiny hands and feet. She tried to remember that she was the patient, not the doctor, but she couldn't help but study all the anatomical markers she learned in residency.

"You're measuring at twelve weeks and four days. Does that sound right?" the technician asked.

"Yes, that's what I figured," Izzy said. "So my due date would be June 8?"

"Yes, give or take a few days."

Somehow having a date seemed to make it so much more real. She was already a third of the way through her pregnancy.

For a moment it all seemed too much. The baby. Telling Ben about the baby. Figuring out how they'd manage to raise a child. But that wasn't the scariest part of all this. The scariest part was that she might be falling in love with the man. Her brain screeched to a halt at that thought. Where had that come from?

No. Absolutely not. She couldn't do that. Falling in love with her baby daddy was the last thing she needed to do. It was a cliché that she couldn't let happen. The two of them had to work together to raise this baby and then they still had to interact as co-workers. Falling in love with Ben would be a disaster. The man was clearly still mourning his late wife. He'd made it plain that he wasn't ready to move on with his life. Hadn't he ran the moment he'd realized he was in her bed?

But was it possible that she could help him not only keep his job at the hospital, but also find his way back to a life where he could be happy again? Maybe he just needed a little push. If so, wasn't she the one to do the pushing?

For their baby's sake she would do this without getting romantically involved. Expecting anything else would only be asking for heartache, something that she couldn't afford with her life already in such turmoil. If she could just forget about the way he'd looked at her when she'd been crying at the end of the movie. He'd been so concerned and he'd offered her a shoulder to lean on.

And there was that chemistry between them too. It seemed to hum in the air whenever the two of them were alone together. It had been present that night. She trusted her own instincts enough to believe that he had wanted to kiss her. But he hadn't. Instead he'd pulled away from her.

And that was what she needed to remember. He'd run the morning after they'd slept together and he'd run away the moment he'd been tempted to kiss her. He had made it plain that he didn't want anything romantic between them and she had better accept that now and move on from what they could have and concentrate on the baby that they soon would share.

By the time Izzy left her appointment, she had come up with a plan. She'd invite Ben on a trip to the Christmas market and once he was relaxed, and hopefully enjoying himself, she would tell him about the baby. It would be awkward, there was no way around that, but at least she'd have gotten it out of the way. The weight of keeping her pregnancy secret was beginning to wear on her. She just needed to get it over with and move on no matter how Ben took the news.

Whatever happened with Ben, she wasn't

going to let it take away the happiness she felt about having this baby. She looked down at the ultrasound pictures she held in her hand and marveled once again at the miracle that was growing inside her. She was having Ben's baby. And nothing could make her happier at that moment.

CHAPTER NINE

"WELL, AREN'T YOU just the cutest little girl I've seen all day?" Izzy said as she entered Janie's room. Standing up in the crib, the toddler was laughing as she bounced on the mattress, no longer attached to the oxygen tubing as she had been the last time Izzy had visited her. It had only been a week since the child's surgery, but she was improving every day.

"Dr. Murphy came around earlier and said that she could be discharged tomorrow as far as he was concerned, but we had to get it cleared by you since you are the attending doctor," Janie's mother said.

Izzy stepped in front of the crib and examined the little girl. Her chubby cheeks, once ashen, were a healthy pink and her brown eyes sparkled with mischief. This poor baby had struggled so much with her breathing before Ben had operated and taken the mass from her lung. She would still need to be followed closely by her local doctors, but for now she had a good prognosis.

"Let me take a listen and then I'll check over her recent vital signs. If everything looks good, I don't see why she can't return home."

Janie's mother lifted her squirming daughter out of the crib and sat down so that Izzy could place the bell of her stethoscope against Janie's chest. Izzy squatted down in front of them and listened to Janie's heart and lungs. When her exam was finished, Izzy looked up at the anxious mom. "She sounds perfect. As long as her vital signs are good and Dr. Murphy says he's okay with her being discharged, I don't see any reason why she can't go home."

Izzy stood and her head immediately began to swim. Clutching the arm of the chair, she steadied herself and waited for the dizziness to pass. She'd done this to herself. She was a doctor. She knew that a pregnant woman was prone to orthostatic hypotension and needed to move slowly when standing.

"Are you okay?" Janie's mother asked as she placed her arms on Izzy's. At some point the woman had placed the toddler back in the crib.

"I'm fine," Izzy said, as her head finally cleared of the pretty dancing lights.

Janie's mother loosened her hold on Izzy's arms, but she didn't let go. "Why don't you sit down for a minute?"

Izzy wanted to refuse, but she was afraid the woman might mention it to the staff if she didn't assure her she was okay. "That would be nice."

"I did the same thing when I was expecting Janie," the woman said, taking the seat across from Izzy. "You'll get used to it."

Now Izzy's spinning mind had nothing to do with her blood pressure. "How did you know?"

"I didn't, not for sure, until now." Janie's mother smiled, looking as mischievous as her daughter.

"I don't understand," Izzy said. Her feeling faint could have been caused by a number of things, such as dehydration. Why had this woman gone straight for the pregnancy diagnosis?

"When you started to feel ill, your hand went to your abdomen, as if you wanted to protect it," the woman said, still smiling. "And since I'd experienced the same problem when I used to get up too quickly when

I carried Janie, it just made sense. I take it you haven't told anyone?"

Izzy shook her head. If this woman who was a stranger had been able to tell she was pregnant, how was she going to keep it hidden from the people she knew? Should she just tell him now and stop all this secrecy?

"That's okay, I won't say anything. I didn't tell anyone for a while either. I didn't even tell my husband that I suspected I was pregnant until after I took a pregnancy test. You'll know when it's time."

They sat for a moment in silence watching Janie bounce up and down on the springy crib mattress. Once Izzy felt she had reassured the woman that she was fine to get up, Izzy slowly stood. She'd have to be more careful now that she was pregnant.

"I'll have the nurses start the necessary paperwork to get you and Janie out of here as soon as possible," Izzy said.

"Thank you, Dr. Jeong. We appreciate everything you've done for us. And please let Dr. Murphy know how much we appreciate him too. I wasn't sure what to think of him at first, but we're so thankful for everything he did to help our daughter. He was so good with her this morning. He even sat on the floor and played with her. She's crazy about him."

"I'll tell him," Izzy assured the woman before heading out to make the arrangements for Janie's discharge.

When she recognized the man coming down the hall toward her as Dr. Bailey, the chief of surgery, Izzy made a point to step toward him when they met. Here was an opportunity she couldn't miss. Putting on her biggest smile, she greeted the man, "Dr. Bailey, I'm so glad to see you this morning. I just left one of my patient's rooms and they were so thrilled with their surgeon that I wanted to pass their praises on to you."

"It's always nice to see you, Izzy. And I'm always glad to hear that our patients' families are happy with the care they're receiving from one of our surgeons." Dr. Bailey's face beamed with pride. Izzy knew that the man really did care about the patients, no matter how much his and Ben's personalities clashed.

"Oh, I just left their room and they couldn't have spoken any higher concerning the care Dr. Murphy gave their daughter. The child's mother was just telling me how he was actually down on the floor playing with little Janie. Of course, it's because of

Dr. Murphy's surgery that Janie can even play now. The poor thing was looking so sick when she first arrived here."

Dr. Bailey's smile faltered for just a second before it returned, still looking as genuine as it had before the mention of Ben's name. "I'm glad to hear that. As I'm sure you know, Dr. Murphy is an excellent surgeon."

"Yes, I do. When they first arrived, they said the doctor who referred them here had told them he was one of the best in the country. We're so lucky to have someone with that type of reputation here on Ward 34, aren't we?" It couldn't hurt to let the man know that Ben was sought out by other doctors across the region. She understood that Ben had many faults, but it still didn't make sense that the board was willing to let him go without giving him a fair chance to make things right.

"I'll make sure that I mention that to Dr. Murphy when I see him next. It was nice to see you, Izzy," Dr. Bailey said, his smile giving her no doubt that he knew exactly what she was doing. He gave her a nod, then continued down the hall.

Well, she'd done what she could. It might

not be enough to change the man's mind about Ben, but it was a start.

For the rest of the day as she rounded on her patients, she kept an eye out for Ben. When she checked with the operating room to see what time his last case was expected, she learned that there had been an emergency surgery added when a young teenage boy had come into the emergency room with blunt force trauma to his chest that required surgery for an aortic injury. If she was a little relieved by the fact that he'd be tied up in surgery for a while, she wasn't going to admit it. Besides, it wouldn't be right to hit him over the head with the news that he was going to be a father after his long day in surgery.

By the time she'd gotten home, she knew that her original plan was best. She needed to ease Ben into hearing about the baby. Telling him at the hospital was out. He was always so tense at work. Leaving a message for him to call her, she changed into a pair of her Christmas pajamas, popped a bag of popcorn and settled on the couch to watch the next movie in her collection. It had just got to the part where the kid left at home alone was terrorizing the burglars, when her phone rang.

"Hi, Ben," she said, then paused the movie. Though she knew every scene by heart, she didn't want to miss any of them. As a pediatrician, she enjoyed seeing the kid take down the bad guys. People were always underestimating a child's resourcefulness.

"Good evening, Izzy. I hope you're doing well," he said.

For a moment, she thought someone might have told him about the spell of light-headedness she'd had in Janie's room. Then she remembered that Ben had been in surgery when Janie was discharged home.

"Izzy? Are you there?" Ben asked.

"Sorry, yes. I'm fine, thank you. I heard you had a hard day in surgery. They said there was a kid with a traumatic injury."

"Car versus skateboarder. There was a small aortic tear that I repaired and some broken ribs. His head CT was clear, so he was lucky." Ben yawned and she was reminded that he'd had an early and late day of surgeries. It was time to get to the point.

"So, I ran into Dr. Bailey today at the hospital," she said.

"He wasn't looking for me, was he?" There was a rustling that sounded like clothing. Was Ben undressing on the other side of the phone? That thought had her heartbeat speeding into the danger zone.

"No," Izzy croaked, trying to keep her traitorous mind away from all her memories of an undressed Ben. She restarted the movie. Maybe watching two grown men suffer terrible injuries by an underage mastermind would help. "Actually, I did bring up your name though."

"I bet that went over well. You'd better be careful, Dr. Jeong. You don't want to get a reputation for taking up for the troubled Dr. Murphy. You might find yourself in front of the board explaining your lapse in judgment."

There was more rustling on the phone and Izzy couldn't help but imagine Ben climbing into bed. She needed to end this call.

"I know you must be tired, so we can talk about it later. Do you have any time off tomorrow?" She'd already checked with the OR and knew it was his day off.

"Yeah, why? More Christmas trees we need to see?" The fact that he was teasing her was a good sign. Maybe this wouldn't be as hard as she'd thought.

"Not exactly. I need to go to the Christmas market tomorrow and I was hoping you could go with me." She caught herself holding her breath while she waited for him to answer her.

"Why?" he asked, suspicion replacing his teasing.

"Well, I need to do some Christmas shopping and I thought it would be a good time for us to talk away from the hospital," she said, pausing the movie again as she waited for his answer.

"Is this another one of your attempts to try to trick me into becoming Christmas obsessive like you?" the teasing was back in his voice. "Because I have to tell you that it's not going to work."

"Is that a challenge, Dr. Murphy?" Were they flirting? Was this what it would have been like if Ben had been willing to give them a chance? If he hadn't run out on her the moment the morning sun had come up?

"And give you more of a reason to torture me with sentimental Christmas movies and hours of threading miles of color lights through painful tree needles?" he asked. "No way."

"What if I promise that this is the last Christmas outing I ask you to take part in? Would you agree to go then?" she asked. Seconds ticked by while she waited for him to answer. Had he fallen asleep on her?

"No more decorating or watching corny movies?" he asked, finally. His voice was soft and sleepy, sending a shiver down her body.

"No," she said, her own voice not much above a whisper now as she pulled her knees up to her chest, hugging them to herself. She didn't know what was going on between the two of them, but it was plain to her that things were changing. Did Ben notice it too?

"Will there be any singing of Christmas carols involved?" he asked.

"I can't promise that there won't be people singing, I can't control that, but it won't involve either of us participating." While she loved Christmas music, singing was not one of her talents.

"Okay. I'll agree to go to the Christmas market. Send me a text in the morning with the when and where." Ben yawned again.

"I will," she said. The line went quiet and she was sure this time that he was asleep. "Good night, Ben," she whispered.

"Good night, Izzy," he whispered back to her.

Izzy clasped her phone to her chest when the call ended while she told herself to get a grip. Even if things were changing between her and Ben, she couldn't forget her first priority was their baby.

Laying her phone down, she turned the TV off. She'd lost all interest in the movie. Unlike her own life, she knew how the movie would end.

Her mind kept replaying her phone call with Ben, looking for any sign that maybe his feelings for her were changing just as hers were changing for him. And if they were? What would happen when she told him about the baby? Maybe it would have been best if she'd just been up-front with him as soon as she'd found out she was pregnant. Ben had closed himself off from the world and didn't seem to trust others enough to let them in. Somehow she'd managed to get beyond those boundaries. But would he still trust her when he found out she'd been keeping their baby a secret?

Or would it end a life that Izzy secretly believed the two of them could have...before it even had a chance to begin?

CHAPTER TEN

BEN WASN'T SURE what he'd expected, but this wasn't it. He'd envisioned a couple dozen stalls of people selling specialized items and maybe some handcrafted gifts. Instead, right smack in the heart of Boston, he'd walked into a winter wonderland filled with over a hundred shops. What little Christmas shopping he'd done over the past few years had been done over the internet. He picked out what he wished to buy for his parents and his brother's family and he had it sent straight to their homes. No wrapping. No going to the post office. It was simple and painless. And you could avoid the endless Christmas carols that were blaring at him from every direction.

"Exactly why are we here?" Ben asked Izzy, as he took her elbow and guided her around a group of shoppers. She was so busy looking at all the decorations and shops that she almost ran into a group of elderly women. Not that they noticed. It seemed everyone here was possessed by some Christmas spirit that had taken over their bodies.

"I need to get something for my Secret Santa gift and I thought maybe we'd get some ideas for Miguel's Christmas wish," she said, now moving through the crowd as if a predator pursuing its prey.

Keeping ahold of her arm, he followed her until she stopped in front of a stall that displayed small glass figurines.

"Aren't they beautiful?" she asked. Her hand went up to touch one, then she pulled it back. "But maybe too fragile."

Her head turned toward the next stall, and she was off again, pulling him along with her.

They stopped at a stall to examine some hand-dyed wool scarves. It reminded him of his mother and the scarves she'd once made for him and his brother. He'd already ordered his mother the latest teakettle to come on the market, but he knew she'd love one of the scarves. He'd just finished paying for it, when Izzy began to wave at someone in the crowd.

"It's Bryn and Nick," she said to him, taking his hand and dragging him behind her, not noticing his attempt to pull back.

It wasn't that he didn't like Bryn and Nick, he just didn't know them very well and he couldn't help but feel awkward being caught out with Izzy. And not just for him. Rumors ran rapidly through the halls of Boston Beacon's pediatric ward and part of him had been serious when he'd warned Izzy about getting on the board's bad side by being associated with him.

"Izzy," Bryn said, waving at them. "And Dr. Murphy. I mean, Ben. It's so nice to see the two of you."

"Bryn and Nick. Checking out the markets?" Izzy asked, her hand letting go of his, then taking his arm. Her hand on his arm felt warm and slightly possessive as it tightened when they reached the other couple. His stomach did a peculiar dip at the action. He didn't know how he felt about all these changes in their relationship recently. It was all happening too fast.

"It's Nick's first time," Bryn said. The woman's hip bumped the other man and she laid her head against his shoulder. "I worry I might overwhelm him."

"This place can be a bit much." Ben gestured at the gathered crowd, feeling a bit awkward.

"Don't worry, I'll keep you safe," Izzy said, then to his surprise, she kissed his cheek.

Clearing his throat, he pulled away. He saw the hurt in Izzy's eyes and knew he'd overreacted.

"I'll keep you safe too," Bryn said, then repeated Izzy's actions, kissing Nick's cheek.

"Well, it was good seeing you guys," Bryn said.

"Have fun." Izzy waved goodbye as she led Ben away.

They stopped when they reached a stall with holiday-themed children's items, and Izzy moved away from him.

"I didn't mean to embarrass you," Izzy said, her cheeks a little too red to be explained away with the cold. "Sometimes I'm a little too spontaneous."

He wondered if she was thinking about when they'd gone out after work and had ended spending the night together. It had been totally spontaneous and a night to remember, though he'd spent weeks trying to forget it.

He felt like he was on some precipice where if he took one step forward he'd fall off into a world he'd never escape from. A world he didn't think he was ready for. Did he take a step back or go forward? He couldn't decide. All he knew was he had to make the decision. And soon.

Or was he just overreacting?

"It's okay," he said, "don't worry about it." It had only been a peck on the cheek.

His eyes caught on a wooden nutcracker dressed in green and red velvet with a wooden sword at his side. He remembered how Izzy had said her mother had taken her to see *The Nutcracker* ballet every year when she was growing up.

Izzy had done so much for him and here he was making her feel bad for just being herself. She'd even gone to bat for him with Dr. Bailey, though from what she'd told him on the way to the market, the surgeon didn't sound too impressed. Still, she'd tried.

He picked up the wooden nutcracker. Maybe there was a way that he could thank her. As she moved closer, her eyes lighting up with that special sparkle only Izzy had when she saw what he held, he made his decision.

"Izzy, how would you like to accompany me to the Boston Ballet to see *The Nutcracker*?"

"The Boston Ballet?" she asked, her brown eyes going almost as wide as the smile on her face.

"Yeah. I'm pretty sure I can get tickets to *The Nutcracker* one night this week. Would you like to go with me?" The way her eyes shone with happiness right then shattered something inside him.

"I'd love to go. But I'm sure I saw that tickets are all sold out." Her smile wobbled a moment before returning. "But it was a wonderful thought."

Oh, he'd get those tickets, one way or another. There were always people willing to sell tickets if the price was right, though he didn't think it would come to that. All he knew, at that moment, it felt like making Izzy happy was the most important thing in his world, even though he wasn't ready to let himself think about why.

"I still can't believe you got these tickets. They've been sold out for weeks," Izzy said as they entered the Citizens Bank Opera House. Surrounded by men dressed in black tuxes and women in long sparkly dresses, Izzy felt more than a little underdressed in a simple green gown.

"I operated on one of the ballet manager's

nephews a few years ago. She'd told me to call her if I ever needed tickets," Ben said, as they moved through the crowd to find their seats.

When Ben had invited her to the ballet to see *The Nutcracker*, she'd been ecstatic. It was a sign that he was starting to interact with the world again. The fact that he'd thought of her and how she'd told him about enjoying this ballet as a child, just made it more special. Especially after the way she'd freaked him out after kissing him on the cheek. She'd managed to cover how much that had hurt her, but it had destroyed all thoughts of telling Ben about the pregnancy. How could she tell him about something as intimate as the pregnancy when just a simple peck on the cheek had almost sent him running away?

Which had made it even more important that she looked her best for their night out. Her confidence needed a boost. It wasn't until she went through her closet that she'd realized most of her formal dresses were too formfitting for her to wear now. It wasn't like she was really showing at three months. She only had the start of a baby bump, but it still would have made her feel self-conscious.

As she tried on dresses, she'd made herself the promise that this would be the last night she hid her pregnancy. She was ready to share the joy she felt with those she cared about.

But first she had to tell Ben. She'd practiced different ways to tell him at least a hundred times before she'd given up. She'd just have to wing it. But no matter what, before the night was over, she would tell him.

They took the stairs up to the balcony and Izzy was thrilled to see that they had seats in the front row, giving her a chance to take in the whole room. Just the architecture of the place was impressive with its ornate curves and gilded trim work.

Moments later, the lights began to dim. As the curtain rose, she was thrown back into a time of childhood wonderment as the orchestra began playing one of Tchaikovsky's greatest works. Two dancers entered the stage and began decorating an elaborate Christmas tree. For the next forty-five minutes, she was entranced as her childhood imagination came to life. She danced every dance with Clara and fought against the Mouse King to save her wounded Nutcracker.

When the curtains closed and the lights

came on, announcing the end of the first act, Izzy realized she was clutching Ben's hand where it lay on the arm of their seat.

"I'm sorry," she said, removing her hand. She had to quit grabbing hold of this man. Hadn't he made it clear at the Christmas market that he wasn't comfortable with her touching him like that when they were out in public? "I'm going to run to the ladies' room."

Ben couldn't help but smile as Izzy retreated down the aisle. The ballet wasn't really his thing, but watching her expressive face had been a show worth watching. He knew she'd realize that he'd planned the outing after hearing her tell of her childhood tradition.

He liked Izzy, more than he wanted to admit. He'd always thought her constant cheerfulness was a bit too much, but now that he'd gotten to know her better he understood it was just who she was. He'd recognized she'd been trying to help him recover from the loss of his family. He just hadn't been ready to let go of all the bitterness he felt at the unfairness of life.

Even now, four years later, he couldn't understand why something so terrible had happened to Cara. His wife had been such a gentle and loving person. She hadn't deserved to have her life ended so soon. And their child? He'd never had a chance to experience life at all. The pain of their loss had driven Ben inside himself, making him unable to share his grief with his family or his friends. As he'd withdrawn, he'd experienced a feeling of security. If he didn't let anyone close, he couldn't be hurt again. It was self-preservation in its most basic form.

But while others had started to avoid him over the years, leaving him alone with his grief, Izzy had been determined to bring a little sunshine into his day every time their paths crossed. It had been annoying, yet he had to admit that a part of him began to look forward to seeing her each time they worked together. That was why it had seemed so natural for the two of them to go out the night one of their patients—a child who'd been given no chance of survival at birth—had received a heart transplant. They'd meant it to be a night of celebrating the surgery's success. Only, when the clock had crossed over into the new day had he remembered the anniversary of his wife's and son's death.

What followed had been a mistake, he'd

known it as soon as he'd woken the next morning and saw sweet Izzy lying beside him.

It had been one glorious night of feeling alive. One night of sharing a passion he'd thought was gone from his life forever. One night that he had regretted the next morning when Izzy looked at him with an innocence that he hadn't wanted to destroy.

But what if he hadn't left? What if he'd stayed and they'd talked things out? Maybe she had been lonely like him? Maybe she'd just needed someone to be there for her that night?

He rose when Izzy returned and for the next act of the ballet he forced himself to concentrate on the dancers instead of her. But still, his mind kept returning to the night they'd shared and the smile Izzy had given him the next morning. And what might have been if he'd just had the guts to take a chance on putting his heart out there again. But not knowing if it would be able to survive another heartbreak had made that impossible.

He looked over at the gorgeous woman sitting beside him. This felt right. She smiled as another group of dancers took the stage and it felt like the sun had come out in the darkened auditorium. His life was changing and he knew it was because of her. Her presence filled him with a happiness that he almost couldn't recognize. Her laughter. Her humor. The way she took his hand when she was excited. The way her touch made his body fill with a need for more. It was almost too much, yet at the same time it wasn't enough.

He wanted more. He wanted to feel her soft lips against his. He wanted to touch and taste every part of her. He wanted to know if she wanted him too.

As the last curtain closed and they stood and applauded, he was filled with anticipation of what the night ahead might hold for them.

CHAPTER ELEVEN

Izzy's hands had begun to shake the moment she'd climbed into Ben's car. The night had been magical, at least for her. She hoped Ben had enjoyed himself too. He was such a hard man to read.

Which made the thought of what she was about to do even more daunting. How was she supposed to know how he felt about her pregnancy when his go-to reaction on anything personal was to hide his emotions? She didn't want him to reassure her that everything would be fine when really he was having a cosmic-sized meltdown inside. He had to be honest about his feelings with her in order for them to make things work for their baby. If it was too much for him, if he couldn't handle everything that being a good father to their child entailed, she needed to know.

And it wasn't as if she couldn't do this

without him. She was an independent woman surviving in a man's world every day she went to work. She'd be a great single mother, she had no doubt about that, but Ben deserved the right to have a place in their baby's life if he wanted it. He might be reserved, but after getting to know him over the last few weeks, she knew he would be a good father.

As he parked the car in front of her place, she drew in a breath and readied herself to make the biggest announcement of her life. When he jumped out of the car and walked around to her side, it threw her off.

She'd had a plan. She'd expected to have a few minutes with them alone in the car, the lights dimmed and the stillness of the quiet winter night surrounding them. She'd thought it would be the perfect time to tell Ben about the baby. It seemed every time she got her nerve up to tell him, something happened to change her plans.

When he came around to her side of the car and opened her door, she had no choice but to climb out. She made the walk up to her home as slow as possible, searching for a way to start this necessary conversation. She'd promised herself, again, that she would tell Ben about the baby tonight. If things kept going this way the kid would be starting kindergarten before she told him.

"Thank you so much for taking me to see *The Nutcracker*. It was magical, wasn't it?" The whole night had been magical for her. The music, the dancing, the costumes...it had all been beautiful and she would remember it for years to come. But the best thing about the night was that she had spent it with Ben.

"I'm glad you enjoyed it," Ben said as they arrived at her door. He seemed to be captivated by the old iron door knocker just above her head.

"I did," she said, trying to think of something, anything, to keep him there so she could find an opening to tell him about the baby.

"Would you like to come inside?" she asked. If he didn't, she was going to end up spilling the beans right there on the doorstep, which just seemed all wrong.

Ben cleared his throat, the sound harsh against the quiet night. For the first time, she realized how quiet he'd become since getting in the car. She'd been so wrapped up in her own thoughts that she hadn't noticed until now. "Is something wrong?"

"It might be best if I don't come in tonight," Ben said, though he made no effort to leave.

They stood there in silence. Her mind racing with the need to find the best way to tell Ben about the baby, and her heart racing from the nearness of him. The soft scent of his crisp, white shirt. The warmth of his body, so close to hers. Her body was remembering the last time they'd stood there together no matter how hard her mind tried to shut out those thoughts.

When his hand came up to touch her cheek, she tilted her head up toward him, hoping to relive the good-night kiss they'd shared once before. But when his lips met hers, she realized this was different. It was soft and tender, almost platonic, and she had to bite back her disappointment. She knew it was better this way. Neither of them needed more complications right now. But then his hands cupped the side of her face, holding her prisoner as his tongue swept into her mouth.

And just like that they were right back to where they'd been their first night together. But still, this was different. This was more. The desperation of that night was replaced by a sensuality that had been missing before and her body wanted to explode just from the feel of his lips. When he slid his hand down her body in a slow, possessive motion, her legs gave out.

He pulled her closer to him, taking all of her weight against his hips as his arm wrapped around her waist. It was happening again. Ben was making her lose her mind. And she didn't even care. All she knew was that she wanted him. Now.

"Promise me that you'll not run away as soon as the sun rises," she asked, turning her body so she could fit her key into the lock. Her hand shook and she dropped her keys. She bent to pick them up, but Ben was there before her, reaching over her and jamming the key into the lock. The doorknob turned as they both placed their hands against it. They fell inside the front foyer as the door swung open, Ben grabbing hold of her before she could hit the floor. He backed her against the wall.

She knew this wall. Knew the path they'd take to her bedroom and all the stops they'd make in between. It was a déjà vu moment, yet still different from their first time. This wasn't two strangers getting tangled up together by desire. She had learned so much about Ben now and she hoped he had learned more about her.

Except he hadn't. She hadn't told him about the most important thing in her life. She hadn't shared with him how the two of them would soon be bound together by another little life. He had the right to know. He needed to know the consequences of the last time they'd made love.

"I need to tell you something," Izzy said when she managed to free her lips. His hands held her against his hard body, the ridge of his erection pressing against the softness of her abdomen.

"Now?" he asked. His hand ran down the back of her dress finding the zipper. He pushed the dress off her shoulders and she shivered as the fabric puddled at her feet leaving her in just thigh stockings and undergarments. His lips brushed against the sensitive spot behind her ear and then began working their way down her body. One of his hands opened the clasp of her bra as his other cupped her bottom, holding her tight against him.

She needed to tell him. She needed… "Oh, yes," she moaned as his mouth tugged at one of her nipples. Yes, this was what she needed.

His mouth moved to the other nipple and his hand palmed the spot between her legs, bringing the ache that had started to build inside her to the forefront. "Don't stop." Her voice was a weak, desperate plea.

"I can't," Ben admitted. He pressed his length against her, pinning her against the wall as he removed her panties. His eyes met hers and she could see the same fever that burned inside her had taken hold of him. She realized then that it had never been *if* they'd repeat the night they'd shared, it had always just been when.

Then he was inside her, his body pressing hers against the foyer wall as she wrapped her legs around his hips and let him fill her. He made her feel complete. Whole. It was something she'd never experienced until now.

And when they came, they came together, her cries filling the small room as Ben's body shuddered against her.

The button on the Ben's tux jacket scraped against her bare chest and she realized then that he'd never fully undressed. Laughter bubbled up inside her, causing her body to clench around him again. His lips turned up into a devilish grin, making her body tighten even more as she felt her arousal begin to build again.

Her heart stuttered for a second as she looked into his laughing eyes. She was in so much trouble.

"I have to go," Ben said, dropping a kiss on her cheek when Izzy raised her head off the bed.

She knew her eye makeup must have melted into a black smear that circled her eyes and her dark hair was a tangled mess.

"No, wait," she said, sitting up and pulling the sheets up around her. "We need to talk."

"So you told me several times last night," he said. His hand ran down the one bare arm she'd left outside the covers.

"And every time you managed to shut me up."

He raised one eyebrow and grinned. "Are you complaining?"

He knew she had no complaints about the night they'd just shared. Still, this had to be done. She would have thought that a night of lovemaking would make this easier. Instead, it made it more difficult.

The Ben leaning over her was relaxed and happy and it felt so good to see him this way. He'd not only stayed the night, but he also hadn't run away. He'd taken the time to kiss her goodbye, something she wouldn't have believed possible before last night.

She wanted to ask him what had changed. Was it her? Was it him? Did he feel safe to share his emotions with her now? Was there a chance they could share more?

But until she got everything out in the open, neither of them could move on. This had to be done. "This is important, Ben. We really do need to talk."

She saw his eyes dart to the door as if he wanted to make a getaway. He probably thought she wanted to have the old *Where is this relationship going?* conversation. He had no idea just how far their relationship had already gone.

She leaned back against her upholstered headboard, dragging the sheets along with her. "I need to tell you something, but I don't want you to freak out."

She looked up at him and saw the moment he began to retreat behind the shutters he'd hidden behind for the last four years. "Stop. Don't do that. Don't close yourself off from me before you've even heard what I have to say."

"I don't—" he began.

"Yes, you do. You know exactly what I'm talking about. You do it all the time. Some-

one gets close and you shut down. You're
afraid of being vulnerable. I get it. You've
been through a lot. But that doesn't mean
you get to live your life in a bubble. You
have to interact with the rest of us. It's called
being human."

"Was I not human enough for you last
night? Did I do something wrong?" he
asked. "Everyone wants me to change who
I am. Is that what you want too?"

"No. This isn't about you changing. This
is about a change that's happening to both
of us." He started to rise, preparing to run
away again, but she wouldn't spend the rest
of her life chasing him. He had to make a decision about what he wanted, who he wanted
to be. He could continue keeping everyone
at a safe distance, or he could come out and
join the rest of the sorry, bleeding bunch of
them. None of their lives was perfect. But
she would make their child's life as perfect
as it could possibly be.

"I'm pregnant." The words tumbled out of
her mouth before she could catch them. This
wasn't the way she'd wanted to say them, but
at least they were out.

"What do you mean? How could that happen? I know I should have used a condom
last night, but I thought you told me you

were on the pill." He looked so confused, his eyes staring at her in worry. Did he think she'd lost her mind?

"Not from last night, Ben. I'm three months pregnant. I was on the pill. I just must have gotten off schedule. The doctor says it happens sometimes."

Ben sat back down on the bed. Though his eyes were on her, his mind had gone somewhere else. She could almost see the wheels turning as he went through the last three months, calculating the weeks since that first night they'd made love.

"Why didn't you tell me?" There was no accusation in the question, though she wouldn't blame him if there was. She'd been wrong to not tell him from the first moment she'd discovered she was carrying his baby. Now, because she hadn't, she was in danger of losing all the trust she'd built between the two of them.

"I don't know. I just found out a couple weeks ago. At first, it seemed so unreal. Then, it was just so early I didn't want to tell you in case something happened. I decided to wait till I had my first ultrasound to make sure everything was okay." She felt so exposed sitting there, hiding behind a wrinkled pile of linen. This was not the way she'd planned to have this conversation.

"And everything is good with you and the baby?" he asked, his voice sharp and anxious.

"Yes," she said. "No problems except for some morning sickness and an occasional dizzy spell when I get up too quickly."

"Okay. Good." He nodded his head and stood. "You're three months pregnant. Three months. Pregnant."

It was plain to see the man was in shock. They might have had mind-blowing sex last night, but this morning she'd really rocked his world.

"I don't know what to say..." He turned away from the bed and took a step before facing her again. "Who else knows?"

"No one. Except my doctor, of course. I haven't even told my parents." Not that she would ever be in a rush to do that. She didn't see her parents being any more interested in their grandchild's life than they were in hers, but they'd be quick to critique her life choices and once more find her lacking.

"Okay. Do we need to tell anyone right now? I mean—" he ran his hands through his hair "—I just need some time to take all this in."

"That's normal. I'm still trying to get used to the idea too." Though, once it had truly hit her, she'd been thrilled. Waiting to tell Ben had held her back from sharing the news with everyone else. "And no. No one needs to know until the two of us are ready to make the announcement."

He nodded then looked down at his watch. "I have to go if I'm going to make the Santa Dash this morning."

The Santa Dash. How had she forgotten? She'd chosen not to run this year; she didn't need to be seen puking in the middle of the road. But the race was for a good cause and she'd planned to be there to cheer for the hospital staff. "I need to get ready too."

"You're racing today?" His eyes filled with concern. "Did your doctor clear you to do that?"

"I'm not racing, though it would be perfectly safe," she said as she pushed back the covers and got out of bed. She didn't have to look at Ben to know he was looking at her body and not for the same reasons he'd studied every inch of it the night before. "I still have some mornings when my stomach is queasy and I prefer not to puke in front of a crowd."

"How did I miss this?" He shook his head. "Never mind. I need to go."

"Wait, I got something for you to wear at the race," Izzy said as she rushed to her closet. She grabbed an old, soft and cuddly robe and wrapped it around herself. Then she pulled the red hat off a shelf before returning to the bedroom.

"Here," she said, handing the hat out to him. "Some of the runners from the hospital are wearing these for the race. I thought it would look good if you wore one too. That way if any of the board members are there, they'll see that you're making an effort to mix with the rest of the staff."

Ben looked at the hat like she was holding out a piece of roadkill instead of a simple Santa hat. Finally, he reached for it, then stuck it on top of his head. But there was nothing Jolly looking about him. She wanted to tease him and ask him to do a *ho ho ho* for her, but all the teasing they'd done earlier was gone now. Without another word, he turned and walked out of the room. Seconds later, she heard her front door close.

Well, all things considered, that could have gone worse. Now she just had to wait and see if Ben was the man she thought he could be. Or if he'd run away once the news of the pregnancy really hit him.

"It's okay, little one," she said as she rubbed the abdomen where her baby grew. "Your daddy will be fine. You're just a surprise he wasn't ready for. We'll give him some time. And no matter what, you will always have me to count on. I'll never run away and leave you."

CHAPTER TWELVE

For a moment, Ben thought maybe he was at the wrong race. Everyone was dressed so much more...festive than the years before. He straightened the hat on his head as he started his stretches. He just had to get through this race and then he could...what? Freak out? Lose it? It wasn't like any of that was going to help. He just didn't know what to do. Or what to think. Nothing had prepared him for this. Was he really so disengaged that he hadn't noticed something was different about Izzy? What kind of man did that make him? What kind of father? Friend?

Okay, now he was getting way too inside his head. He needed to concentrate on this race. He always enjoyed running and this race was for a good cause that he supported.

Nick Walker, dressed in a full Santa suit, and Bryn, one of the new nurses on staff, who was dressed in a tutu and snowman shirt, came up beside him. Even the therapy dog Bryn brought to hospital was dressed in a Christmas sweater and a pair of reindeer ears.

"You don't think it's too much?" Nick asked.

"Not at all," Ben said, as he rolled his shoulders and moved to the starting line. "Maybe you should stop and see the kids when we're done. I bet they'd love that."

"Did I miss the memo on the Santa hats?" Nick said, laughing.

"This was Izzy's idea," Ben said as he adjusted the hat once again while looking to see if Izzy had made it.

"Where is Izzy?" Bryn asked.

"Not feeling up to a race this morning," Ben said. "She's meeting me...us...at the finish line."

"Smart move," Nick said. "If it's going to be this cold it should at least be snowing. When are they firing the starting pistol?"

Ben was ready to start the race too. He needed to blow off some of his pent-up emotions ever since Izzy had informed him that she was pregnant.

Bryn's golden retriever barked and Nick pointed to her. "She's ready to be warm too."

"She's ready to move," Bryn laughed and

kissed Nick's nose. "There are a lot of people here and she's very excited."

The two of them seemed even closer than they had been the last time he'd seen them. He'd have to ask Izzy about it. It was probably one of those things everyone besides him already knew. Maybe Izzy was right. Maybe he had alienated himself too much from the rest of the staff.

"Santa," a little boy cried out and pointed to Nick. It was funny how just a man in a red suit could make a child happy.

"All right, I think Ben is right, we should stop by and say hi to the kiddos," Bryn said.

"I am usually right." Ben stretched his arms across his body. He was ready to do this.

"Runners ready!"

"Yes!" Ben cheered with the rest of the crowd.

The starting gun sounded and they were off.

Once Ben crossed the finish line and caught his breath, he easily found Izzy talking to a group of nurses, most of whom he recognized from the hospital. The run had felt good as the sharp cold air rushing in and out of his lungs had kept thoughts of Izzy's pregnancy buried under the need to keep his legs pumping at a rhythm that would carry him all the way through to the end.

But seeing Izzy, all the disorientation he experienced from her announcement rushed back. He hadn't felt this terrified since the night he'd lost his wife. He didn't like the feeling at all.

He liked to have total control of his life. It was something that had become very important to him since that night. If he controlled everything in his life, he could make sure no one was hurt. Including him.

Now that control had been taken from him. He didn't blame Izzy, it wasn't her fault. They'd both been in the bed that night. They had made this baby together.

A baby. They were going to have a baby. His knees started to go weak right when he joined Izzy with the group of nurses and it wasn't from the race. He had to get a hold of himself. He needed to put everything to the back of his mind until he was alone.

"There you are. I was just telling everyone that I've got to run to the store and get everything to make my white chocolate and raspberry cookies for the staff bake sale. I want to bring them in Monday morning," Izzy said, her smile uncertain when his eyes met hers. He loved the deep mahogany color of her eyes. Would their child have her eyes? Or would they be blue, like his?

It was one of the things he'd wondered about when he and Cara found out they were expecting. Would their child have his blue eyes or Cara's green ones? He'd never found out the answer. That thought sent a chill over him. He couldn't go through this pregnancy with Izzy while the past still clouded his thoughts.

Over Izzy's shoulder, one of the nurses, he thought her name was Sheri or maybe Carrie, started shaking her head at him so hard that he couldn't ignore her. When another nurse joined her, he realized they were trying to tell him something. He looked back at Izzy, who was still talking about her weekend plans of baking.

"And they sold out really fast. I was so glad everyone liked them. It was my first time baking them," Izzy was saying.

Then Izzy's words finally hit him. She planned to bake her white chocolate and raspberry cookies? Even he had heard about the super-dry, syrupy sweet cookies that she'd baked last year. At first, he didn't believe they could be as bad as he'd overheard one of the staff members saying, until he tried one himself. Then, not wanting Izzy to feel bad when no one bought them, he'd bought the lot of them and dumped them into the trash can, hiding them under some old magazines.

"We told Izzy that she didn't need to worry about doing that. Not with her not feeling up to running in the race today," one of the nurses said. The two nurses behind Izzy who had been shaking their heads now nodded enthusiastically.

"It will do me good. I loved baking them last year. It's one of those things people love to do at Christmastime that I didn't have any experience with," Izzy said, her smile now bright as she spoke of a tradition that he felt sure her mother had never shared with her.

"You know, I'd like to help with the bake sale too. Maybe you could help me. I could make some of the chocolate chip cookies my mom used to make." He forced a smile on his face, trying to show some kind of enthusiasm about the chore. The last thing he wanted to do was bake cookies with Izzy right now. He wanted to go home and hide in his office and review his patients' charts on the computer until his mind calmed down enough to begin comprehending what Izzy's pregnancy meant for them. But from the way the two nurses behind Izzy smiled at him, he'd done the right thing. He'd thrown himself on the sword, sacrificing his peace of mind, instead of taking a chance Izzy might get her feelings hurt if someone said anything about her awful cookies.

And it made him feel good to do this for her. She'd done so much for him. They'd actually started to build something between the two of them. He just hadn't been given all the information about what was going on. Now he didn't even know if Izzy had agreed to help him for him, or if she was helping him because of the pregnancy. Having a jobless baby daddy would probably be hard on her.

More reason for him to work on keeping his job.

"Really? Of course I'll help you," Izzy said, her smile even brighter now. "Do you have your mother's recipe?"

No, but he knew where to find it. It was typed out right there on the bag of chocolate chips that his mom always used. All he had to do was call his mom and find out the brand of chips. "Sure. I'll pick up everything today and we'll decide later on a time to make them."

"That sounds great," Izzy said. "I can always make my cookies after Christmas."

He coughed to cover the moan of the two nurses standing behind Izzy. He'd worry about that later. Maybe he could hint that he didn't like white chocolate. Maybe he'd tell her how great the chocolate chips were and that everyone was asking for more.

"I need to get home and clean up," he said, ready to make his escape.

"I thought you might stay for the after-race get-together. We're headed over to that Irish pub for lunch." Izzy said.

Ben watched as the other nurses moved back into the crowd that was still waiting for the last group of runners to cross the finish line. He could follow them and sneak off as he did every year. Or he could force himself to go to this lunch thing. He remembered Izzy telling him that he ran away every year after the Santa Dash and that he needed to mingle with the staff to make a good impression on the board.

Maybe he could have done it if it hadn't been for her announcement this morning, but right then he'd had about all the socializing that he could take. The ebbing adrenaline from the race was being replaced with anxiety about the fact that in a few months he and Izzy would be parents. While he couldn't deny the excitement that being a father would bring him, it was the fear of what could happen to his child and how he could mess it all up that was forefront in his mind. He'd felt the excitement of having a baby before. He'd also experienced the loss of his unborn child. The two emotions were at such polar opposites that he almost hadn't survived the terrible grief. He knew he had to find a way to put the past pain behind him, but he'd lived with it for so long that he didn't even know where to start.

But in light of the board's ultimatum, did he really have the choice of running away this time? Izzy would be disappointed if he didn't make the effort. But still...

"I can't, Izzy," he said, his voice low as he bent down to whisper in her ear. The smell of vanilla and sunshine teased his nose. It was sweet but not overpowering. It was a comforting smell that reminded him of his mother's kitchen mixed with the scent of cotton sheets dried outside in the summer sun. Yet the scent was uniquely Izzy. "I just need a little time alone today."

The light he'd seen in her eyes as she'd excitedly talked about her plan for baking cookies disappeared. Was that hurt he saw now? The last thing he wanted was to hurt Izzy. She didn't deserve that.

But before he could take back his words and agree to go with her, the sunshine in her smile reappeared and her eyes lit back up. "Of course, I understand. You need some time to…adjust to my…news. It's okay. Besides, we're getting together to bake those cookies, right?"

"Sure, how about we get together tomorrow afternoon? I'm off for the rest of the weekend unless they need me for an emergent case. Just text me and let me know what time."

"I will," Izzy said. Her hand came up and skimmed down the side of his sweat-drenched face. "Everything is going to be okay, Ben. I understand that it was a shock. I should have said something earlier, especially before last night. We'll work it out together."

As she walked away from him to join the crowd that had begun heading down the street to the pub, he thought about the night they'd just shared. He'd taken a big step by not running off that morning. His first big step into a relationship he'd made since his wife's death.

And now she was asking him to make

another step, one that led to parenthood, with her assurance that everything would be okay. Izzy was an optimist who always saw the best in people. She even saw the best in him. But she hadn't lived through what he had. She might believe that everything would indeed be okay.

But he knew better. Everything did not always end up okay.

CHAPTER THIRTEEN

"AND THEN LISA—you know, the tall, blonde respiratory tech—she climbed on top of the table and began dancing this Irish dance. We were all impressed until her foot slipped on a saltshaker and she fell into an ortho doctor's lap. It was one of those disasters you see coming but you can't stop," Izzy said. "You should have seen the look his wife gave Lisa. Watching the woman's face was like watching one of those mood rings go from pink, to red, and then to purple. But when Lisa jumped up and took a bow, the wife calmed down."

Izzy knew she was talking too much, but Ben had been so quiet since letting her into his house that she couldn't seem to stop herself. There was an awkwardness between the two of them that hadn't been there before she'd told him about the pregnancy. It certainly hadn't been there the last night they'd spent in her bed together.

She knew she couldn't expect Ben to accept the news of her pregnancy as easily as she had, not that it hadn't been a shock for her too. But once the shock was over, she'd been thrilled at the thought of a baby, their baby, growing inside of her. Now she just had to give Ben the time to get used to the idea. Only that was turning out to be harder than she thought. She wanted to move forward with letting everyone know about her pregnancy. She wanted to share her happiness with her friends. But Ben had asked her to wait, so she would. He needed time and she would give it to him. The loss of his wife and baby still hung over him, so no matter how hard it was she had to give him a few days to come to terms with his new reality. Their new reality.

"Everyone asked about you at the pub though. I told them you had work to do." Wasn't that the excuse he'd always used when she'd invited him to different hospital functions? "I told them that they'd see you at the staff Christmas party on the twenty-first though."

"I won't be at the party." He took down two white metal canisters, one labeled Flour and the other one labeled Sugar in bold black print, and put them in front of her.

"Why not?" she asked, trying to keep her disappointment from her voice. He had made such progress. She didn't want to think that the news of her pregnancy, something that she had secretly hoped might heal the pain inside him, was driving him back into his solitary existence away from those who cared about him.

"I have Dr. Geller's patient, Jiyan, scheduled for his surgery that day," Ben said, as he walked over to the big stainless-steel fridge and began removing eggs and butter.

"Maybe you can come in later, if the party is still going," Izzy said. She wasn't giving up on Ben no matter how painful it was for her to keep fighting for something that she knew he might not ever be ready for.

"I'll see," he murmured. He moved over to a cabinet and pulled out two mixing bowls then opened a drawer and dumped some measuring spoons inside the bowls.

He'd been this way ever since she'd gotten there. He'd barely looked at her, instead choosing to busy himself with all these preparations. He acted like he was preparing for a complex heart surgery instead of an enjoyable day of baking. He was taking this all too seriously. Hadn't all the Christmas movies she'd watched shown everyone having fun as they made cookies? Maybe it was Christmas music they were missing.

Pulling her phone out of the back pocket of her jeans, she went to her Christmas playlist. When Ben gave her an evil eye, she just shrugged. Not everyone appreciated the true creativeness of the three chipmunks.

"Please tell me you don't have a whole album of that stuff." He'd finally stopped for a moment after taking a couple packages of chocolate chips from the cabinets, along with brown sugar and a bottle of vanilla, and placing them beside the rest of the items.

"My Christmas playlist is very diverse. Of course, we can listen to yours if you would rather." She'd bet her whole investment portfolio that he didn't have one Christmas song on his phone, let alone a playlist. The look he gave her told her she'd have won. Then his lips quirked up for just a second and her world began to spin. Even his grumpy Scrooge act was beginning to have an effect on her.

"Let's get started," Ben said. It was clear to see that he'd made the decision to take charge of this project. "The butter needs to soften, but we can start adding the dry ingredients together. Do you want to mix or measure?"

"Dry ingredients?" she asked. She saw that he was studying the bag of chips in front of him. "Where is your mom's recipe?"

Ben picked up the package of chips and held them out to her. She looked at the back of the bag and read the instructions. "This is your mom's recipe?"

"That recipe is the original recipe that has been used since 1930 by millions of mothers, including mine."

"I talked to my mother to make sure I bought the right chocolate. And, I bought the butter and vanilla that she recommended. If we do everything by the recipe on the back of that bag we should be able to duplicate my mother's cookies." Ben had that determined look about him, like he was daring the cookies not to turn out the way he expected them to.

She went back to studying the bag of chips. "Okay, I'll measure and you can mix."

An hour later, Ben looked around the room in horror. His normally pristine kitchen was a mess. His cleaning service would likely revolt. And he'd never had so much fun.

It hadn't taken him but a few minutes

to understand that Izzy didn't know what she was doing. When he'd realized that she was using the tablespoon instead of the tea-spoon to measure, he'd switched jobs with her. When she'd turned the mixer on high to cream the butter with the sugar and vanilla instead of starting at a lower speed, the mix-ture had been splattered onto every surface of the kitchen, including them.

Now his sink was full of bowls and spoons and his counters were covered in flour, but Izzy looked so pleased with the only slightly burnt cookies that sat cooling while the last batch was cooking, that he knew it had all been worth it.

He adjusted the temperature on the oven, determined to get one batch perfect, though if Izzy saw him she would be horrified that he was going against the recipe.

"I think you should take some of these to Dr. Bailey," Izzy said as she sneaked a look at him before taking another cookie from the rack.

"If you keep eating those there won't be any to sell." Not that he really cared. If she wanted to eat them all he'd just stop at the bakery and pick some up to replace them. "And I don't think a plate of cookies is going to fix the problem Dr. Bailey has with me."

"I don't know. Chocolate is the cure for most things that irritate us." She took another bite, leaving a dab of melted chocolate on the corner of her mouth. He'd never been as hungry for something as he was for that tiny bit of sweetness.

He looked away. Those were not thoughts that he needed now. The pregnancy changed everything between them. He couldn't let himself forget that. He had responsibilities to her now. He'd been willing to take things slowly with Izzy. He hadn't been ready for any type of commitment. Now he didn't have a choice.

"I think the two of you are too much alike. And you both are used to getting your way. Maybe if you just sit down and talk it would help." Izzy looked up at him, her eyes hopeful while that smear of chocolate still tempted him.

How did he say no to her when she looked so adorable? "Okay, I'll drop the cookies off at his office tomorrow, but that's all I'm promising to do."

The timer dinged and Izzy rushed to the oven.

"Put both of the oven mitts on your hand this time," he said. As she pulled out the cookie sheet, he began to load the dishwasher.

"That's all I'm asking. Of course if you get a chance to talk to him, you might want to mention that you also baked some of these for the bake sale," Izzy said. "It won't hurt to show him how much you're trying to become a part of the staff."

"I've always been a part of the staff. I shouldn't have to prove that. There have never been any complaints from the surgical staff that I work with and I'm always happy to see the patients that I get consulted to see."

"I think Dr. Bailey wants the staff to work together as a team and he doesn't see you as a team player. Showing that you are working together with the staff to help raise money for Camp HeartLight would be a good way to prove him wrong. Administration is very supportive of the camp for our pediatric cardiac patients."

They worked together quietly, him cleaning up the kitchen while Izzy boxed up the cookies in Christmas containers she had brought over. By the time they were finished, the afternoon sun was setting and Izzy looked dead on her feet.

"Go home and get some rest," he told her

when she started to pick up one of the rags he'd been cleaning with. "I'll finish up here."

"We still need to talk," she said, pulling out a barstool and climbing up to the island. "I know this has all been a shock for you. The pregnancy, I mean. But eventually I'm going to have to tell the staff. I'll need to schedule some leave in a few months and the other docs will have to plan coverage for me. And after all the cookies I ate today, I'm not going to fit in my clothes for long. People are going to notice."

She was right. They had to talk about the baby. Why was it so hard for him to do that? Was it the memories of him and Cara preparing for their baby? Was it the guilt he felt at the hope of a new baby in his life? He was being given a second chance with not only a baby, but also a possible new life with Izzy. Was he so scared of losing someone again that he couldn't let himself feel the joy that he knew he should feel?

"Can we just wait a few more days?" he told her, turning away when he saw that flicker of hurt cross her face. He didn't want to hurt her. He cared for Izzy. He just needed time to figure everything out.

"Okay," Izzy said as she slid off the stool

and picked up her purse. "Just don't wait too long. Time is running out."

As he watched her car pull away from the curb from his kitchen window, he silently counted down the days he had left before the board made their final decision. Izzy was right. His time was running out. He had to find a way to ensure that he stayed at Boston Beacon. And he had to find the way to get over his fear of living in a world where at any moment you could lose everything. Because if he didn't, he was afraid he'd lose Izzy and their baby before they even had a chance.

Ben felt ridiculous standing in front of Dr. Bailey's secretary holding a plate of cookies like he was Susie Homemaker welcoming the newest neighbor to the subdivision. "I just wanted to drop these off for Dr. Bailey."

The secretary eyed him up and down suspiciously. "I'll be glad to give those to Dr. Bailey when he returns———"

The door opened and Dr. Bailey walked in. Ben wasn't sure who was surprised the most. Ben, because he had called to make sure the man would be out of the office until after lunch? Or the chief of surgery, who would never have expected his most antisocial surgeon to voluntarily visit his office?

"Ben, it's nice to see you. What do I owe this visit to?" Dr. Bailey said, before smiling down at his secretary. "Can you hold my calls, Shannon?"

When Dr. Bailey walked past him, Ben assumed the man meant him to follow. Looking down at his watch, Ben was glad to see that he only had fifteen minutes until his meeting with Jiyan's mother to get the consent needed for his surgery.

Dr. Bailey sat down at his desk. He was a large man, over six feet tall, and even though he was now in his sixties it was rumored he still worked out every day. His size alone would be intimidating to some people, but it was the dark green eyes with their bushy salt-and-pepper eyebrows that gave Ben trouble. The man had a way of pinning you in place with those eyes, like a bug to a corkboard. For some reason the older man seemed to find Ben fascinating and Ben didn't like it.

"Have a seat," Dr. Bailey said, motioning to one of the upholstered chairs in front of his desk.

"I have a meeting with a parent in a few minutes," Ben said.

"Sit down, Ben. This won't take but a minute," the chief of surgery ordered.

Ben took the chair. When Dr. Bailey looked at the plate in Ben's hand he held out the forgotten cookies to him. "Dr. Jeong asked me to bring these by."

It wasn't a lie. He wouldn't be stuck here in the chair about to get dressed down if it wasn't for Izzy. But when the man eyed the cookies suspiciously, he realized the fame of Izzy's white chocolate and raspberry cookies had spread throughout the hospital. "They're good. We made them together."

Dr. Bailey smiled and took the plate. "I've heard rumors that the two of you have become an item."

An item? It seemed that the rumor mill at the hospital had been very busy.

"I'm friends with Izzy." It would soon be plain to everyone that they were more than friends, but he didn't have to share that with his boss.

"Good. I'm glad to hear that. You need friends. We all do."

The room became silent as Ben sat there, once more feeling like that pinned bug while Dr. Bailey studied him.

"I've been worried about you, Ben. You suffered a great loss when your wife was killed. I'm sorry for that. I know what a loss like that can do to a man. It almost cost me my military career."

Ben tried to understand what the man was saying. What had Dr. Bailey lost? "I don't understand."

"I was gone out of the country, sent on assignment to Afghanistan, when my first wife had a brain aneurism. By the time the Marine Corps could get me back, she'd been declared brain dead. They kept her on life support until I could get back, but I knew before they told me that she was gone. It was like some part of me had been ripped out. I didn't know what to do. We had two little boys, one two and the other one four. I needed to be there for them. But I couldn't handle it. I sent the boys away with my wife's parents and I started to drink. It wasn't until I got thrown into jail for disorderly conduct out of country that I realized where I was headed.

"Actually, it wasn't until my best friend punched me in the jaw after bailing me out of jail that I started to see the light." The man rubbed his shadowed jaw as if remembering the pain.

"Why are you telling me all this? I don't have a drinking problem." Ben never should have listened to Izzy. Did the man think that because he had shared his story with him that Ben was going to suddenly bare his own soul? It wasn't going to happen.

"I know that. In most ways you've handled yourself a lot better than I did. I admire that about you." That was probably the first positive thing he'd ever said to Ben in the years they'd worked together.

"There's nothing to admire. I lost my wife and son. I've handled it." Ben rose to go. He had things to do that were a lot more important than swapping sad stories with the chief of surgery.

"Ben, if you want to talk, I'm here. Thank Izzy for the cookies and don't mess up what you've got going there. She's good for you," Dr. Bailey said as Ben walked out the door.

He'd come to Dr. Bailey's office hoping to break some of the tension between them with an offering of cookies. He'd never dreamed their conversation would take such a personal turn. Not that Ben didn't feel for the doctor, he'd been dealt a hand just as bad as Ben's.

But Ben didn't need to hear the chief of surgery's opinion on how Ben had handled the loss of his wife. And he didn't need anyone telling him how to handle his relationship with Izzy.

CHAPTER FOURTEEN

DRESSED IN HIS sterile gown and gloves, Ben settled his hands on the blue drape in front of him as once more Kenny G music filled the operating room. He was beginning to get used to the smooth calming sound of the music during his OR cases. He still couldn't say he was a fan of most Christmas music, but he had learned to like this.

He'd been preparing for this surgery for several days. He and Dr. Geller, Dylan, had studied the images of Jiyan's heart over and over until Ben felt he had all the information he needed to plan the surgery. He'd explained the artificial shunt he would place between the aorta and pulmonary artery to increase the blood flow to the lungs. And then they'd gone over the patch he would need to make to prevent right-to-left shunting and finally, if Jiyan was tolerating the surgery, he would widen the right ventricular outflow tract. It would be a complex surgery, but it would make a world of difference in this child's life.

Ben looked behind the drape and saw the little boy sleeping comfortably. He liked to be reminded before starting surgery of the life he held in his hand. It didn't make it any easier—there was no way to make having the responsibility of a life in your hands easy. Just like assuring Jiyan's mother that he didn't expect any problems while still going over all the things that could happen wasn't easy. He wanted to promise every parent that their child would survive and thrive. A lot of these kids had never experienced a normal life. And a lot of the kids were like Miguel. They had started their life with a regular childhood just to have it taken away from them. But he couldn't promise any of the children that life. All he could do was use all of the surgical talents he had and believe that it would be enough. It had to be.

He nodded to the anesthesiologist who had intubated and sedated the child. Then he nodded to the circulating nurse who started the required time out process. Once that was done, Ben took one more look around the room. Everyone was in place. He had all the equipment necessary. He held out his hand for the scalpel. As always, the weight of the instrument in his steady hand felt right. He'd known the first time he'd held one that he was meant to be a surgeon.

He took a breath, relaxed his body and made the first incision. It was all up to him now and he wouldn't let this child or his family down.

Izzy walked through the doors of the elevator before it could close and pushed the button to take her to Ward 34. The staff Christmas party had been still going strong when she'd left, but it hadn't seemed right without Ben there, even though he'd never attended before. She hadn't been able to relax and enjoy herself. She'd gone to the OR first to see how the surgery on Dylan's patient, Jiyan, was going only to find that they had finished the surgery and Ben had left the OR. It had been the same way for the last three days, with her continuously missing Ben each day. Except for the emoji of a thumbs-up after she'd texted him to see how dropping off the cookies for Dr. Bailey had gone, they'd had no contact.

She might think that someone else was just too busy to contact her, but with Ben it was worrisome. He was pulling away from her and she didn't know how to stop him.

"Merry Christmas, Dr. Jeong. Is the party already over?" one of the nurses called out to her the moment she stepped out of the elevator and the other woman stepped on.

"Merry Christmas. No, it's still going. I was hoping to see Dr. Murphy. Have you seen him?" she asked.

"He might still be in Miguel's room. I saw him there a few minutes ago," the nurse said before the elevator doors closed.

The nausea and the dizziness that had threatened her all morning caught up with her again. She stopped in the hallway and steadied herself against the wall while forcing herself to take a slow deep breath into her nose and then letting it out her mouth. She repeated the process until the walls lost their scary carnival mirror maze effect and she felt safe to continue down the hall.

Looking into Miguel's room, she saw Ben sitting on the side of the bed talking to the boy. Whatever they were discussing, they both had their serious faces on. Had Ben decided to discuss the possibility of a heart transplant with Miguel? Not wanting to interrupt them, she stepped back and started to turn when the room began to spin. Grabbing the doorframe, she slid down to the floor. As the darkness took her, she heard Ben call her name.

Ben looked over at the door just in time to see Izzy slide to the floor and her eyes roll back. Fear gripped him, holding him in place for a mere second until his training kicked in.

Hitting the button of Miguel's call light, he shouted for help before rushing to Izzy's side. With her eyes closed, her face pale and her dark hair fanning the floor under her head, she looked like a fairy-tale princess waiting to be awakened with a kiss.

Only he wasn't a Prince Charming. He was something better. He was a doctor, which was what she needed instead of the lovesick fool he was acting. He checked her pulse while he watched her breathing. They were both regular without any sign of stress. He couldn't say the same for his own vital signs. He pulled the stethoscope from around his neck and listened to her lungs, the task made more difficult by the pounding of his own heartbeat in his ears.

Two nurses rushed up the hall, followed by their charge, Leigh. Stopping at the door, the two nurses looked down at Izzy with surprise.

"Call the rapid response team," Leigh ordered one of them before turning to the other one. "Go get a stretcher. They'll want to take her down to the emergency room."

"What happened?" she asked Ben as the two nurses rushed off.

"I don't know," he said. Izzy's color was returning now and his own heart rate began to slow. "I saw her slide down to the floor."

He heard the announcement over the hospital intercom for the rapid response team to come to Miguel's room.

"Did she fall? Hit her head?" the nurse asked.

"I don't think so," Ben replied. He brushed his hand across Izzy's cheek and saw her eyes flutter open.

At the same time the area outside the room suddenly filled with people. A young resident arrived and started spitting out orders until one of the ICU nurses reminded the man that Izzy wasn't a patient.

Ben saw one of the nurses go to Miguel and take his hand. How had he'd forgotten about the little boy?

As Izzy's eyes finally opened, the nurse was explaining to the young doctor that he couldn't order a stat EKG on her. "She's not a patient yet. You have to have a patient number to order tests. We'll take her down to the ER and the doctor there will order it."

Izzy's eyes went wide as she looked around the room, taking in the half a dozen people who had responded to the RRT call. When she looked up at him, Ben saw that she was about to go into panic mode.

"I need everyone to leave," he said, raising his voice and adding the authoritative tone he used in surgery.

The room quieted and everyone looked at him like he was crazy, but he didn't care. "It's okay, Izzy. You fainted. Don't try to get up yet..."

He settled her head against his arm and curled his body around hers when he saw her eyes widen more. A pale pink flush of color filled her cheeks. He knew being the center of attention like this was the last thing Izzy would want.

"Dr. Murphy, the team really needs to take her down to the emergency room to get checked out," Leigh said. "We need to find out what's wrong with her."

"*We*," he said, emphasizing the word, "know exactly what's wrong with her."

He looked into Izzy's eyes. He'd wanted

more time to come to terms with everything that was happening in his life before having to deal with all the attention from the hospital staff, but his time was up. When she nodded in silent agreement, he said the words he'd never thought he'd say again. "We're pregnant."

The room went silent as this news took everyone by surprise. Even Leigh, one of the few charge nurses Ben had known since he'd arrived in Boston, seemed speechless. Then Miguel broke the silence. "Dr. Ben, I didn't know Dr. Jeong was your girlfriend."

The room exploded with voices congratulating him and Izzy and wishing them well, and it took another ten minutes before the room was cleared. He'd helped Izzy into the chair beside Miguel, who had been silent the whole time. While Izzy talked to the boy, assuring him that she was going to be fine, Ben accepted awkward congratulations and assured the insistent ICU nurse that he would have Izzy follow up with her obstetrician.

"I'm sorry," Izzy said when the last person left the room. "I know you didn't want to tell anyone yet."

"It's fine. I'm just glad you're okay. And you were right. It was time." Izzy didn't need to be stressed out about him. Then a thought hit him: she'd been stressed ever since she'd found out she was pregnant and struggled to tell him about the baby. It couldn't have been easy for her to go through all of the first trimester by herself.

He owed it to her and the baby to get his life together. He just didn't know where to start. It was hard to change the way you thought about your life in less than one week. He didn't want to disappoint Izzy like he'd disappointed Cara the night she'd died.

"My momma has a baby. His name is Angel. They had a party for him last week. He's two now," Miguel said, breaking the silence that had fallen between the two adults in the room. "Momma says he looks like me, but I don't think so."

Izzy had explained to him that she'd fainted because she was going to have a baby and that sometimes happened. For once the boy's eyes had shown something other than worry and resignation. He had seemed happy that Ben and Izzy were having a baby. Now the boy looked more troubled than before.

"Why don't you think he looks like you?" Izzy asked.

"His face is all—" The boy demonstrated

by puffing out his cheeks so that he looked like a chipmunk whose mouth was stuffed with acorns. "Besides, I don't want him to look like me. He could have a bad heart like me too."

"Are you worried about your brother?" Izzy asked, then looked up at Ben where he stood beside them. "The problem you have with your heart isn't something he could catch from you or something that he would get because he's your brother."

"Is that right, Dr. Ben?" the little boy asked.

Ben never knew how much to explain to a child, so usually he left that up to the child's parents. With Miguel's mother not there, all he could do was answer it as simply as possible. "That's right. You don't have to worry about your little brother. Let's just concentrate on getting you better so you can go home and play with him soon."

He didn't know why he said the words. He still didn't know if Miguel's cardiac tumor was operable. Giving the boy false hope was wrong.

"How about you tell us what you would like for Christmas?" Izzy asked the boy.

When he shrugged, Ben felt something crack inside of him. Maybe Ben wasn't into

Christmas like the rest of the staff, but he could still remember the excitement he'd felt at Christmas when he was Miguel's age. This wasn't normal. The boy seemed to have closed himself off from all the things other children enjoyed. There was just so little happiness in this child's life. The only thing Miguel seemed to enjoy was his books, especially the one about the zookeeper and the snake.

Maybe there were more books about Miguel's favorite characters that Ben could find and bring in for him. And if not, maybe there were other books about the zoo that he would like. "Miguel, what is your favorite part of the zoo?"

The boy looked at Ben curiously. "A favorite part?"

"Yeah, when you go to the zoo what part do you like the most?" Ben asked.

"I haven't been to the zoo yet. Momma says as soon as I'm well we can go." The look on Miguel's face wasn't the one Ben would have expected from a child looking forward to the trip. Instead, there was a sadness about it as if the boy believed that the trip would never happen. "But Bernie says all the animals at the zoo are special even though Sam the snake thinks he's the most special."

Ben looked at Izzy and her eyes met his and he knew she was wondering the same thing he was. What could they do to help this child?

"I always liked the monkeys when I went to the zoo," Izzy said, filling the silence. Neither of them wanted Miguel to know how shocked they were that he hadn't experienced this simple childhood pleasure. "What about you, Dr. Murphy?"

Somehow it sounded ridiculous to have Izzy call him Dr. Murphy after the announcement they'd just made. "I think I'd have to agree with Sam. I always wanted to hurry to the reptile house so that I could see the snakes. There's just something special about the way they slither around and flick their tongues."

"Can you tell me about the snakes you saw?" Miguel asked. His eyes were lit with an excitement Ben hadn't seen in them before.

"Of course," Ben said. "Do you want to hear about the boas first or the cobras?"

"I don't think I want to hear about either one," Izzy said, performing an exaggerated shiver before standing. "I'm going to leave the two of you to your discussion while I take care of a few things."

Izzy's hand rested on Ben's shoulder for a moment before she left the room, the warmth of her touch reassuring. The fear he'd felt when she'd crumpled to the floor, so pale and lifeless, had almost been more than he could handle. He'd had to force himself to take control.

"Okay, so which one will it be?" Ben asked the boy. Leaning over the bed, Ben picked up Miguel's book about the zookeeper. Another idea of something he could do for the boy had begun to form in his mind.

Thirty minutes later, when he left Miguel's room, he found Izzy in the doctors' lounge bent over a computer screen.

"Hey," Izzy said, as she motioned him over to her. "I've found the Christmas wish we need to grant for Miguel."

Ben could have told her that with the pregnancy she already had enough to handle, but he knew it was useless.

"I think Miguel wants to see his family, especially his mom. He just doesn't want to say it because he knows his mom has his brothers and sisters to take care of. It's not going to be easy, this late, but I think I can have them here before Christmas. I've already called his mom and she was so excited she started to cry." Izzy wrote something down on a pad of paper then went back to the computer screen.

As Ben listened to Izzy explain how she'd found a local B and B that would help lodge Miguel's mother and three siblings, he worked to form a plan of his own. He agreed that having Miguel's family visit was a great idea, but he wanted to do more. For the first time since he'd come to the children's ward to work, he felt the need to help a child experience something special. Something that he might not ever have another chance to do.

For Ben, granting wishes had always felt like he was giving up on the child, but this was different. He wouldn't, couldn't, give up on Miguel. He had to agree with the other doctors that had assessed Miguel for surgery, the operation the little boy needed was almost impossible to perform. He could do it, but the chances of the boy surviving the surgery were less than 50 percent. Those odds made the surgery too dangerous for him to attempt.

He did still have the hope that a donor heart would become available soon. But if it didn't, Ben would always carry the weight of knowing Miguel had never had the childhood experience of actually seeing all the animals he'd come to love from his books. He didn't want that. He wanted to give the boy a reason to smile. A reason to keep on living. And he had an idea of how to make that happen.

And Izzy was going to hate it.

CHAPTER FIFTEEN

"IF THE BOARD, or even worse Dr. Bailey, finds out about this they'll have a coronary." Izzy stood in Ben's office, trying to get him to see reason. They'd argued over this for the last two days. She appreciated the fact that Ben was into granting Miguel's unspoken wish of having his family visit him in Boston. He'd helped arrange the flights for Miguel's family, insisting on covering the cost while she took care of the group's lodgings. But he refused to listen to her whenever she told him how crazy his idea was.

"I won't get caught," he insisted. It was the same reassurance she'd gotten every time she'd tried to make him see reason. "The zoo knows it can only be a small non-poisonous snake. It's not like we're bringing in some sixty-pound boa constrictor."

"There is no *we*. I'm not going anywhere near a snake. And I can't believe the zoo is going to let you do this." She couldn't believe *she* was going to let him do this.

"It's fine. I operated on one of the zoo board member's grandsons. Once I explained the situation to him, he was happy to help out."

"Did you explain the part where you weren't going to get the hospital board to clear this first?" They had gone over and over this, but she couldn't let it go. No matter how determined Ben was that no one would discover his covert operation, she wasn't so sure.

Both their phones dinged, as the hospital intercom system went off with a call for the rapid response team to go to Ward 34. When the operator announced the room number they looked at each other. They knew that number. It was Miguel's room. The boy was in trouble.

Izzy was at the door before Ben but she moved aside, knowing that he would be able to make it down the halls faster than her. By the time she made it into the room, Ben had already taken control.

While he studied the EKG someone had printed out for him, she rushed to the boy's side. Miguel was conscious, but he appeared to be in pain, though he still didn't complain.

His breathing was shallow and labored and his eyes looked up at her with a fear that no child should ever have to experience. While a tech from the lab drew blood from his arm, a nurse was busy applying monitor pads to his chest. Izzy took his hand, the palm damp with sweat, and squeezed. "Me and Dr. Ben are here, Miguel. Hold on. We're going to fix this."

What they were going to fix, she didn't know. Ben hadn't given her much optimism as far as the surgery that was needed. They were putting all their hopes on a last-minute donor heart becoming available. But for now, all she knew was that the boy was all alone and she needed to comfort him somehow.

"Can you please increase his oxygen?" she asked the respiratory tech, who was at the head of the bed with her. "And get everything together in case we have to intubate him."

She looked over to where Ben stood studying the heart monitor. "What is it?"

"He's gone into V-tach. I'm going to have to shock him," Ben announced to the room.

V-tach? It wasn't a rhythm you usually saw in children. This had to be caused by the tumor interfering in the heart's electrical paths.

Izzy ordered the nurse beside her to draw up a dose of morphine for the pain. "I've ordered some morphine. Can we sedate him before we shock him?"

The look that Ben gave her answered her question. "V-tach in the two-twenties. We don't have time to wait for anesthesia."

"Give him a dose of diazepam, three milligrams," Izzy told the nurse in charge of medication, then looked back at Ben. She didn't want to think about what she had to do next. "Just give them a minute to get him medicated."

She couldn't do as much without sedation and anesthesia, but at least the medications she'd ordered would help.

A nurse pushed the morphine Izzy had ordered earlier while the other drew up the diazepam. Izzy clutched Miguel's hand tighter. "Dr. Ben has to make your heart slow down. It's going to hurt, but it will only last a minute."

"We're going to use two hundred joules," Ben told the room as soon as the nurses finished giving the ordered medication. "Izzy, move away from the bed."

The nurse in charge of operating the defibrillator looked around the room. "I'm charging. Everyone clear?"

Izzy let the little boy's hand go and moved back from the bed with the rest of the staff. She was relieved that the medications had begun to work as the boy's eyes drifted shut.

"Shocking!" the nurse announced.

Miguel's body jerked and Izzy felt the pain of the shock deep in her soul. The room went silent as they all waited for Miguel's heart rate to adjust.

Izzy prayed they wouldn't have to repeat the shock as she moved back to the boy's side.

"He's converted to a normal sinus rhythm," Ben said. "Good job, everybody."

As Ben began ordering the team to transport Miguel to the PICU where he could be watched more carefully, Izzy brushed the boy's damp hair from his face. Between the stress he'd just gone through and the medications she'd ordered, the child would sleep for the next few hours.

The two of them decided the best anti-arrhythmic drugs to order for Miguel, and followed their patient to the pediatric intensive care unit. "I'm going to call his mother and tell her what happened. She's arriving tomorrow and she needs to be prepared."

Ben stood beside her, staring through the window into the boy's room. This child had touched something deep inside of him. Something that Izzy knew had been dead for a long time. Ben cared for all his patients—she'd seen that herself. But there was something special about this little boy. In some ways, Miguel reminded her of Ben. They both appeared so strong, neither wanting to admit they needed someone. And they both denied the pain they felt. Did Ben see it? Was that why he felt so in tune with the child?

"I don't know if I can fix him," Ben said, the pain and uncertainty in his voice tearing at her heart.

"You know this is just the beginning. As the tumor grows there's going to be more and more arrhythmias until…" She didn't say it, couldn't say it, but Ben knew what she was thinking. They both knew that there wasn't any hope for this boy if Ben didn't operate soon. The chance of Miguel getting a new heart before his own quit was getting less likely every day. They didn't have the time to wait. "You're his only chance, Ben."

The look of hopelessness he gave her tore at her heart. She felt as if she'd kicked a dog while he was down.

When he walked out of the PICU, she didn't follow him. She couldn't. As much as it hurt, she'd had to say it. Now she just had to find a way to help him make the only decision that would give Miguel at least a chance. If things went bad, she knew that it was likely Ben would never forgive her.

She looked back at the little boy lying so still against the white hospital bed while monitors and machines surrounded him.

It was a risk she'd have to take.

Ben sat in his office examining the images of Miguel's heart. He'd spent most of the night going over and over all these images. Nothing changed. He was a cardiac surgeon. One of the best. He should be able to find some way to save this child.

He slammed his laptop closed. There was a way, but it wasn't a good one and he knew that. But the chances of Miguel surviving were not in the child's favor. How could he open up the kid knowing that it was likely he wouldn't survive?

Yes, he'd operated on children whose chances were slim, but he'd always felt confident that he could handle whatever complication he faced in the OR. But it was different with Miguel. Since the first time he'd studied the boy's scans, he'd had this deep belief that something would go wrong if he chose to operate. A feeling that whatever he encountered in the operating room wouldn't end well.

When someone knocked on his office door, he knew it was Izzy. He recognized her knock now. He could ignore her. Let her think he had left the building or gone to see another patient. It was Christmas Eve. Shouldn't she be home doing some Christmas thing?

"Come on in, Izzy," he said.

She stepped into the room and her eyes met his. He knew what she would say. She'd remind him once again that Miguel's only hope was for him to operate. He knew she was right. He could come up with no other choice. So why was he hesitating? Because of some feeling that he couldn't even explain?

"Okay, I'll help you get a snake inside the hospital tonight, but only if you'll agree to come with me somewhere."

"I don't understand," he said, then stopped. "What did you say?"

"I said I'd help you get that stupid snake inside the hospital, which I might remind you will be even harder now that he's been moved to intensive care, but you have to agree to come with me somewhere. Today. As in right now."

"But…" He started to explain that he needed to stay at the hospital in case something happened with Miguel. But what was he going to do if it did? Any doctor could do what he'd done when the boy had gone into V-tach. What Miguel needed was a doctor that could perform the surgery he needed.

"I've already rounded on my patients and I've got someone to cover for me the rest of the day. I've also checked with the operating room and you don't have any surgeries. Please do this for me." She looked up at him with those big brown eyes of hers and he knew he was a goner.

"I'm not in the best mood for this. Besides, I thought you promised me that you wouldn't make me do any more of your Christmas activities."

"This is different," she said. "Don't make me threaten to tell Dr. Bailey about your plan to sneak dangerous animals into the hospital."

He shook his head. "I never would have believed that the sweet Dr. Jeong would lower herself to blackmail."

"Desperate times call for desperate measures," she said. "Besides, I'm not as nice as everyone thinks I am."

"I'm beginning to see that," he said as he rose and exchanged the white coat he wore in the hospital for a heavy wool jacket. "Where are we going?"

"I want you to see someone," she said, then added, "just be patient. Okay?"

He nodded his head in agreement. He didn't want to hurt her feelings, but there was no one he wanted to see today. Watching Miguel get shocked had taken everything out of him. He felt empty inside. Too empty to even argue with Izzy about whatever she had planned for him this afternoon.

The sky was turning gray as they walked out of the hospital and headed to Izzy's car. They'd finally gotten a good snow a couple days earlier and it looked like they could expect more. He liked snow. Or he used to like it. He wasn't sure when he'd quit enjoying the simple things in life, like snow, but he was sure it was after Cara had passed.

Cara. Would she even recognize the man he'd become? He was sure she wouldn't like him. Half the time even he didn't like himself.

He couldn't understand why Izzy was bothering with him today. Usually when he was in a foul mood, he'd just snarl at someone and people would leave him alone. He had an idea that if he snarled at Izzy, she'd snarl right back at him. He smiled at the thought.

"What's that about?" Izzy asked as she parked in front of a large church that sat on the corner of a small street. The parking lot was full of cars and as this was not a Sunday, he knew that this had to be another one of Izzy's crazy Christmas traditions she was dragging him into.

"Izzy, I don't think this is a good idea." The last thing he needed was to be around a bunch of people right now.

And a church? Wasn't that a place of hope and peace? He wasn't feeling either one of those today.

"I want you to see someone. Please, Ben? Just come with me." Once more those big brown eyes of hers captured his. How could he tell her no?

Izzy hoped that she was doing the right thing. The moment she'd seen the invitation to the choir performance clipped to the calendar on her office desk, she'd felt that it couldn't be a coincidence. This was meant to be.

And it might be her only hope for Miguel.

She had no idea if Ben knew that she was Zachary's pediatrician. She wasn't even sure that Ben had seen the boy after he'd performed the operation that had saved Zach's life, which was the same night that Ben's wife had been killed in a car accident.

From what she'd been told, Zach had come into the hospital after suffering from a blunt force trauma when he'd been hit by a baseball in the sternum. A team of emergency medical techs had been on the sideline and they'd brought him into the emergency room where they discovered a large aortic dissection. She'd been told by Zach's family that the only reason he was alive was because Ben was already in the building when the boy arrived. Even as Zach was crashing, he'd been rushed to the operating room. Izzy had heard that everyone in the operating room had given up on the boy but Ben wouldn't stop, insisting that they keep transfusing him with blood even when he went into cardiac arrest. Ben didn't give up.

She just hoped seeing the boy would remind him of the man he'd been and not about what he'd lost that night.

The performance had already started, so they took a program and a seat in the back of the church. They sat through several carols sung by a group of elementary children before a group of teenagers joined them.

Izzy spotted Zach. He was in the middle of the back row and when he stepped forward and began to sing a solo of "Silent Night," she couldn't hold back the tears as the boy's voice filled the chapel. Ben sat beside her so still she couldn't tell if he was breathing.

Was it possible he didn't recognize the boy? It had been four years since the operation and Zach had done a lot of growing since then.

After the last carol was sung, they managed to sneak out the door before Zach's parents could spot them. She didn't want Ben to be put in an awkward position if he didn't recognize the teenager. Once they were back in her car, Ben turned toward her.

"Why did you bring me here, Izzy?" His voice was almost lifeless. Had she made a mistake? Maybe he wasn't ready.

"I wanted you to see him, the boy you saved that everyone else had given up on." She didn't know what more she could say.

"You mean the boy that I saved while I should have been with my wife?" he asked.

He looked away from her, but not before she saw the pain in his eyes.

"Is that what you think? That you lost your wife because you weren't there? Wasn't it a drunk driver that caused that wreck?"

He didn't answer her and she was at a loss of what else she could say or do to make him quit this internal dialogue of self-loathing that she now knew he'd been living with.

"Surely you don't blame Zach for your wife's death," she said, the idea horrifying her.

"Of course not. I understand what you're trying to do and I know you meant well, Izzy. And I'm glad the boy is doing well. I want to save Miguel. I do."

"I just wanted you to see what you are capable of doing. I was told everyone in the OR gave up on that kid. Everyone but you. His parents told me that the staff said the operation you performed should have been impossible, but you wouldn't give up. And they are so thankful that you didn't. We just witnessed the kid that you saved singing a beautiful carol. He's going to college next year on a baseball scholarship. You made that possible."

The crowd had exited the church and the sun was going down. Soft flakes of snow fell against her windshield. "We both know that you are Miguel's only hope. We can't give up on him. You have to give him a chance."

Ben turned toward her, desperation in his eyes. "And if I can't? If he dies on the operating table?"

"And if you don't try to save him? How can we live knowing that we didn't give him a chance?" she asked.

"We?" he asked.

"Yes, we. I can't operate, but maybe if you explain the problem to me I might know someone that can. Or maybe I'll see something from a different perspective. It can't hurt," she said as she started backing up the car.

"Okay." Ben let out a sigh as he leaned back into his seat. "You're right. Maybe someone else looking at this might help."

She glanced over at him as she put the car into Drive and was surprised to see a teeny, tiny smile on Ben's face.

"That doesn't mean I'm letting you out of helping me with the snake," he said, before turning serious again. "Let's head back to the hospital so you can take a look at the images on my computer. Then we have a zoo-keeper we need to meet."

On the way back, they began to discuss the case. From what Izzy understood, it had always been the placement of the tumor that had been the problem with Ben operating on Miguel. "Did you talk to any of the oncology surgeons about the tumor?"

"A biopsy was done before he arrived. It's noncancerous," Ben said.

"But still, it's a tumor, right? Maybe there's an oncology surgeon here at Beacon that could help.".

When Ben didn't say anything, she was afraid she might have insulted him. Surgeons were strange that way. But when she looked over at him, the smile was back.

"I didn't think of that. It isn't cancerous, but it is a tumor and an oncology surgeon might see something or know a procedure I don't."

For the first time, Izzy saw some hope in Ben's eyes. She just hoped she hadn't sent him on a wild-goose chase.

But by the time they were back in his office, Ben had contacted the oncology surgeon on call and she'd agreed to look over Miguel's scans and give Ben an opinion on whether it was operable. Now they just had to wait to hear back from her.

"Why don't you go on home?" Ben asked. "It's Christmas Eve. I bet there's some movie you're supposed to be watching right now."

He was right. She did usually watch *Elf* on Christmas Eve.

She'd gone by the PICU to check on Miguel and found the boy doing well. Only the IV antiarrhythmic drug was keeping him in the intensive care unit. That and the fact that he could go into a fatal arrhythmia at any time.

Also, Izzy had learned that his mother had arrived while she'd been gone and one of the staff had watched her other children while she'd visited with her son. It wasn't the visit Izzy had hoped to give the boy, but as long as he was in Intensive Care it was all they'd allow.

Her work at the hospital was done for the night. There was only one more thing that she needed to do before she could sink into her couch and enjoy one of her favorite Christmas movies.

"I thought we had to go by the zoo to pick up a snake," she reminded him. She couldn't wait to see how he planned on sneaking a snake past the staff when they wouldn't even allow Miguel to have his siblings visit.

"I was just joking. I don't need you to do

that." Ben's phone rang and Izzy's breath caught. Maybe this new surgeon had some good news.

She waited as Ben discussed the case some more with the woman. From what she could tell, they were discussing a new technique used to remove difficult tumors that Dr. Edison had been trained in. By the time Ben hung up, she could see a spark of hope in his eyes.

"So you're going to do it?" she asked.

"If you can get in touch with Miguel's mother and have her here tomorrow morning by seven? Dr. Edison and I will be ready to operate," Ben said before standing. "And now you need to go home so you can't be accused of being an accomplice in the crime I am about to commit."

"Oh, no you don't. I promised to help and I'm not backing out. We are in this together." Izzy just hoped Javi would be willing to bail them out with the board if they got caught.

"I'm not taking you with me," Ben said, using that surgeon stare of his. She was sure it scared all the new surgery techs until they learned his glare wasn't as deadly as he tried to make out. But unlike most recipients, Ben's glare had never intimidated her.

"I'm going," she said as she grabbed her purse and followed him out the door. "And nothing you can say is going to stop me."

CHAPTER SIXTEEN

"I'M GOING," IZZY SAID as Ben parked his car in his reserved spot. They'd argued all the way to the zoo and back, including when they'd stopped at her house to grab a decorated box to place the snake inside.

He had to admit when he picked up the box from the back seat that it had been a great idea. No one seeing them carry the silver-wrapped box would think it contained anything more dangerous than a fruitcake. It seemed there really was more to Izzy than that sweet-as-sunshine reputation she had. She could be pretty devious when she wanted to be.

"You're pregnant, Izzy. You should be at home in bed, not sneaking a snake into the hospital."

"It's only eight o'clock. And neither one of us should be sneaking that snake inside the hospital. I'll be happy to go home if you will."

He wanted to lie and tell her that he would forget about this, but he couldn't. He could never lie to Izzy, though he was sure there would be times over the following years as they raised their child he might want to.

A child. With Izzy. It still seemed unreal. They'd both been so busy that they hadn't even had a chance to discuss the baby, something that would have to change as soon as Miguel's operation was done.

He still wasn't sure if he could get all the tumor without damaging Miguel's heart, but Dr. Edison's new procedure gave him hope.

They used the staff entry instead of going past security at the front entrance. They didn't need a nosy guard asking them to remove the lid.

They'd almost made it to the elevator when Izzy grabbed him by the sleeve. It was Dr. Bailey coming down the hall toward them.

"Well, I didn't expect to see you two here so late on Christmas Eve," the man said when he reached them.

"We didn't expect to see you either," Izzy replied, her smile not quite as bright as it usually was. "We just wanted to come see a patient. He's having surgery tomorrow morning and we wanted to give him his gift early."

The chief of surgery turned to Ben and for once Ben had no witty comeback for the man. The snake had begun to shift inside the box and Ben was scared the man might have seen the movement. If he asked to see what was inside, he and Izzy would be in a world of trouble. Especially him. He'd been warned that he might be let go by Christmas. His days could already be numbered, but he didn't want to take Izzy down with him. "We don't want to hold you up. I'm sure you have plans with your family tonight."

"That's actually why I'm here. My aunt had to be admitted and I promised my wife I would check on her before I headed home," Dr. Bailey said.

Izzy looped her arm in Ben's free one. "We need to go too. Ben's got surgery early in the morning."

"A surgery on Christmas Day? It must be emergent," Dr. Bailey said.

And before Ben knew it, he and the surgeon were involved in a discussion of the procedure that Miguel needed. The older surgeon had some good ideas of his own on how to proceed and he recommended Dr. Edison highly.

"I hope everything goes well. And I'm glad to see that you and Dr. Edison are collaborating. I'm pleased we ran into each other tonight. I was going to call you tomorrow, but I might as well tell you now. I've decided to recommend to the board that we continue your contract. Over the last few weeks I've seen an improvement in your attitude. I suspect some of it comes from being around Izzy. Just don't do anything foolish and make me look stupid."

Ben thanked the man, and he and Izzy started back down the hall. They'd barely made it around the corner and into the elevator when Izzy broke into laughter.

"I can't believe that just happened," she said when she finally stopped. "And he said he was going to recommend they continue your contract. Isn't that great news?"

"He also said not to do anything stupid. If we get caught after the speech he just gave me, we'll both be looking for new jobs." He'd known bringing Izzy was a bad idea.

"Then we better not get caught," Izzy said as the elevator doors opened on the hallway to the PICU. "We do it just like we planned. I'll keep the staff occupied while you go check on Miguel. You'll have to ask him not to tell anyone about your visit, but he's a smart kid and I think you can trust him."

He wasn't worried about Miguel. The boy would keep their secret.

Ben used his badge to get them into the PICU and he headed straight for Miguel's room. Izzy headed for the nurses' station where she planned to tell the nurses that Ben wanted to explain to Miguel about the surgery and that he shouldn't be disturbed.

Miguel was asleep when Ben entered the room. They both had a big day tomorrow and needed their rest, but first Ben would make sure that Miguel had a chance to see a snake like the one in his book.

After showing the man at the zoo a picture from Miguel's book, it had been determined that Sam the snake was just an everyday garter snake. Nonpoisonous and plentiful in the outdoors, the one he'd been given was only a foot long.

"Miguel, wake up," Ben said, moving closer to the bed when the boy's eyes opened. "Look what I brought for you to see."

Once they'd made it back inside the elevator and were headed down, Izzy's heart rate began to slow. She'd never had to worry about getting caught at something she wasn't supposed to be doing before.

She'd always been the good kid in school, never pulling pranks or getting in trouble. She'd even been good through college, applying herself to her courses while she worked toward her goal of getting into medical school. And once she'd made it that far, there had been no time for anything except working, studying and occasionally sleeping.

Tonight had been an adrenaline rush that she had no desire to repeat.

"Are you going to return the snake tonight?" she asked Ben.

He hadn't said anything since he'd come out of Miguel's room and found her entertaining the whole nurses' station with stories about the weird objects she'd had the pleasure of removing from toddlers' many orifices. He'd only nodded once toward the doors and disappeared.

"I'm supposed to meet them at the zoo entrance in—" he looked at his watch "—thirty minutes."

"I can't believe we pulled that off. Did he love seeing the snake?" Izzy asked, though she already knew the answer by the smile on Ben's face.

"He was blown away. I think me telling him we had to keep it a secret just between the three of us made it even more special."

The elevator doors opened and they headed back to the staff entrance. Izzy stopped when Ben started toward his car. "I'm parked this way."

"Okay, I'll walk with you," he said.

They walked in silence, the tap of their footsteps the only sound. It was a Christmas Eve like she'd never had before. And next year would be even more different. "I can't believe that next Christmas we'll have a baby."

"I'm having a problem wrapping my mind around that one too."

"It's okay. We don't have to talk about it now," Izzy said. She started to berate herself for bringing up the baby. Then she stopped. This had to end. She needed to know if Ben was going to be able to handle being a father.

"No, wait. That's wrong. We do need to talk about the baby. I need to know how you feel about being a father. I need to know what part you plan to play in this baby's life." She stopped and turned toward him. She'd put this conversation off long enough. It was time that she was totally honest not only with him, but with herself. "And that's not all. I want to know where I fit into those plans."

Ben looked down at her, his eyes warm one moment and then cool the next. He was starting to do that thing where he pulled away from her. She knew the signs now. "Ben Murphy, don't even think about locking me out. I want to know how you feel. I need to know what you want from me. You make love to me like I'm your world. You laugh with me. You even flirt with me. But the moment I bring up the baby or us, you shut me out."

She turned to walk away. She was tired of fighting for this man. She'd done all she could. She'd even risked her job for him tonight. And she would do it again if only he'd tell her that he cared for her. But if he couldn't see that he needed her and their baby in his life, she couldn't do any more.

"Izzy, I..." He let the words trail off and Izzy couldn't take any more.

She turned to face him. "There was a time when all I wanted to know is that you wanted our baby in your life. But somewhere between helping you win back your job and the two of us spending the night together in my bed, I realized I wanted more.

I deserve more. And if you can't give it to me, I need to know that."

"I care about you, Izzy. You have to know that." Ben's eyes were no longer shuttered, but still there wasn't the love she'd hoped to see there.

She turned to walk away again and was glad that this time he didn't follow her.

Ben tried to concentrate on the operation he was about to begin, but his mind kept going back to Izzy. There were so many things he needed to tell her last night, but he hadn't been able to make his lips move. He was scared. Scared of taking the next step into a life that Izzy had shown him he could have.

But why? His life was much like the surgery he and Dr. Edison were about to perform. Miguel had no chance to live as long as the tumor inside his heart was there. He had to have the surgery, but the surgery itself might kill him.

But if Miguel died on this table, something Ben had no intention of letting happen, but if he did at least Ben would know he'd done everything he could to save the boy.

So why was he so scared to take a chance on a life with Izzy? If he didn't take the chance, he'd lose her. He just had to take that first step into the unknown with her.

"Dr. Murphy?" the surgical tech said.

Ben looked around the room. Everyone was in their places. The time out had been done as per protocol. It was up to him now to make the next move.

He nodded to the anesthesiologist and to Dr. Edison, the oncologist, then held out his hand for his scalpel. He stared at Miguel's small chest that had been prepped and draped. He could do this. He was ready.

It was a grueling surgery. For two hours, Ben and Dr. Edison worked to remove the tumor that had grown into the boy's interventricular septum while the bypass machine continued to provide the boy with oxygenated blood.

By the time Ben was closing the incision he'd first made, he should have been drained, but instead he felt more alive than he had in years.

Once Miguel had come off the bypass machine and his heart had returned to a normal sinus rhythm, Ben headed to the waiting room to speak with Miguel's mother and hopefully have a chance to see Izzy.

But only Miguel's mother waited for him.

"He did great. After he gets out of Recovery they'll be taking him back to the intensive care unit for the night. But tomorrow, if he does well, I'll get him moved out to the ward so you can spend more time with him."

"My Miguel is a strong boy. I thank you for all you've done for us."

"It was a pleasure. Your son is very special." He decided to wait a couple days before he mentioned to the woman that he wanted to buy the boy a pet snake of his own. "Do you know where Dr. Jeong went?"

"She took the children back to the hotel. They were too tired and fussy."

The woman thanked Ben again before he left her and headed to Recovery to check on his patient. By the time Miguel was safely returned to his room, it was almost noon. It was Christmas day and once again Ben was all alone.

Izzy propped her feet up on the couch and pressed her television remote again. None of the movies she'd planned to watch on Christmas Day could keep her attention. She'd shared lunch with Miguel's mother and his brother and sisters. It had been a rowdy meal at the restaurant in the hotel with all the little ones excited about the Christmas presents that Izzy had delivered.

And now all she wanted was to be swept away into the magic world of Christmas so that she could quit thinking about Ben and how he'd let her walk away.

Her doorbell rang and she checked the camera on her phone. Her heart rate sped up when she saw that it was Ben. And he'd come bearing gifts.

Did he really think that she could be bribed with a couple of gifts to let things continue as they had before she'd demanded to know his intentions?

She opened the door, not even caring that she wore her rattiest, though most comfortable, flannel nightgown. "Ben."

"Izzy, how are you this evening?" Ben asked.

She couldn't believe he was using her own lessons on her. "It's late and I'm tired and cranky. That is how I am tonight."

"I see. Can I come in?"

She wanted to be rude and slam the door in his face, but she couldn't. It was Christmas. She had to at least let him in and see what he wanted. Besides, she was becoming curious about the two boxes in his arms.

She held the door open for him, then followed him into the family room before taking her seat back on the couch.

"I know it's late, but it's Christmas and I wanted to give you something," Ben said.

"I didn't get you a gift," she said, though she had. She'd hidden it deep in her closet last night when she'd gotten home. She hadn't wanted to look at it under her tree like it belonged there.

"This is just something to show you how much I appreciate everything you've done for me."

She opened the box he handed her and pulled out a wooden nutcracker dressed like the dancers in the ballet they'd attended. The memories of that night weren't ones she wanted to dwell on. She'd thought that they were moving toward a real relationship, even though she'd denied it to herself. Deep down, she'd always hoped that she and Ben would someday have a future together. It was a romantic dream that she'd wasted too much time on. She needed to concentrate on her baby and making a life for their family of two.

She put the nutcracker back in the box and closed it. "Thank you."

He held out another box, this one small and square. "What is this one for?"

Ben took a breath then reached for her hand. "This is another thank-you present, but I hope it will be more."

"I don't understand."

"I shouldn't have let you walk away last night, Izzy. I need you and our baby. I've just been too scared to admit it." He stood and walked away from her, then turned back to her. "I think I fell in love with you that first night when we went out to celebrate and ended up in your bed. Or maybe it was before that. You used to drive me crazy with all your cheerful morning talk, but I secretly enjoyed it."

"I find that hard to believe. You made me chase you all over the ward so that I could tell you good morning each day." Something inside her began to sing.

"So you admit you were chasing me?" Ben asked as he came to sit next to her, his lips turned up into a smile so sweet she thought she'd burst with happiness. Seeing Ben smile had always made her happy, especially when he was playing the part of the grumpy doctor.

"Do you admit that you're tired of running?"

"I don't want to run," he said, his tone now serious. "Your sunshine has driven away all the shadows I've hid behind for the last four years. I'm not going to promise I'll always be as cheery as you, but even when I'm grumpy I want you to know that I love you."

It was more than she had ever hoped for. "I love you too."

"So, what's in the box?" she asked. "You said it was a thank-you gift, but you were hoping it would be more."

"I had to say that, in case you turned me down. It's an ego thing. I hear we surgeons have a problem with them."

He opened the box and a gold band with a heart-shaped diamond lay in a box lined in black velvet. "Will you marry me, Izzy?"

For once, Izzy Jeong was speechless. She'd always dreamed of getting engaged on Christmas.

"I'd love to marry you, Ben. But I have one question," she said as Ben pulled her into his arms. "Where did you get a ring on Christmas Day?"

"Well, there's this jeweler whose god-daughter I operated on…"

Grabbing his face, she kissed his lips. She'd spent half her life trying to make the perfect Christmas, but there was always something missing. Now she had Ben and her Christmas was perfect.

EPILOGUE

Izzy handed Ben their daughter as the happy couple came into the room. It was almost Christmas and she knew there was nothing like a Christmas engagement. Bryn smiled at her and waved as Honey sat by her side. When Nick wrapped his arm around Bryn's waist, Izzy's eyes began to tear.

"You can't blame those on your hormones," her husband said as he handed her a tissue from the diaper bag.

"I'm so glad they decided to announce their engagement at Christmas," Izzy said. "Look at the screen. It's Ailani and Javi with Mabel. I hate they're missing this, but I can't blame them. The sun and sand of Hawaii would be heaven right now."

"No snow for Christmas? Isn't that one of Izzy's Christmas requirements?" her husband teased her, but she wasn't fooled. He might deny it, but he had loved every minute they'd spent decorating their home this Christmas. He'd even been the one to buy their daughter's first Christmas stocking.

When Kalista and Dylan joined the crowd, they both looked thrilled. "What's going on with those two?"

"Dylan told me they were looking at houses today. It looks like they found one," Ben said.

The future groom's brother raised his glass of champagne to toast Bryn and Nick. While they all took a drink, Izzy looked around the room. She was so lucky to work with this amazing group of people.

Then her eyes came to rest on her husband, who held their beautiful daughter, little Joy. Closing her eyes, she made a Christmas wish of peace, comfort and joy for all the staff and all the children that night on Ward 34.

* * * * *

MEDICAL
Pulse-racing passion

Available Next Month

All titles available in Larger Print

A Daddy For The Midwife's Twins? Tina Beckett
Cinderella's Kiss With The ER Doc Scarlet Wilson

....

Surgeon Prince's Fake Fiancée Karin Baine
A Mother For His Little Princess Karin Baine

....

Second Chance For The Heart Doctor Susan Carlisle
A Therapy Pup To Reunite Them Luana DaRosa

Keep reading for an excerpt of a new title
from the Western Romance series,
A FAMILY FOR THANKSGIVING by M. K. Stelmack

CHAPTER ONE

NATALIA GARIN GLARED at the watercolor, scarcely a foot square, that hung in the art gallery. The painting depicted a wide curve in the Peace River, the mighty artery that cut across Northern Alberta. Cliffs bound this section of the river, rising and then leveling off to the suggestion of meadows and pines beyond, unmarred by human presence.

"Pretty," Brock Holloway said, beside her, his voice echoing through the sloped gray-walled walkway where other paintings of the Peace Country were exhibited.

"That's because it's missing the flies, heat, cold, swampy smells and crazed bison."

"True. Painting would need to be bigger to get all that in."

Was he making a joke? Humor in conversation threw her like a stick in wheel spokes. But then, most everything about this man threw her. His very presence in the Grande Prairie courthouse had sent her, dry-mouthed and shaking, into the women's washroom to regain her composure. On top of the heartache of the past few days, he had walked in and proposed to take away the one good thing that remained from her brother's sudden, recent death.

He had applied for guardianship of her four-year-old niece, Sadie Garin. Technically, their niece. Sadie's mom and Brock were siblings, until Abby had died from childbirth complications. Natalia was sister to Sadie's dad, until Daniel's death eight days ago. Drowned in the frigid April waters of the same river that flowed wide and gentle in the painting before her. His body was found two days later caught up in shore debris. Local police had identified the body. She was spared that particular horror.

Natalia turned away from the canvas with its misty blues and greens and browns, and pretended interest in another painting of trees in autumnal shades. This one showed a sturdy log cabin amid dense, tall trees, not much different than the prison she'd grown up in. Daniel and Abby had taken it over after marrying, a wedding gift from the Garin parents who retreated farther north into the Yukon wilderness. A chamber of bad memories for her, as it had to be now for Sadie. She'd sat with her doll for hours, waiting for her father to return before calling for help on the ham radio.

These false images sickened Natalia, but the gallery provided a quiet space for her to hash it out with Brock. The judge had cleared both of their applications and turned it over to them to come up with a workable solution.

They'd left the courthouse and begun walking together because, Natalia supposed, together was what the judge had ordered. Half a block away she'd glanced over at the art gallery, and he'd asked if she'd wanted to go inside. It was starting to rain and she had no idea where else to go. So yes, she'd gone inside with Brock, and they'd drifted into the exhibit.

"Too bad we can't hear from Sadie what she'd like," Brock said. He'd stayed at the first painting, perhaps sensing her desire for space. "I'd like to know her thoughts, and take them into consideration."

It irked her, too, that the authorities hadn't allowed either of them to see their niece. Both her parents and Brock's parents south in Arizona had declined to travel, and had shown no interest in their grandchild. Her own parents had gone so far as to tell her that death was not to be mourned and Daniel's remains should be returned to the wild. He rested in an urn in her hotel room because she would not abandon him to bug-infested muskeg.

Brock and Natalia had asked separately and together to see Sadie, who currently resided with a foster family. But to avoid more turmoil in Sadie's life, the deal had been that they would first hammer out an arrangement. Dangling a carrot, the judge was.

Sadie would choose Brock. He was a typical handsome cowboy—tall, broad-shouldered and lean-jawed. Not that Sadie would register his good looks, but she would pick up on how Brock hooked onto a person, as if you were the only one in the room, as if you mattered above all else. Anyone who might feel alone or...unloved would blossom from just being around him.

In the end, though, she was better for Sadie. But how to convince him? She could sell candles and home décor like there was no tomorrow. If she had to sell herself, she'd gather dust before expiring on some discount table.

She touched the ammolite pendant on her necklace. "I'm not sure how much weight we could place on her thoughts right now. She's grieving."

Again, his warm gaze rested on her. "You are, too."

There, that...pull, reeling her into his orbit. She wrenched herself away to focus on a stylized map of the local area, part of the exhibition to show where each of the paintings came from. There was no marker even close to where Daniel and Sadie had lived, thirty miles east of Fort Vermilion, which itself was a hamlet of a few hundred. Most were clustered around Grande Prairie. The first time she'd come here when she was seventeen, Natalia had really believed it was a city. Until she'd rode the bus farther south to Edmonton. In the fourteen years since, she'd traveled on holiday to Singapore, London, Buenos Aires and dozens of other spots, including Amsterdam, when the Canadian embassy there contacted her about Daniel. Those were cities. This so-called city was a scraping out of streets and buildings from the surrounding wilderness.

"I'm fine," she lied. Her last visual contact with Daniel had been four months ago, at Christmas. She had sent Sadie a huge box of gifts she'd wrapped in rolls of thick glittery gold wrapping paper with intricate red bows, and Sadie had opened them over a video call from the Fort Vermilion library, where there was cell reception. They'd talked regularly since then over ham radio. The last time she heard Daniel's voice was when he extracted a promise from her to do a video call when she arrived back from Amsterdam. Among all the promises she had broken to him, this was the one she would've loved to have kept.

"Still," Brock said. Abby had been torn from him the day of Sadie's birth. He must have had the same aching hole inside she now had. Might still have it.

But mutual sympathy would not resolve their present dilemma. Best get on with it. She forced herself to look into his mesmerizing eyes and say her piece. "I don't doubt the sincerity of your intentions, but I think I'm a better fit to be Sadie's guardian. She wouldn't be alone. I work, but I have found a day care close by. There are other kids her age and programs, lots of stimulation."

"That in Calgary?"

"Yes. I manage a warehouse there. I also make sales calls."

"What do you sell?"

He didn't know? Then again, how would he know that his chance remark at their siblings' small wedding eight years ago had sent her career on a completely different trajectory? "I'm a partner in Home & Holidays. It's a home décor company. We sell into shops."

"Sounds as if it keeps you busy."

She detected censure. "No busier than your work. You still on the rodeo circuit?"

He shook his head. "I got out of that racket last fall while I still had all my body parts. I'm working full time at a ranch near Red Deer."

"Oh. Is that…stable?"

From the slight thinning of his lips, he had understood the bend of her question. "My position is secure. I know the owner well and we get along." He paused. "You?"

She had single-handedly pulled the business operating out of her landlady's triple-car garage into a going concern with twenty employees. A landlady and roommate who became her boss and was now her partner. "My company is secure, too."

The corner of his mouth flicked upward. "I guess we're even on that score. What hours do you work?"

"It's not a nine-to-five job," she said. "But the day care has flexible hours."

"After the kids go home, Sadie would be there, waiting for you?" Brock stood higher up the sloping walkway, making him rise above her even more than he normally would.

Natalia leaned against a railing to appear relaxed, though really it was for support. "They close at seven, so obviously it wouldn't be for too long."

"Seven. That's practically bedtime. Definitely past supper time."

He was right. "It wouldn't be every day. Once a week at the most. What about you? I imagine your hours aren't regular."

"I spoke to that in the report. I stay on the ranch. It

comes with its own support system. Knut—the owner—already said he'd back me up. And his daughter, and her husband. They've got a boy. A one-year-old. And then in a pinch, there are families around. There'd always be someone around."

He had her there. She was pretty much on her own. She had Gina, but she had no experience with kids and probably wouldn't want to babysit during her precious free time. And she had no friends close enough to call upon for emergency childcare.

Natalia crossed her ankles to bolster her relaxed vibe. "I don't intend to raise Sadie apart from others." With its one and a half million residents, Calgary must have some kind of support for single caregivers. "Far from it. She'll be fully immersed."

"Immersed?" Brock walked down the tilted walkway toward her, slow and easy. She tensed.

"Given opportunities. Allowed to make friends. Go shopping. Use playgrounds. Go to the zoo, the science center. I will see to it she has everything she wants."

Brock leaned against the railing alongside her and stretched out his legs. Was he trying to project the same ease? No. Nothing rattled him. "What if she doesn't want that?"

Natalia blinked. "Not want what?"

"What if she doesn't want to live in the city? With all the people and noise? What if she wants a life closer to what she had here?"

"You have obviously not led the life she has or you would not even consider the idea."

"What are you saying?"

"Daniel's—Daniel was a great father, but there was nothing, nothing for her in that place."

"It might've been quiet, but then again she's only four—"

Natalia pushed off the railing and paced the flat portion of the walkway. "Four is old enough. You stay in the bush too long and you're stunted forever. Any ability to communicate with others, to laugh in the right spots, to make friends, to…anything." Her voice was quivering. She clutched the ammolite. Its deep rainbow colors complemented her every outfit, and her every mood. It never failed to calm her.

"The ranch isn't isolated," he said softly. "Sadie wouldn't be alone. If she didn't want to be."

And if he made a point of socializing Sadie, which she didn't trust him to do. Still, he had an available network and she needed time to build one of her own. "If she stayed with you," she said, "would she have her own room?"

"I already talked to Knut. We can live in his house, and there are three available bedrooms."

"And how far from the nearest town are you?"

"Quarter of an hour along graveled roads and pavement. Town's population is around ten thousand. Stores, schools, playgrounds."

"Would you take her there?"

"If she wants."

"Oh, she'll want. Trust me. And is there a chance for her to socialize? A kindergarten or a prekindergarten?"

"I imagine so. One of the moms up the road takes her daughter into some classes. I could find out."

"I'll find out. And I'll pay for that."

Brock stiffened and blew out his breath. "Fair enough. Are you saying that I get her, then?"

Natalia had been grinding through her own mental calculations. "Three months. How about you have her for the first three months, until the end of July? I will take the next three months to the end of October, and then we can reach a decision about her permanent home. This way Sadie will see both kinds of life and we can feel assured that her wishes are rooted in knowledge."

Brock looked through the wide windows at the lazy spitting rain. Finally, he brought his gaze back to her. He had the darkest brown eyes she'd ever seen. She hated all shades of brown. It reminded her too much of the spring mud in the Peace River. But there was a quality to his brown. "That works."

Natalia found herself smiling, without even trying to. "Then let's go tell Sadie that she has a home now."

SADIE WAS A dead ringer for his sister. Brock had visited Daniel and her a couple of times, but seeing her now on the couch in the foster parents' living room, he was struck by how she seemed like a smaller replica of Abby. Same thin face, same watchful dark eyes, same boniness, same quick, birdlike hands. Only her hair was different, redder and curlier, like her father's. Like Natalia's. A reminder that as much as he might not like it, Sadie was not his alone.

The foster parents had a busy household. There were toys, backpacks, kicked-off shoes everywhere. A bike lay on the carpet with its front wheel missing. Some kind of long vine crept along the back of the couch above Sadie. Natalia, sitting next to her, had repeatedly eyed that plant, as if it might lunge and strangle their niece. Protective… or paranoid.

A social worker sat in a kitchen chair off to the side, pen over notepad, poised to record the slightest misstep. Brock kept forgetting her name, but he did recall how she'd said three times in five minutes that she was retiring in less than four months. In other words, she was counting the days and Sadie was just one more kid to deal with. Good thing he and Natalia had worked out an arrangement to get Sadie away. One that made him the caregiver of a small child he'd only met three times before, and talked to for as many minutes on the phone. Three months under the scrutiny of her suspicious aunt. Nothing in his thirty-three years had prepared him for this pressure.

"So, Sadie," Natalia said, her long, pale fingers coming to rest on the cushion above Sadie's head in such a way that the vine fell down behind the couch, "what do you think of our plan?"

If possible, Sadie hunched her shoulders even more and darted a look upward to Natalia before staring down again, her knees pressed together so hard they'd leave red marks. She opened her mouth but clamped it shut again. In awe of her aunt. Brock could relate. The first and only other time he'd seen her in person, at his sister's wedding, she'd left him dry-mouthed, heart racing. Like he'd slipped onto the back of a bronco.

He crouched down in front of Sadie, taking a page from his friend and neighbour Will who did this when reasoning with his three-year-old daughter.

Up close, Brock saw that maybe it wasn't just his sister's looks that Sadie had inherited, but the same fear that the entire world was about to crush her. He had failed to rescue Abby from that fear. He wasn't about to fail her daughter, too. Even if it meant dealing with Sadie's intense, determined aunt.

He remembered a technique from when, as kids, he'd try to draw Abby, three years his junior, into conversation. "Do you want help saying something that's hard to get out?"

A sharp nod.

"Okay. Is it something you want to tell me or Auntie Lia or us both?"

"Both," she whispered.

"Both, then. Is it okay to tell us here or do you want to go someplace else?"

The social worker shifted, probably to state some policy, but Sadie whispered again. "Here's okay."

"Okay. Do you like it when you answer my questions? Or do you want to talk on your own now?"

Sadie pointed at him. "You ask me."

"I can do that. Is it about staying with me or Auntie Lia?"

A nod.

"That's good because it's important to both of us you say how you feel about our plan. We can always change it."

Sadie nodded again and then shook her head. "I want to stay with you, but... I don't want to live with Auntie Lia."

He saw Natalia stiffen and take hold of the gemstone at her throat.

"That's honest. That's good. You want to tell us why?"

She pulled on her T-shirt until the hem stretched over her knees and said nothing. Natalia was biting her lip so hard that it had gone white around the dark pink skin. Her hand still over the gemstone, she said quietly, "Would it be easier to talk to Uncle Brock, if I left?"

Sadie swiveled to her aunt. "No! Don't leave me!" She gripped Natalia's sleeve. If she hadn't, Brock might have himself. Whatever their disagreements, he most definitely wanted Natalia to help Sadie and him hash this out.

Natalia relaxed in her seat. "Okay. I'll stay and listen."

Still holding on to her aunt, Sadie turned to Brock. "Auntie Lia lives in the city. And Dad said we can only go to the city together."

There it was. "You don't want to do anything your dad might not have liked."

Sadie's face cleared. "Yes."

"But he didn't say you couldn't go to the city?"

"No."

"Well, since your father has…is—Since your aunt and I are looking out for you now, you don't need to worry about disobeying your father. It's on your aunt and me to make sure we respect your dad's wishes. All right?"

Sadie nodded and then addressed her aunt's knee. "Is that all right with you?"

"It is."

Natalia's support emboldened him. "And Auntie Lia is welcome to visit us anytime. Okay?"

Sadie's grasp on Natalia turned into a full-on hug. "You can come stay with me and Uncle Brock, too."

Over Sadie's head, Natalia's eyes widened on Brock. "A visit," she said quickly, "is a short stay. One or two days."

Sadie sank back and her lower lip trembled. Brock and Natalia exchanged looks of mutual fright. She fussed with the stone on her necklace and then, in a single swift motion, removed it, the stone nestled in her hand. "This is the first time you've seen it for real, isn't it?"

"It's the most beautiful thing in the world," Sadie said with all the conviction of a four-year-old.

"I think so, too," Natalia said. "I don't know if I told you that ammolite is only found here in Alberta. Down south of Calgary. It's that rare. I think this piece has every possible color."

Sadie studied it. "Blue. Red. Orange. Wait, I see purple! It does have every color." She reached out a finger, then stopped.

"You can touch it," Natalia said. "It won't break or scratch."

Sadie stroked it softly, as if the stone were a kitten.

"Remember the story of how I got it?"

Sadie curled into Natalia and her arm banded around

Sadie in a half hug. The tension in Natalia's posture eased, and Brock returned to his chair. *There, all good.*

Sadie drew a deep breath and, on the exhale, began. "You were shopping for a wedding gift for Mom and Dad, and you saw this necklace and you told Dad about it, and he called up the store and bought it over the phone for you and said that you had to come to the wedding in person to thank him for it. Only you came to the wedding but forgot to thank him. And every time you talked to him since then, you thanked him. I remember you thanking him. And Dad would always say, 'About time, Lia.'"

Natalia clipped the ammolite around Sadie's neck. "You keep it while you live with Uncle Brock. It's a little magical. When you feel stuck, it will help you find a way through. There are lots of pretty things like that where I live," Natalia said. "When you come to see me, I will show you them."

Lots of pretty things where Brock came from, too. Providing he kept Sadie safe and sound to show them to her. Hopefully some of that magic rubbed off on him, because he was pretty sure he'd need all the help he could get for the next three months.

CAROLYN'S COLLECTIBLES LOOKED like Black Friday after closing. Brass gargoyles peeked out from under throws, plaques were slotted together like books instead of their words of wisdom facing out, candles were jumbled into a bin, a stack of hats curved up from the floor like a wobbly palm tree. Natalia ached to right the retail chaos.

But she would focus on her job or, in this case, that of her salesperson who had begged off from dealing anymore with Carolyn presently slouched behind the store counter.

"If you would like help displaying our merchandise, I'm more than happy to help," Natalia said brightly.

Carolyn rolled her shoulders as if she had an itch square in the middle of her back. "I don't need help. I need time."

"The former often produces the latter," Natalia said as she gave into impulse and plucked Home & Holidays soaps out of a very not-H&H ashtray and re-homed them in a company glass bowl. The owner watched like a drugged sloth. This was not like Carolyn. She was normally an A-list client; her reorders came in like clockwork. The drop-off two months ago on the spreadsheets had alerted Natalia, but she'd never supposed Carolyn would let her shop fall into such disarray.

"We would like you to be able to show off the Home & Holidays line, and we could assist with that so you can concentrate on other…things." Like folding throws or hanging pictures or mopping the tacky floor or doing something about the smell of wet dog.

Limp, gray hair flopped over Carolyn's smudged glasses. "I can't focus. I'm worried to death, is the thing. It's my son and grandsons."

Oh, no. She was going to tell Natalia a sad tale and expect kind words in return, a shoulder to cry on or something that would make her feel better and not as if life was hopeless. "I'm so sorry to hear that," Natalia said. "How about I just slip to the back, then, and bring out our merchandise?"

She didn't wait for an answer but scooted around the counter and dived into the dim cavern of the back room.

Her phone rang. Brock.

She held her breath. Since Sadie had taken up residence with Brock a month ago, she'd talked twice weekly to him, and he'd reassured her that everything was going well. Sadie, too, seemed happy enough and kept asking when Natalia could come up. She had put her off. Brock had never renewed the invitation, so she'd supposed that he'd only said it to pacify Sadie at the time. Besides, she was swamped with work.

For the first time, he was calling her. "Hello? What's the matter?"

There was a breathy pause on the other end and then came a voice strained and wavery. "Auntie Lia?"

"Sadie? Are you okay?"

"I'm okay."

Natalia sank onto an authentic cow stool. "Hey, sweet daisy-do. Good to hear from you." Natalia had read that kids liked pet names, and she and Sadie had spent ten whole minutes coming up with one. It was the most satisfying conversation Natalia had had in years.

"Good to hear from you, too," Sadie repeated back.

"What are you doing?" Natalia had learned the usual "How are you?" proved to be an astonishingly abstract question for Sadie. "Besides talking to me." She stuck to small talk, hoping the reason for the call would naturally tumble out.

"Nothing much. Sitting on my bed."

"Oh. How was school?" Natalia had enrolled Sadie in a morning prekindergarten program.

"I don't know. I didn't go."

"Why not?"

"Uncle Brock didn't take me. He said I didn't have to go if I didn't want to."

Natalia didn't think he had made much of an effort, either. Never mind that she had paid for those classes. "I see. What did you do instead of school?"

"I visited the kittens, and me and Pike went for a walk." Pike was the Australian shepherd and lab cross puppy Brock had bought her from a local rescue sanctuary. Apparently, Daniel had told Sadie that he'd get her a dog for her fifth birthday, and they'd settled on Pike for a name.

MILLS & BOON

Want to know more about your favourite series or discover a new one?

Experience the variety of romance that Mills & Boon has to offer at our website:

millsandboon.com.au

Shop all of our categories and discover the one that's right for you.

MODERN

DESIRE

MEDICAL

INTRIGUE

ROMANTIC SUSPENSE

WESTERN

HISTORICAL

FOREVER
EBOOK ONLY

HEART
EBOOK ONLY

Subscribe and fall in love with a Mills & Boon series today!

You'll be among the first to read stories delivered to your door monthly and enjoy great savings.

WE SIMPLY LOVE ROMANCE